Zoyla Sexton's
Other Novels:

Soul Warriors
Book 2 of The Story of 3

Soul Tribe
Book 3 of The Story of 3

Soul Hunters
Book 1 of The Story of 3

Zoyla Sexton

To the missing and those left behind
waiting, wondering and praying may
they one day find peace.

Chapter 1 Soul Hunter

Elsa crouched between the headstones. Her head bowed as she leaned forward with one hand on either stone. Midnight in the boneyard and she was home this was her Texas. The wind flowed over her, the pain in her calves pulsed. This was the best part of her every day. She caressed the tops of the rough stones. The breeze delivered the promise of rain as she shifted her braid fell over her shoulder. "How pathetic is this?" She turned, and a man stood at the end of her mother's grave. His face was covered in a black mask painted with a white skeleton skull. He wore a cape like a superhero on Halloween. He frowned, and she fell forward. Her parent's graves were gone. She stumbled over her feet. The former home of her dead relatives was freshly dug earth.

She exhaled. She was homeless. She stepped around him and moved toward the gates. He blocked her exit. "No, response, nothing? I'm disappointed in you." His eyes were deep green lights in the darkness. To his right, another man stood among the shadows. The thief turned to where she gazed. "I'm the leader you deal with me, am I clear?"

Elsa walked passed him, and the gates crashed open and slammed shut in his face. She leapt forward and a second later she arrived to find that the home she grew up in with her old aunt was missing as well. Nothing, but the barren stone from the mountain remained. She sat upon the ground to wait.

Raymond waited in the master's house. "So who made the decision to take the graves and her home?" The master's face was passive as she asked the question. Her hands clasped together. Raymond glanced at his brother and then at the master.

"I made the decision, I'm the leader," Raymond said.

"He is leader, but I came up with the plan," Alexander said. His younger brother was a hot-tempered idiot on a good day and on a bad was an emotional little girl.

"Which was what?" she asked.

"My intent was to break her, mother," Raymond said. Alexander came up with the plan, but had stopped short as to what to do next.

"And you would do this how?" she asked. Mother was slender and tall, very tall for a woman. Her plain, pale face reflected no emotion, no signs as to what she thought.

"A woman whose whole life is to visit the dead wouldn't be hard to break."

"I thought we would get her cooperation if we said we would give it back," Alexander said. Small time plans that was Alexander.

"That is why I'm the leader, little brother," Raymond said, "The plan is to break her to my will."

"And you would do this by taking a couple of old graves and a shack?" she asked. She sat behind her desk. Her hands folded.

"We followed her for months that is all she ever does. They must have some value to her mother," Raymond said.

"Why do you insist on calling me mother?" she asked.

"Because you hate it when we call you master. Mother is more fitting somehow."

"I see, so what you did was take the sole earthly possessions of the only person that has ever loved me?" she asked. The words sank into his head and jetted to his gut. Raymond fell on his knees before her and expected punishment.

"Punish me mother," he said. He lowered his head and waited for the sword to separate his head from his body, but instead a trembling hand raised his face.

"Nothing I do will be worse than the suffering you will experience in your future."

"You don't care if we break her?" Alexander asked. Mother patted his face as he glared at his brother.

"Of course she cares idiot!" Mother helped him up.

"The problem is that you can't break her. No one can, but let us speak of your suffering for a moment longer. Elsa is an addiction, more powerful than any ever known and that is where your suffering shall come from," she said. Raymond paced.

"The solution is not to become addicted," Raymond said.

"It's too late for second guessing. Your actions have trapped you, and only death will release you from this burden. There is a young man who you will rescue, and he will become a Black Cloak like you and your brother and another will be found and another until you equal twenty-seven in total, Raymond what job do you want in reference to Elsa?" He wouldn't disappoint mother a second time.

"I want the hardest job you have," he replied.

"As you wish you will have the hardest job, and that will be as her protector, your job is to keep her alive," she said. Alexander inhaled.

"I will find her enemies and kill them," Raymond said.

"She has many enemies, but she will be your biggest challenge, how do you stop a monster from killing herself?"

"I don't know, mother, how?" Raymond asked.

"By feeding it what it needs the most," she said.

Elsa moved around the grounds and found a spot to await the return of her kin. The men had power that was true, but what did they want from her, for there would be a price for the return of family. The three graves, her mother, her father, her father's aunt, who were these people? How could she love people she couldn't remember? Somewhere long ago they were. Some place lost deep inside her. She just had to find that place, and she would be home. She leaned against the tombstone and inhaled the scents of the night. "Get off my foot!" She met eyes with an old man. Deep wrinkles set into his square face. He was more ghost than man, more dead than alive, but here he was flesh and bones in front of her. She kept her foot in place. "You got to go, otherwise there will be trouble. He doesn't like many people."

Elsa shifted off the ghost's foot and curled up in front of the grave and close her eyes. He shook her, and she inhaled. His scent was like a smoky cherry tobacco pipe. His fingers slid over her face. "You're cold as death, go home," he said. She got up and went to the barren spot of earth where her kin once lived. The ghost scooped her up and went back to the small grave, and she leaned against him. His arms encircled her. "Now that I think of it, maybe you're just what he needs, and you certainly need a hero. That's what he is my son, a stubborn, hard headed man. He's powerful, but nothing like you little one, you will drive him out of that Hell he's made for himself. Sleep now little one, soon he will come, what day is it?" She raised her head. "Monday, that's right he'll be here very soon, sleep, sleep."

Raymond glanced around as they came up to the gate. Alexander pulled on him and he caught sight of the woman, curled up on the ground, her face pale, her lips a bluish color, as if she were dead laying there in the darkness. He moved, and Alexander snatched him back as a towering figure loomed into sight. A flash of light brushed against the still woman, and then the man peeled her from the ground. He held her close as his face slid against hers. Raymond shifted into position just as the stranger kissed her. Elsa stirred and snuggled closer to the big figure. Just what they needed another complication, that was the last time they would try one of Alexander's plans. Raymond drew his pistol. They couldn't lose the woman now. He aimed, and they blinked away. "Damn me to Hell!" Raymond shouted. A light flashed, and they were back to mother's sitting room with the expensive furniture and grand elegance. All of it meant nothing to her or them.

"His name is David Gracia, a powerful man, a powerful Warrior that is what they are called," mother said. She towered above them.

"I'll find her," Raymond said.

"Already it is too late for that. He kissed her and now he is infected with her sweet poison. It really doesn't matter Raymond for you see what is happening is what should be happening," mother said.

"It is fate that will guide us mother?" Alexander asked.

"Guide you no!" mother snapped. She didn't like Alexander and Raymond was glad of it. He approached. Her posture indicated pain, anxiety, and he was the cure at least for a bit. He bowed his head, and mother grasped his neck and the scream of pain echoed through the room as she ate of his energy, of his power. Alexander came to them, never wanting to be left out, mother, held his brother off. Her power shrieked into him, and he fell. His eyes fluttered as Alexander took a turn with his power. The screams of pain came out of him, but they were not his pain. They belonged to others, mother's victim's, mother's sins shrieked out of him like a thousand lost souls with nowhere to go, trapped in the pain of the existence that she gave them through her torture. He and his brother were alive because they had use, mother needed them, but one day it would end just as it had for all the others, another scream entered his mind.

Elsa's pale face floated into his vision, her mouth no longer blue, but a bright red, he wanted that mouth to kiss him to take his pain, and he leaned toward the image and a jolt of pain brought him out of his dream. "If you allow yourself to be seduced by her kindness, by her neediness you're lost do you hear me

Raymond!" All the world should have heard her as the sound of her voice vibrated into his being, and he convulsed on the ground in pain. He flipped over, and his brother suffered the same. How many times could they feed her and not die, soon they would know the answer to that question. The darkness came, and he was lost.

The air choked its way up as Elsa fought her way out of the darkness she longed just to have a moment of peace, of gentle sleep without the violence and consequences of the nightmares. She gasped as a hand grasped her arm, cold and stiff the fingers pulled at her, and the old man ghost stood over her. She lay in softness, like a fluffy cloud of warmth. "What the Hell has happened with my son? This is not the life we planned for him?"

"Who is your son?" she signed. The old man watched her hands. He was known as father. "Who is your son father?" She lifted out of the covers, and he watched her.

"You're deaf?" She jumped as the voice vibrated against her.

"I'd say that means no," a woman said.

"Who are you speaking to?" the man asked. The old ghost took a position between her and the giant with the glowing gray eyes.

"My name is Nellette Cameron, miss who is father?" Elsa eased out of the bed and moved toward the window.

"No one said you could leave, and you didn't answer my question."

Elsa signed. "She wants to know who you are," Nellette asked, "My Grams was deaf that is how I know to read sign, and I read lips as well." The petite blond smiled, warm and sincere.

"Here are the rules. You will never trespass on my property again, or I will have you thrown into a jail, and no one will ever find you again!" The windows exploded, and the house shook. Elsa reached for Nellette and covered her as the room imploded and furniture bounced into the air.

"You're no one to give orders boy!" The shock wave of sound vibrated across her skin as she held the other woman to prevent damage from the tornado of debris. A shelter of mattresses stood in a teepee to protect them. The old man wanted to keep them safe. "You all right little one? You saved the only one in this group worth saving." Elsa wiped her palm against the pale face of Nellette. The mattress flew away, and the giant jumped at her.

Elsa signed as she scrambled out of his reach. "Why do you want to hurt me? What have I done to you?" Nellette asked. The giant skidded to a halt in front of her.

"Nellie did she hurt you?"

"No, sir she saved me, but she's frightened," Nellie said.

"Of what?" he asked.

"Of you stupid, moron chasing her like you're crazy, come on little one. I thought you would be safe here I was wrong." The old ghost tore through the wall, and Elsa ran as the building where they had taken her rumbled and shook.

Morning dawned, and Elsa waited by the small tombstone. The night was quiet as she rested among the dead. The name on the stone was John Dalton, loving father and friend. It was the plainness, smallest stone in the bone yard as if the owner didn't want to be noticed. A brown stain leaked down the left side. "I arranged to have this stone. He wanted to waste money on something no one would see. I wouldn't let him. I planned the whole thing. I should have gone with the cremation, regrets, regrets. Hey, come on, he's sending his goons to find you."

The police car rode up through the graveyard, slowly coming around to where she hid. It stopped and the giant from the night before stepped out and glanced in their direction. She stepped toward him an old John pulled her back. "He'll have them take you away. I don't want that Elsa." She nodded and stayed back. The car doors slammed, and the vehicle rode through the gates. When she could no longer see it she came around to the front of the tombstone of John. She cleaned the weeds and brought with her powers a vase of the reddest roses.

"I knew you wouldn't come out until they left." She scrambled to her feet as he towered over her.

"I won't let him hurt you little one," John said. She smiled at the ghost, but when her gaze came back to the giant, he frowned.

"I have found throughout my life that there are many explanations for things that can't be explained. Take you, for instance, dressed like an old bag lady, with your holey shoes and no coat, and yet…"

"Why did you kiss me?" Elsa signed. He watched her hands.

"It wasn't personal," he said. John laughed and rolled to the ground. Elsa went to the ghost as the fits of laughter shook him.

"My ass it wasn't personal. He wants to kiss you right now, and if you get close enough he will," John said. Elsa stepped back.

"What is his name? I don't like him John," Elsa signed.

"John? No one is here, but you and me! What is your name woman?"

"I don't like you. You're mean and weird and strange looking, and I got to go," she signed. He snatched her up.

"Am I ugly is that it?" he asked. Maggots swelled up on his face and ate his skin, and she screamed. She struggled, and they blew apart.

The scream pelted Raymond's mind, and he glanced at mother who shoved him hard. He sailed through time and space and found himself back at the cemetery. Alexander appeared a moment later and with him came another scream. He leapt at the man who held Elsa. He separated them, and the man pulled two 9mm's and aimed. Several other men came out of the trees as the giant let loose. Elsa jumped between him and the firing man. He held his breath as the bullets jumped at her. He took hold of her, and the scene changed, and they were at her old home, the barren earth where her shack had once stood. He released her, and she went to a pile of wood. She didn't look at him. She only added a small twig to the pile as if she was building a fire on the bare, cold stone. He stomped away and a moment later they were back with mother. "Is she all right?" mother asked.

"Yes, I had to touch her to get her away from the men shooting at her. I didn't like the feel of her."

"What didn't you like Raymond?" mother asked.

"She…smelled of death," Raymond said. Mother stood and went to the window to gaze out at some unknown enemy.

"Since when does death smell of sweet flowers?" mother asked.

"It wasn't death you smelled, but fear," Alexander said. He glared at his brother.

"Yes, maybe that is what fear smells of, roses," mother said.

"She was afraid mother, but it was confusing since she could easily kill the men, why fear them?" Alexander asked.

"You'll figure it out. For now let's go get your new brother," mother said. She wound the coat around her frail arms. Raymond traveled next to mother as his brother trailed behind them he matched her steps even as he was a good foot shorter than she. He inhaled her scent soft, fragrant roses. She met his gaze and they leapt across time to arrive at an alley. The smell of human waste enveloped them. He stepped in front of her and she held him back. A figure lay in the shadows.

"Come on kid, its easy money all you have to do is kill Elsa de las Almas. We'll take you where she is and all you have to do is pull the trigger," the woman said. Raymond couldn't see the woman's face.

"If it's so simple why not do it yourself?" Mother nodded as she came into the light and another figure entered the light with them, another woman with a gun.

The boy pulled a knife and Raymond slammed him into the alley wall. The speaker aimed at mother and Raymond stepped into the line of fire, but mother wouldn't have it. She snatched the woman off the ground and a second later the first woman stared up as her head dangled on the end of mother's bloody fist.

"Your kind of woman gives the rest of us a bad name, and then we have to deal with all the crap from the men who want you instead of us. Guess it's your unlucky day, Ana," mother said. The woman dropped her gun and stared wide eyed.

"Please I have children two little boys," the woman pleaded.

Raymond sensed the shift in mother. "Where are they? You left them alone to whore your ass for the wolf man?" mother asked. She had the woman by the throat.

"Please mother think of her little boys," Alexander said. Raymond's gut twisted. How could he question her and not think there wouldn't be consequences. Mother adjusted her grip. All Alexander saw were the pretty woman's curves and ready smile.

"Her children are better off without her," mother said.

Alexander approached with care. "Times are tough mother. She has to feed them." Mother's eyes went to blue slits. She loved to play games, and he would teach his little brother a bitter lesson this night.

"I believe mother. However, since you are doubtful brother, let us test your theory," Raymond said. Mother nodded, and he blinked to where the little boys slept. Rats, roamed the window ledges as he came to their sleeping forms. They huddled together, thin and afraid. Mother had known this, so he collected the two boys and returned to the alley. Their little heads lie on his shoulder as he reappeared, the woman was startled to see them.

"My babies let them go," she pleaded.

"I will make a trade," mother said. Ana shifted. "You live and I kill your children."

"Do what you want I never wanted them anyway!" The woman tried to run, but mother was fast even for an old woman. Blood splashed into the air as mother gutted her. The boys stirred as their mother's blood splashed against their back.

"Take them to love, Raymond, she will know what to do with the little orphans," mother said, "Alexander and Gabriel stay, we always clean up our messes."

Elsa adjusted the forty-five beneath her shirt. She jogged along farm road 1421 and inhaled the afternoon heat. The dust hung on the air from a traveler come before her. She took in the scene. She was ten miles east, out of El Paso, Texas.

Wild flowers suffocated in the heat. The barbed-wire fence strung on either side of the road kept the land marked for ownership. An occasional tree reached to the sky. An open gate with a faded wood sign, swayed in the hot breeze, read: Sanchez. 'No man stands alone'.

She jumped the metal cattle guard and onto the dirt road. As she passed beyond the gate a wooden sign with peeling paint said: Welcome to Nowhere, Texas. She grinned, Nowhere wasn't even a dot on map, not any map anyone could find.

A few feet into the property the weeds grew tall down the center of the road. As she traveled on, the untamed terrain trapped her. The sunlight disappeared as the branches, crowded together to form a canopy. Within the murky shadows, she imagined movement. Grasshoppers bounced in all directions as she eyed the barren space.

That house was old Romalia's home, the place she grew up. This was the place where she escaped the nightmares the place she could hide when the memories of her failures grew too strong. She moved to the far end of the stone. This was her Texas. She tapped the stack of logs and twigs where her fireplace used to burn. The clouds roiled, and the scent of rain flowed over her.

"People are born and from that moment, they move toward death. That's the way of things, we live to serve. Your Papa asked me to be your Godmother because we're alike. We've this gift, this power. It runs deep in our family.

I'll teach you the ways of the nightmares, and you'll become a soul hunter. You've been chosen. You've no choice. We're not the only ones in these difficult times. There are many," Romalia spoke in the past. From that day, she learned of her curse. Romalia saw it as an honor, a privilege, but for Elsa, it was different. She served, but many times the outcome was unfair and without justice. It brought pain to have so much power and yet so little control.

With the graves and the house gone all she had was a few old memories of an old woman. A scream brought her attention back to the living. "Help! Help! The monster, he's a monster!" Elsa moved, and the man from the other night ran at her with two wailing boys. She jumped up and hammered her foot into the man's chest. The two boys dropped and ran to hide in the brush. He jumped back. She motioned to them and to her surprise, they ran to her. She embraced them and went back to the spot where her home had once stood. "You not a monster," the older one said. She shook her head. "You are a monster?" She nodded.

"I not care she soft and warm and that one he was a monster," the other said.

"Jaime I'm hungry," the younger one said.

"And I'm thirsty, but we just got to wait and see…uh, Mama, she not come back, lady. For a lot of days, we hid in the room when the man comes to get the money." Elsa reached inside her pocket and found two candy bars, and she gave them to the boys.

"No we not take you food, what you going to eat?"

"We not have candy in how long Javier?" Elsa reached inside her pocket and next came two packets of crackers. She motioned for them to reach into her pocket and when they did they found even more. She sat them in front of the fireplace. The cloaked man appeared across from her, and his eyes went to the boys. She smelled the death on him even from so far away. The two little ones were orphans. He turned and ran away. She wanted to follow him to see what it was he wanted, why had he thought he could bring her these children?

Elsa approached the small grave and settled in with the two little boys. They glanced around at the cemetery. It was late, and she wanted them to sleep. "Why would you bring lice covered little creatures to my grave. Do you know how hard it is to get rid of lice?"

"We not smell like…rotten chicken," Javier said. The ghost eyed them and then Elsa.

"How can they see me or smell me, for that matter?"

"We not dumb, we just got lice and…were not dumb," Jaime said. Elsa touched their matted hair. A second later they were bald.

"That's how you get rid of lice," John said.

"Why you got to be mean, huh?" Javier asked.

"Elsa they need to have a home. This is where the dead stay, cause resting isn't something I'm allowed apparently. They need to go where?" John asked. Elsa signed.

"What she do with her hands?" Jaime asked.

"She's mute. That's how she communicates…talks," John said.

"Is she sick?" Javier asked.

"No, she just doesn't speak like you do…" John turned. "You've got to go or else he'll get them sent to the orphanage. He's lost his damned mind." Elsa escaped the cemetery with the two small children.

Chapter 2 Loba Madre, Mother Wolf

Elsa entered the dark foyer, and a priest came up to her. "She will see you now." Elsa followed him down a dark hall to a room. He opened the door and allowed her to pass and closed the door. She paced. "Your little friends have Sister Maria upset. Telling everyone that they have lice." Elsa embraced the tall blond.

"They're afraid Isabella. What have you discovered of their family?" Elsa signed.

"They don't have any family. They lived in Mexico City with their mother. The landlord said that he hadn't seen her for nearly a month. He would go into the apartment and leave little bits of food. He hadn't the heart to throw the boys out." Elsa nodded.

"Their mother is dead," Elsa signed.

"I will take your word for that since what I found is that she disappeared."

"She didn't want them, maybe she just abandoned them," Elsa signed. Isabella came around the desk.

"What I hear is that she disappeared, like vanished, a man reported seeing her go down an alley and never come out. She was looking for an assassin to kill you."

"In an alley, who would look for a homeless person to kill me?"

"Someone that's really dumb or someone who doesn't know you. Rumors say that the Black Wolf wants you dead."

"Alejandro's nephew, what is his name?" Elsa signed.

"Wow that would tick him off, since everyone knows the great Manuel Rojas Villanueva, he's the leader of the wolf clan, a bunch of low end outcasts, mostly drunks I know one of them," Isabella said.

"How do you know one of them?" Elsa asked.

"Saved his life once, he was drowning, splashing around below one of my little dark caves. I gave him mouth to mouth. I got a little carried away, and he got a power boost, now every time he sees me, he wants more. He's a greedy giant," Isabella said.

"I don't like that, can the boys stay until I get a class started?" she signed.

"A Fighters class, sure whose teaching it this time?" Isabella asked.

"We'll see, call me if they need anything," Elsa signed. Isabella embraced her, and she climbed out of the window and ran down the alley. She loved coming to Mexico and her adopted people. Many of her friends were here. Texas was lonely. She crossed another alley careful not to be noticed. A cat snarled, and she stumbled over a body. Strong, soft hands steadied her.

"Hello." The woman was too well dressed to live in the alley. Elsa shivered. "You are definitely a hard woman to find, Elsa de las Almas." Elsa stepped back. Loud voices came in their direction, and she took the woman's arm, and they ran down into the street. A long black car pulled up, and the door opened. "Please come with me. You're safe I promise." They entered the car, and it moved slowly forward. "I am Maria Rojas Leon. I am Loba Madre."

"You're related to Alejandro Rojas?" Elsa signed.

"He is my brother," Maria said. Elsa shrank back. "I learned to read the sign many years ago, one of my charities is for special-needs children, in memory of my sister who died as a child."

"We are enemies," Elsa signed.

"Because you are a Fighter, no? One of two female fighters of Abrim Stein?" Elsa nodded and rubbed her hands together. Maria lifted a thermos from its holder and poured a cup of coffee. The steam and the aroma enticed Elsa. Maria took a long drink and made one for Elsa. She accepted the brew, and it warmed her. "Well, as far as I am concerned, I believe Alec did your leader a favor, by taking that bitch. All we've had is suffering because of her stupid, selfish ass. I hate it when men think they're smarter than women. He won't bring that bitch near me. However, that cancer is spreading. Since she's taken up with my son." Elsa glanced at the pretty face of the older woman.

"You have a son?" Maria rolled her eyes.

"I have several, but you wouldn't know it. They never call, maybe I should be glad about that, no news means I don't have to know the truth, but it also means I'll never have grandchildren, which leads me to how you can help me. Now don't worry what I ask won't compromise your ethics, I wish we had more ethics in the wolf clan."

"I'm not sure what you've heard about me, but I won't kill the leader's wife for you."

"They're divorced, but anyway, no, if that bitch dies it's going to be because I kill her," Maria said.

"All right," Elsa signed.

"What I want is for you to clean house," Maria said.

"I don't like dusting, but I like dishes and to cook, making beds. It would be a change," Elsa signed. Maria laughed.

"No, mija, I want you to go to Alejandro's house and get rid of the chippies, the mezcal and the wasted lives. We've suffered enough, and I believe there is a plot to kill off the wolf clan, now as to pay." Elsa held her cup out, and Maria refilled it.

"I have money," Elsa signed. She drank the contents in the cup.

"No, what I have you want you'll see," Maria said.

"What's happened?" Elsa asked.

"Patricia killed a family in your leader's village and took the only surviving member hostage thinking that she could lure you to her. I have her. I have Leticia Marras," Maria said. The air sucked out of Elsa as she leaned back against the seat. Jose Marras was Abrim's best friend, a man without equal. The tears fell, and Maria came to comfort her. The warmth of the other woman's embrace was powerful as she wept without sound. "I'm so sorry I would have stopped her. No one knows what she has done, but you and I and Leticia. Patricia did this to bring Abrim Stein to slaughter the wolf clan. We've suffered too much Elsa. I won't let this happen. I have Leticia in a safe place, and she must go to where my brother and sons are in order to prevent all of this. I know that this will put you cross ways with your leader, but there is no other way, please I beg you." Elsa nodded as Maria wiped the tears from her face.

Day four, Tuesday, what month March and still no relief, no way to sleep. One day removed from her encounter with the Wolf mother and how would she free Leticia? The cold of the stone seeped into her legs, and her fingers hurt. A light flashed through the darkness, and the stone changed to solid wood shiny and deep brown. A heavy sigh broke the silence, and she leapt to her feet.

To her left, a fireplace held a fire and a across from it a tall back chair. Next to it was a huge desk of shiny cherry wood. In a glass jar floated a pinky finger with a golden ring. A strong hand flickered over the wood to a row of shot glasses of clear liquid. A long finger ringed the glass in a slow, steady motion. The door swung open. "Master, your Uncle wants to know when you will join the party."

The curvy blonde swayed against the doorframe and smiled. Her firm pale breasts peeked out of her red dress as she posed. The man seated never turned. "Come on Master all the beautiful ladies wait for your arrival. They can't wait to worship and adore you as is your right." The shot glass disappeared and blasted into the fire. Elsa jumped as the flames protested the assault.

"Let them wait," he said. He fingered the next shot.

"But Master you can't disappoint them," she said. A gunshot burst over the back of the chair and bruised the doorframe next to the woman's flawless face.

"I won't miss next time," he said. The blonde closed the door. Elsa appeared in the darkness next to the wood pile. She peered over the stack. The man wore a tuxedo. All parts of him were perfect except for the fact that he sloughed in the chair. He was grace and beauty. He shot the drink back and sniffed. In his right hand, he fondled a Glock and his left went to the row.

She perched on her tiptoes and the pistol came up, just as he did in one fluid motion. His eyes remained on the wood as she emerged. He stepped on, and she stopped. Her shirt caught on a length of firewood. The pistol winked at her, and she reacted. The fabric ripped from the force as she jetted back. He brought the barrel to his side, and she walked to him. He spun it to his heart, and she came within hands reach. He stepped back and she with him until they arrived to the chair and the brighter light from the fire. He sat and she hesitated, but then sat on his lap. The gun came up and she pulled away, a moment later it disappeared and his fingers came to her mouth.

Her head jerked to the door, and he followed her gaze. The door crashed against the frame as he searched for her. Their eyes met from her hiding place in the woodpile. "Angel said you don't want to be bothered?" Elsa's gaze drifted to an old man.

"No, Uncle," he said.

"Mano, there are many beautiful women out there," the old man said. The Commander sat back in his chair.

"So go and enjoy them Uncle and leave me be," Mano said. His fingers slid over his eyes and he rubbed them.

"There are many young women your age," the man said.

"Alejandro, my dear, leave Mano if he wishes to be alone with his thoughts so be it," Patricia said. Alejandro eyed the woman.

"Too much competition for you Tricia? So much young flesh to savor, so little time," Alejandro said. Patricia glanced down.

"Youth is underrated isn't it Mano my dear?" Patricia asked. Mano's eyes searched the dark, and he didn't find her. He stood and paced. "Are we interrupting you?" Alejandro glanced around.

"You've a woman in here?" Alejandro asked. The skin on the General's face was pale and mottled with age spots, but he was still a handsome man.

"Yes," Mano said. Patricia frowned as she swept further into the room to a row of cabinets with cut out windows.

"I doubt that, you'd be in a better mood," Patricia said. She reached inside the cabinet and withdrew a bottle of mezcal and placed it on the desk. "Come along Alec our guests are waiting." Alejandro leaned over the desk.

"Where is she?" Alec asked.

"Hiding in the woodpile where else?" Mano said. Alec straightened and sent a glance in her direction as he left with Patricia. Mano opened a drawer and pressed a button. A loud click and the door locked. He gathered the bottle and stepped to her. He reached in and pulled her from the dark. Her eyes went up the shelf where the bottle came from. He took her arm and dragged her along. A thick white worm swam in the tan liquid in each of the bottles from the shelf.

They entered a bedroom, and the light caught the bottom of the bottle. She pushed him hard, and he jerked her back. She kicked the bottle, and it tumbled onto the floor. The clear contents poured onto the carpet and dissolved the fabric in a jagged stream. It sizzled inward to the bottom and splashed forward to disappear more fabric.

Elsa stumbled back as Mano glanced at the reactive liquid he was to consume. He pulled her tight and pressed a number into his phone. "Uncle come into my room…alone," he said. She slipped away and he let her go, but his gaze remained on her destination as she hid and Alec entered the room.

"What should I send some girls?" Alec asked. Mano nodded toward the bottle and tipped it with his boot. Mezcal gushed out and ate carpet. Alec withdrew his Ruger. "I'll kill them until someone confesses."

"Let them try I'm not so easy to kill," Mano said. Patricia selected the bottle, and the thoughts reflected in the commander's eyes. Patricia was his lover as well as his uncle's.

"I will not have treason in my house," Alec said, "They kill you. They kill me!" The old man left. Mano came to her. He cupped her face, and a gun blast erupted in the hall.

"Stay here until I return," Mano said. She shook her head. "Yes, you will I command it." He gathered his weapons as more fire rang out. Elsa ran into the wall, and the pain brought her to know she was in this place awake and in person. She hadn't traveled here on her own. Someone had delivered her, maybe the wolf mother. She searched the doors and found a closet. She crawled into the back of it and found a pillow and blankets. She lay with the wall at her back and accepted the gifts. She closed her eyes and found sleep, dreamless sleep.

A door slammed, and a light crashed into her vision as she scrambled to the corner of the closet. The beautiful man glared. "At least you can follow orders." He snatched her off the floor and carried her to his bed. Her gaze went to the door. "It's locked, why were you hiding in the closet?" She signed, and he frowned. She pushed his chest and signed the word no and shook her head, and then she pushed him again and signed the word for yes. She pushed him and did it again. "I got it the first time, who are you and how did you get to this room and passed the guards?" She pushed further away from him.

She signed.

"That isn't going to work are you dumb?" he asked.

"No," she signed.

"Well you're not deaf, so you're a dumb mute," he said. She got on to the bed, and he laughed. "I've insulted a homeless, mute woman I guess I can scratch that off my bucket list, now come here."

"No," she signed.

"No one tells me no, now come here," he snapped. She stood her ground, and he pounced at her. She easily avoided him, and he roared like a beast as she ran up the wall and landed on his bed. "We're getting closer. I've never had to chase a woman, especially not an ugly little homeless woman." She slid to her knees on the soft bed and fell face forward and sobbed. Her whole body shook as she grieved for something she never had. He peeled her up as the tears streamed down. "You don't even know me to have this reaction to my insults, and you have skills as a fighter…"

"Yes," she signed.

"You agree with me?" he asked.

"No," she signed.

"It doesn't matter, go away!" he snapped. She stumbled off the bed, and her foot caught the blanket. He caught her. "I don't want you suing me cause you busted your head open in my house." She kissed his cheek and her tears smeared against his face. She went into the closet. "That's not the way out." She jumped into the closet and slammed the door. She shifted time, and she appeared in another closet, but this one was filled with beautiful clothes and shoes. She turned, a pillow and a blanket waited for her. Somehow she felt at peace and lay down. A soft hand touched her face. Maria looked down on her.

"It seems that I owe you for my son's life, but he will need you again mija, sleep now," she said. The wolf mother was hard to resist, and she drifted away.

"Oh master come now, stop working come and enjoy." Elsa raised her head.

"I'm busy Angel go annoy someone else." The dark-haired man from last night snapped. If he was Maria's son, he was the Black Wolf and the clan leader, Manuel Rojas Villanueva the man who sought her death. Elsa rose and crept around the bed. Angel swiveled her hips and lean legs to position herself in front of the man.

"Look you've dropped your pen," Angel said. She leaned over and her skirt rode up smooth, pale skin. Manuel never turned, and Angel pouted. She pushed his chair back and dropped onto his lap. A tall drink of thick liquid in her hands, she smiled.

"I've brought you a treat," she said. She twirled the drink, and a neon green ribbon appeared in the white and slid into the bottom of the glass. The ribbon pulsed, and Angel pressed it to the man. Manuel Villanueva was a torturer, a killer, if anyone deserved a painful death, it was this evil man. The ribbon disappeared. She rose, and he snapped in her direction. He shoved Angel away and the drink splashed, but never left the glass. The beautiful Angel of death jumped up. She flipped open her phone. "Rico come in here! A beggar has gotten into the master's room!"

She walked to the clan leader, and Angel shoved her. Elsa dodged her and reached Manuel. She raised her palm to him, and his came against hers. His thumb caressed the back of her hand. "Get your filthy hands off of the master!" Manuel kept her back as he towered over Elsa.

"Are you hungry little one?" Mano asked. Elsa nodded. The guard entered the room and reached for her. Elsa mashed against Manuel. His heartbeat pounded as he steadied her. A single ripple emitted from him, not of evil, just plain, ordinary, a hum. His every evil should have merged across her skin, but only a cool peace remained. He took the drink from Angel and Elsa frowned. "If you think it poisoned I shall drink it first." Elsa shook her head.

"That drink can't be appreciated by a peasant only a man whose tastes are of the highest quality can find it good," Angel said. Elsa eyed the milky drink.

"You don't want me to drink this little stranger?" Manuel asked.

Elsa shook her head as she stepped back. "Why should I trust you instead of my own people who wish me nothing more than the best?"

"Get away ugly thing," Angel said.

"Is she ugly Rico?" Manuel asked. He twirled a strand of her dark hair.

"No, Senor she's not," Rico said.

"Shut up," Angel said. Manuel put the glass to his mouth, and Elsa jerked it down and it splashed his brown leather vest and ate the edge away. Manuel exhaled.

"Take Angelica to the dungeon, Rico," Manuel said. The guard wrestled the beautiful blond away. Manuel removed the vest and laid it across the chair. A gunshot brought Elsa in front of Manuel as Angel blasted into the room 9mm drawn.

"Had to do it the hard way you bastard fine by me!" Elsa put her hand up. Angel blinked as the long knife drew through her. Rico's face appeared over her shoulder.

"You weren't even a good fuck stupid bitch!" Rico said. Angel slipped onto the floor, and Elsa raised her hands as Rico fired at

Manuel. The bullet ripped against the invisible barrier and lanced into Rico's shoulder as he bounced against a wall. A gun blast exploded from his weapon, and the bullet flew into a light above them. Manuel grabbed her, but she held the protective barrier as the shower of splintered glass dropped in spears around them. She spun free as the door bent forward with force.

"Stop it or you'll deal with me!" Manuel shouted. The door moved again with a massive force. He dialed his phone. "I said to quit. No, I don't need help, and yes we have at least one dead body, no leave me be! Yes, that was a threat!" He slammed the phone on the desk as Elsa moved backwards. "Why have you save me three times?"

Elsa shrugged. "Only one hero could do this…Elsa, Dear One of the Fighters. I am a monster among your people why?" Elsa lifted her hands.

"No," Elsa signed. She leapt through time and came to be back at the place of her former home. Manuel's energy pulsed in her as she tried to catch her breath, it misted in the cool air.

"What is this place?" Manuel asked. She stood as he moved forward, the moment he tried to cross into what was once her home he bounced back. "Let me in now!"

"No," she signed.

"That is a bad habit, I'm going to break you of, no one tells me no woman!" he said.

Lightening pierced the sky and the rain came as she lay on the cold stone. "This is not done!" The second he was gone Maria appeared with an umbrella.

"He likes you mija. He's a bit rough, but keep telling him no. He's not used to that. I'm afraid you have to go back. Lettie is locked inside a room, and they're trying to get in. They can't of course. I wish to make a trade," Maria said.

"No," Elsa signed.

"It's the only way to save Leticia," Maria said.

"No," Elsa signed. Maria's deep-blue eyes sparkled.

"My request won't compromise your ethics. I'm sending you back as soon as you stop them you'll sleep without the nightmares," Maria said. Elsa leapt through space just as the door ripped off the hinge, and men poured through the room.

Elsa exhaled. Her mind crashed forward. Sweat clustered on her forehead, trails of salty liquid soaked into her blouse as she fought the nightmare to no use as it dragged her away. The mist cleared, and she stood in the living room of a house.

A shot shattered the peace. Elsa turned as the room changed. Raised voices erupted from another room, and then a child screamed. A lean figure crossed the room with a young woman, Leticia? The woman handcuffed her to a chair. A soldier dressed in the gray of the militia stood over Leticia. "Make her talk Jorge," Patricia said. She returned with a baby and girl and dragged them to another room.

"Come on pretty girl, tell Jorge what he needs to know, and I'll talk to the Commander, and she might go easy on you," he said. He leaned close and the young woman spit in his face. The solder slapped Leticia and grabbed her chin. "If you want this hard I'm game. Elsa was seen talking to your father. Where is she?"

"Go to Hell!" Leticia said. The soldier's fist smashed into her face. Leticia glared. Chains appeared to snake around Elsa as she tried to get to Leticia. Screams burst through the house. Leticia sobbed and when the soldier touched her breast, she kicked him. Elsa shook as she reached to kill the soldier, but instead she shifted forward as shots ripped through the house, and she landed. A woman Ana Marras, Eloisa her ten-year-old daughter and baby Jose lay dead. Their blood mingled with the dirt floor. Their future was canceled. Her screams echoed through the silence of her mind. A face appeared.

"Mama, make it stop!" Manuel shouted. Elsa fought the sheets only to slip away into the darkness.

Elsa was hungry. She was always hungry. She paced to a nearby mirror, and the reflection changed. She grew into a creature with red fire eyes and lightning bolts for arms and boulders for legs. She blinked, but the monster that she was remained in the mirror. She would have to report soon. She was back at the mansion of John's son.

She pushed her bare feet against the beige carpet. Dark clouds moved beyond the mountain range. She inhaled the smell of the rainstorm and leapt to the windowsill. She closed her eyes and popped onto the other side of the glass. The thunder rippled through her body, and she squeezed her fingers together and came into the next room. It was past midnight, and she dripped on the master's carpet. No one was about as she slipped down the hall. Elsa moved through the kitchen of David's home. The mansion was still.

Lights blasted, and the vision came. A terrified scream burst into her mind. She cracked her knees as the sound chewed her nerves and only then did she realize it was her voice. Her vision blurred. It returned seconds later. Leticia sat in a hard chair. Arms and legs tied to the back. Blood soaked Leticia's blouse. Elsa forced the air into her lungs.

Leticia said, "I don't know Elsa." A hand made contact with her face. The sound of flesh against flesh sounded like thunder. She covered her ears and scrambled from the horrible noise. The girl would be killed, and she jumped to the girl's defense. Her hands moved through the attacker as if she were a ghost. She screamed, but no one heard as Patricia beat the girl. She wrapped her arms around Leticia and shared the young woman's pain.

The tremors shook Elsa. Death and despair clutched her heart. Soft, strong hands gripped her as she fought blackness. Water drops dripped on her. The roar like the wind blasted over them.

The blackness came again with a flash of light. Let me die a voice whispered and Elsa agreed. Powerful talon's gripped her arms and snatched her up. Elsa slammed her head away from the furnace of heat that drowned her. Elsa let go and fell to the pit, but she wasn't allowed freedom as a hard mouth pressed into hers and breathed fire into her. She opened her eyes, and David's gray ones stared into hers as he kissed her mouth and crushed her body to his.

"I will own you," said the man's voice. Her mind erupted with anger, and she shoved back, not physically, but with mental tenacity and David launched across the room and through the wall.

"I'll die if I want!" The deep abyss came, and she leapt into it full of rage.

Chapter 3 The House of Gracia

Elsa's head ached as she leaned against a wood-frame shack. Her left eye twitched as she stepped to the corner. A stream of cold wind ripped through her clothes as she made the turn. A boy stepped back from a trashcan with two large rocks. His blond hair a jumbled, tangled mess and he aimed for the nearest window. His shirt and pants were more rags than fashion and were small on his huge body. The back door opened. "Hey boy, its cold are you hungry?" The boy's gray eyes turned to suspicious slits as he nodded. "Well come in then."

Elsa followed the boy into the shack. A fire burned in a small pit across the room as the old man gathered a bowl and spoon. Elsa came to stand by the table. "All I got is soup, but it's more than most. What's your name boy?" he asked.

"David," the boy replied. The old man cut the one potato in his bowl in half and of the four pieces of meat in the broth, he placed three in David's bowl. He ladled steaming broth over the mix.

"I'm John Dalton, wash your hands boy and come on." David swallowed as he glanced at the supper.

"I was gonna bust out your windows mister," David said. The old man planted himself at his spot.

"Well, it's a blessing you didn't for both of us. It's mighty cold here at night and there's a northerner on the way. Damn knee is better than any weatherman," John said, "Go on and eat before it gets cold." David took up his spoon and tasted the broth.

"It's good," David said.

"It's crap, but it's warm, you know what would be good a small loaf of bread, wouldn't care if it were that fresh either," John said. David glanced around.

"Where do you keep it?" David asked. John slurped a spoon of the soup and pointed at a counter that was in shadows. David rose.

"No sense in looking ain't anything over there, but some cobwebs," John said. David pushed around some old containers and turned with a large loaf of bread.

"Looks like bread to me," David said. Elsa smiled at the teen that would be the Warrior and the old man who was now a ghost.

"All right now I'm old, but…well we won't ignore a blessing now will we?" John said. He smiled as David opened the plastic sack. The fresh-baked scent came to Elsa.

"It smells good," David said. John smiled.

"Yes, indeed, when I was a boy my Ma would make butter, we had an old milk cow," John said. David nodded.

"Like in a churn, she churned butter?" David asked. John laughed.

"No, boy that's in the movies we were so poor all we had was an old jar with a metal lid, and she would pour the cream into it, and I'd sit at the table and shake that jar until the bits of butter came up. That was the best butter not like that stuff you get at the store."

"Did you put it on bread?" David asked. John sighed.

"Oh, yes, one of my favorite things." David glanced at the refrigerator. It was old and a dingy white. John's eyes drifted to the box and back to David.

"Not much in there boy." David got up and went to it. He reached in and fished around, and a light blinked on. John turned as David returned with butter and jam.

"Where can I find a glass?" David asked.

"You want some water boy?"

"No milk I want milk," David said. John Dalton glanced to the wood floor of his old home, shame filled his old face.

"I'm sorry boy, I ain't got any milk, see…" David went back to the box and came with a gallon of whole milk.

"If we finish it, I'll go get more tomorrow," David said. John stood and went to the icebox it was empty, but the light was bright. He went into the cabinet and took down two glasses.

"I'm going senile I guess cause this morning, I got one potato and one old piece of meat and now…" John said.

"Maybe we shouldn't question blessings," David said. John sank to his chair as David poured him a full glass of milk. Elsa came to the old man as he was deep in thought.

"That's what old Enrique used to say," John said. David sat down and buttered a piece of bread and ate the whole thing.

"Was he your friend?" David asked. Elsa laid her palm on the old man's shoulder. John nodded as he took a thick slice of the white bread and spread it with butter and jam. He bit the piece and grinned.

"Man I sure miss bread I forgot how good it tasted. Yeah he was the most important person in town, back then this place was called Lawson's," John said. David nodded.

"Your friend he was the mayor?" David asked.

"More important than the mayor," John said. Elsa rubbed the gnarled old shoulders.

"The sheriff?" David asked. He ate the soup.

"No, boy he was the grave digger." David frowned.

"Oh, cause either rich or poor he's the last one to see you huh and the widows don't want to see their husbands going back to dust in the streets," David said. John laughed.

"True enough can't move on without the grave digger. He was a wise man that one."

"You think he would like to have a kid?" David asked.

"No, David, nothing left of Enrique, but memories and…"

"His name," David said.

"Yeah that's right, he never married, and he didn't have any kids that I know of why?" John asked. Elsa came to stand next to David.

"I never had any parents, so he and I have something in common, except, he has a name, and I don't," David said.

"Everybody has a name boy." David scraped the last bits of potato out of the bowl.

"I don't, someone left me at the orphanage, and I don't have a real name," David said. He buttered another piece of bread. John put his spoon down.

"I always liked Enrique's last name who says you can't have it. He would understand," John said.

"What if the name don't fit me?" David asked. He shoved the bread in his mouth. John stared him straight in the eye.

"Then you got to live up to it. That's what your name will be somehow I'm going to make it happen," John said.

"You don't even know me mister, and I was going to break your windows remember?" David asked.

"All I remember is not having enough to eat this morning and now cause of you. I'm full David Gracia." The younger man laughed.

"Gracia means…" David said.

"It means Grace. David filled with Grace you'll have to live up to it, but you made a start tonight." Elsa squeezed David's shoulder as the name sank into his heart.

Lightening blasted through the room, and she was thrown against the floor. She shielded her eyes as another round creased the midnight sky, and she crawled to her knees. The thunder roared, and another light struck and stayed to illuminate the darkness. An older David leaned on his knees in front of a grave. John Dalton's name engraved against the stone. David's black suit, tailored and expensive, five carat diamonds gleamed at the cuffs to hold the shirt closed. A golden ring gleamed in the darkness as he bowed his head. "Father I'm sorry I…failed you." Elsa stumbled and moved closer.

The nearby trees swayed in the night. "Why could I not stop this disease!" he shouted. He spun off the ground and ripped the nearest tree from the earth and tore the limbs from it like they were leaves. His rage pulsed, and he changed from a man to a huge gray beast with claws and scales. His head turned toward the sky, and he roared as he ripped all the surrounding trees from the earth and pitched them in the air. When there was nothing left to tear he crashed his head into the headstone of his dead, adopted father. Blood splattered the gray stone of the marker.

Elsa came from the ground and spun up and grasped the beast's head. He roared and pressed her into the sky. Some parts of him were man and others were a creature as he held her aloft. She gazed into his gray eyes as they pulsed. She reached her hands to him and descended into his embrace. Her face connected with his, and he turned his mouth to her lips, and the kiss brought him peace. "Boss we got some…shit!" Wayne said.

David pulled away, but his mouth was bright red, and his expression different as he pushed away from her and left the room. Bob and Wayne went after him. "Sorry we interrupted David…" Bob said.

Elsa turned and appeared at the front door as David reached to leave. She gazed up as his hand came over her face and his mouth crushed hers. His cold rage filled her, and she shivered as he kissed her neck and ripped her shirt to taste her shoulder. He pressed her up to the wall as he tore her clothes. "Son of a bitch!" Bob said. David turned and stomped away. "I'm sorry sir!"

"In my office now please," David said. Maria appeared and turned her face.

"It's time to leave Hunter Elsa. You must protect yourself from this Warrior. He has tasted his escape, and now he will do whatever he has to find a greater bit of it," Maria said. She turned back, and the old shack from the past appeared as a tiny corner of the grand mansion. The room in the present was David's bedroom. A sharp pinch drew her to the top of her right hand. Two marks welled up, and blood trickled. Another bite and the shadow image of a rat appeared. Elsa blinked, and Leticia's head twisted. Rats jumped from place to place within the prison.

Elsa burned them and those that remained ran from the carnage. Pain echoed through Elsa's hand, and then her hands burst into flames. She leapt into the darkness, and a distance roar turned her head. A wicked howl burst the silence of the nightmare, and her eyes snapped to the right. A tidal wave crashed toward her. It devoured the ground and swept her up. She swallowed the vomit. She floated, helpless in the murky water. She burst from the water and gasped for air. A shoreline appeared, in the distance, the only land in sight, and she swam to the beach.

"Elsa…Elsa, come to me." The voice called from a distant place as if the person was in a tunnel. She pushed forward and forced the panic down. The vomit gushed out. She clenched her fists. "I don't know if I can do this. Sweet Jesus, help me," she thought. Her voice bounced through the stillness and startled her. Seldom had she been allowed the privilege of hearing what her voice might sound like. She made it to the shallow water her legs heavy weights. Her wet clothes pressed against her as the wind froze her.

The coldness that squeezed her heart wasn't due to the weather, but to the memories she had of the victims of Patricia's evil. The horror and pain Patricia brought them made no sense; no words described what happened to them. She swallowed the lump that threatened to choke her. Her bravado splintered and fell into the sand.

Lightning flashed, and she was sent into the house. "Elsa…I want to die." She covered her head and crouched down. Again, she shifted forward after a moment, she raised her head.

The room was dim; chairs littered the floor. The walls were crucified with shackles and the once white surface stained, brown. No natural light was allowed in, just a bare bulb placed on the ceiling. There was no place to hide; no place to run, no knob to the door; no escape, only madness and death. The air was foul with human waste and vomit. The smell of death filled this nightmare from Hell, in this place of no return.

"Elsa…" She turned toward the sound of her name. In the corner across the room, a woman was chained to the wall. In her years of travel in the nightmares, she saw many horrible sights. She had never been a coward, and she wouldn't begin this day.

Long, red hair hung over the face. Crusted, dried blood covered her hands and her feet were blistered. The sight moved her to action. She brushed away the hair. "No you must not be here this is a place of death. Mama saved you for a reason. You're important without you people die," Leticia said. She stared at the defiant young woman. "Please leader go don't make my mother's sacrifice a vain one. My mother was never wrong, and she won't be this time. The angel told me you would come if I called."

The voice she had moments before had now retreated and she was left her only form of communication, to sign. "I'm here. I had no choice."

"No one who comes here is given a choice," Leticia said, "I told Patricia I didn't know where you were, but she wouldn't believe me. I only wanted you to come here to let you know one thing. You've no blame for their deaths. Their time my time was at hand, don't suffer for a sin you had no part in, please promise so I may die in peace my leader." Elsa touched the beautiful bruised face and pressed her head to hers. Elsa hated the words she would say. Her stomach knotted as she knew the truth of them.

"The only peace I'll know is if you come out of here alive." Leticia's eyes closed.

"What worth do I have now? My life is over, kill me and end this. You would do as much for an animal," Leticia said.

"No, you're not finished. I need you," she signed. Elsa bit her lip. Didn't she want the same fate as this young woman? If she gave up it would solve her problem and Leticia's. She knew in her heart it wouldn't be allowed.

"No," Leticia said as her head dropped onto her chest.

Elsa pulled her face up. "I'll come for you very soon. I promise." The sweat ran down Elsa's face. "That's an order, Marras!"

"I'm no longer a soldier, not one that wants to live," Leticia said. The force of Elsa's power penetrated the fog in Leticia's mind.

"Stay with me," she signed. Leticia tried to pull away. Elsa held her face in a vice grip as her power sank into the dying girl. Leticia jerked. "A part of me will remain to give you strength." Elsa released her face as the girl fell into her eyes. "Think of me. I'm with you." Elsa jerked back.

"Just another second please," she prayed in her mind.

She took a step back. Leticia's face glazed over as the hope died. "Don't waste your effort my leader…you'll never make it in time."

Elsa shifted backward. "Wait for me Lettie!" The thought screamed through her mind as the water claimed her. The strong current yanked her down. She gained her balance as the water fought to take her life. "I want to die." Leticia's voice whispered through her mind.

Elsa jerked awake as a kiss came over her mouth, she pushed him away and the beautiful man frowned. "Don't you want me baby?" She squirmed out of his grasp. Lettie was here, locked in the room. Maria had stopped them.

"No," she signed.

"Wow that's what it's like when I tell the beautiful women, I no longer want them. It's not that bad and that's not what you said last night, you're a beast. It was kind of different I liked it."

She ran passed him and down the hall where Leticia was, she came to the door full force and opened it. The group of men glanced at her as Manuel caught her arm. "Easy, bebe…" She smacked him and entered the room. Lettie lay pale and still.

"Hey, the leader has a girl?" one of them said. Elsa pressed her forehead to Leticia, and the woman came to and grasped her. Lettie jumped into the Fighter's stance.

"Is she threatening the leader?" one of the men asked.

"Back up black wolf and take your little dogs with you, have you no idea who she is?" Lettie asked.

"Who are you?"

"I am Fighter Leticia Marras, and she is Fighter Leader Elsa de las Almas, wolf," Lettie said. Elsa came around her.

"Stand down," Elsa signed. Lettie dropped into an at ease position and raised her head. The weight of Lettie's grief dropped into Elsa like an anchor, and she went to her knees. Lettie's legs shook as she resisted the need to help her, she waited for the command to move and Elsa couldn't give it. She collapsed on her face, and Manuel came to roll her over. Elsa raised her hands. "Help, me Lettie." Leticia shoved the wolf leader away.

"Now you want to help?" one of the wolf clan asked.

"Unlike you I am a soldier I have to be commanded to move, Del Rosa," Lettie said. Her fighter wouldn't be able to lift her with her current injuries. "My leader is asking whether your leader will lift her since I am injured."

"We're ready for the party, Saul," a woman with very little clothes said, "Oh, who invited the reaper? Is it a costume party?" The reaper entered the room, and Elsa smiled as she leaned over them. Smooth cool hands ran over her face. Elsa pushed the cloak back and light blond hair spilled over her shoulders.

"Isabella?" The giant named Saul charged them, and Elsa pinned him to the wall with her power. "Leader let me down I have to kiss her a dozen times."

"No," Lettie said.

"All right two dozen and after that I'll stop," Saul said. Manuel peeled him off the wall, and he stopped him from coming near them.

"I will pick her up if she goes where I want her to," Manuel said. Elsa sat up and signed to Lettie.

"She said to forget it, and she'll be down in the dungeon with the two of us until you remove the chippies," Lettie said. Isabella helped Lettie, and they followed her.

"He's the leader he doesn't have to listen to you," Chino Del la Rosa said. Lettie grasped her arm as they went down. Elsa decided the dungeon was too good a place to wait, and so she arrived at a location known as the pit. The two women sat at her side in coldness. A light blinked on, and she glanced at Manuel. Elsa signed.

"The leader wants to know what you want." Lettie asked. Manuel glanced around. The rats danced across from them, but the creatures wouldn't come near them.

"I'm not sure I want you in my presence if rats won't have you?" he said. Elsa signed.

"Leave then," Lettie said. A moment later Chino and Saul arrived.

"Damn its cold down here, what's with the rats?" Chino said.

"They're afraid of death," Isabella said.

"You're not death you're just a little creepy," Saul said. Isabella leapt at him, and he spun around and when the spinning stopped he was pressed against the wall, a wicked curved knife to his throat.

"You smell like the swamp outside of my father's house, damn I love that scent," Saul said. She released him, and he laughed. "You like it when I say sweet things to you." Lettie pulled Isabella down next to her and glanced at her face.

"He's weird, stay away from him," Lettie said.

"Why would you care Fighter Marras?" Isabella asked.

"Because I do and believe me when your sibling finds out I'll catch Hell for even speaking to you, but that will be his problem not mine," Lettie said. She sat closer to Isabella, and the blond leaned against her. "Whatever you want it's not here, move on."

"We got rid of the chippies for this?" Chino asked. Elsa signed.

"Leader said she would have thought better of you, but I was right you're a liar."

"You've no right to question me in my own home!" Chino said.

"You will find wolf that I am the opposite of your desperate little chippies, nothing you have frightens me, so go on then," Lettie said. Chino charged her and Lettie raised her arms, the red, bleeding scars on her wrists glowed bright. He spun away and stomped toward the door. "And unlike you I am not afraid of my truth." He circled back.

"In my clan women aren't expected to be men!"

"Since you and your leader have a hard enough time being men I imagine that you would have to have weak women, it makes sense that is why you're losers," Lettie said. Manuel glanced at his soldier.

"You believe me to be weak Elsa of the souls?" Manuel asked. Elsa signed, and Lettie glanced down.

"Has she nothing to say soldier?" Chino asked.

"She said when you grow up and learn to sign she will speak with you, if her leader, Abrim Stein needed to learn you sure as Hell do," Isabella said. Lettie glanced at her. "What? She ordered you not to speak to them."

"Come with me Isabella and I will make it worth your while," Saul the giant said. Isabella threw a rock at his head, and he dodged it.

"You can't buy me pendejo!" Isa shouted.

"I told you," Lettie said. Isabella frowned.

"You're not smarter than me just because my brother says you are, Fighter Leticia," Isabella said.

"Your brother thinks I'm a privileged woman and not an equal, so your opinion that he thinks I am smart is wrong," Lettie signed.

"You'll find that the two of you have much in common," Elsa signed. Manuel glared.

"If I want to be ignored, I'll go find my mother," he snapped.

Elsa signed. "So go," Isabella said. The three wolves left and Elsa leaned against Lettie and Isabella.

Chapter 4 Demons

Anga shivered despite the warmth and comfort of her beautiful home, in Mexico City, there was nothing she couldn't have or buy. Nothing was out of her reach except immorality and peace. The cold drifted down into her limbs. Her fingers shook as her plans took shape all she needed was patience. It was too bad that she wasn't patient, just the opposite. She ground her teeth. The door swung open, and she snapped a glance to the intruder. It was Raymond with some comfort. Coffee wasn't what she needed. He placed the cups and coffee pot in front of her. Alexander shifted to his left, why was it when one found something good, something dreadful came with it, that was Alexander the bad part of Raymond, the stupid part of Raymond. She detested stupid. "When the three men arrive send them to me right away."

"Should I go and look out for them mother?" Alexander asked.

"Unless you have something better to do," she said. He had that puzzled look like his brain shut down whenever he had to have something more than a small thought. She ground her teeth.

"Get out!" Raymond shouted. The two men left, and she patted Raymond's arm.

"Thank you, I'm fine," she said. He knew she was lying, but had the good sense to keep his opinion to himself. The door bell rang, and he moved away. They were here. Within a moment, they were delivered the lowly Wolf clan and their leader. She always liked helping the underdog, but especially this group would work well to her advantage. The leader approach, he was a beautiful man indeed.

"I have heard that you have ownership of something I need," he said. She leaned back and waited.

"I own many things Senor Villanueva, what would I have that someone like you would be interested in?" she asked.

"You have a skill that I need," he said. She nodded.

"Which is?" she asked.

"I want to learn to sign, to learn the sign language of the Fighter's," he said.

"I see, well it would take some time…" she said.

"You don't understand I want to be able to sign by this evening," he said. She sighed, ah, well the addiction of Love had the vain man in a powerful grip.

"It would cost…well, you wouldn't want to pay it," she said. He stepped closer.

"Any amount of money I will deliver," he said. She glanced at the other two men.

"All three of you want this gift?" she asked.

"Yes, name the price and it will be paid," he said.

"I have money and there is nothing that I want, so even if you could find something that I would want…the transfer would be…painful at best at worst you die," she said.

"So you can do it, make us learn sign by tonight?" Chino asked. He too was handsome, the younger brother of Manuel.

"Yes, but it would require that you submit yourselves to me."

"You want us, physically, not that I would be against such a trade. You would never forget me, and I would ruin you for all other men," Manuel said. Anga sat up.

"I've always liked older women," Chino said.

"Tall blonds are my favorite," Saul said. She smiled.

"There would be pain, horrible pain," she said.

"So we can play rough," Manuel said, "Anything you like sweetheart that's what we do best."

"So who will be first gentlemen and just as a disclaimer, there will be side effects."

"There always are, I'll go first," Saul said. The other two blinked away and he lifted her out of the chair, and they appeared in a room with long curtains on the bed. Silk sheets and candles glowed throughout the room. Anga shook her head. He leaned in to kiss her, and he was gentle and kind. He stroked her face and the next moment he was on his back as her power roared into him, and she grasped his power and drank deeply of the richness. A scream ripped around them as she took his love, and she delivered her promise. He stared up into space, his blue eyes lost in some other place. She closed his eyes and kissed his cheek. "Sleep and when you wake you will find that your desire has been granted. You will also find we will be forever connected," she whispered.

Anga appeared again in her office, and Chino came to her, and they disappeared. A cool breeze fell over them as they lounged in a sweet meadow of clover, surrounded from all sides by billowy covers. He smiled and pressed a soft kiss on her face. She pressed him back and again, she delivered the promise and took his love, sweet and gentle for herself. His green eyes pulsed as her power grew upon his mind, and he found the gift he needed to conquer the Fighter woman, poor bastard, he would never conquer Leticia. "Sleep when you wake it will be as you wanted."

Anga returned to the office and found that Manuel waited for her. He smiled, and her heart fluttered. He was at her side. "Poor dear, no one loves you what a shame. You're so sweet." His words were sincere, and she felt the heat rise into her face. A door slammed, and she turned. A whip rang out, and chains clicked. She swallowed. "You think a man like him would ever find you beautiful or special? He will be something one day, and you're nothing, but a dirty animal!" Anga stood and searched the room. Father, was back, no, not yet, not yet! Manuel grasped her hands, and she forced him back and pressed her lips to his in a violent kiss. Her power blasted through him, and she gave him all she had and he disappeared as she fell upon her knees. "Dirty filthy animal, I'm going to make you pay for being alive, for being a failure!" She shook her head as the first blow crossed her head, and he ripped her clothes. She scrambled around on the ground in search of an escape, in search of the darkness. A small dark space appeared beneath the couch, and she rolled into it to hide.

A clock chimed ten times and Elsa woke. The darkness blanketed the mountains, in the distance. A fire popped opposite the window where Elsa hovered. The room was a mixture of shadows and low light. Her eyes adjusted as she gazed at the yellow and orange flames. One day had passed since she had been to the Wolf's mansion.

Elsa turned, and dark descended. She stood on the edge of the grave. The women huddled in groups as their children cried and the men clawed at the earth that bound them in the darkness. One step forward, and a skull rolled away.

"Miss, help me please." Elsa glanced up at the gentle voice. An old man held the hand of a child. The boy no more than ten stared dead eyed into space, a row of perfect bullet holes crossed his chest.

Elsa's breath misted in the cool air as her eyes came back to the man, and he smiled. She nodded. "Yes, you see the child, the boy he's my grandson, Antonio. He must leave this place. The darkness is no place for a child to learn and grow." She nodded. A burst of energy sparked against Elsa's arm.

"Elsa we must talk," David said. The old man eyed the Warrior.

"Rule number two, Hunters should never, ever invade, intruder or otherwise enter the conscious, unconscious or subconscious thought, nightmare, dream or such other event without permission in writing thirty days in advance of said invasion and or occupation. Punishment for said violation is...what is the punishment, never heard of anyone breaking that rule?" Isabella said.

"Who are you?" David snarled. Elsa pressed the Warrior back, and his eyes slid to her hand on his chest.

"I was invited. How about you?" Isa asked.

"Miss please I'm in need of your help," the old man said. Elsa nodded as she came back to the dead.

"No one can help you. You're dead," David said. The old man shook his bald head.

"You're insane. I can't be dead. I'm talking to you." Isabella nodded.

"So what?" David asked.

"Are you dead?" the old man asked. Elsa blinked.

"No, but you are," David said.

"If I'm dead and you're not. How can you hear me and speak to me. It doesn't make sense, not logical, now I was here first," he said. Elsa lowered David's arm.

"Sir, can you see out of your right eye?" Leticia asked. The old man's right eye was a fleshy red hole. The Fighter's healer and young hunter still needed to come to terms with her new gifts.

"No," the old man said.

"Why is that?" Leticia asked. The old man sniffed.

"I've developed a cataract. It happened to both my parents, they went blind, now as to the boy," he said.

"Elsa attend to the living and leave the dead to their fate!" David shouted. He reached for her, and she blasted him away. He roared and the wind tossed the residents of the grave about. She shielded the old man and gathered the child in her embrace. He laid his head on her shoulder. David stomped across to them. She raised her arm and dropped a bolt of lightning on David.

"Whoa that's gonna leave a mark," Leticia said.

"Only on his ego. We don't have to do what they say," Elsa said in her mind. She soothed the back of the trembling child.

"He's a nasty one I don't think you want him for an enemy Leader Elsa…this is the weirdest dream I've ever had," Leticia said.

"It's not a dream. You're here in person," Elsa said in her mind.

"Then that would make this a nightmare and me…what would that make me Leader Elsa?" Leticia asked.

"A Soul Hunter," Isabella said in their mind. The corpses rearranged and came back to their positions in the dark. The old man watched them.

"This David can't be as bad as Leader Abrim. You are the Leader of the Hunters," Leticia said.

"There are no Hunters to lead," Elsa said in her mind.

"There will be," Isabella said.

"If I am dead, then so is Antonio," the old man said.

"What is your name?" Leticia asked.

"My name what is my name?" he asked.

"Mario," the child whispered. Elsa glanced at the boy.

"Yes, that's right Mario Luis Jimenez what has happened to all of us?" Mario asked. The boy shifted.

"They made us disappear," the child said. Mario swallowed.

"I will stay here to be a witness, but Antonio he must go. He deserves better than this worm hole," Mario said.

"No one deserves this Senor Jimenez. The leader shall take him some place brighter," Isabella said.

"Like Heaven?" Mario asked. Elsa shook her head.

"Maybe someday for now, he's bound to earth by the chains of the crime committed against him and you," Isabella said.

"Is that a promise that he'll go to Heaven?" Mario asked. Isabella's eyes met Elsa's.

"If she could promise that she would be more than human, but she will not lie," Leticia said.

"Fair enough," Mario said.

"Fairness and justice in a pit of the unknown doesn't exist," Isabella said.

"I might agree except that she's here, and Antonio is leaving. I pray I see you again my dear boy, be good and brave as you always are," Mario said. The child shifted.

"I love you Poppi," he whispered.

"I love you too," Mario said. The old man's eyes remained on the others with them. He hobbled away.

Isabella's rage rippled through her as she shifted time, and they came back to the houses with the signs where the group in the death pit had originated. People milled about talking and laughing and Isabella shouted at them.

"Get out of here! You're going to die!" They shook their heads and ignored her. "Why won't they listen?" Elsa adjusted the child and took her arm.

"Would we believe if someone told us of our future, of our deaths?"

"No, where will this all end?" Isabella said.

"I'm not sure," Elsa said in her mind.

"I believe my ignorance about these things was better than the knowledge I now hold my leader," Leticia said.

"Reality is worst than any fiction, Fighter Leticia and I agree ignorant bliss is better."

"And much more dangerous," Elsa replied in their minds.

"As dangerous as the wolf clan when the Fighters hear of our...association with them," Leticia asked. The railroad tracks spread out before them as Isa jerked her arm out of hers.

"When Warrior full of Grace comes to he's going to be Warrior full of piss, and you're going to have an additional problem. Leader Stein won't like him," Isabella said. She took the child from Elsa, and the boy shivered in her arms, only for a moment and then disappeared to walk with the others that Isabella harbored.

Three days passed since the ghost child Antonio came to his new keeper, his new host. The clouds hid the stars from her as she perched in the spot where her family should be resting in peace. She adjusted the few little stones left as the wind moved the dust around. She jerked backwards and was caught in a talon's grip. "I knew you'd come back here!" David shouted.

She spun out of his grasp, and a bolt of light blasted him. He staggered, but came on, and she blasted him again. He took it like a woman and kept on. Another strike and smoked issued off his coat. His jaw clamped together. She scuttled back and ran into his father's headstone. He stopped. "I don't want you to be afraid of me!" She was weak from lack sleep and no food. Leticia hunted for something to feed them. Her eyes caught that of her soldier's and stopped her. Leticia hid and watched, but it was only the girl's nightmare image as her body remained trapped in the mansion of the wolf clan.

"I need…you…I need a…fix," he said. She struggled and managed to disappear half of her body. "No, no don't disappear again." He spun in place and ran his thick fingers through his short blond hair. "What do you want for me to beg?" he shouted. The ground crunched as he hit his knees. She exhaled and reappeared. She shook her head. He laughed, and the sound grated her nerves. It was desperate, and maddened. His eyes were carved in deep, dark circles, his lower lip clenched in his teeth.

He dropped his head, and she scrambled to him. Her hands spread across his back, and his power surged into her. She held it back the best she could, but it overpowered her. She shifted time, and they appeared at his bedroom. She floated him from the floor to his bed and laid him back. She took the sweat from his face and placed her mouth on his forehead. She drained down until light spots flashed in her vision. A surge of power blasted back as she exhaled. He sighed and slept.

She rose, and four guns aimed at her. "We're sorry Miss, but he would want us to take you hostage," Nellie said.

"He hasn't slept for days," Bea said.

"He's losing his mind over you," Wayne said.

"I've never seen him so lost in all the ten years all of us have been together," Bob said. Elsa moved.

"We don't want to hurt you, Elsa, but without him, we're done," Wayne said. Elsa's gaze slid to the prone man.

"He's saved us a life of misery," Bob said.

"This is our life, and if he dies…we die," Nellie said.

"Without him we go back to being nothing," Bea said. Elsa eyed them.

"What are you with him?" Elsa signed to Nellie. Each looked at the other. She jumped through the air and aimed for the window. The alarm shrieked as she broke the glass barrier. Gun shots whistled and then a roar of wind. David was awake and very pissed. She was invisible as she floated to the carpeted floor of his bedroom. A small sting pierced her arm.

"What the Hell are you thinking what if you hit her?" David shouted. The quartet backed up from the heat of his anger. His face was no longer the desperate hollow shell of earlier in the evening.

"We couldn't let her escape David. We can't let you die," Nellie said. She frowned. "We need you." Nellie spoke the truth the others were afraid to expose.

"So we take what's not ours?" David asked.

"That sounded like a question it wasn't was it Wayne?" Bob asked.

"Only in the hypothetical sense cause the answer is yes if we need it, yes we take it. We pay for it, but we take it," Wayne said. David glared at the broken glass.

"How would we pay her for what we need?" Nellie asked.

"Maybe someone needs her more than we do," David said.

"Give us an example of someone who needs her more than us?" Bea asked. The others nodded.

"Yeah cause if you die, we go back to being homeless, a con artist, a drunk and a person without care or fear. We're done. We're worse than three-time losers. No one wants us, but you," Bob said.

"She asked us what we were with you." Nellie said.

"What did you say?" David asked.

"Nothing," Bea said.

"That's when she escaped," Bob said.

"We had an answer," Wayne said.

"Yeah the answer is we're cowards," Nellie said. Elsa pressed her fingers to her arm as the blood dripped. A single drop flew free. David's eyes followed it, and he pinched between his fingers. Elsa spun and landed in the wet grass.

"Oh dear we hit her!" Nellie shouted.

"Maybe we killed her?" Bea said.

"No, where is she?" Wayne asked.

"Yeah cause if we hit her. She'd be here!" Bob said.

"What will I do if she dies?" David asked. Elsa pitched a stone into the middle of them. Their eyes drew down as she appeared. David's gaze came over her face.

"You didn't shoot me! It was the glass, I scraped the glass." Four guns came up.

"Come back in Miss you look hungry, and I should know," Nellie, the homeless said.

"Yes, it's warm in here," Bea the con artist said. Elsa stroked the blood away.

"You're safe here with us," Bob without care or fear said.

"Stay here and you can be strong," Wayne the drunk said.

"Why do you need me heroes?" Elsa signed. Nellie glanced toward the others and they stared at her.

"Heroes we never saved anybody, we can't even save ourselves," Nellie said.

"You struggled alone, we all struggle, but together you became heroes to one another, and you even helped David keep a promise," Elsa signed. She took two steps back.

"What promise did we help David keep?" Nellie asked.

"The promise of his last name, David full of Grace, you've forgotten about earning that grace. John hasn't," Elsa signed. She stepped away.

"The promise of David's name," Nellie said.

"Only two people knew of my name and one of them is dead, how did you know?" David whispered. She turned back, and the guns were down.

"She said you opened the door David and yanked me in Warrior," Nellie said. David didn't like that he couldn't understand her.

"Who's John?" Nellie asked.

"He's David's adopted father," Bob said.

"You some kind of psychic witch?" Wayne asked. Elsa grinned.

"Something like that. The dead are just waiting to be heard those that are still around," Nellie said. Elsa walked backwards.

"You can't leave Elsa!" Bea screamed.

"Yes, I can and so can you, hero," Nellie said. A blast of lightening hit the ground and she disappeared. Nellie screamed and they poured out of the window, but all they found was charred earth. The sky lit and bolts crashed, and they were thrown back.

"Get in the house!" David shouted. They scrambled through the window as the storm pounded the house. She used her power to cross the miles and return to her soldier. Leticia grasped her when she saw the blood. She ripped a piece of her blouse and wrapped it around.

"I thought you left me," she whispered.

"I can never leave you, until I am dead," Elsa signed. Leticia jerked to her face.

"What does that mean Leader?"

"Only death can separate us. We are hinged together like a door."

"And what about the blond one?" Leticia asked.

"My name is Isabella, Fighter," Isabella said, "And we are hinged together as well. My brother will not be pleased with you, not that he ever was. He's such a baby. Elsa you must free our physical forms from the wolf mansion," Isabella said.

"Why would I care what he thinks?" Leticia said.

"That is a question only you can answer, Lettie," Isabella said. Elsa helped her fighter off the ground, and they went on their way. John Dalton's ghost remained hidden. She wondered what he thought as she turned away from his final resting place.

Chapter 5 Master

Raymond entered the study, and Gustavo glanced up. "I've brought your dinner master," Raymond said. The master glanced behind him. Gustavo was nothing like his twin Anga, where she lacked confidence and power Gustavo was nothing but power.

"I have some new Black Cloaks Raymond?"

"Yes, master, your sister has added to her guard. His name is Gabriel and he's still learning," Raymond said.

"Is he smarter than Alexander?" Gustavo asked. Raymond smiled at the insult leveled at his brother, who shifted in discomfort. He poured the red wine into a shot glass and drank. He then set it front of the master. He ate a large spoonful of the rich meat and potatoes and passed them to him.

"No, master he isn't any smarter than Alexander, he is faster than him."

"Is there more of this it's delicious, will I get dessert? You know I hate it when you're gone!" Gustavo said.

"Yes, master I know and I made extra as always."

"How is my dear sister, weak as ever?" He shoved large amounts of meat into his mouth as he closed his eyes.

"She is the same." The plate was licked clean and Raymond repeated the ritual and served him again. The wine was next, and a whole chocolate cake waited with one huge bite taken out of it. Raymond swallowed the sweet chocolate along with the vomit that threatened to choke him. He hated rich foods. He could never get used to the textures and flavors, but the master needed to be satisfied at all costs. He wiped his mouth.

"Have you ever killed a woman Raymond?" Gustavo asked.

"No, master." The plate was clean and Gustavo attacked the cake with vigor.

"They are so easy to kill, even with the crying and begging. I have an assignment for you. Her name is Elsa de las Almas." Not one bit of crumb or frosting was missed when the master enjoyed the cake. Raymond straightened as he waited.

"You wish for me to kill her master?" He shoved the empty plate away and drank the last of the bottle of wine.

"You can't kill her. No one can, not even I, not that I want her dead, I don't. I want her brought to me, but here is the kicker. I want her brought to me by you, but she can't know who you are, and she must come willingly," Gustavo said.

"How soon will you want this done?" Raymond asked.

"As soon as you can, however, I won't hold my breath since I believe this is an impossible task. Do I have new recruits to review?"

"Yes, master," Raymond said.

"Good let's see how much blood can be shed," Gustavo said. The man rose, over six feet tall as he strode to the gaming room. The doors were opened, and they passed through to the line of new recruits. Raymond eyed them and at once knew which one would die. Gustavo took a seat as Raymond stepped forward. "You on the end leave!"

"Why am I not given a chance?" the man asked. Raymond knew well why, but the master liked games, and so it would be that way for this poor bastard. Raymond turned and bowed before the master.

"Give him a chance then Raymond. Here are the rules, you must take all that the leader can take if not you die," Gustavo said. The big man looked round the room.

"Who is this leader?" he asked.

"He is right there before you," Gustavo said. Raymond straightened, and the man laughed.

"Him this little man?" he asked.

"Yes, that little man is the leader so what say you? Will you compete against him?"

"I will beat him!" came the reply.

"Excellent, let's hope that you are right," Gustavo said, "The first trial is lay across the bar there to your left, little man." Raymond

removed his shirt and lay across the rail. He
caught the eyes of Alexander and Gabriel
because of him they wouldn't need to suffer the
trials of Gustavo. The master rose and raised the
rider's crop. He hammered the straps against his
back. Raymond exhaled the pain and waited for
the next one. He shifted his thoughts away, to a
beautiful face and sweet red mouth of the
woman he could only have in his dreams. Elsa
put her hand on his face as the next blow ripped
his flesh. He wouldn't fail, and the boastful
newcomer would surely die at the hands of the
master.

Evening arrived once more, and Elsa drank
the noodles and broth. She sent the two women
to wait for her return, there would be enough
trouble when her leader found out of her deal
with the wolf mother to save Leticia, she would
go to him to clear the way for their return. She
arrived at the village entrance. She hadn't seen
anyone from the village in several months. She
hadn't seen her leader Abrim Stein in that time.
Just to hear his voice would give her comfort, to
see his smile or know he was somewhere
nearby. She sighed all she needed was just a
moment of his time. He always had time for her.

"Ramon what's taking so long?" Abrim
shouted. Elsa approached and peered into the
next room. Abrim paced by the phone. "Yes I
heard you just a moment!" Elsa ran to him, and
he frowned. He turned his back. "Well what do

you think?" She reached up to kiss him, and he stepped away. "Not now I'm busy! Ramon!"

She went around the table and poured him a coffee with cream and sugar, a piece of ice so it wouldn't be too hot. She brought it to him and smiled. He glanced at it and took it. His tan face squeezed together. "Its ice cold, I hate it!" She took the cup and went back to the cupboard. She pressed her hands around it, and the heat came up. She made another for Ramon.

She brought the cup to Abrim and passed Ramon his. The Leader's second sipped his coffee. "Wow I needed that thanks Elsa," Ramon said. He smiled, and Elsa nodded. Abrim took a sip.

"Damn it. I just burn my mouth!" he shouted. He slammed the cup on the floor. One of her pretty cups broke into a million pieces, just like her heart.

"I'm sorry…I just needed to see you for just one…" Elsa signed.

"I don't have time for you!" Abrim shouted. The broken pieces of Elsa's heart dropped to her stomach.

"You always have…" Elsa signed. He got right in her face.

"What don't you understand? My best friend and his family are dead, and now I have to figure out how to keep this village from going crazy with vengeance when all I want to do is the same!"

"That's what I want…I think I can…" Elsa signed.

"You can do nothing woman!" he shouted. The phone hung on his hand. His face was gray with grief and anger.

"Let me help you, please…" Elsa signed.

"This is for men to handle," Abrim shouted. Tears ran into her mouth as she tried to get a hold of herself. "Fighter's don't cry!"

"Abrim stop hear her out," Ramon said.

"No, I'm handling this my way!" Abrim shouted. She ran in front of him and forced him to look at her hands.

"I can help Leticia," Elsa signed.

"She's been gone five days if she's not dead, maybe it's better to let fate take its course," he said. She slapped him. Her tears ran free as she stared him down.

"If there's a chance to help Leticia, I'll do it."

"Don't go against me!" Abrim shouted. Elsa bit her lip and tiptoed to his face.

"You're not man enough to stop me," Elsa signed.

"I've never had to punish a woman Fighter, but I will," he said.

"Abrim, no," Ramon said.

"Do anything you want. Her life isn't forfeited on your word. She is my sister. She is a Fighter, and I will spill my blood to bring her home," Elsa signed. She walked away.

"Elsa stop!" Abrim shouted.

Elsa leapt forward in time. A red-brick mansion loomed into the air three stories tall. She approached the double doors, and they opened. A butler appeared. "Is your luggage in the car?" he asked. He was round faced and spoke English. She shook her head. "Well, never mind the master will see to your every need. This way." She entered a dark room and walked over the blood stained carpet to a chair. The damaged leather vest and a shirt lay together. The soft leather smelled of rich woods and burned almonds.

"That would have been a painful death," Alec said. She placed Mano's shirt on the chair. The elder leader came around shirtless, his chest, chiseled and carved like a much younger man. He stood above her and grasped her hair. He pulled her face up and smiled.

"Abrim wouldn't listen to you would he?" Alec asked. He touched the worn fabric of her shirt. "He admires you because you're unique, you don't care about his money like all the other women in his life. I can understand his point of view. A man is vain, well this man is vain." Her clothes changed and she was bare of foot and a long, black gown slipped around her. She reached for the dress. "Give me at least this one favor, I owe you, four lives and no it's not a hand me down." She tried to change it, but all that changed was the color to red, then to pink, then to purple. She stopped it, and it returned to black. He leaned closer. "I like black too." He freed her braid and ran his fingers in her hair.

"Uncle dinner is going to be served in…" Mano said. The younger commander slammed the door.

"I have plans make some excuse," Alec said. Mano's square jaw twitched as they watched him.

"What would you like for me to tell Tricia your lover?" Mano asked. Elsa glanced at Alec who grimaced.

"We do have that thing tonight don't we? Some kind of honor for her, something about orphans and widows what a load of crap? Tell her the truth."

"Which is what Alec?" Mano asked.

"That I'm having an evening with the younger much more beautiful Elsa. I have some plans for you that you might like my dear," Alec said. Mano's cheek jumped.

"You deliver that message old man, and I'll stay so she doesn't escape," Mano said. Alec shook his head.

"I never leave the fox with the chickens. I made a picnic dinner we can have by the fire on the mink rug. Move along son."

"Maybe he wants to join us?" Elsa signed.

"Who is she?" Mano asked.

"Like you don't know. You tried to have her killed by that boy, Gabriel, poor lad with no family. You try to raise them right, but look at who he's sleeping with. You sleep with rats you get the plague, go!" Alec said. Mano slammed the door. Alec entered another room and sat the basket on the rug. A fire burned. He sat down and pulled her next to him. She put her hands up.

"You can understand sign?"

"I understand many things, not so much the Hunter's rules or ethics," Alec said. He leaned back and propped himself up.

"Where is Maria? You're a warrior," Elsa signed, "You can do many things."

"Except live forever and not suffer with the frailty of age and disease. Which is where you come in, I am in need of a Hunter. I told Maria you would come here if she asked."

"Warriors don't need anyone," Elsa signed.

"Not true, we need many people we're very vain. Vanity can't work without a crowd, but in your group, you do what I need."

"There are no other hunters," Elsa signed.

"The other group, the Fighters you're responsible for the women and children that's where I need the help," Alec said. He reached for a sandwich, and she examined it and took a bite. He took it from her and ate it and removed another. The bread was fresh and the ham sweet. She handed him the other half. He rubbed mustard off her face.

"Does it bother you that Mano sleeps with…"

"I've never been a fool all right I was a fool, but when a young man looks at a woman he sees what he wants, not always the reality of things. Long before Mano came along I was replaced, but I made…well I kept my family separate until recently, another mistake," Alec said.

"Forbid him to ever go to her again," Elsa signed.

"That sounds like warrior talk," Alec said. Elsa adjusted the dress and passed another sandwich to him.

"We must never fight our nature. You're family, you say what happens, and loyalty is never cheap. He should have said no to begin with just because it was a conflict of interest," Elsa signed.

"Hunters are so black and white," Alec said, "And evil that's a nice surprise. Problem is he's leader and I'm just an old has been." She frowned, and he laughed.

"Uncle!" Mano said.

"What?" Alec asked. Elsa glanced up.

"I heard laughter, I thought someone was being tortured," Mano said. Alec winked.

"Someone is me. New rule no more whoring yourself to the old lady, oh and call your mother and tell her," Alec said.

"What? You're jealous of Tricia and me…" Mano said. Alec ran his finger over Elsa's chin.

"Sure I am when I'm sitting by the fire with a beautiful woman who doesn't care about my money whose sweet and soft with a pretty full mouth and…" Alec said.

"Uncle!" Mano shouted.

"Why are you shouting at your elder?" Alec turned angry eyes at his nephew, and Mano glared back. Elsa touched his chest.

"Don't touch him girl!" Mano growled.

"She can touch me anywhere she likes go call your mother!" Alec shouted. Mano left.

"It's nice when a young man is jealous of you. I like it."

"Tell me why I should help you?"

"I want your promise as a Hunter, that you'll protect the women and children of this family if…something should happen to me."

"General…" Elsa signed.

"I don't like that name. Call me anything, but that," he said.

"If something should happen to you the best person to protect your family is Manuel not me," she signed. Alec nodded.

"You think he's handsome?"

"He's hairy, and black and nasty, and I don't see him like most people do. It's an inside out thing."

"Does he frighten you?" Alec asked.

"No."

"Everyone is afraid of him," Alec said, "Except me."

"They should be," she signed. He rose.

"Well, that's what I want do we have a deal?"

"Why should I deal with you?"

"So that your secret is safe," he replied.

"What secret?"

"That you saved the life of the enemy which is what you did when you saved Mano? I made him the leader. We'll see if he can manage. Abrim is a bitter and jealous man he will not be pleased and at his best he's a devil at his worst not even you are safe," he said.

"Blackmail is that it? So go on and tell him," she signed.

"He will come after Maria is that what you want?" he asked. Abrim had no love for the Wolf clan and when he found out that there was a price on her head, he would wipe them out, including Maria.

"I will protect them with my life," she signed.

"That's all I need," he said. He went to the door.

"Why are you..." she signed.

"You can't change what people think. I stole Abrim's wife, my mistake his gain consequences sometimes you just have to die with them," Alec said. He disappeared beyond the door.

Chapter 6 Wolf Men

A door slammed, and Elsa jumped up. She glanced down at the drive. Patricia stood at the open door of a limo. "Where were you with some little whore?" Patricia shouted. Alec wore a white shirt with the sleeves rolled up. Mano joined them on the landing.

"No all your friends were with you. I was with a real woman, a special woman, a woman with qualities no man can resist," Alec said. Patricia bit her lip.

"So you were with some young girl with a perfect body," Patricia snapped. Alec laughed and smiled, a smile of sweet memories.

"No, not so young and definitely not perfect, oh, but she was so soft and sweet and she reminded me of what was," Alec said.

"Are you smiling you had sex while I was with our guests. How could you?" Patricia asked. Alec shifted.

"Same way you can fuck every young soldier who walks by your door, but no it was better than sex, maybe later," Alec said. He grinned at Mano.

"You're hopeless!" Patricia screamed.

"No I'm number one bastard, and tonight I saw reality more clearly and so should you," Alec said. He pulled a mirror from behind him and presented it to her. She refused to take it, and he grabbed her head and made her look.

"Do you know what I see an old, pocked face woman with deep lines and spots allover." Patricia gasped as her face changed. Her fingers flew to her face as she whimpered.

"You're so cruel to me," she said.

"You smell like rotted chicken and old piss. You asked me if I was jealous of you and her Manuel not at all. No amount of nothing is worth what she is, take care how you live boy, or you may build a Hell you can't escape," Alec said. He jerked away from Patricia as she continued to examine her face.

"I'm leaving come on Mano," Patricia said.

"No, not this time."

"Why? Come on I demand it," Patricia said.

"No!" Mano shouted. Patricia retreated to the car, and it sped away. Alec glanced up at her. Mano turned, and Alec slapped him.

"Do not look upon the sacred you are not worthy!" Alec shouted. Mano turned more, and his Uncle slapped him again. "You want to challenge me boy you better grow some balls!" Alec stomped away. Elsa pressed her palm to the glass as Mano squinted at her. She turned away from his anger and went back to the fire.

Leticia and Isabella were locked in the room by Maria. She wouldn't leave without them, and the wolf mother knew it. She arranged the meeting with Alec to make the deal, to give the old leader some peace before…what? It was midnight and she should be home with her kin, but instead she paced the small room and waited to hear news of the women. A ripple passed through her, and she followed it. Lettie was tied to a hospital bed, and Isabella was on the next one. Lettie tried to free the restraints. Elsa ran to her, and they worked on it. "All you needed was a scent," Mano said. He grasped her and pressed her head to his chest.

They appeared on a bed full of soft, warm blankets. Candles were lit all around the room, but a light shone bright. He pressed her against the big pillows as he lay on top of her. He leaned down, and she rolled away. He caught her and ripped her shirt. He exhaled. "Listen I don't want to force you...I never had to force a woman, but this has to happen do you understand?"

She shook her head and moved her hands to sign. "I don't care what you have to say let's try to do this easy all right there should be passion, not anger it will make for a better one." She flipped him on his back. "You're taking this very well go on do what you want." He gripped her hips, and she opened her mouth. Tears ran down. "No, screaming, stop, stop," he cooed. She rolled beneath him, and his mouth came over hers. She closed her mouth and licked her lips, but his tongue touched hers, and she froze. He flew away, and she scrambled to the window.

"What the Hell are you doing we're not animals!" Alec shouted. Alec raised his fist and Elsa caught his arm, but faced Mano. His eyes went down the front of her. She put her hand over her bare breasts. Alec's arm came around her waist, and Mano came unhinged.

"Don't touch her!" Mano shouted. He spun her out of Alec's grip. Fear, grief, pain exploded in Elsa, and she caught Mano's knife. She spun through the air and sliced open her wrist. A stream of blood followed her as she spun. "No God damn me!" Mano shouted. She drove the knife to her heart as she looked into his eyes.

Lettie woke in a bed, her bloody scarred wrists no longer tied. Pain, grief and failure ruptured her heart. She spun from the bed and yanked the lamp off the table. She wrapped the cord around her neck and stood on a chair. A clothes hook on the door would do the trick. She wrapped the end around and stepped off.

A mouth pressed to Lettie's, air rushed into her. A sweet taste spilled into her mouth and her hands went to his face. She turned her head and kissed his mouth. She came off the ground and landed on a soft bed. His hands slid under her shirt. She turned her face. "I've never made…Chino," she whispered. His green eyes flashed a curious light.

"I know what to do my baby girl," he whispered. She trembled.

"I'm afraid…I don't even know how to kiss you," she said. He rubbed her bare skin with his big hands.

"You were doing all right. I thought you were dead," he said.

"I want to see my Ma," she said. His eyes looked away.

"She's dead baby girl…I'm really sorry. Mano's flipped out, and I don't know what to do…" Chino said. Lettie spun off the bed with his knife. She drew the wicked edge against her wrist. "Oh, fuck no!" Her blood splashed his face as she drove the knife to her heart. He picked her out of the air and caught her by the wrists. She fought him.

"Let me die! Elsa was my last hope, my Elsa, my Ma everyone else is dead let me go!" Lettie screamed.

"Somebody better help me here!" Chino shouted. She bucked against his body, and they crashed together. "Leader, Mano somebody!" Elsa appeared over his right shoulder, and Lettie screamed and pitched him off. Elsa grasped her in a death hold.

"He said you were dead. He did. He did!" Lettie screamed.

"She slit her wrist can someone do something?" Chino said. Lettie jumped and kissed the man. He hauled her off the floor and went to Elsa. "Fix it now!" Elsa's index finger turned white hot, and she held out her arm.

When the finger touched her skin, Lettie inhaled and squeezed Chino tight. Her flesh burned closed and Lettie held on, but even after the finger was lifted free the pain remained.

"Seal my wrists, Ma," Lettie whispered. Elsa held both her wrists, and the pain jerked into her mind. "Wait...for me Chino..."

Elsa swept the sweat from Lettie's face. Chino De La Rosa held the girl in his embrace. Lettie's wrists were scarred red beyond repair where she tried to escape the manacles that held her prisoner and now a jagged scar on her right forearm glowed where she tried to take her life. A red, bluish bruise appeared at her throat. Elsa slid her fingers over the skin. "How did that happen?" Alec asked.

"She tried...to hang...herself, but I don't know what saved her," Elsa signed. She pressed her forehead to Lettie's.

"I did, don't thank me. It was an accident I came to check on our prisoner and knocked her away. Can I keep her Leader?" Chino asked. Elsa smacked him.

"What kind of menso are you? She's not a stray cat," Alec said. He laughed, and Elsa frowned. Chino stroked Lettie's face.

"Maybe she could teach me to be decent," Chino said. Elsa signed.

"Girl ain't got that kind of time. You'll learn that like everybody else does on the street," Alec said. Alec laughed again.

"She likes me leader," Chino said. Elsa signed.

"She thinks you have pretty eyes and a really hot kiss…" Alec said. Chino grinned.

"That's enough for me," Chino said.

"But not nearly enough for her," Elsa signed.

"What did she say?" Chino asked.

"Follow Lettie's lead," Alec said. Elsa frowned and ripped the bandage from her arm. Mano crossed the room, and she lit her finger. She drew the white hot fingertip down the injury and held on until the end. When the black came she leapt into it.

The smell of Mezcal woke Lettie. The glint of the bottle flashed as the green-eyed man tilted it up. Lettie wrestled the bottle from his hands. "Give it to me!" Chino recovered the bottle and eyed her. He sighed and dropped the bottle on the nightstand.

"You told me to wait so I did," he said.

"You thought you'd get drunk in the meantime do you know what that shit does to your body?" she asked. She was on her knees next to him. He pulled another bottle free.

"Makes me drunk?" he asked. She straddled his body.

"No!" Lettie said. He kept the bottle out of her reach as his hand slipped up her hip.

"Mezcal which this is gets you high, I've had enough to know, and I need it after what happened tonight. I'm getting stoned out of my mind." His hand was at her neck.

"That stuff will kill you, do you know how many people I've treated for…" Lettie said. She counted the empty bottles, five bottles. "Did you drink all of this?" She ran her hands over his face.

"Yeah so what?" he said.

"You should be dead!"

"I don't even have a buzz yet," he said. She took the bottle and put it to her mouth. "No, that's not good for you." He shoved the bottle away and pulled her close. He kissed her mouth and held her tight. The heat rose in her body as she jerked away.

"I need to see Ma," she said.

"Can't she's…asleep and Mano's in the pen," he said.

"She's unconscious, not asleep." She sprung from the bed, and he caught her.

"If you wake her Mano is going to flip out. It's going to be ugly, and then I'm going to the pen," he said. She tasted the tears. "Ah shit come on." They crept up the dark hall and entered a room. Lettie ran to Elsa and touched her face. Elsa signed.

"Mano's in the dungeon?" Lettie asked. Elsa evaporated. "Where did she go?"

"To find Mano, where do you think, genius," he said. She yanked him along, and he snapped her back. "Where are you going?"

"To Ma and the dungeon you torture people in your house?" He walked away, and she ran in the opposite direction. She slammed into him at the door. "You're not drunk?"

"No, but…" he said. A roar erupted. "That would be the Black Wolf the meanest, nastiest bastard in the world." Lettie ripped the door open and tripped down the stone steps. Chino caught her and stomped forward. The door bent outward and blasted across the hall into splinters. Chino sheltered her.

"Where is she?" Mano shouted.

"She's not with you?" Chino asked.

"Don't make me hurt you!" he whispered. Lettie got between the two men. Mano stopped. "What is this?"

"You're not going to hurt him," Lettie said. Chino's arm came around her waist, and she cleared the floor.

"Chino tell her who I am!"

"You're a sorry excuse for a human being not worthy of the One, but then no one's perfect. Maybe if you died a hundred times and came back a hundred more you could be a flea on the mongrel dog outside her house!" Lettie shouted, "You're not touching the hot man with the green eyes unless you want me to cut you and shoot you and poison you and chop you into little bits to feed to the rats!" Chino turned her head into his shoulder.

"Was that a threat medicine woman? Where is your mother? Make her tell me Chino. I don't want to get nasty," Mano said.

"I'm gonna bite you!" Lettie said. Elsa appeared. "Ma!" Mano grabbed Elsa. "No don't take her away please!" Lettie screamed. Elsa held her and stroked her face. "Chino said it would get nasty I should have let you stay away I'm sorry."

"It's all right," Elsa signed.

"Why are you out of the pen?" Alec asked. Mano grabbed Elsa. "Why do you want to hurt her Manuel?" Mano pushed Elsa away and slammed the door on his cell.

"That's all he knows Elsa he knows nothing of…well it's my fault," Alec said. Elsa disappeared, and Lettie ran up the stairs.

Elsa appeared in the cell. Night came and a small light from above lit the small space. Mano crouched against a wall, and she slid in front of him. She leaned forward with a bottle of Mezcal. She drew the open bottle to her mouth. "No, that's not good for you," he said. She offered it to him. "If this is poisoned, I'm just going to die." He turned it up. She pressed her mouth against his and scooped a bit of liquid out with her tongue. The smooth liquid tingled. He took another drink and she leaned in, and he stopped her. "No why are you here?" he asked. She put her hands up. "I don't understand that so don't do it. Are you here because you pity me?" She shook her head and signed no. "I don't want to learn your language go away."

She shifted against the opposite wall. A rat jumped at her hand, and she burned it to ash. "You're here because you think I'm hot?" She fished in her pocket and went to sit between his legs. He looked in the mirror. "So what I see myself. I need to get some sleep I'm looking a little rough." The image changed, and he turned into a creature with long black hair all over his face and arms. His teeth were jagged points of ripping death and his eyes deep blue. She pointed to herself and then to him and then to the mirror. "You see a monster when you see me?" She nodded and signed yes. "Everyone else in the world thinks I'm hot, and you see a monster how is that?" She turned her sleeve inside out and pointed at the inside of the sleeve. "You see the inside of me? I'm ugly to you?" She shook her head and signed. "No, that means no. I see a monster, and you see what?" She pointed at him and stroked his face. "You see me and you don't care that I'm a nasty, ugly wicked monster who scares little children and old ladies and men and everyone except him," Mano said. She pointed to herself and smiled. "And you I don't scare you this isn't going to work. You see the rules say fear motives people to do what I want, and I thrive on fear and…" Another rat jumped in her hair, and she snapped it's neck and burned it. She smiled and gave him a bag. "What is this? I hate sandwiches. I smell beans and tortillas you give a king the food of the peasants?" She reached for the bag, and he snatched it back. "Did you make these for me?" She nodded. "Go upstairs it's damp and cold and then there's the rats one could bite you," he said. She turned her hand and showed him a scar. "A rat bit you…one of these rats?" She nodded. "Go upstairs this is no place for you…for a lady go on," Mano said. She walked to the door, and the rats were back. She closed her eyes, and a loud pop echoed. She went to the door. "Elsa," she turned to him, "Thank you." She smiled and came to be in the room Alec gave her.

"I've never seen him like he is with you," Alec said.

"We can't change our nature he's still who he is. Nothing will ever change that."

"You don't believe people can change?" Alec asked.

"What I believe doesn't matter what he knows is what will count to your family."

"If a great hunter can accept him, then who can say? So you like him, Hunter Elsa?"

"He scares people. He's nasty and arrogant and cruel. He's got skills what's not to like?" Elsa signed. Alec raised an eyebrow.

"If he's to survive your reign among my women and children a sense of humor will help you," Alec said.

"I did not agree to him, Warrior Alec. He does not need me." Alec squinted.

"Well here is the problem, they're his women and children as well as mine, and he's a lot like me. You may have to take them from him to keep your promise," Alec said.

"You believe you tricked me into accepting him. He doesn't want me or my help." She adjusted the dress.

"So I had to pull him off of you because he has no interest that's not logical."

"Forcing a woman to be with you is about power, not desire. Manuel is nothing but power," she signed.

"So why did you take him something to eat and drink?"

"He was hungry and thirsty, and you weren't going to do it, and everyone else is afraid of him," Elsa signed. Alec frowned and disappeared.

Elsa paced, Lettie was asleep. She went into the next room, but it was empty. It was some sort of office. A huge desk, a fireplace and tall cord of wood, a string blew off a piece of wood. This was the room where she first saw Mano. She freed the string and went to the desk. The glass with the finger was gone. A black packet lay on the table with a shiny glint at one end. She opened it and a group of steel surgical knives lay in the velvet pouch. On one other occasion, she had seen a set just like these. She turned from the painful memory. Next to them was a pearl handled switchblade. She took it and went back to the room. She stripped away her clothes and entered the bed, knife in hand. She popped the sharp edge free and slid it against the pillow. "I forbid you to speak to the old man! He told me what you said. What kind of power do you think you have that I would want?" She slid the knife beneath the blanket.

He slipped in with her, and his fingers curled around her shoulders. Her arm tensed. "I know a hundred women that would kill, and otherwise destroy to be where you are right now. Celia de Villa she's an actress, oh, the twin models from Peru and…" She slid the knife to her left wrist. "You've been sheltered and you don't know the rules, here's how it goes. I tell you all the beautiful, perfect women that adore me, and you cry and beg and plead. Like this, no Mano, no you have to like me, or I can't go on!" Elsa turned in his arms. She slid the knife to her heart. The sharpness pushed against her. His black eyes went blue as he sobered.

"I see the pain in your eyes. Death isn't your only choice you can grieve and cry."

"No." His fingers slid up her arm.

"I said you can and you scream and…" She shook her head and moved her fingers across her throat.

"Why because no one can hear you? I can see you, scream and cry Elsa…please," he whispered. She opened her mouth and closed her eyes and strained to set her grief free. His mouth rubbed her face as he drank her tears. "I taste your pain." He kissed her face, and she snapped the knife closed and laid it on the pillow behind her. She pulled him in, and his arms tightened as she wrapped her legs around him.

She gazed into his blue eyes. "That's Alec's favorite knife you have to put it back," he said. She shook her head. "He's going to punish me if I let you take that. Keep it, now you're only wearing panties, and your legs are wrapped around me in my world that means yes. Tell me no, oh that's right you can't speak I love it. I hate yappy women!" She bit his neck. "I like that dulce bebe do it again." She pinched him. "Ow it's getting better." She glanced into his face. "Oh alright I'll slow down. This doesn't leave the room, and no one knows I'm a monster." She tilted her head. "What all right that I look like a monster." She slid against his hard chest. "I really hate you." He rubbed her shoulders, and she nodded. "And you don't care, great."

Chapter 7 Fighter's Leader

Lettie helped Elsa up the slope. "The Fighters are skilled in this village," Elsa signed. Elsa glanced up. Isabella was on her other side, and they moved forward painfully.

"They should be they're grown men, and these have graduated no? Who is the teacher Ma?" Lettie asked.

"Ramon Maldonado and Abrim are their teachers. Do they lack some talent Leticia," Isabella signed, "Can you feel their presence? Above and around us?"

"Yes, I can hear them breath and smell them which I could do before, but now everything is so bright. They're all right, but the best teacher is…was," Lettie said. Elsa held her arm as they went.

"Your father was our best teacher with his patience and wise words, but then again, he had your mother to go home to every night which he did without fail," Elsa signed. Lettie tightened her hold on Elsa's arm as a tremor went through it.

"I've always wondered one thing about you why are you involved in all of this? In a country that's not your own?" Lettie asked.

"My grandfather was a member of this tribe. They wanted the land his father owned, so they killed his family and took it. He moved to Texas and never came back. When my aunt Romalia died, I found his letters in her things, and he regretted not fighting for what was his," Lettie wiped the sweat off of Elsa's face, "The nightmares brought me to this place to fulfill an old man's wish."

"The nightmares that is what happens to you when you sleep. You are sent to places to help?" Lettie signed. Elsa stiffened.

"Sometimes all I can do is...nothing," Elsa signed.

"But witness and remember that's more than nothing," Isabella signed.

"It's not enough for me," Elsa signed.

"It has to be because it's all you have," Isabella signed.

"I'm sorry for my failure and the loss of your family, there are no words to repair what has happened just to save me, but if there is something, anything you want from me just ask and I am at your command," Elsa signed. Lettie glanced at the trees, and they stopped to rest.

Isabella glanced around, days of walking in hard terrain and now Elsa's use of invisibility drained her, and Lettie needed help. They all needed help. Handsome Marcus Nunez stood in wait a few hundred feet ahead of them. One of her father's strongest fighter's and her brother's best friend she was nothing to him. She came up on him and stepped around him. "I need your help," she said. He turned away, and she followed him. He wouldn't look at her. She was known as the curse, the curse of her father and brother's lives. She grabbed his hand and for a moment, his eyes came to hers and then looked away. "Come on your Ma needs help." To her surprise, he followed her with his hand in hers. He jerked his hand away when he saw Lettie and Elsa.

"Ma, Leticia?" he asked. Elsa nodded her face strained.

"We…they need help," Isabella said.

"Does the Great Dear One need help?" Elsa gasped in her mind.

"You are great and dear and the one, but you're still human and four days of no sleep and this invisible trick is wearing on you," Isabella said. Marcus went away and returned with all the men.

"Marcus help me!" Lettie called. The regal man turned and leapt from the ground at them. He swept his mother up.

"She has a fever. Javier go ahead to the village and tell the leader my mother has returned, and she was successful!" Marcus said. Elsa shifted, and Lettie kept her still. Isabella stood back as they ignored her. Elsa froze.

"You'll not be forced to see anyone you don't want, Ma," Lettie said. Marcus eyed her and he frowned.

"Ma why are you calling my mother, Ma?" he asked.

"Why do you call her mother?" Lettie asked. She brushed the hair from Elsa's face.

"Because she rescued me from death, because she is my Ma," he said. He lifted her, and Elsa fought him.

"Let her down boy, you think I escaped on my own? She is my Ma now," Lettie said. Elsa was free and hooked arms with Lettie.

"I don't like it. She's my mother," Marcus said.

"I shared mine with you," Lettie said.

"Yes, but…Leticia I'm…" Marcus said.

"Don't say words to me that won't change a thing just bring your men and let's go. You all need to bathe you stink. I could smell you for miles," Lettie said. Marcus sniffed his pits and grinned.

"That's man scent," he said. He had a ready smile, and all the women loved him. Isabella watched them as they left a moment later Marcus stood in front of her. She glanced up. "I was ordered to escort you to the village." She moved forward as he stepped along with her, for such a handsome man he stunk. They struggled along, and Isabella stumbled. He caught her, and she turned her head and vomited. Lettie came next to her and pushed him away.

"You all right he smells can you make it?" Lettie asked. He frowned and Isa nodded.

There hadn't been much talk the rest of the day and as the sun slipped through the trees, they crested another ridge. They traveled south and higher into the mountain. Elsa stood next to Lettie and searched the terrain. The men arrived ahead of them, and a crowd stood waiting below in the valley. A runner broke free and ran toward them. Elsa tensed. Abrim Stein wasn't going to wait for them to arrive. Lettie helped her down, and they continued. Two steps down and Abrim blasted passed, and Elsa disappeared in his arms. Lettie hit her knees and the rocks' bit her. Marcus helped her up. "He's a little anxious to see her," Marcus said. Abrim returned and Elsa struggled to get free.

"Hey let her go!" Lettie said. Abrim held firm, his face grim. "You didn't have time for her, and now you want her to just forget that?" Abrim let Elsa go, and she slipped to her knees. Lettie came to her and helped her up. Isabella moved closer, and Marcus blocked her way. Isa took several steps back, and Elsa reached for and pulled her closer. Marcus straightened.

"You told the girl what I said?" Abrim asked.

"She speaks of you as if you're a god," Lettie snapped. Lettie struggled to get a handle on Elsa.

"But I am just a stupid man," Abrim said. Abrim took her up, and Elsa's arms went around his neck.

"I'm convinced," Lettie said. Abrim walked and they followed.

"The One is wise to not criticize her leader to his face in public something you might learn one day, Leticia," Abrim said.

"Lucky for me the One is wise enough not to listen to you and leave me for dead," Lettie said. Marcus pulled her back.

"He's in a bad mood best not to tempt him to punish you," Marcus said. Lettie sniffed, and Isabella wiped her face.

"He's got to get passed Ma first," Lettie said.

"Your Ma's a little weak right now," Abrim said.

"Just try to punish me see what happens," Lettie said.

Within ten minutes, they entered Abrim Stein's village. Each of the houses was built of clay blocks with tin roofs and about the same size. Isabella inhaled the evening scents of earth and meat. This village was her home. Elsa reached for her hand. Flowers grew in patches of blue, red, pink and a variety of shades of white. Their green leaves pressed together as if they were cold and needed the warmth of their neighbors.

There were no fences to separate the yards. Each family seemed to respect their neighbor's space. They passed homes where women worked looms to create colorful fabric. The men toiled in gardens with crops of tomatoes, peppers, onions and potatoes. Isa had watched her father, and his men build many a house like these.

They passed a group of children being taught a lesson by a tall, red-headed woman. One of the boys in the group read a section from Hamlet in perfect English. The rest of the class listened.

Elsa's memories flashed into Isabella's mind, but they were someone else's memories, David Gracia's. Memories of David's childhood of a lesson his adopted father taught him on the very same subject. He read the work so many times he could recite it from memory. His father had been so pleased he spent countless hours telling the story instead of reading it. In his father's final hours, the words seemed to bring him comfort and peace. His father died in the middle of the story, David continued to the final verse.

Isa stopped. The boy stopped. The beautiful moment ended. "Please forgive the interruption it's just that the child's voice and the verses reminded me of my childhood. Please continue," Elsa signed. Isa glanced at her.

Elsa squeezed his hand. "His name is David. He's an orphan," she said in Isa's mind. The boy's thin face and serious expression twisted Isabella's heart.

Abrim bent so Elsa was level with the child. She patted the boy's face, and his brown eyes blinked. "You have the voice of an angel. I see in you a great man. You'll have to work hard, much harder than those around you," Elsa signed. She pressed her palm against the boy's chest. "In your heart, in your mind is where your spirit lives. You must allow your soul to guide you. Fear not for our God has a special place in His heart for you. He will give you the strength to fulfill your destiny," Elsa signed.

Abrim rose. The boy's serious expression remained etched on his face. Elsa bowed to the teacher as Lettie took her arm, and they continued. A sound like the cry of an eagle ripped through the air, and then a voice sang the words of William Shakespeare's Hamlet. The sound filled Isabella's mind and heart, more memory than sound came from Elsa. She stopped and turned back. The orphan boy's eyes were closed as his soul roared and touched every living thing with its greatest. The boy completed the verse, and his eyes slid open. The child's hands moved through the air. "May God's grace comfort you, lady." Elsa nodded.

"May we all find His mercy," Elsa signed. The boy nodded, and a smile emerged on his serious face. He didn't know who she was, and it was just as well for Elsa. Elsa pulled Lettie along, and the children went back to their lessons.

They approached the largest house in the village, and a group of women crowded at one of the windows. Several children clung to their dresses. Concern rippled through Isabella. Elsa's face was strained. Lettie folded her arms together, and her fingers encountered the jagged scar of her suicide the same mark glowed on Elsa's arm.

"Allow the Leader to pass," Marcus called. Isabella sensed a shift and turned back to Elsa. "Ma, are you all right?" Her heart thumped.

"Yes," Elsa signed.

"Leticia?" She turned and stared into a pair of intense gray eyes. Isabella tried to reach Lettie and came face to face with her brother. She was yanked back, and she fought Marcus and shrieked as he tried to restrain her. His powerful hand came over her mouth, and she bit him. She struggled and his grasp tightened, and she screamed. Lettie was next to them. "If she would just be still!" Lettie freed her, and she jumped up and punched the handsome man. He glared at her. Lettie pulled her along, and Elsa's son, Samuel approached them.

"Are you all right, Leticia?" he asked.

"Ma where's Ma?" Lettie said. He swung Lettie up, and she closed her eyes. Isabella raised her fists, and a large hand covered hers. She jerked away from Marcus.

"Steady, linda, my mother's right here, do you need some mouth to mouth?" Sam asked. Isabella stepped back, and her knees knocked together. Elsa took her arm.

"Elsa!" Abrim shouted. Lettie came around gun drawn.

"Do not shout at Ma ever!" Lettie said. She pressed Elsa behind her.

"Your Ma's…dead," Adam said. Her brother's gaze was angry and hurt.

"Shut up you want to tell me what I already know I was there and his wife…showed me…Papa's…death, however, my mother was never wrong, and she saved Ma and Ana Marras is never going to be wrong in life or death. I'm a little shaky and Ma's needs help," Lettie said. Abrim stepped up to Elsa. "Not you, she doesn't want you to touch her. You with the gray eyes and short blond hair, Gracia, come and help me, listen so I don't have to shoot you and then fix you up. Hold her like you would a little injured bird come along," Lettie said. Elsa's gaze came on David as he approached.

"What happened to your arm?" David asked.

"No questions just go!" Lettie said. He lifted her, and Lettie took a step and tilted. Samuel caught her. Isabella separated them.

"Steady rough angel," Sam said, "I am so happy you're alive." She swayed to the left as she followed Elsa. Samuel scooped her up.

"Put her down!" Adam commanded. Lettie closed her eyes.

"I'm going to need help," Lettie whispered. Adam swept Lettie up, and his orange scent came around Isabella. "No, no!"

"Be still or they're going to have to break the door down to get to you," he whispered. They filed passed Isabella, and she took several steps back and went to a nearby tree and waited. An hour passed and when night fell she would leave. A smooth, clean scent came to her, and she raised her head. Marcus glared at her.

"What?" she asked.

"Ma, asked me to return you to the house and…"

"Don't you mean ordered?" she asked.

"When my mother says to do something I do it, now you are to stay in my room until she is ready to see you," he said.

"Why am I being punished?" she asked. It offended the handsome man that she would question her good luck at getting to stay in his room. He was very popular among the women, beautiful and otherwise.

"Just come along so we can be done with this," he said.

"Make me," she said. He leapt at her, and she jumped away. She was going to make him have to tell his mother that he failed. She jumped up and caught a limb. She scrambled up the tree, and he came after her. Too bad he was so slow.

Elsa smelled blood and rushed forward. She caught the man's arm. "Leader I smell blood," Isabella said. A spot of blood came up on the back of the man's shirt.

"Where are you from?" she signed. The man's eyes widened. He was a stranger in Abrim's village.

"You're mute?" he asked. His green eyes were dull with pain. Why hadn't he asked if she were deaf, which would be the more logical of questions? "Forgive me Senora, I mean senorita…I am looking for work."

Elsa signed to Isabella. "She wants to know who injured you."

"Uh, it's a long and painful story. I should go." Isa stopped him.

"Do you know who you are speaking to?" Isa asked. Lettie appeared next to them.

"No I did not mean to offend," he said.

"I want to treat him," Elsa signed. Lettie and Isabella had him cornered, and she ripped his shirt off his back. Elsa frowned at the damaged flesh. He shook as she reached to touch the uninjured flesh.

"Please let me go. I'll call the police," he said.

"How will you clean his wounds without him going crazy? I could go and find something in…" Elsa shook her head.

"Please I've no money for a doctor," he said.

"She said it will be free and painful to clean your wounds, unless she treats you…with what?" Elsa nodded. "She says she will not force you, but she must kiss you in order not to hurt you further." He jumped back.

"What is this some witchcraft? I…she wants to kiss me?"

"It is for medicinal purposes only…and there are side effects," Lettie said, "She understands that you would not want her to kiss you since she is poor and ugly."

"Who is poorer than me and who's ugly?" he asked.

"So you'll do it?" Isabella asked.

"No," he said.

"You would rather die?" Lettie asked.

"No, all right, but I will not like it," he said. Elsa leaned closer and when her mouth touched his, he passed out.

"Wow, we'll talk later about how that's done," Leticia said. They hauled him closer to the tree, and Elsa examined his back. His flesh was a mass of damaged skin and swollen welts. Her index finger lit up, and she touched it just to the most damaged of the flesh. Leticia brought her supplies, and she went to work on him.

Lettie stared at the wall. She had been awake most of the night. She made Abrim send Adam and the others away. Elsa was in the room next to hers, and she was alone, but the old man had been with her. Lettie rolled out of the bed as the door swung open. Sam came in and stopped. His blue eyes traveled. "Grandfather is pissed, he wants to know when he can see Ma?" She pulled on her shorts.

"Now he's in a hurry. He didn't have time before. He can wait."

"Did you sleep?" he asked.

"Our ma is upset and you ask stupid questions."

"She's my mother," he said.

"Why can't she be my mother?"

"Cause I'm not your brother," he said.

"I don't want you for a brother."

"Good we're in agreement. That's not what I want with you," he said. She pulled at the sleeves of her shirt to cover the scars.

"Tell grandfather when I'm ready he can see her."

"I want to discuss a debt, I owe you and the way I intend to repay it," he said. She glanced up at him.

"You gave me nothing."

"It is a debt, I owe to your father. I was the last one with him, and I told him when you were rescued, I would see to your protection," he said. She opened the window and looked down at the stone yard below.

"I don't want that."

"I will be your protector until one of us is dead, but my debt goes further I believe I know the reason you were captured was to get to me, so I offer you any amount you choose to pay back what you have lost and if vengeance is what you want I will spend my life on it." She exhaled and smiled. What an ego this one had, the truth wasn't what he wanted. He came to her, and she leaned against his broad chest and stroked the fine fabric of his shirt.

"You're so generous, everyone says how brilliant you are and handsome, but you're better in person than any rumor." She gazed up at him, and he smiled.

"All I want is to be there for you," he said. He almost sounded believable and she searched his face. "You don't remember the first time we met do you?"

"I do, you were seven and I was five, and we visited your grandfather. You played with marbles and you shot a blue one at me, and I caught it. It was the color of your eyes. I gave it back," she said.

"I made you keep it," he said, "I guess you don't have it anymore."

"It's in my jewelry box back…" she said. He stroked her face.

"I'm flattered so tell me what amount, and if I have to borrow, steal, or spend the rest of my life earning I'll make it happen."

"How about a dollar?" she asked. He frowned.

"I'm serious Leticia," he said.

"As am I. What are four lives worth to you in coins or paper money? How much is a brilliant soldier and a teacher worth? How about a trusted medicine woman whose knowledge defied reason or a young girl whose dream it

114

was to create worlds out of words or a boy who had yet to express his dreams how much Stein does all that come to? I don't know do you?" she screamed. He stomped away, and she fell against the window frame. She opened the window and put her foot on the ledge.

"If I had given you one more long kiss you wouldn't have been captured," Adam said. She turned from the window.

"If I hadn't been with you, they would be alive," she said.

"You're blaming me?" he asked. His long blond hair pulled into a ponytail, and his head shaved save for that long piece. His hard jaw cut the air in defiance.

"No, I'm to blame for being selfish and needing…"

"How could you have made a difference?" Adam asked.

"There were only three soldiers and the commander I have taken out ten fighters at one time, many times, including you," she said.

"That was in practice," he said. His gray eyes flickered to the left. He felt shame to know a woman could best him, even more because it was her. For the first time, she sensed his conflict of desire mixed with envy for a woman better than him and what would people say if he chose her for a wife? The knowledge cut, and her heart bled.

"Go away," she said.

"We need to talk," he said.

"No." She cried and he took a step, and she pulled her weapon, and she put it at her head. He backed up to the door.

"Why didn't you kill them if you could Lettie?" Adam asked.

"Do you really want to know?" she whispered. He slammed the door, and it opened a moment later. Abrim stared at her and turned away. "Go to Elsa, she needs you, think of her instead of yourself for once!" He left her. She dissolved to the floor and rocked.

"Angel, my angel, I'm sorry," Sam said. She scrambled back. He held his hand out to her. "Here is an American dollar, a peso, a yen, a mark and my signature to everything I own it's yours." She shook her head and slid backwards. He pressed them into her hands. He pushed the blue marble into her palm on top of the rest. "Try to remember some of the good. I'm grateful you're with my mother." He kissed her head and retreated. Lettie fell back on the floor and cried herself to sleep.

Elsa rolled over in Abrim's bed. She was so sleepy. Juan sat on a chair across from the bed. He leaned back arms crossed. His eye's half closed. "You sleep hard, never saw you sleep before? Why are you wearing my father's t-shirt?" The tan shirt was huge and fit like a dress. She freed her legs, and he raised an eyebrow.

116

"Where's your father?" she asked. She put her legs over the side.

"No pants what happened in here last night?" He frowned, and his eyes narrowed. As black as midnight on a moonless night his eyes searched for clues, and she sighed.

"Where is my leader, Juan?" Elsa signed.

"Your leader is right here. What can I do for you?" His expression dared her to question him. He was a King, beautiful and strong, carved chest and his arms guns of power. He was tall, and his hard chin cut the air. He had one dimple when he smiled, which wasn't often around her. He hated her and wanted her, and the feelings whirled in his mind drove him to madness. The battle raged every time he was in her presence.

If her eyes remained too long on his face, he would cross great distance just to shout at her. Any excuse to reprimand or put her in her place he took full advantage. Any time he could shame her in front of Abrim was a day of celebration for him.

"Go to Hell," she signed. She stood as he leapt out of his chair.

"I'm already there when the old man can spend the night with you behind closed doors and all I get is that you're back. Father said I'm the leader!" he snapped. He didn't put his hands on her even though that was his only desire. He only saw her cry once, and it drove him to unspeakable rage and not even his father could silent his anger.

"He also said you're not my leader," Elsa signed.

"Cause you're the pet show some dignity will you?" Juan said.

"Where is he?" Elsa signed.

"What no kiss good-bye?" Juan asked. He caught her hand and entwined her fingers. "The rumors were that you'd been captured and killed. I searched everywhere for you." His mind wanted her gone forever, but his heart disagreed.

"Did Abrim?" she asked. He flung her hand away.

"Ma's awake," Marcus called. Sam and David came across the room.

"Where's your father?" Elsa signed to Marcus.

"He was called away he told me to let you sleep. He would see you soon," Marcus said, "He finally slept last night when he was in here with you. I checked on both of you." She pulled at the shirt.

"Where did he sleep?" she asked. Marcus smiled.

"With you on his bed, he held you, and he was peaceful like I've never seen him before, why? Don't you remember?" Marcus asked. She didn't remember anything of the night before.

"Was he all right when he left?" Elsa asked.

"He got to hold you while he slept. What do you think?" Juan asked. David floated in the background.

"He was a little distracted, but he was happy, well as happy as I've ever seen him, no, he was happier," Marcus said.

"Where is Isabella?" Elsa signed. Marcus glanced down. "I see there was an injured man last night. Where is he?"

"He's in the room by the kitchen," Marcus said.

"What are you doing here Senor Gracia?" she signed. Sam glanced at David.

"I asked grandfather if David could stay a few days more we've consulted on a few business issues. He's great Ma," Sam said. Her son defended the Warrior, the kid needed to grow up.

"There is nothing Senor Gracia can teach us that would benefit the Fighters, Samuel. I'm sure he's busy and needs to get back to his life," Elsa signed.

"But Ma you always teach us to learn from different experiences and perspectives. David's a billionaire. He should have some tips we can use," Sam said. Elsa exhaled.

"The devil knows how to steal souls, but unless your intention is to be one of his minions that's not a skill you'd need, right?" Elsa signed. David stared at her hands.

"Ma you're comparing him to the devil that's a little harsh. He's your friend," Sam said. Elsa walked passed to Lettie's door and stood watch. A scream erupted. Adam, Sam and Marcus moved toward her.

"Back up," she signed.

"Aren't you going to check on her?" Adam asked.

"She's asleep," she signed. Another scream and Juan and David joined the men.

"Shouldn't you check that?" Juan asked. Elsa opened the door, and Lettie slept upon the floor and screamed.

"Checked, go away," Elsa signed. Elsa swallowed the exhaustion that ebbed in her. She exhaled. Juan stepped away with Adam and Marcus.

"When was the last time you slept?" David asked. She never noticed how dark this hall was. Reality sharpened everything and made it uglier. She swallowed, and Lettie screamed again. David touched her arm, and it stopped. She pushed him off, and Lettie screamed again. He caressed her neck. Elsa shoved him, and Lettie erupted again his hand came over her face.

The door opened behind them. "Will you quit!" Lettie said. Elsa pushed away from David. As Isabella came up the hall and passed into the room.

"I can help you sleep without the nightmares, just one kiss and then," David said. Lettie separated them.

"Never heard that line before, no thanks," Lettie said. Elsa clutched her hands and was dragged into Lettie's room.

"Where is the stranger?" Elsa asked.

"He's gone, Ma. I couldn't find him this morning," Isabella said. Elsa nodded as she went to the window and looked out into the courtyard, down below, a torn bloody shirt waved with the breeze.

Chapter 8 Vanished

Raymond waited down the hall next to Antonio, the master's adopted son held a tray with food and wine. Antonio shot a glance at him. "He's hungry. He hasn't eaten since you went away…to do whatever peasants do," Antonio said.

"He won't eat it," Raymond said. Alexander and Gabriel stood at his right and waited. The door swung open and Raymond moved forward. Antonio passed him and put the tray in front of his father.

"Raymond who is the only man I trust?" Gustavo asked.

"I am the only man whom you trust father," Antonio said, "Raymond has returned and made you something to eat." Gustavo's blue eyes landed on Antonio. Raymond moved to test the food and Gustavo stopped his hand.

"Have you completed the mission?" Gustavo asked. The younger man shifted.

"No, I had to stop to do Raymond's jobs," Antonio said.

"He has returned see that my request is completed!" Antonio stepped away, and Gustavo's hand tightened on Raymond's wrist.

"I smell sweet mercy why is that?" Gustavo asked.

"Because unlike Antonio, I have completed the mission that you sent me to do and the only man whom you trust master is yourself. How may I serve you?" Raymond asked. He released his wrist.

"Make this trash disappear and…" Gustavo said. A second was all it took to make the poisoned food disappear, and another second brought the feast his master needed. He took a bite from each of the dishes and drank an entire goblet of red wine. He passed a fresh glass to the master who leaned back to enjoy his refreshment. "I don't like it when you are away so what did you learn?"

"That you were right master she helped me as you predicted, she is very powerful this woman named Elsa." He pressed the napkin over his arm as he served the meal.

"She used her gifts to bring you comfort?"

"Yes, master and she showed me a great deal of mercy, even though it compromised her comfort level."

"What did she do?" he asked. He took an overloaded spoon of meat and gravy and shoved it in his mouth.

"She kissed me to…make me pass out." Alexander shifted across from them.

"Would she help me Raymond?" Gustavo asked.

"No, master she would not."

"Oh," Gustavo said.

"The very last conversation I had with my mother…before she disappeared…that is the key to Elsa's aiding you master," Raymond said. He put more food in front of him and moved away. The two other men followed him to the door.

"What did mama say to you?" Gustavo asked.

"She said that humans, all of us are connected to each other by invisible threads, and that these threads are strong, stronger than any force in the universe." A tiny wave of hesitation filtered to Raymond from the master. "The answer master then is that you will need to yank on the threads of the people that matter to Elsa. She may not help herself, but she will never walk away from those that love her, no matter what happens, she will defend them to the death."

"You are a wicked man Raymond there may be hope for you yet. Return to me with a plan and we shall see what reward you deserve."

"As you wish master." He strode through the door and walked passed Antonio. The boy glared at him, and Raymond laughed.

"You are a cockroach Antonio nothing you do will ever work against me," Raymond said. Antonio's face reddened.

"We shall see who is left standing peasant," Antonio said.

"You cannot even lure the woman you want, boy, see to it that you walk with women who are your equal you're aiming too high!" Antonio clenched his fist. He could only hope that the little coward tried to fight him, and then he would be able to rid himself of the pest. He went down the hall and entered his room.

Elsa paced the tiny room at the end of the huge house. There was a double bed, a small dresser with a cracked mirror and chipped drawers, an old rocking chair with cushions by the window. This was her room in the master's house, and she loved it and he hated it. Even Abrim Stein's servants had better rooms. Abrim prided himself in his generosity. He was renowned for his ability to share his wealth. Rewards were constant and grand in Abrim's world. No one was ever forgotten for a good deed and the higher the accomplishment the greater the gifts and accolades.

Elsa dusted the top of her dresser chips of dark brown came away, as she patted the piece of furniture. She rescued it one day from the back of Abrim's house. She brought it in and cleaned it up, shined up the mirror and the master had been pissed to know his most important ally saved a piece of trash. He had carted it out himself to the trash pile and broke the mirror. She cried like a fool in front of him and went back to her reality, back to Texas. She fought the sleep that time for a week and when she dreamed, it wasn't of this place or of him. She didn't return for three months.

She snatched at her backpack and dragged it to the bed. It was heavier than usual. Her jagged reflection stared at her on the bed. She returned on the last day of that third month to this room to find him, asleep in this bed with the broken mirror back together. The king of her world slept in a tiny room in a creaky, rusty old bed with hand me down blankets and old pillows. She sent him back to his expensive bed and crawled into the warmth he created. The peacefulness lasted only a second when he blasted into the room and shouted. He frightened her, but instead of offering comfort he stomped away.

Elsa unzipped the pack and a silky black cloth rippled around her. Her old clothes disappeared, and the dress caressed her skin. A brand new pair of black leather, short heeled shoes popped on her feet. She glanced into the pack and a glint caught her eye. She slid her hand in and caught the rolling object.

Light caught on the silver ring. How had it gotten there? She turned it and a diamond glittered, round, but within the stone was a crack, a small imperfection. Elsa smiled. She never liked jewelry before, but something about the ring enticed her. She slipped it on the fourth finger of her left hand. She leaned back against the pillows. She fought the sleep for so long.

"Mama this milk stinks!" Elsa blinked. A teen boy held a carton of milk. "The expiration date is for Friday. This is Tuesday damn the box isn't working again!" He kicked the bottom of the refrigerator, and the light blinked.

"Mr. Rincon said he would look at it Thursday why do you want milk?" a voice said. The tan face frowned.

"That old man is a liar he can't fix this, slum lord. Mimi wants milk with her cookies. Why can't things be different?" he asked.

"Lauro speak up I can't hear you Mimi has the T.V. too loud," the mother said. Lauro poured the milk in the sink.

"I'm going to get more milk," Lauro said.

"No you're not, it's ten at night. It's too dangerous," his mother said. Elsa nodded.

"Ma I'm not a baby, I'm fifteen you have to let me grow up. You worry too much nothing is going to happen. Senor Dominguez always watches out for me. I do favors for him," Lauro said.

"What kind of favors?" his mother asked.

"Ma, he's a good man," Lauro said.

"Just tell me!" she said. Elsa watched the young face.

"I take out the trash and sweep," Lauro said.

"You need to finish school Lauro. You're the man of this house son," she said. Lauro filled the sink with warm water and soap and did the few dishes and dried them.

"I know ma can I go, I'll be right back."

"I don't have any money," she said. Lauro nodded.

"I have some from sweeping today."

"No mijo that's your little money," she said.

"So you can pay me back when you can. Mimi needs milk," Lauro said. A young girl entered the room.

"It's o.k. I'll eat them dry this time," Mimi said.

"Who's my favorite sister?" Lauro asked. Mimi frowned.

"I'm your only sister," Mimi said. Elsa smiled.

"Lucky me I'd be sweeping all of Long Drive to get milk for them," Lauro said, "Ma, please?"

"All right come right back," she said.

"Lauro I'd rather have a candy bar than milk," Mimi said.

"You eat too much candy it's going to rot your teeth." Mimi sighed.

"I haven't had one in three weeks please," Mimi said. Her round, thin face and big brown eyes stared.

"No, go sit with Mama."

"Don't talk to strangers and look both ways before you cross that street boy!" his mother called.

"Ah geez ma you'd think I was an idiot."

"Lauro?" she called.

"All right."

"Wear your jacket its cold," she said. Lauro grabbed his jacket and flung it over his shoulder as he left the small apartment. The street lights blinked above them as they walked across. Lauro looked both ways, no cars only an old plastic bag. They stepped onto the concrete of the store. A man filled his car and nodded at Lauro as he passed. Lauro nodded back.

"Hey Lauro it's late what you're doing out here, your Mama, she's not going to like this," a round man said. He sat behind the counter.

"She knows stupid box spoiled the milk, and Mimi can't eat dry cookies Mr. Dominguez." The glass door swung open and Lauro checked for the oldest date. He got the one he wanted and went to the counter. He looked at a rack with candy. He took the smallest one.

"That is Mimi's favorite?" Mr. Dominguez asked.

"Yeah, she hasn't had one in three weeks." The round man reached over and grabbed the biggest one and put it on the counter.

"Mimi likes to share, that isn't enough," Mr. Dominguez said.

"I don't have enough and she needs the milk more."

"So I pay for everything," Mr. Dominguez said.

"No sir, you're kind, but we can't take any free stuff. My Dad always told me nothing was free. We have to earn it, and Mimi has to learn that too." He put the candy bar back and took the smaller one. Mr. Dominguez shook his head. Elsa could see the distress on the man's face. He liked the young man. He had been this young man years ago, and now he wanted to make things different for Lauro.

"You swept my place so good today you deserve extra," he said.

"You paid me and you give me work that's more than most people do for us," Lauro said. Mr. Dominguez swallowed.

"All right I have this old Mama, and she has these weeds in her flower beds. It's two streets passed Kendall, but she's old and I'm always here so you take Mimi the big candy bar and the milk and I pay you for the weeds uh?" he said.

"Yes, sir," Lauro said. A white van pulled into the parking lot as Lauro walked passed her. It parked across the two lanes of the road Lauro would pass. The skin on Elsa's neck rose, and her skin crawled as they grew closer. Lauro hesitated and stepped down from the location of the van. He crossed without looking at the vehicle.

"Lauro." He turned at the sound of his name. A woman squatted at the back of the van and held a girl by the back of the neck. The girl's hands were bound in front of her, and tears ran down her face. A gag sealed her mouth. "Come here boy," the woman called. The young girl was thirteen. She was Mimi's age. Lauro stood his ground and glanced back at the store. Mr. Dominguez couldn't see them. A thump brought their attention back to the van interior. The woman had the girl by the hair. Lauro took a step toward them.

"No, no don't do it," Elsa thought. She raced after him.

"Stop Lauro take off your shoes," the woman said.

"Why?" Lauro asked.

"You're a lot slower on this rough terrain of broken glass. Put the stuff down you won't need it," she said. Elsa pulled on Lauro, but it was of no use. Lauro stopped and a green glow appeared around the woman, and Lauro could see it. The boy was cursed as a Hunter or Warrior, he was underdeveloped, but he knew of his curse. Lauro's eyes went to the girl. The space around her gleamed bright and he frowned. The young woman wasn't a hostage, just a decoy. The woman yanked him into the vehicle. "Go Esteban." Elsa climbed in as the door closed. The plastic bag on the milk fluttered in the breeze.

"Just be still and they'll feed you. My name is Eva." She pulled at the straps of cloth on her hands and grasped his arm and shifted it around her, so he could hold her. "How old are you?"

"Fifteen how old are you?" Lauro asked. Elsa watched a patrol car drive in front of the van, and then the light turned green.

"Thirteen, you're old enough to be a man," Eva said. Lauro blinked as Eva kissed him. He retreated to the back of the van a padlock held the doors closed.

"I get him first right Sylvia?" Eva asked.

"No this one goes to the master," Sylvia said. They passed a green sign with glittering white letters that read leaving Houston. Elsa glanced at the backdoor as they traveled away from Lauro's neighborhood. Elsa grabbed the padlock, and she jerked awake.

Rough hands yanked Elsa from the bed. "Who gave you this dress?" Abrim asked. She stared into his angry face. She dangled in the air and struggled to get free, and he dropped her. "Answer me that dress is new and you look…beautiful!"

"It came out of my pack," she signed. The light caught the diamond on her hand, and he grasped for her fingers.

"Where did that ring come from? Why are you wearing it on that hand?" he asked. She glanced at the ring and smiled.

"It's mine it was in my pack. It's mine!" she signed.

"It's a wedding band take it off this minute!" he shouted. She walked out of the bedroom, and Marcus smiled at her.

"Wow Ma you look beautiful, uh that's a new dress?" Marcus asked.

"Yes, it's mine," Elsa signed.

"You bought a new dress?" Marcus asked. Samuel and David joined them in the hall.

"Why are you wearing a five carat engagement ring?" David asked.

"Hey the shoes are new as well," Marcus said.

"They're mine…I didn't buy them. They were in my pack, so they belong to me so what?" Elsa signed.

"Your shoes are more holes than shoe and your clothes are always old and outdated…not that it looks bad on you or makes you look like a bag lady or…well, you don't care about those things," Marcus said.

"What is his name Elsa this man whom you allowed to buy you things?" David asked. Elsa blinked and smiled. Magic dresses weren't purchased they just existed no one could explain them.

"Some man put his ring on our mother? Do we know him?" Sam asked. Lettie traveled up the hall in a flowing dress of emerald. A ring graced her left hand. Isabella joined them in a dress of deep purple and Marcus took notice.

"Who gave you that ring girl?" Adam asked.

"Ma, I'm ready to leave," Lettie said.

"We have an arrangement Leticia," Sam said.

"What arrangement?" Adam asked.

"Ma it's getting late," Lettie said. Abrim came around and yanked on the ring. Elsa smacked him.

"You're coming to my room, and you're removing that ring and that dress is coming off, and we're going to bed!" Abrim said. Lettie pressed between her and the leader.

"You are a nasty man. Ma isn't going anywhere with you!" Lettie said. Elsa moved down the hall the exit was less than a hundred feet. She would be hard-pressed to explain why she dealt with Abrim's enemy and rival to free Lettie. Abrim's world was black, no white, no gray. She and Lettie and Isabella made it to the front door.

"If you leave this house you can never return Elsa!" Abrim shouted, "I won't take you back we're done I mean it this time!" Elsa blinked, and her foolish side emerged full force. The tears wiggled down her face. The clouds roiled to life, and the thunder echoed, in the distance. Abrim opened his mouth, but was drowned out by a blast of thunder.

"It's so easy for you to put me out of your life, maybe it's for the best I never return."

"He doesn't mean it Ma," Marcus said, "When did the curse, I mean your sister get engaged Adam?"

"Grandfather's had a hard day in the saddle. He had a difficult mission. He's just tired," Sam said. Elsa turned away.

"Elsa wait!" Abrim shouted. She looked into his blue eyes.

"You wait and I'm tired of your shit!" Elsa signed. The anger slipped from his face. She stepped into the pouring rain.

Elsa stepped into a hole of mud and water. Her blistered feet sore and bruised as she inched forward in the drenching rain. Lettie stepped with her. "We must look like idiots dressed in evening gowns trekking through the jungle. I liked these shoes when they first popped on my feet," Lettie said. Isabella stopped them. Elsa eyed the trees ahead all the world was a blurred mess. She flung her left shoe.

A tree caught it and turned into Marcus. He ran up with a wide grin. "They looked prettier without the mud Ma," he said. She took the shoe and replaced it.

"Whatever you want the answer is Hell no!" Elsa signed.

"Wow and I thought we were going to have to defend our leader's actions," Sam said. Lettie glanced around. "Are you missing someone Leticia?" Lettie moved closer to Elsa.

"Why are you here?" Elsa signed. Her left foot sucked into a hole, and she fought the vines to get free. Isabella took her knife and freed the pretty bow.

"He wants you to come back," Sam said. Lettie glanced at her and laughed. They stepped on.

"I'd rather die in the mud," Elsa signed.

"That's not what he said you would say," Marcus said.

"He'll accept your apology, and all will be as it was when he left the other night," Sam said. Elsa stopped.

"I don't remember the other night and all I have been told is that he snuck off like a thief," Elsa signed.

"We shouldn't repeat that to the leader, oh and the ring it has to be gone, but if you're good he'll replace it with another of his choosing because you don't know about diamonds and such, but it will be in accordance with your stature among the Fighters it's going to be big cause like you're the top right?" Marcus asked. Isabella shook her head and pushed passed him. He jumped back when her hand touched his chest.

"You're really dumb," Isabella said.

"You can keep your little trinket just come with me. I just want to talk to you," David said. Elsa met his gray eyes. Dark circles ringed them. His gaze darted to the right. He needed a fix. She moved on, and Lettie followed her.

"Ma we've got to tell him something," Marcus said.

"Tell him things have changed, and he can fuck off!" David said.

"Ma?" Sam asked. Elsa stopped and pressed her fingers to David's temples. His eyes slammed shut and his power surged back into her, and she jerked. He clasped her arms and embraced her. Her feet sucked out of the mud as she came into the air against his giant mass. He opened his eyes and exhaled. He put her back. "Ma what are we going to say to the leader?" Sam asked.

"Tell him…what David said," Elsa signed.

"He's going to blow a vein," Marcus said.

"You get what you give, Marcus," David said.

"If we tell him that he's coming after her," Sam said.

"If he can catch me, we'll talk." She snatched at the ruined fabric of the dress.

"Whoever this new man in your life is, hope he likes fire," David said.

"Anyone who can deal with Ma should be able to deal with any of you," Lettie said. David's face relaxed, but his gray eyes turned to slits. Elsa moved and Lettie with her, Isabella on her left side. They passed a tree and disappeared.

"It's going to take a while to get used to that," Lettie said. The Fighter's shelter was cold and Lettie went to the fire circle. Within a minute, a small blaze erupted and Elsa sat next to her.

Elsa brought lanterns, and the space lit up. "This is one of the best hideouts I've been in," Isabella said. Lettie raised her pistol. "Easy

Fighter I'm one of you." She held her hands up and grinned.

"You're a Fighter?" Lettie asked.

"No I'm a…never mind what I am," Isabella said. Lettie glanced at Elsa.

"I don't like secret's Ma?" Lettie said. A pot went to the edge of the fire to boil water. Elsa wished for some tea. Coffee would be better.

"There are no secrets between us as you will come to know. All you need to do is ask a question and you have all the answers that you need to know who Isabella is."

"The legendary and only second of the female Fighters, Leticia Maria Marras why would she want to know anything about me, Leader de las Almas," Isabella said. Lettie jerked to her face.

"You are Adam Maldano's younger sister and…" Lettie said.

"I am many things' Fighter Marras my brother would be pleased to know of your obsession with him, although I don't understand it since he is shamed of the feelings he has for you…well you know it," she said. Lettie shifted in the dimness. "Sometimes it is better not to know what people think." Isabella eyed her hand.

"You found the Black wolf's ring?" she asked. Elsa pulled her hand back.

"It's mine," she signed. She rolled the ring on her finger.

"Indeed it seems to have found its home and what an odd finger to land on. The commitment finger, the death finger and you Lettie your ring is on that finger as well, how interesting I wonder what that means? If I were the men whom you received the rings from, I would assume ownership of what, you?" Isabella asked.

"There was no ring in your pack?" Lettie asked. Isabella shrugged.

"Maybe, however, I am not as free to enjoy something so personal for it speaks of Saul's intentions to me," Isabella said. Lettie glanced at the ring on her hand.

"It's just a silver ring" Lettie said.

"It's platinum not silver," Isabella said.

"Platinum is an expensive metal, no?"

"Yes the most, but to the man, who gave it, well the ring means nothing compared to who holds it. Do you like your new powers Leticia?"

"I've no powers, girl I am the same as, I have always been."

"Except for one important thing, you we're closed, and now you're wide open and you're attached at the mind and heart to Elsa, no wishing, nothing, but death will change that," Isabella said. Elsa swallowed and added a log to the fire.

"You make it sound like a bad thing to be connected to Elsa, maybe someone else might see it as prison, but me, I see it as home," Lettie said. She shifted to draw leaves into the boiling pot.

"You're a wise Fighter, and I approve of your involvement in my brother's life, even though he doesn't care what I think."

"His loss as I see it," Lettie said. Isabella bowed. She shifted into the shadows and left them.

Elsa adjusted, and the rock slipped closer to her shoulder. Sleep would come soon whether she liked it or not. "Do you have any idea what you have done imbecile?" Alec shouted. Elsa spun and peered over the stacks of wood. Manuel dropped into a chair in front of the fire with a bottle in his hand. The worm glowed white in the dim light.

"What have I done great Leader?" Mano asked.

"That crazy old bastard is tearing up the world, and it will lead right to your door and all because you think you're important you stupid ass!" Alec shouted. Mano's eyes remained on the fire.

"What are you talking about? Can't I get drunk in peace?" A wicked yellow beam bounced off the ground at Mano. Elsa caught it and pitched it to the ground where it shattered like a light bulb.

"You won't make me break my promise," Elsa signed.

"Get out of my way! I will correct him anyway I see fit!"

"No, everything is different now," Elsa signed. Another bolt came at her, and she knocked it away. Mano disappeared from the chair. "Where is he Alec?"

"I sent him away. He's not part of the deal."

"What deal have you made with this old man?" Mano asked. The handsome commander appeared in a large metal cage.

"He's a child of this clan, and I will protect him whether you like it or not. How can you cage him like an animal?" Elsa signed.

"Now I'm pissed what did she say?" Mano shouted. He couldn't stand in the cage, but he kicked at the door.

"Learn the language dumb ass what I have said. The enemy can only be conquered if you understand them, but you're too good to learn the sign. I'm not helping you!"

"Your words mean nothing to him. He's like a brick. However, that is not the point I gave my word, and I shall keep it," Elsa signed.

"The young commander doesn't need your protection Hunter Elsa," Alec said. Mano melted the door and jumped out. Alec picked a fight for her knowing the prideful man wouldn't want her help.

"Protection you made a deal for her to protect me? That's like asking a little girl to protect the devil," Mano shouted.

"I'm not stupid like you this little girl is a monster that even you will not conquer. Did you notice she doesn't fear you how will you control her great Commander?" Alec asked. Mano clasped her.

"Why do you smell of mud girl?" Mano asked.

"Better question for me is why does the smell of mud arouse you imbecile?" Alec asked. Mano shifted closer.

"My dress is ruined. Where are your shoes? You've mud all over the hem look at you?" Mano asked. Elsa pulled away.

"Do I not please you Commander?" Elsa signed. The light caught the ring on her finger. He grasped her hand.

"You're wearing my ring on your left hand," he said.

"It's mine you can't have it. Anything in my pack is mine," she signed. She hid the hand behind the fold of the wet dress.

"You think I would take it from you. It's my ring," Mano said. She shook her head and pointed at herself.

"Do you know now why the old man is pissed?" Alec asked. Mano trailed a finger down her face to her chin.

"He can fuck off who cares," Mano said. Elsa slapped him.

"Do not curse in front of me Black Wolf," Alec said. Mano gazed at his uncle and then at her. He leaned in for a kiss, and she stepped back.

"You dare to reject me after my gift?" She stepped back and signed.

"If you want the ring take it from me," Alec said. The old man laughed, and Mano stepped up. Elsa blinked and raised her hand. She went to remove the ring.

"Keep it who cares, I don't need your protection insignificant woman," Mano said. Alec slammed a light at her, and Mano blocked it. "Who saved who little girl?" The next bolt Elsa caught in the chest, and she flew back. She dropped upon the ground.

"Damn you what is wrong with you?" Mano shouted. Elsa signed.

"Why do I want to know you…Black Wolf?" Alec asked. She faded, and Mano roared in anger. Lettie appeared over her.

"Ma tell me what to do? How do I fix this?" Lettie asked. The dress sizzled, and Lettie pulled it away. A bruise appeared over her heart. "Don't die please. I have a something for pain."

"No and don't take it either," Elsa signed.

"Why it can't harm…only a developing fetus, please Ma," Lettie said. Isabella appeared over her shoulder. She leaned down and rubbed her head. Lettie glanced at her.

"Do something," Lettie said.

"I can't. Sleep Elsa you won't return to where you were I will keep watch," she said.

Elsa closed her eyes as the pain drifted in and out. Alec could have killed her that hadn't been the point. The pain flowed into the darkness, and she followed it.

Chapter 9 The Good and the Bad

Lettie shifted on the stone. Isabella sat next to Elsa, who was at present asleep, no it was more unconscious than sleep, and the girl had some part of it. "You should sleep."

"I don't trust you," Lettie said.

"You don't trust anyone and the few people you did trust are dead, so what?" Isabella said. Lettie rolled against the wall. The jagged rocks rippled beneath her fingers.

"Rule number three do not read others people's thoughts." Isabella shifted behind her.

"So you follow all the rules all the time?" Isabella asked.

"Rules are created to prevent chaos," Lettie said. She was cold and tired.

"Chaos happens anyway," Isabella said.

"If everyone broke the rules then there would be nothing," Lettie said.

"You have killed a man," Isabella said. The connection between them and Elsa grew with every passing moment and this girl, was strong with power, a power new to Lettie, a power, she could not get comfortable with.

"He tried to kill my mother and the other women of the village," Lettie said. She rolled her shoulders in and pulled her legs up.

"You protected them?" Isabella asked.

"I am a Fighter, and my oath is to protect the members of my clan," Lettie said. She rested her chin on her knees.

"You had just taken your oath the day before, and are you not a medicine woman as well?" Isabella said.

Lettie rolled her head. "I am both, yes if you ask about regret there is always regret it's a difficult load to carry, but the greater regret would be to allow innocent women and children to die," Lettie said.

"Better to do wrong in the name of good than to let fate play out her role?" Isabella asked. Lettie sighed.

"Fate is a male and who is to say I was not left behind to defend them was that not fate as well. My little brother was fussy and Mama had a pregnant patient, and the other fighters went on training. I was always ahead in my lessons I stayed behind."

"Maybe," she said. She shifted sleep drugged her, and she let it take her away.

"The two of you have brought that old bastard to my door!" Alec shouted. Lettie blinked. Chino stood at attention and Manuel paced. "We were fine until…"

"You started this," Mano said.

"I took something he didn't want! Not his most precious possessions, do you have any idea the problems this causes me?"

"If they are so important why are they starved for everything from attention, to love, to food? I've never seen a needier woman than Leticia?" Chino said. Alec paced.

"Was she different for you?" Alec snapped.

"I will not speak to you of my time with her," Chino said.

"You were her first did you know?" Alec asked. The elder man frowned as he paced. Lettie shifted further into the shadows.

"Yes," Chino said.

"Was that something new to you?" Alec asked.

"I've had a virgin before," Chino said. Chino's gaze shifted to the window. Alec stepped in front of him.

"But Leticia was different wasn't she?" Alec asked. Chino looked at his leader.

"She was afraid and so hurt because that whore that you call commander…" Chino growled. Alec searched Chino's face.

"You showed her love?" Alec asked.

"There was no love. How can I love a woman I just met? Love comes with time."

"You are a rough nasty enforcer, but with her, there was gentleness and kindness. What has she done to my warrior?" Alec shouted.

"Just because I didn't act like some animal you think I'm weak?"

"You're no Fighter?" Alec said. Lettie swallowed the insult. "No because they are the best warriors in skills, wealth, in power everyone wants to be a fucking Fighter!"

"I don't," Chino said.

"Do you think you could pass their trials and be matched to them? Do you know that the woman you took…the woman you made love to is one of their very best Fighters?" Alec asked. Chino grinned.

"I made love to a woman not a soldier, and she may be the best fighter in the world, but she let me comfort her and she respected me and showed me her strength the rest doesn't matter to me!" Chino shouted. Lettie jerked when he disappeared.

"Let's see how defiant he feels after being in the pen a few days," Alec said. Mano ran his hand over his hair.

"You are such a hypocrite," Mano said.

"I left the door unlocked so what? I like that he speaks his mind unlike those others," Alec said. The old man dropped into a chair.

"He won't leave that cell until you say, and you know it," Mano said. The Black wolf drank from the bottle and passed it to his Uncle.

"I know he is a man to be trusted," Alec said.

"There are only six other men that have my trust besides you and him," Mano said. Lettie was against a wall with bottles. "I wonder how the woman is?"

"She's unconscious, and Stein is coming after her," Alec said.

"Young or old? I'll give them some trouble," Mano said. Lettie took a bottle.

"Abrim will bring everything he's got to defeat you," Alec said. Mano stood, and Lettie shifted.

"It seems my brother the Green Wolf may have an angel?" Mano said. Alec glanced in her direction. They couldn't see her. She appeared in a dirt hole.

"Leave!" Chino said. She turned and pressed the bottle to him.

"You sleep with me one time, and now you're a thief?"

"I paid for it. I left five hundred dollars on the table," she said. He frowned.

"Where the fucking Hell did you get that kind of money?" She slapped him, and his green gaze came to her face.

"My father did not curse me and no man ever will," she whispered.

"Did Stein give you that money?" he asked.

"You know Sam...Samuel?" she asked.

"You took money from Stein?" he asked.

"He gave it to me." The door to the cell blasted out and splintered against the wall across the hall.

"And you think that makes it o.k.?" Chino shouted.

"He gave me a dollar, a peso, a yen and a mark oh and a blue marble like his eyes and a paper that said I own everything that is his, I'm not sure what that means I'm thinking I'm not going…" Lettie shifted to a path of stone stairs that lead up.

"Out and don't let me hear you drank out of that bottle girl!" Chino said. Lettie turned the bottle up, but kept her mouth closed. Her eyes remained on the cell. He ran at her and slammed to a halt at the entrance. "Son of bitch, mother fucking girl don't test me!" She flew at him, and he grasped her. She slapped him again, but her heart fell as the welts came up on his face. She pressed her mouth to them, and he pushed away. "Are you sorry you hit me?"

"Don't curse me. I don't like it, no, I'm not sorry," she said.

"Then don't send mixed signals. That's what I hate about women like you," he said.

"There is only one other woman like me," she said. His eyes pierced her face. "You think I'm a decent woman that I'm good you're wrong. I know the rules, but if my leader asked me I would break every rule that exists."

"Abrim Stein or Samuel is your leader?" Chino asked.

"Elsa is my leader," Lettie said.

"You're a Fighter that makes the men your leader," Chino said.

"I'm a woman first that makes Elsa my leader. She is the keeper of the women and children as decreed by Abrim Stein," Lettie said.

"So he gave her the crappy job of women and children," Chino said. Lettie capped the mezcal and it dropped to her side.

"We're not crappy we're us," Lettie said.

"Women and children are the ones with the problems. Where did the money come from?" Chino asked.

"It was the prize given to the last fighter standing at graduation," Lettie said. Chino dropped to the dirt floor.

"So how would the brilliant Samuel Stein feel to know you traded your hard-earned money for a cheap bottle of mezcal to be given to an even cheaper bastard that's not recognized by his own father."

"If I cared what they thought I wouldn't be a Fighter. I don't know your father, but it's his loss not knowing you," Lettie said.

"Do you think your goodness is ever going to outweigh my badness?" She stared up the stairs.

"I was hoping some of your badness would seep into me and make me not so black and white. I like you," she said.

"You like bad men?" he asked.

"No, I like monsters. I always hoped I'd find one under my bed or in the closet turns out monsters look like hot green-eyed men never saw that one coming," Lettie said.

"Don't drink that mezcal, Leticia," Chino said.

"I'm old enough to drink in Mexico," Lettie said.

"I don't care don't do it!" She took the steps two at a time.

"And I'm going to obey you why?" She cleared the spot where he was imprisoned.

"You like me do you think I like you?" She jerked to a stop.

"I don't want to know," she replied. He laughed.

"Coward," he cooed. She fell into this new world known as nightmares.

Raymond waited as the master licked the plate clean. He brought another to be consumed by the starving man. "Antonio has a plan. He seeks to capture the girl known as Isabella what do you think?"

"He will fail as he always does," Raymond said. He cleared the used plates as the master indulged in every type of food provided.

"Maybe I should intervene," Gustavo said.

"His failure will lead to your success." The master laid the spoon down and stared out the window.

"What a burden it must be to see the end of your life to know the last day and minute that you will have, to have such details…is a curse, a damnation," Gustavo whispered.

"Yes, master, but I cannot change what is, so ask me what you wish to know, and I will answer if it is your will?"

"Will I suffer?" Raymond exhaled.

"Yes," Raymond replied. Alexander and Gabriel shifted if they had his powers they would lie, and it would do them no good as the master would know of their deceit. "But the time shall be short, very short, and it will not compare to your present suffering."

"Why do you give me hope, when all I deserve is…punishment?"

"I do not decide who deserves what I am but the messenger, so knowing will not matter," Raymond said. He shifted the fabric of his cloak to extend his arm to the master. The weakness came over the master, and his power would be required. Gustavo took his arm and squeezed. The pain jumped into Raymond's head as the master drank of his power. Stars flashed into view as he held on, and he motioned Gabriel to his side. He transferred the grip to Gabriel, who dropped onto his knees and screamed until he passed out. Next came Alexander and he too came to his end. He moved the two men to their rooms where they would need at least two days of sleep to recover if they lived they became a part of the food chain and there was much to gain from that chance. Gustavo jerked, and his eyes rolled back.

"Please…please do not…leave me…son…" Gustavo pleaded.

"I will never abandon you master, sleep now, find peace." He lifted the tall man and brought him to rest on his huge bed. He placed the cover over him and stood in watch. The darkness swallowed the light, and he remained vigilante. The door swung open and Antonio entered. He raised the blade and hammered it toward Gustavo. Raymond shot him across the room. He pinned him to the wall, but the other man spoke not a word. He glared into Raymond's eyes.

"One day I'll succeed..." Raymond gripped his face.

"You have a little over a year, and then you will be turned to ash. You will die by the one that you wish to defeat," Raymond whispered. Antonio squirmed as the truth snaked into his mind. When Raymond dropped him, he ran like a frightened child and Raymond grinned in the darkness.

Elsa flipped over, and her vision cleared. Samuel stood over Lettie, who cradled a bottle of mezcal. Her eyes snapped open as he moved to her. "Where did you get that bottle?" he asked. She shifted away and kept the bottle out of his reach. Lettie's eyes met hers and a moment later, were replaced with David's intense gaze. His fingers whisked over her bruised skin.

"Who hurt…" Elsa rushed forward with her powers and gathered Leticia. Isabella was gone. They leapt through time. She crashed to the thick tan carpet. A pair of shiny black boots gleamed in the fire light. She scrambled back and was caught. She yanked away from Manuel, but he kept his grip. Lettie was cold and unconscious.

Elsa flipped out of Mano's grasp to appear in a dirt hole with Lettie and Chino. The green wolf touched Lettie's face. He shook her, and she remained out. He gathered her and sank against the nearest dirt wall.

Elsa spun in place, and Mano ran into her. She stepped back. "I need help?" she signed. He pulled her further into the room to the fire. A small group of men sat at a square, dark table. "Mano I need help now!"

"Whatever you're trying to say I don't understand so stop it. Why are you so cold?" Mano asked. She jerked her hands around and the tears came, no stop, no crying in front of him. He swallowed and turned away. She yanked on his arm, and he glanced at her. She pointed to him and shook her head. She folded her hands and rocked them. "What the Hell is this?" A dimple creased his chin.

"Charades, the gringos play this game for fun it's…" The man's eyes were light brown and lines extended from the creases. He was young, but somehow life aged him.

"I know what charades are Alfonso!" Mano shouted. Elsa nodded.

"Maybe if we play we can help the leader's lady, and then we can get back to getting drunk and playing cards." This one was a red head with gray eyes and pale skin.

"Who said she was my lady Pepe?" Mano asked.

"She is cause no one we know is hung well enough to snatch at you like she just did and not get their damned head blown off." This man grinned, and his blue eyes sparkled.

"Her eyes they kiss your face," Alfonso said.

"That's disgusting Brown Wolf it frightens me when you use those sticky words," Pepe said.

"When you speak to a real woman you need those words," Alfonso said. Elsa eyed the small group.

"The women we know don't care about any pretty words, they just love us because we are Wolf Clan," Pepe said. Elsa looked at them. Blue-eyed Pablo dropped his head.

"We don't get any women we're just a bunch of poor bastards with nothing," Pablo said. Mano frowned.

"Hey don't tell our secrets!" Mano said.

"Maybe you have some nice friends who would speak to us?" Alfonso asked. Elsa shook her head and made a mean face.

"All her friends are mean and nasty hey that would work out, no?" Pepe asked. Elsa smiled, and Pepe looked away. Elsa folded her arms and rocked them.

"O.k. uh, baby?" Pablo asked. Elsa nodded and touched Mano's chest. He watched her. "Leader is a baby?" Pablo asked. Elsa nodded and shook her head. She rocked her arms again and touched Mano and then pointed at herself.

"Baby, leader, woman?" Pablo asked. Pepe pushed back from the table.

"No, leader and woman make baby," Pepe said. Elsa tilted her head. "I'm thinking if she has your baby leader you better get it back she looks like she would keep it."

"We didn't know you had a baby leader. It's a boy right?" Alfonso asked. Mano slammed his fist on the table.

"I don't have a baby!" Mano shouted.

"Still if she has your baby, she's going to keep it, I agree with Pepe," Pablo said. Elsa put her hand at the top of her head and shifted to the right and did the cradle and pointed at herself.

"Her baby you have kids?" Alfonso asked. She held up four fingers. "Four kids that a lot of kid's leader." Elsa made varying sizes with her hands in the air.

"Big kids they're not going to like you leader," Pablo said.

"Are they boys or girls?" Pepe asked. Elsa squeezed her fists together and shook. She swayed. Mano steadied her. She jerked her hands around, and he cocked his head. She cradled her arms.

"Samuel and Marcus I've heard they call you mother, and I guess Leticia…" Mano said. She hammered him on the chest. She pointed to each of the Wolves and held up one finger, and she pressed one down.

"We're missing a Wolf, Chino," Pablo said. Elsa nodded.

"Leticia is with Chino," Alfonso said.

"The pen ain't no place for a lady. It's no place for a man the only one that's ever lasted in there for more than a few days is Mano and now Chino," Pepe said. Elsa shivered.

"It's cold down there I know," Mano said. Elsa sank to her knees, and the men stood. Mano pulled her up. "He won't leave unless Alec tells him." The nightmare pulled at her, and she fought it. She placed trembling fingers at Mano's temple. A tiny heartbeat echoed between them. Her eyes closed, and he snapped her awake. "It's Chino's?" She nodded, and her head snapped back.

The cold wind cut through the thin evening gown. "Damn lock won't shut again!" Elsa glanced at Mr. Dominguez as his eyes jerked around to look for trouble. The lock clicked, and he snatched at the trash bag. He stomped to the bin and flung the bag. A fly buzzed his head as the smell of rotted milk assaulted them. He spat on the ground and zipped his jacket over the round of his belly. He raised his hood and turned to his vehicle. Elsa searched for evidence. She prayed he would notice, but his head was down.

Elsa ran to the site and blasted a beer bottle on the sidewalk. She stared in his direction, and his eyes came over the top of his car. He stood long moments, and she fluttered the bag on the milk. He got into his car and started the engine. Smoke issued from the tail pipe, and Elsa sent her power to that weak engine. It sputtered to a halt. "Son of a bitch not tonight!" he said. He emerged and this time she rolled rocks in the breeze as he lifted the car's hood. She pitched a rock at his fender, and he turned to see. She ran passed the bag and was only able to appear for one moment.

He crossed over to the bag and the shoes and Mimi's favorite candy. He flipped open his phone. "Tinker where are you? Come to the store now, yes now!" A moment later a police cruiser's flashing lights raced up and a man jumped out.

"You all right brother?" He wore a suit, not a uniform.

"Yeah little bro look at this," Mr. Dominguez said.

"What is this Oscar?" he asked. He snatched on some gloves.

"I sold this stuff to Lauro at ten, five hours ago and now here it is with his shoes this is wrong Felix," Mr. Dominguez said.

"Lauro wouldn't run off look at all the broken glass," Felix said.

"Somebody took the kid, make an Amber Alert, do something," Mr. Dominguez said. The officer used his phone.

"This is Detective Felix Dominguez. I need a patrol car and…" Elsa jerked from the nightmare as Mano shook her.

"Listen to me! Wake up now!" Mano shouted. Elsa signed. "No, Alec give me the power to understand her now!" Elsa fought the sleep.

"It will hurt like…it's not that simple!" Alec shouted.

"You will do it old man because I say!" Mano shouted. Elsa shook her head as he slipped away from her.

"I could kill you!" Alec said.

"I don't care do it!" Mano said. Elsa found Alec.

"Please don't…don't hurt him." Mano got in her face.

"Let me tell you something baby girl, I am the man. I'm the Leader. I am Warrior, and I am top Wolf in this clan, and he does what I say!" Elsa shook her head. "You don't run me like you do that sorry old man, but he will not know more about you than I do ever!" Mano turned to Alec, he had read the sign? "Your leader commands you to give him the curse of sign now!" Alec's fist crashed against Mano's cheekbone, and Elsa jerked away.

Elsa faced the street. "Senora Ortiz hello?" Elsa turned toward the voice. A few feet away Mr. Dominguez and his brother stood at an apartment door. The Detective pulled out his badge. He pounded on the door, and it cracked open.

"Who is it? What do you want? I have a gun!" Mr. Dominguez moved closer and stared into the crack.

"Senora Ortiz I'm…" he said.

"I know who you are what do you want at this time of night? This is no hour for decent people to be out," she said.

"Yes, ma'am is Lauro home?" Mr. Dominguez asked.

"Whatever work you want him to do at this time of night the answer is no, decent people do not go out this late and…"

"Mama Lauro isn't in his room. The bed is made?" Mimi said. The woman swung the door wide.

"I'm Detective Dominguez Oscar's my brother, and he called me because…" Felix said.

Mrs. Ortiz' eyes fixed on the fluttering bag, in the distance. She ran barefoot across to the bag, and Elsa was right with her. She stared down at the shoes and screamed. She dropped, but somehow Mr. Dominguez lifted her into his massive embrace. She struggled with him.

"Your feet are bleeding!" he shouted, "Mimi stay in the apartment!" Mrs. Ortiz stared at him as he held her up.

"Lauro's dead," Mrs. Ortiz whispered. The tears spread down her broad cheeks, and his eyes squinted on her face.

"No, you're wrong. He's coming back. We'll find him. I know we will. Felix for the love of God help us!" Mr. Dominguez said.

"Oscar we need to take her to the hospital," Felix said.

"I don't have any money," Mrs. Ortiz said. Her reddish-brown hair came loose.

"I have money Laura call the ambulance Felix now!" Oscar said.

Her slender body shivered in his massive hands. Her eyes moved away from his face. Blood dripped on the plastic bag with the milk. Elsa watched the man.

"Lauro says you're a good man, but your woman would not like this I wouldn't if you were my man. I have to find my son."

"I don't have a woman, I'll help you find him," he said. Elsa turned to the apartment where the young girl stood.

"I don't know your name I can't accept," Laura said.

"I'm Oscar Dominguez, you're Laura Ortiz your husband died three years ago. My brother is Detective Felix Dominguez. My mother is Liliana Dominguez, she lives across the street can Mimi stay with her? Our mother is a strong woman she'll take…"

"Why would you do this for us? We're strangers," Laura said.

"My brother and I were once Lauro until my stepdad, my dad found us, payback Laura. The faster we fix your feet the faster we find Lauro," Oscar said.

"Mommy I'm scared," Mimi cried. The ambulance rolled up. Felix came around the corner with an elderly woman. Her hair pinned to her head in flat circles.

"I'm here mijo what can I do?" she asked.

"Mama ride with Felix and Mimi to the hospital," Oscar said. The old lady smiled, and Elsa's heart crashed to her feet. She collected the child and moved with Felix.

"I'm scared," Mimi cried.

"Me too, but it's o.k. we'll see your mommy when we get into the hospital, and I know where the candy machine is I'll buy you a treat," the old woman said. Mimi burst into tears as they got into the patrol car. Laura's gurney entered the back of the vehicle, and Oscar followed it. The young man stared at him.

"I'm her man, she's afraid. Our son is missing I'm coming do I need to call your boss?" Oscar asked. He got in, and the doors closed. Laura's tears flowed as Mr. Dominguez held her hand.

The wind blasted Elsa, and she turned as the evidence was collected. A white van inched its way to the light as it went red. A man looked at the police activity, and the light went green. The vehicle moved, and Elsa closed her eyes.

A hiss turned her head. Mano lay next to her. His eyes closed arms crossed over his chest. His face a ghastly pale, a cut swelled on his right cheekbone as tremors echoed through him. Elsa raised her hand. "Don't touch him," Alec said.

"Bastard why did you do this?" Elsa signed.

"He did…what I commanded unlike your old bastard of a leader…I do what I want," Mano said. She placed both hands on his face, and the tremors transferred. "No, no!" She blacked out.

"That old lady is no match for me." Lauro vomited into a bag. The woman forced his face against the window, and they looked out. "Her name is Mimi right?" Lauro ignored his captor. "If you don't cooperate I'll take her as well and make her into Eva," the woman said. Lauro dropped on the van floor. Eva applied red lipstick and gray eye shadow. She winked at Lauro, who puked into the bag. The van moved, and Lauro's eyes went to the back door. Elsa went to the padlock and took hold. She closed her eyes to break the lock.

"Wake up girl!" Mano said.

"Damn you to the deepest level of Hell!" Elsa signed.

"I'm thinking that's where we're going to live," Mano said. She leapt from the bed, and he caught her mid-air and held her above him. "Go on sign to me." A tremor lanced her left arm, and he frowned. The door crashed open and Lettie raced in chased by Chino in a tuxedo.

"Blast him Ma!" Lettie said.

"Go ahead blast me baby girl," Mano said. Chino laughed. Dropping a bolt of lightning would please her, but he wasn't worth the strain. He put her on the ground, and Lettie ran to her. "I have a question? What happens to Leader Elsa for consorting with the enemy?" Elsa took a step back.

"We are not enemies with the Wolf Clan," Lettie said.

"You'll find that I am the enemy of your leader Abrim Stein and my Uncle, well, Abrim should thank him, but alas Stein is an ungrateful bastard. My point is what is the punishment among the Fighters for treason?" Mano asked. Elsa glanced at Lettie.

"Death," Elsa signed. Mano's eyes slid to her hands.

"He would kill his most important ally for making a mistake?" Chino asked. Elsa's gaze remained on Mano. Chino now read the sign, but Alec hadn't hammered his fist into the man to gain the knowledge.

"How can you read our sign?" Lettie asked. He ignored her.

"What part would be a mistake?" Elsa signed.

"You're just a woman, he's the Black Wolf you couldn't resist him," Chino said, "When he wants something it's his way."

"I made a choice and I'll stand by it," Elsa signed.

"To the death how does that make sense?" Chino asked.

"Leticia's life is…my purpose is to serve and this time…I made a choice, I will not deny it to anyone," Elsa signed. Lettie gripped her hands as the tremor bumped along.

"You criticize Leader Abrim, but wouldn't you do the same if someone did what we have done for whatever reason?" Lettie asked.

"Am I not in the same position as your beloved leader Abrim Stein?" Mano asked.

"How is that?" Lettie asked.

"When she leaves she will return to him has my trust not been betrayed?" Mano asked. Lettie sighed.

"We're getting strapped to a pole and set on fire, and he's betrayed!" Lettie said.

166

"In my world since I am the King he would die not her, why punish myself?" Mano asked. Lettie pulled Elsa along. "Just so you won't worry I'm telling him."

"Why would you do that?" Lettie asked.

"I'm bored, go on when I want to see her, I will plan an abduction. We have a party Green Wolf," Mano said. They disappeared, and Lettie entwined her arm. Elsa popped shoes on their feet.

"Where is Isabella?" Lettie asked. They stepped across the hall, and Isabella appeared. Lettie took her hand. Elsa freed her toes into the expanse of the old canvas shoe. Each small toe sprung through the holes. "Well, these feel better than those pretty ones, and they're clean I'm good," Lettie said. They crossed the beautiful patterned carpet arm in arm. Loud music jumped at them, and they stopped at the entrance to a grand ballroom. A group of beautiful women laughed together dressed in elegant gowns. "Do you ever miss being like them? They're so lovely?" Lettie asked.

"Yes sometimes, do you?" Elsa signed.

"Being recognized as a woman among my Fighter brothers would be nice."

"So they can dance we can do many things they can't. The clan doesn't look impressed," Isabella said. The women smiled at the Wolf Clan, but the men just drank and looked away. A song played and several of the women swung out onto the dance floor and whirled their hips in rhythm.

"How about dancing do you miss…" Lettie said. A broom crashed into Elsa's back and Lettie snapped away. The broom came again, and she blocked it. A sting pulsed, and her wrist bled. "Ma!" Another swing caught Isabella on the side of the head. The man drove the broom to their heads again. A black arm twisted around the man's neck.

"You're going to die slow and painful," Mano snarled. The knife gleamed in the kitchen light. Lettie moved them away.

"But master they're dirty nasty peasants!" Mano's eyes dragged down to her shoes. Lettie steered them to the back door. A broom hammered Lettie on the arm. Elsa turned, and the man was pinned against the wall a knife stuck in his sleeve.

"You're mine bitch and I'm pissed," Chino said.

"Master Chino they're thieves," the man pinned against the wall whined. Chino turned to Lettie.

"How do you figure that?" Chino asked.

"The red head is wearing your monogrammed shirt and the little one look she has MRV on her shirt. Those are tailored shirts, they're expense I buy mine in Mexico City, and that dirty little one has Master Manuel's shirt," Mano's captive said. Mano stuck him to the wall. The Wolf clan entered the kitchen. Saul glared at Isabella. His expression changed when another man whacked her with a broom. He roared like a beast as the man came up and was pinned to the ceiling.

"We're going to be late for confession…again," Pepe said.

"All this killing and punishing it makes us run late for the card game and then there's not enough time to get drunk enough," Pablo said. Alfonso nodded.

"We have to get really drunk to come up with some new confessions for the Padre. We don't want him to get bored," Alfonso said.

"We're his only escape from the sacred life," Pepe said.

"What did they do?" Pablo asked.

"We beat those nasty, thieving peasants. They stink!" The Wolf clan glanced at Elsa.

"Ah geez not those peasants?" Pablo asked. The other man nodded.

"We took the brooms to them. I bet they're hungry!" Mano's glance fell on Elsa.

"Are you hungry little peasant?" Mano asked.

"Yes," Elsa signed.

"She's one of them beggars who need coins for their little pens, nasty liars!" Chino's captive said.

"You hate us because we are dressed in old clothes and hungry?" Isabella asked. The man frowned.

"You don't belong in a place like this among these great men. You're low life little whores!" Saul's captive said.

"You don't know us," Lettie said. Elsa signed.

"You're all the same trash!" Chino's captive snapped.

"We went from being peasants to thieves, to liars to whores in less than ten seconds what kind of man are you?" Isabella translated.

"He's a tortured man," Saul said.

"He's a dead man," Chino said.

"He's a forgotten man," Mano said.

"He's a dissolved man. I would for once like to have a party with no dead bodies involved," Pablo said.

"If you screened the idiots, then maybe we could!" Mano said. A woman swayed into the kitchen. Her black hair in perfect order.

"Who ordered the squirrels to my party?" she asked. Elsa smiled at the wolf mother.

"I didn't order any squirrels," Pablo said. The elegant woman took a breath.

"How am I supposed to teach you proper manners when the women you invite to the party eat like starved squirrels, what am I saying squirrels have more brains than that group out there. What part of decent, pleasant, and well-mannered didn't you understand?" she asked. Lettie approached the woman and put out her hand.

"I am Leticia Marras and this is Elsa de las Almas, and Isabella Maldano, we're sorry if we caused any trouble," Lettie said. The woman's eyebrow arched. Lettie wiped her hand and presented it again. The woman took it, and Elsa shook her hand as well. Isabella bowed to her.

"Maria Rojas, you're bleeding," she said. The elegant woman took a tissue from her purse and wiped off the blood. "Do you have any idea what it's like to raise a wolf pack? Evil, wicked I get it, but stupid, no, we will not add that to our gene pool." A bandage came out of her purse and went on the cut.

"No madam, don't touch them. They're nasty, stinking, dirty hungry peasants!" Mano's captive said. Maria eyed the men.

"They're polite. They don't smell, and if they're hungry why didn't you feed them?"

"We beat them with the brooms just like they deserve," Chino's captive said. Maria bit the corner of her lip. The wolf mother wished to keep her secret with Elsa and she would be accommodated.

"I know this is going to be a bad question, but…" Maria asked. Elsa signed, and Lettie nodded.

"We're Fighters," Lettie said.

"You like to fight I get it," Maria said. Elsa signed.

"No, we're the Fighters," Lettie said.

"The only THE Fighters I know are Abrim Stein's Fighters, and he only has two female, top notch Fighters, they are his…allies, greatest fighting potential are you nuts?" Maria shouted. She flung her purse at Mano, and Elsa leapt into the way. She caught the shiny black object. The woman raised her arm, and Elsa blocked her from Mano. Maria swung, and Elsa braced for the impact that never came. Mano caught her arm. Maria spun away and hyperventilated. Elsa and Lettie patted her back. Lettie took her pulse.

"Her heart rate is high, Ma," Lettie said. Elsa stroked her face and signed. "Ma says it's fine to just relax."

"Do not tell Padre Ignacio about this!" Maria said. Elsa signed.

"We don't know a Padre Ignacio," Lettie said. Maria held Lettie's chin. Her fingers went to the girl's hair.

"No sweetheart, not you and her, and the ghostly little blond, the dead bodies what is rule number five, wolf clan?" Maria asked.

"Never tell the preacher the real stuff," they chanted including Manuel. Elsa turned and smiled at him. He exhaled.

"She's your Mami?" Elsa asked.

"What did you think I didn't have one?" Mano snapped.

"She's beautiful like you," Lettie said.

"And you think I care what you think?" Mano shouted. Elsa signed.

"Not one bit," Lettie said. Elsa glanced down and then at Maria.

"What in the devil's name is holding up my dinner?" Alec shouted as he stomped into the room. His eyes landed on Maria and Elsa and Lettie and Isabella together. "Aw crap!"

"Does someone want to tell me why these three beautiful, decent women are wearing your monogrammed shirts?" Maria asked.

"No, now you're going back to Mexico City what's wrong with the girls in the ballroom?" Alec asked.

"Nothing if you like squirrels? I want filet mignon not squirrel damn crazy old man. We have enough stupid genes, we need to mix it up Alejandro, but no you want to get drunk, play cards and lie to Padre," Maria said. He hauled her away from them.

"You asked me to invite beautiful, articulate and…" Alec said.

"And you go to the park and pick up squirrels!" Maria shouted, "You see them that's what I want!"

"You're unreasonable!" Alec said. Maria stopped and glanced at Elsa, a slow smile came to her face.

"You're right of course," Maria said. Alec stopped pulling her.

"I am?" Alec asked.

"Yes, what I want is them, those three Elsa and Lettie, and Isabella you have friends right?" Maria asked. Elsa nodded. "Excellent! I want to meet all of you very soon!"

"You've lost your mind do you know who they are?" Alec asked.

"Abrim's Fighters I know make it happen, Manuel," Maria said.

"You're going to pick a fight with the biggest dog in Mexico what in the Hell chance do you think you have of winning?" Alec asked. Maria hammered her purse at Mano. Elsa caught it and slipped to the floor. The rough stone rushed up to meet her as she slammed to a halt. Mano set her on her feet. She kissed his face, and he frowned. She took Lettie's and Isabella's hands.

"That is why I think we're going to win, although we have to talk about your manners boy! No blood in the house. I want an update on your progress in two days! Take me home I think I'll be able to sleep tonight," Maria said. Elsa glanced back as they slipped into the moist night air. Alejandro Rojas grinned, sweet and evil as he escorted the woman away. Mano's mouth creased into a snarl as he slammed the door.

Elsa dipped her hands into the stream. The cool water crashed against her fingers as she brought the water to her face. The breeze shifted, and she turned. Juan stared and Adam stood to his right with another man. Lettie and Isabella ran to her. "The Leader wishes to see you, whatever problem you have get over it!" Juan said. The two women flanked her. Juan crossed his arms.

"I'd like to speak to you Elsa." David and Sam emerged from the foggy shadows. David's strained eyes fixed on her. Bob came to stand next to his employer. Elsa stepped into the water, and each of them took steps backward.

"Father wants to talk can't expect him to change. He won't even for you," Juan said. David came further, and she moved to the middle of the stream.

"You're exhausted. How long will you fight?" David asked. Elsa moved to the other side, and the fog swallowed them. She moved, and the tremors echoed in her legs.

"Ma, you have to stop soon," Lettie said.

"We have to rest and I need to return home," Isabella said. Susa Mendoza joined them. She leapt forward, and they followed. Isabella backed up, and Elsa ran into her. "Who you?" Susa held her arms wide to stop them. Alfonso held up a pistol.

"You a friend of the Fighter Elsa?" he asked.

"Me her soldier, me die for her," Susa said.

"She's your leader?" he asked. Elsa searched the terrain.

"Move on me not want hurt…hurt…" Susa said.

"You think you have that kind of power?" Alfonso asked.

"Not have power, only skills, bad ones," Susa said.

"Is this one mine Leader?" Alfonso asked. Mano and Chino came into view, and Saul trailed behind them. Elsa stepped in front of Susa. Three days had passed since they left his mansion.

"What can two assassins make?" Mano asked.

"The pretty one is like me?" Alfonso asked.

"They make war," Susa said.

"I want her Leader," Alfonso said. Susa glanced at the dirt.

"She trusts no one leave her alone," Lettie said.

"Trust like love is earned," Alfonso said.

"Love Hell and trust prison," Susa said.

"I don't agree," Alfonso said. Susa stepped closer to Elsa.

"Not like him," Susa said. Alfonso grinned, and a wolf howl crested the night air. Elsa blinked, and she was in a room. She raced for the door and yanked hard. She turned a large old bed shimmered to her right. Soft blankets and fat pillows and a fireplace burst to life to warm the room. A shaggy rug appeared, and Elsa held her arms out. She forced every last bit of

176

strength to rupture the walls, but they held as she collapsed to the cold wood floor. The ceiling drifted away.

"Bus leaving for Laredo in five minutes!" Elsa spun around. A hand shoved her away, and a small boy kicked her.

"Get off of Linky!" he said. Beneath her foot, a ragged stuffed bear with a missing eye lay crushed. The child pulled hard, and Linky lost his arm. The boy burst into tears. His father took hold. Elsa grabbed the ragged bundle and the discarded arm and attached the toy with her gift. Linky even got a new eye, a brown one to match his blue one. She pressed the toy at the boy, and his father frowned.

"I'm sorry I'm lost…" Elsa signed. The child took the toy and his father fished out a dollar and gave it to her. She passed it back and pulled her pockets out.

"If you're of out pens, well, just take it," he said.

"Poppy, how did Linky grow a new eye?" the boy asked. The father glanced at the child, and Elsa stepped away.

"Two minutes to departure to Laredo!" Elsa searched the crowd and her gaze fell on Eva, whose arm was linked with Lauro. The boy stared into space as she led him onto the bus. Elsa ran to the platform, but she was too late as it pulled away. She ran around and saw the sign. Houston to Laredo. She willed her curse to put her on that bus, but the darkness ripped her away instead.

The crackle of thunder woke her. She sat in a corner of a huge room. A large desk graced a far wall covered in papers and a computer. She got to her feet and went around the table. A blue plate covered in the remains of some crackers. One sole piece, a half with a smear of peanut butter lay discarded next to a half of a discolored apple. Her fingers trembled against the edge as she stole the cracker and apple.

The salty piece crunched as she devoured it. "I believe I am capable of providing better than an old cracker," Abrim said. She jumped back, and the apple flew. He caught it. His eyes traveled to her hand where the ring still remained. She put her hand behind her back and glanced at the floor. Bits of the apple dripped from his fist. She walked away. "You came to see me?" His voice was nails on a chalkboard.

"I had no choice…" she signed. She regretted the words even as they fell through the air between. His breath scraped through his teeth.

"Cause given a choice you'd rather go against me than for once do what I say?" His deep blue eyes glowed.

"I wouldn't turn my back on Lettie what happened to her was because of me…"

"You're the almighty Elsa, the Dear one who can do no wrong!' She turned and ran. He stepped in front of her, and she crashed. His hands were on her waist, and she met his gaze for a moment. "Why won't you ever look me in the eye?" She followed every line to its end and came back to his eyes. "I want you to…" She pulled away.

"The ring is mine. You said whatever was in my pack was mine, and it didn't matter how it got there. It was mine…cause I don't have too much of anything."

"Did I say that?" Abrim asked.

"I'm not a liar." His palms pressed together.

"I'm trying to recall when I made this decree?" She shifted.

"When Juan was trying to cheat and take my rations. He said that the stuff in my pack should be his since he's my leader and everything I had was because of him." Abrim bit his lower lip.

"As I recall you stated that everything you had was because of me and the only man whom you would follow was me."

"Yes," she signed.

"I wonder if that has changed?" he asked. His hands dropped at his side.

"Without your help I wouldn't have been able to help the villages or get the medicine to the children or the books or shoes or clothes. You always give me what I ask for."

"You ask for a lot," he said.

"Yes, sometimes I feel like it's too much, so I try not to ask unless I really need something, but you've done so much more than everyone else." He stood straighter.

"You never ask for anything personal," he said.

"I don't need anything." She turned the ring on her finger and smiled.

"Maybe you want something from me?" he asked.

"Like what?" A shiver ran through her.

"I could give you a ring," he said.

"I already have this one."

"But I didn't give it to you," he said. She brought her pack and held it in front of her.

"Why does that matter to you leader Abrim?"

"You should be grateful that I am a forgiving man!" His shoulders pulled together, and his face clenched.

"I am grateful for your help," Elsa signed.

"Do you think I am senile and don't know where you've been? Who you've been with?" His voice shredded the air between them.

"I will tell you whatever you wish to know leader…"

"You will be silent! I am an honorable man and as such my bond to you will not be broken even as others will criticize me for my weakness. I will bear the shame and disgrace you bring for both of us for to…"

"Maintain honor one must often suffer and sacrifice." She ran, and he appeared to block her. A tear fell into the lines of his hand. She walked around him.

"Elsa, wait…" he called. The darkness delivered her back to the room and the fire. She blinked, and the smell of warm tortillas came to her. She put her pack on the floor. A brown sack lay among her things. She pulled a silver packet out and consumed the soft, fragrant meat and bread, he sent to her.

"You saw that old bastard?" She glanced at Mano. He snatched the brown bag from her hands and flung it into the fire. "You take nothing from him ever!"

"He said whatever is in my pack is mine, he's leader, his word is the law to me!" Elsa signed. Mano's eyes went blue as he ripped the room apart, and she appeared in the middle of the jungle. A steady rain hummed down, and she was soaked. Her Hunters were still trapped with the Wolf Clan, her Hunters? She leapt through the air and entered the room where Lettic held off the Green Wolf. The younger woman jumped against the wall and caught her hand, and they twisted into the next room. Susa pressed fingers to her mouth. Alfonso glanced up. Anger and frustration blasted across his face. He pounced at Susa, and Elsa raised her arms to blast him. Elsa leapt to the room of the purple wolf, and he glanced up. "Where is Isabella, I want…" She spun with the women in tow.

Mano and Chino appeared next to their brethren and powered up. Susa gripped her arm and Elsa back peddled as the balls of light slammed at them. Lettie whipped them around and they landed in the dark, wet night. Elsa ran and never looked back.

Chapter 10 The Crown Prince and the Angel

Elsa glanced to the right as Susa and Lettie came up. They followed Juan onto the path that led out of the trader's market. For two months, they kept pace with the younger leader of the Fighters. He traveled all over the country to visit distant villages and allies just to check on their progress.

The first night they encountered Juan was two days from the flight from the Wolf clan. Her need to be alone was overshadowed by the two women at her side whose confusion and stress crushed her mind. The market was filled with energy. Three homeless women didn't make a difference to anyone they met. No one spoke to them, and they kept to themselves. Juan came to the edge of the jungle and looked back. He didn't see them and turned back to the trees. She adjusted her pack and pressed her mind to move them forward and stopped as men emerged from the trees. Juan raised his arms as they raised their rifles.

The man in front grinned at Juan and held up his weapon as if to slam it into Juan's head. She shifted, and they appeared behind the men and stepped from behind a tree. Juan smiled at the men, and their guns were down. Juan saw her, and his expression changed. She turned to run.

"Hold it or I'll shoot him!" barked a male voice. She stumbled to a halt and fell upon her knees. "Come on you, into the open where I can see you," a man said. Lettie and Susa obeyed the soldier.

"Mundo, Raul, Jaime over here. Look what we've caught in our little trap?" he called. The three soldiers came to the area, all dressed in the uniforms of Paticia's militia.

"Big deal a bunch of peasants, so what Jose," Raul said.

"Three beautiful women and a stupid man. So you've found us some entertainment," Mundo said.

"We'll, show you a very good time, baby," Jaime said. He slid his rifle against Susa's face. Elsa glanced at Juan, and he avoided her eyes.

"Come on," Jose said. He indicated the direction with his rifle. Elsa took the lead and pulled her hair back, as her hands came down she signed, "Not alive." Lettie coughed, and Susa sighed in agreement. Elsa stepped forward.

The soldier stopped. The jungle was quiet. Two of the men took up positions in front of them, and the other two took up the rear of the line. Soon the sun would set and they hurried to make camp before dark. The man at the lead went ahead a bit and disappeared from view. The others stopped. Elsa ran into the back of a man.

"Help! Help me!" Jaime screamed. They moved with care toward the voice. The man was waist-deep in quicksand. "Get me out," he called.

"What do you think men?" Jose asked. The others didn't reply.

"Every man for himself, Jaime. You know the rules. You just lost your turn," Jose said. Jaime stared in disbelief.

"But we're friends," Jaime begged.

"Listen I can hear the voices of the dead call you," Jose said. He yanked Elsa forward. The others followed close behind.

"No! I'll see you in Hell, Alvarez. Jose do you…" he screamed. They moved toward the mountain.

"Wait!" Mundo called. They stopped.

"What is it Mundo?" Jose asked. Mundo pulled at his pant leg. A light flashed on him. Two puncture wounds on his calf bled. Jose caught the movement in the dim light and fired his weapon. He flashed the light on the ground as the snake moved through the night. He turned to Mundo and fired. Mundo's head blew apart as his body fell back.

"Let's go," Jose said. Again, they continued their journey. He called a halt and made camp. "You tie your friends to that tree." He pointed his rifle at Lettie. Juan's gaze drifted to Jose's face. Lettie tied Juan and Susa together. "Now you tie her over there until I'm ready for her."

Elsa placed her hands on Lettie as she took the rope around and placed in it her hands.

With the others tied Jose came at Elsa. He made no rude comments, no gestures to degrade his mind was set to one goal. "Listen friend I can give you money for a real woman, not some smelly peasant," Juan said. Jose trained over her, his breath warm as he licked his dry lips. "Come on I've got a thousand dollars, we'll go party," Juan said. Jose inhaled and closed his eyes. His hand trembled as he reached toward her face. "She's not the kind of woman you want to take a chance with, you don't know where she's been."

Jose whipped his rifle into Juan's face. Tiny lights flickered as the sleep threatened Elsa. She swayed, and Jose caught her.

"Gather wood for a fire, Raul," Jose said. His green eyes pierced her flesh.

"Then after we've eaten we'll start the party?" Raul asked. Jose didn't answer as Raul moved through the darkness in the opposite direction. Jose pressed her forward away from the others. Elsa stumbled back as they moved. She blinked, and a black hood and cape appeared to cover his body. Her vision blurred. "Son of a bitch. Jose, Jose!" Raul shouted. Elsa's vision cleared, and Jose without the cloak searched her face. He dragged her back.

"Stupid bastard is going to wreck this? I have got to recruit better people," Jose said. He clutched her shirt as they entered the camp. To the left against a tree was the headless body of Mundo with a live snake curled over his shoulders. To his right Jaime, his mouth opened in a final scream, quicksand dripped from his chin.

Jose pulled his knife and split her shirt open and tore at her pants. "They're all around us, Jose. Come on, come on," Raul called.

"Shut up! I'm trying to work here," Jose snapped. He shoved her backward.

"Jossseee!" Raul screamed.

"You smell like the flowers of my Texas home in the early morning when only God and I are awake," Jose whispered. Elsa blinked as his thumb worked against her lower lip. "I had to tell you I will not allow anyone to harm you. My sweet Texas rose." The lights flickered again. He adjusted his hold. Raul raced passed and dropped a few feet away. "Stupid, crazy bastard," Jose said.

Blood rained on Elsa's face. Whose blood could it be? The tick of a clock marked off time, and Elsa inhaled the aromas of rich meat. At the stove, Laura stirred a pot. She flipped a tortilla into a plastic container. Tears fell and sizzled on the comal. The hot griddle protested the grief. She turned her slender body back to the task at hand. She twisted the rolling pin to yield the perfect round of bread. She needed more information to rescue young Lauro and all she had was the last names of these people, Dominguez and Ortiz, he may as well have been named Smith or Jones.

A sigh escaped her, and she stepped to allow the tears to fall onto the clean green tiles of the large kitchen. They splattered shiny and bright. Whispered voices echoed and Elsa went to the sound.

Mr. Dominguez sat behind a computer in a large room with a desk. His old mother to the left of him. The woman glanced up and reached to close the door. "Have you spoken to her mijo?" she asked. The large man exhaled and pushed the laptop aside.

"What would you like for me to say Ma?" he asked.

"It is difficult losing a child, I know my heart has known this pain. No one will ever replace Lauro, still after all this time I can't speak of…" the old woman withered. Mr. Dominguez rose and held his mother as she sobbed.

"Of Tim I know Mama. I'm sorry," he said. She wiped her eyes.

"Yes, well I still had you and Tinker, but my grief blinded me to your needs. Do you see little Mimi. A girl needs her mother, mijo at every age, but Lauro is her brother, and she's afraid to lose her mother." The old woman straightened all of her thin frame.

"What can I do Ma, what more will she let me do?" he asked.

"Speak to her of your love, mijo," she said.

"Ma don't do this," he said.

"Don't speak the truth is what you mean no?"

"Ma, no please," he said. He ran his hand through thinning black hair and sighed.

"She is a young woman, she needs a man for many reasons why not you?" she asked. Mr. Dominguez looked out to the street.

"Laura is beautiful and me not so much. What do I have…"

"You're a hard worker. You're kind and generous…"

"Not to mention fat, old and never been married, you just described me in every way, but by my appearance so my own mother thinks I'm ugly," he said. Elsa smiled.

"What has that got to do with Laura?"

"Look at her and look at me. We're a ten, o.k she's a ten I'm a zero," he said. His mother frowned.

"Tell her you love her, or I will," she said.

"Why would you?" he asked.

"Cause Mimi is the closest I'm getting to a granddaughter from you, and if you don't tell her…I want them safe now go!" Oscar Dominguez stared at his old mother and left. Elsa followed him to the kitchen where the grief dance continued. He sucked in his stomach and entered the room. Laura wiped her face and turned to the stove.

"Your supper is almost ready. You seemed to like the frijoles, and I know you love the tortillas…" she said.

"You think I'm a fat pig don't you?" Laura turned her brown eyes with their lashes washed down and stared. Elsa inhaled the sopa.

"I think, that you're the nicest man I've ever known."

"Pigs are nice. They make great bacon," he said. He looked down into the bowl on the counter.

"Why do you not like me?" Laura asked. Elsa smiled.

"You've been living at my house with your daughter for sixty three and a half days, twelve minutes and fourteen seconds, not that I'm counting, but my own mother never lived here," he said.

"I cook and I clean, and I wash and I press clothes and I make tacos for the store, and I do the books and I change your bed everyday. I dust the little beer steins from only God knows where. I put out the paper for you so when you come home it's ready. I put all the money from the tacos you give me in a jar for you! I even draw you a bath and what do I get ignored that's what I get!"

"Free rent and food and my connections and everything that comes from my money!" he snapped. She ripped off the apron and limped away. Elsa patted him on the back. "Smooth Oscar really smooth." Laura returned, and he looked at her.

"I'm leaving, but before I go, I'm going to do one last thing for me something I've wanted to do for ninety days," she said. She leapt into his arms and pressed her mouth to his. Elsa grinned. Oscar held her, and she wiggled free. She limped away.

"Ninety days would be…hold on," Oscar said. Elsa ran after him as he searched his home. He came into the bedroom that was hers, and it was empty. He went into his room, and she finished the bed. "Laura…"

"I saw the stuff…your stuff," Laura said. Elsa wondered if maybe there should be a rule about eavesdropping on private conversations.

"My stuff?" Oscar asked.

"In the closet to the left, brown box with the words Private Oscar's stash," Laura said. She fluffed the pillows. Oscar laughed. "You think it's funny I hate that I love you!" Oscar sobered. She stomped away, and he caught her and laid her on the perfect bed.

"Don't be mad. I don't like it," he said. Elsa looked away as he kissed her face.

"I saw what you have. How could you?" Laura asked. Elsa glanced at the closet.

"It's a man thing," Oscar said.

"Quit you player," Laura said. Oscar laughed. "You need to keep looking cause I don't have boobs like the ones on your made-up woman, mine are little and…"

"Let me see beautiful what you have," Oscar said. Elsa turned her back on them.

"You're not going to see anything. I'm not that kind of woman!"

"Marry me baby, please," Oscar said. There was silence, and Elsa turned as Laura stumbled off the bed.

"You think I don't know what you're doing? You pity me and Mimi. Lauro was right you're a good man, and I won't do this…" Laura said. She ran out of the room.

"Laura wait!" Oscar called. His mother and Mimi stood in the living room with Laura. Felix came into the room. "I do want to marry you, and it's not about pity will you listen!"

"I have and never mind…Mimi stay with Grandma Dominguez," Laura said. The woman ran away.

"Laura please…" Oscar called. He never moved.

"Why didn't you tell her how you feel?" his mother asked.

"I don't know what I feel, I…" Oscar said. Mimi cried and ran the opposite direction.

"Oscar I have some news about Lauro," Felix said. The dark ripped Elsa away.

Emotions raged and burned Elsa. David shook her and Jose came at them, a wicked gleam blasted the captor into a nearby tree. Jose grinned and winked as he bounced from the ground and ran. Jose's blood splattered her clothes. She searched for Juan.

"You were right again David. How did I do, maestro?" Samuel asked.

"Excellent you put your skills to good use they will serve me well in the future, son," David said. Elsa spun, and the darkness blasted her. She fought the wave, and David held her. She let go, and it washed her away.

"Find them! I know they're here somewhere. This is their kind of handiwork," Patricia screamed. Elsa floated above them as they searched the dead bodies at the camp. The commander stomped around the clearing. Her rage beyond reason; they went free for far too long. A young soldier approached her.

"They're gone," the soldier said. Patricia turned as the rage snaked onto her beautiful face. She emptied the weapon into the young man. "I'll have Almas' head! Do you understand me? Find her! I'll have her if it's the last thing I do in this Hell," Patricia shouted. The soldiers scurried to comply with her will.

Elsa jerked. "Your grandmother searches for your mother Samuel let me help protect her," David said. Elsa shook her head.

"Yes, you're right. What should we do? She won't be safe in Mexico, we know that."

"Don't make decisions for her Samuel…" Lettie said.

"I am her son I know what is best," Sam said. Elsa fought the sleep and still it wrestled her soul.

"I'm going to help you Elsa let me in," David said. He pressed his mouth to Elsa's and she fought him. The sticky liquid flowed against her fingers. "Use any weapon you want it won't stop me Elsa. I will bleed for you if I must." His kiss came with fire and then ice. Her peacefulness whisked into him, and he groaned against her as the nightmares were laid to rest for a time.

"Who are your friends, David?" The speaker was a big man with gray hair and a thick mustache. David's arms tightened.

"Doctor Beto Lamb this is Elsa de las Almas, her son Samuel Trevino Stein. Leticia Marras is the young woman next to Sam this young woman is Susanna Mendoza," David said. The man nodded and smiled. His big hands slid over her face, and she jumped free. The front door was a few feet away. Lettie and Susa were trapped by Sam and Bob the only way to be free was to hurt the men. Elsa swallowed the fear and dove into the dark.

Lettie remained frozen as Elsa dropped to the shiny wood floor. Her face pale and the next second Elsa convulsed. Her leader needed escape, and she would help her leave. Lettie inhaled the pain, and Elsa flew away. David spun in her direction. "What just happened?" David shouted. Susa pushed passed the security man and stepped around so that they were over the fallen Elsa. Lettie reached down, and they recovered her.

"Let him help her Leticia, Senorita Marras have mercy on the only person that cared enough to save you!" Sam said.

"What do you know of mercy you would sell your soul to the devil in a second for a profit," Lettie said.

"David's not the devil, even though Ma said he is, he's just different, "

"Were we speaking of your new teacher brother Stein?" Lettie asked. The handsome soldier frowned.

"I'm not your brother," he said.

"My brother is dead you are my Fighter brother as close to a brother as I will ever have, no? The Fighter's line of defense is our family values, brother, you have not been away from our traditions that long to have forgotten them," Lettie said. Susa clasped Elsa under her arm. Lettie took hold of the other side.

"Where are you going?" Sam asked. They turned.

"We're baking cookies want to join us?" Lettie asked, "Stupid ass, why can't they be smart and pretty?"

"Me think ugly ones better," Susa said.

"Which door?" Lettie asked.

"How me know, they too many," Susa said. They continued on.

"Where was her room last time?" Lettie asked.

"She not have one," Susa said.

"All right this time I need a bed for her. Why aren't they following us?" Lettie asked.

"They plot to sneak up and boom," Susa said.

"I'm going to boom them, which one?" Lettie asked.

"May I help?" Lettie turned to a petite blond.

"Who are you?"

"I ask myself that question all the time. Who are you Nellette Cameron? Am I someone I don't know, you know like, maybe I haven't awakened to my true purpose?"

"You are what you have allowed to touch you," Lettie said.

"Oh, my that's good, but what about the things I've no control over?" Nellette asked. She crossed in front of them and opened the door. They entered and followed as the woman pulled down the blankets. Lettie laid Elsa upon the fluffy pillow and a pain issued in her own neck. She removed the pillow and the pain eased.

"What…things?" Susa asked. Susa removed Elsa's old shoes.

"Well like the two of you. I can't control you and you're in my life," she said.

"You decide what do," Susa said.

"Or not do with us, Nellette," Lettie said. She dug through her pack and found the tea.

"Call me Nellie what if I wanted to do what you do?" Susa glanced out the window.

"How we stop you?" Susa asked.

"I'm not like you," Nellie said.

"We're women. How are we different?" Lettie asked. The medicine cup came from its pouch.

"I'm not dangerous like the two of you," Nellie said.

"Yeah we're dangerous I need to make tea," Lettie said.

"Oh I can do that," Nellie said. The blond left them.

"Not without fire like you," Susa said. Lettie eyed her.

"I need fire, not one-word Susa. I'm going to find fire, uh a stove," Lettie said, "You can't imagine what being like this is like."

"Me can't?" Susa asked.

"You want me to bring you something?" Lettie asked.

"You know man name Esteben Cortez, he Fighter?" Susa asked.

"Yes, why?" Lettie asked.

"Me want kiss back," Susa said.

"That's who you saw when we were at Leader Abrim's never mind," Lettie said. Susa sighed and leaned against the bed.

Time seemed to standstill in this palace known as the house of Gracia. Elsa slept as she tried to decide how to free them from this place. The day and a half since they arrived brought no resolution to that issue. Lettie exhaled. "I am a…bird?"

"When will I see my mother?" Sam asked. She tried to gain her balance.

"I am a crazy bird," she said.

"Senorita Marras I am certain you are aware of my position in the Fighter's group, now I command…"

"You're blocking the sun boy, move!" Lettie said.

"It's ten p.m." he replied. She glanced at him.

"Go away Crown Prince Stein," she said. He dropped in front of her. Lettie inhaled his sweet male scent.

"I am your superior," he said. Lettie exhaled.

"You are an ass, wow that's working," she said. He grasped her arms, and she hammered him onto his back. "See what you did you broke

my concentration, and now I have to start over."
Her braid slipped over her shoulder. He ran long
fingers over her head. A cascade of reddish
brown surrounded him. His blue eyes changed
to dark seas.

"All I want is…"

"To get your ass kicked, Fighter Stein, I am
your equal not some little jungle rat you found
along the trail," she said. She maneuvered out of
his grip.

"You're not a regular woman, there is truth
in that," he said. She glanced away. "Wow did
that hurt you Fighter Marras?"

"Only if you were a man, but you're just a
boy," she said. He pinned her to the floor
beneath him. His white teeth clenched. "What
do you want Samuel?" He leaned in his breath,
sweet and fresh his mouth came to hers and
stopped.

"I want only to see my mother, girl," he
said. Her hand opened, and his fingers spread
across hers. He spoke the truth. He thought she
was nothing more than a rough woman with no
manners or sense.

"I will come for you when she has more
rest," she said. She slipped free of his hold, and
he left.

Three am found Lettie in the large kitchen.
The stove had more buttons than directions, and
it looked mean. She would forgo the tea of
strength and wandered down the long hall. She

located the door and knocked no one answered, and she entered. "I did not say to enter," Samuel said, "I locked that door." The room was in shadows, as he lay on the bed. She glanced at the knob was there no door she couldn't open? "Out!" She approached the bed and dropped the sack on his bare stomach.

"I will not accept your arrangement to pay a debt you do not owe. I have returned all of it, check if you like," she said. He clutched her arm and pulled her down.

"No woman refuses me," he said. Her palm pressed against his chest, and she sighed.

"And certainly no man looking thing with scars."

"How can you not comprehend why I am doing this…"

"As a favor to a beloved teacher who saved your life, who helped you be a man. You're a few years from your claim of manhood friend," Lettie said. He devoured her mouth in a hungry kiss, and she suffocated beneath him. Her hands moved through his hair, and he squeezed her. He ripped her shirt open and kissed her shoulder. She struggled to free her body from its desire for him. She rolled off the bed and went to the door. He got there first.

"I am only your guardian nothing more. I am honor bond to protect you from…nothing more," he said. She closed her shirt, but the pieces were tatters, and she did more damage.

She released the fabric. His eyes raked her skin. He leapt forward and covered her.

"Sam," Bob said. His hands slid against her bare back.

"What I'm a little busy," he said.

"Yeah, sure," Bob said. The man retreated, and the Crown Prince stepped back.

"I know you think I'm like a man. It didn't mean anything, the kiss. You owe me nothing Crown Prince you have enough problems without me," Lettie said. She covered herself and stepped to the side. He followed her. "You can see your mother in four hours." She stepped to the right and he followed. "Only because at that time, she'll be better you won't even have to see me." He nodded, and she moved to the left. He was right there. "I don't know what you want!" He leaned down. "You said you didn't want that, liar." He snatched his shirt from the bed and smoothed it down her body.

"You can leave," he said.

"Thanks," she replied. Lettie exhaled. "I'm a worm."

"Angel, Leticia why a worm?" he asked.

"It's going to take a lot of life forms to get me to relax better start low and work my way up," she said. Her hand landed on the knob, and he laughed. She turned, and a big grin graced his serious face. The Fighters saw so much suffering, there was little laughter much less happiness to celebrate. She ran across the room and touched his face, she wanted to always remember the look.

"What is it Fighter Angel Marras?" he asked.

"A Fighter's life has little joy to capture one moment is like the warmth from the sun on a cold winter day," she said. His grin broadened, and his body relaxed.

"You are definitely worth my time," he said.

"A Fighter's pride is his crown, but a Fighter should be careful not to overlay it with too many stones lest it breaks his neck when he tries to wear it," Lettie said.

"You do remind me of a man," Samuel said.

"I'm not surprised most of your brothers are reminded of a man when they see me," Lettie said. She pulled the door open.

"Your father had all those saying you remind me of him," Sam said. Lettie closed the door and wound her way back to Elsa's door.

Seven am where was that Crown Prince of the Fighters. Lettie shifted to the left her feet hurt. Samuel was a genius and he couldn't tell time, no, he played games, strategic games. He knew nothing more than she did. The reality was she knew more. His treasured teacher was her hard father. The lessons he taught her were established to conquer even his most beloved students. The sunlight merged onto the glass in a room across from her. Another day and another night without sleep.

"Listen to every word, measure them for meaning and compare them to the speaker. What does he say to you beloved daughter?" She remembered the words, but somewhere had lost the sound of his voice, the infliction of his tone. "Leticia if you are to be successful you must be better than the men. Your work must be more challenged, more intense, or you will fail." A stream of light cast the dust particles into a narrow beam to stab a dark wood table with two chairs. Lettie crossed her arms in back of her. Tea at that table would be nice.

"Humans are meant for failure my husband without it, we cannot evolve," her mother's words in memory. Powerful words spoken with her mother's convictions, what color were her eyes?

"If I am meant to fail Mama, and yet I must be better than my brothers Papa, how can I win?" Lettie asked. A black bird landed on the sill outside the window of the room in David's house. Its black eyes searched. It hopped along and pecked at the grass.

"Winning is not the goal," her mother said.

"For this isn't a game?" Lettie asked.

"Success is what is at stake," her father said.

"But if I beat them, I will win," Lettie said.

"If you beat the men you will be alone," her mother said.

"And why is that?" her father asked.

"Because your most treasured students are a bunch of peacocks who will not tolerate a woman besting them," her mother said. A pain cruised through Lettie's leg.

"Not true a true man can tolerate competition," her father said.

"Not from his wife, take care my daughter that you not find your road to glory lonely. All things have a cost be certain you can pay it before you take the trip," her mother said.

"I like that one may I use it mi vida?" her father asked.

"Everything I have is yours amor," her mother said. A glint of light bounced into her vision and the world burst apart. Lettie struggled to stay conscious. She fought it and slid against the wall. A tiny thumping rippled into her thoughts. She heard the sound from patients when her mother let her hear through a stethoscope. She inhaled and another stronger, faster set of thumping echoed. Her vision cleared as her hand slid to her belly.

A gray uniformed arm reached for her. The man smiled, but in his green eyes there was intent. He touched her arm and pain ripped through her, someone else's pain. Lettie screamed. "Ma! Ma!" His uniform similar in color and design to Patricia's militia.

"Hold on Miss, I'm Joel Byars, I'm your guard, please don't scream. What in the name of all that is good in Heaven has happened to make you scream like that, please stop!" Joel Byars was a short man.

"Ma!" Lettie shot against the door. Elsa pointed two 9 mm's at the man.

"Hold on lady, I was just trying to help," Joel said. Elsa aimed at his head. A red head skidded around the corner and put her hands up. Lettie clutched Elsa's leg as the feelings generated from the man subsided. The woman smiled.

"Byars what did you do to make Miss de las Almas want to hold a gun on us?" she asked. Joel approached Lettie, and she screamed. Elsa took four quick steps toward him.

The woman snatched him back. "I'm Beatrice Stone I guess you don't remember me. Get the boss now!" Elsa stepped back and pulled Lettie up. Lettie leaned on her and cried. The tears soaked through her leader's thin shirt as Elsa patted her head and held her gun on Beatrice. The fast thumping jumped in intensity as Elsa held her. Lettie pressed her fingers to Elsa's belly. Lettie wanted to see inside of Elsa. An image appeared of a floating fetus. Lettie trembled as she transferred her hand to herself. A similar image appeared in her mind.

"Which boss?" Joel asked.

"The one you think can fix this idiot," Bea said.

"Which is?" Joel asked.

"Get David now!" Bea snapped. The red head smiled.

"Miss Marras, Leticia, Lettie remember me, Nellie." The blond didn't wait for an invitation. She moved to them and smiled. "You're so shaky how bouts a cup of tea. I've lemon, chamomile and peppermint."

"Those teas won't work to steady nerves…it's a placebo effect. A person thinks they work so they do," Lettie said.

"I love tea. I believe I would, even if I wasn't English. My Grams used other kinds of tea for medicine. I know a few," Nellie said. The woman's presence soothed her. Nellie was calm, but when Beatrice approached Lettie jumped back. Her nerves tingled and vibrated in a way that confused her. Nellie spread her hand down her back.

David ran up behind Bea with another man. Wayne Reilly's angry blue eyes reflected revenge. Elsa pulled her guns down. Beatrice's emotions pelted Lettie. Her hunger for the security man drown Leticia. Elsa pulled her into the room and sat her at a table. In the window the trees in the distance swayed, clouds boiled in the sky as a storm approached. Elsa smoothed her hair and the raging emotions shifted away and she was free once more, ordinary once more and she sighed.

Chapter 11 The price of love

Elsa strolled down the hall and came to a desk. A tall, muscular blond sat to the left. Melvin Hickory wrote upon a sheet and made her wait. He looked up with perfect teeth and a ready smile. Melvin looked like a starved rat, scrawny and diseased, but most people's insides weren't for show. On the outside, he was model perfect. "You must be the lovely Miss de las Almas," he said. He stood and held his hand out. She signed. "You must forgive me as I don't know that language yet although Miss Beatrice is trying to teach me a few words." She glanced beyond him to the door. "I'm sorry Miss, they're in a meeting. However, if David knew such a lovely lady waited for him, well I would certainly cancel the meeting."

Elsa turned as the other guard came up, Joel Byars stared into her eyes. His expression calm and sincere. "Miss de las Almas, I hope Miss Marras is better I apologize for earlier," Joel said.

"Well since my relief is here I would be honored to take you for a coffee or tea," Melvin said. Joel lifted the sheets from the clipboard and stacked them together.

"I'm ready for our meeting Miss de las Almas let me just drop these forms off with Wayne," Joel said.

"When did you ask her for this meeting Joel?" Melvin asked.

"Earlier," Joel replied.

"Before or after your mistake?"

"After," Joel said.

"And she agreed why would she?" Joel straightened not much taller than her.

"She's probably going to shoot me later," Joel said. Elsa glanced at the door. David wasn't in the room beyond only Samuel.

"How about dinner?" Melvin asked.

"Sorry Mel I asked first," Nellie said. She came up and engaged Elsa's arm. A strand of blond hair fell across Nellie's face. Elsa brushed it away, and Nellie turned her. Joel passed them as he hurried down the hall.

"Mel's a prick. I don't like him," Nellie said, "Well, here's your room. I'll bring your dinner around in a bit." Elsa located David and appeared in his bedroom. The old shack of his youth was in this place.

"All I'm saying is that we don't know her. What kind of woman has no past, she doesn't exist?" Beatrice said.

"Well it never stopped him from taking people in before now, Bea," Wayne said. Beatrice frowned.

"Just because you think she's beautiful is no reason to trust her. We don't know her," Beatrice said. David rubbed his neck.

"How bad could she be?" Wayne asked, "Not any worse than us?"

"I don't like something about her," Bea said.

"What you don't like is her, that's no reason not to shelter her."

"Your judgment is clouded," Bea said.

"It's the same argument I used before you were allowed to stay." Bea exhaled. David turned, and Elsa met his gaze.

"Grandfather, yes I know where my mother is, yes sir," Sam said. He stopped short when he saw her. "No sir, uh, no she wasn't."

"What wasn't I?" Elsa signed.

"Given a choice to come here," Sam said, "Yes you see I thought..." Elsa took his phone and broken it in half. She stomped the two halves into pieces. "Mother that was our leader he's going to be so pissed."

"You have bigger problems than him right now. Why didn't you listen to Lettie?" she signed. Sam looked to David.

"Now you need his help to handle this?" Her gaze went back to David. "No you thought he would handle it for you?" David's half smile emerged and disappeared. Maggots ate his flesh and then all that was red turned a milky white and still the bugs fed on him. Elsa stumbled back as she watched them swarm. The clip, clip of the bites resounded. He reached for her, and a bug fell. It squirmed and wiggled in a slimy mess as it ate her skin. She whipped her hand,

and it jumped back on him. She blinked, and a scaly hand gripped hers. The leathery skin moved, and she pressed her fingers to the edge. He jerked back as it pricked her skin.

"Elsa!" David said. A flash of lightning crossed the window and blasted the ground. She exhaled, and he was back to his street image. She ran fingers over his mouth and face. Blood smeared his cheek. Elsa ran from the room as the storm hammered the house.

A line of red cards merged in front of Elsa. The red and white squiggles blurred together. Lettie's emotions roiled inside her. The images from Bea's mind of her desires for the head of security burned her. She turned them and placed them at the back of her mind. Lettie's conscious eased. She laid another card on top of a line. "Never seen anyone play solitaire like that before. I'm not much for cards you got to play by yourself," Nellie said. A steamy cup of coffee sat to Elsa's left on a tray. She swallowed the need to shoot the entire cup. Nellie's gaze roamed the cards. She moved one from the farthest stack to one closer and another to its place. She moved two more. "The cards are marked I see the pattern, here." The cards were plain ordinary and, a brand-new pack.

"Let's see how you did?" Elsa flipped each stack, and all were in perfect order.

"See I got them all right," Nellie said. Elsa shuffled the cards.

"Is the coffee for me?"

"Oh yes, one cream, one sugar is that right?" Nellie asked.

"It is, how did you know I liked coffee?"

"It's a gift I can always tell the coffee drinkers from the tea drinkers. They've certain characteristics. Coffee people are more direct, and I find more emotionally balanced than tea drinkers," Nellie said. The blond laid out the four cards face down and started the game again. "I like playing like this, even though it's cheating." Elsa watched Nellie lay out the cards and one by one she made all the right choices.

She drained the cup, and Nellie reached over and filled it. The perfect brew poured out of the pot. Nellie's fingers moved faster as she laid cards down. Elsa reached for a card to misplace it on a stack, the Joker's spade on a two of hearts. Nellie smiled and retook the piece and placed it on the right one. Elsa put the Joker's spade on a five of diamonds.

"That's where it goes Miss Cameron."

"No it doesn't a Joker doesn't go on a five, nor a two. May I take the cards to study?" Nellie asked. Elsa stacked them together and passed them to her.

"Thanks for the coffee," Elsa signed.

"Miss Lettie didn't eat today…uh I'm not snitching on her, well, I guess I am. She doesn't sleep either. People need to sleep otherwise you go crazy," Nellie said.

"I'll speak to her." Nellie pocketed the cards and left the coffee. Not a gallon of coffee could keep the sleep at bay. Nothing stopped the nightmares from their victim. Elsa lowered her body to the floor and leaned against the wall.

A screech whipped into Anga's consciousness. The sound mellowed and became the hoot of an owl. The creature winked at her from the window. He waited for some prey. A scream pelted her with pain. The owl ruffled its wings, and its eyes went red. The smell of alcohol raced into her nose. The screams continued as she tried to turn. "Mother, easy you're safe, now." Raymond smiled but it never reached his eyes. She blinked as he pulled her from beneath the sofa.

The world shifted and she was blind, arms strapped in place. A dim light emerged beyond a white fabric. "Do you feel sleepy?" Anga exhaled and shook her head to clear the confusion. The screams came again and retreated. The man laughed and a feminine voice joined his. The female voice she knew. The sweet sound and gentle words of love could have been spoken from the mouth of an angel, if they hadn't been lies to gain freedom from her duty and put the suffering on her daughter. "She would be more cooperative if you spoke kind words to her dear, husband."

"Anga you're to fulfill your purpose in just a few minutes," her mother said. Anga struggled against the powerful hands that forced her onto the bed.

"No, not again…" Anga's heart raced as the danger crashed into her mind.

"Why am I here?" she screamed. Cold metal slid against her breast to her heart and moved up to her throat. Anga struggled against the restraints as the drum of her pulse pounded. The pain took hold and dragged her down.

"Raymond…help…" she muttered in her mind as the darkness freed her.

Anga jerked awake. Her eyes shifted in the dark. Her clothes soaked with sweat. Her heart raced. She climbed out of the window and circled around to a little garden. The stars winked in a clear morning sky. The grounds quiet and all seemed right in the world, but she knew better. Her soul froze as the memories of her dream replayed.

Elsa moved passed the prickly brush. She dunked under a low branch in the path. "You can't escape them." She caught the image out of the corner of her eye. The masked man returned.

"Who can't I escape?"

"The Hunters, your hunters they will always find you, one way or another," he said. He decided to speak to her, he was powerful enough to prevent her from finding out anything about him. Elsa released a branch, and he burned it.

"What do you want?"

"Listen you need to do something with little miss boring, she's tracking you, and she's not bad. That will serve you well in the future," he said. Elsa glanced back and continued. "You don't want one of your hunters falling over a cliff do you? What she knows Nellie is a hunter. Want to know who I'm talking to?"

"No, leave," Elsa signed.

"You could crack my head like an egg and dig my brains out and find out?" he said. She frowned.

"Find something to do boy and stop bothering me."

"I'm tired of chasing ghost's master. Let me tell her, she'll love it. I know she doesn't have a sense of humor. I gave you that information, yes, no, yes, no! I'm telling!" he shouted. He disappeared, and Elsa shook her head. She jumped down again and came upon a road. Nellie came out a few feet away.

"Hello," Nellie called. Elsa joined her on the dirt road.

"Are you a stalker?"

"Oh, my no, a stalker is a big burly someone, man with an eye patch and a limp. He's quite the beast he is," Nellie said.

"Where are you going Nellette Cameron?"

"I asked myself that question just this morning? So you know what I did?" Nellie asked. Elsa tilted her head. "I made a left in the

214

hall and saw you cross the yard." The worn dirt path flowed away from them.

"Why are you here Nellie?"

"I asked myself that question too, and then I followed you, but you looked back and you had this look like you wished to be left alone," Nellie said. Elsa clasped her hands. "But Susa said I could do what I wanted."

"And what do you want to do?" Nellie stopped.

"My word I'm a stalker, but then who is the chap with the limp and the eye patch?"

"An old friend."

"You know someone like this? Is he the mean sort?" Nellie asked. Elsa shrugged and continued along the road. A few feet ahead they rounded a corner. A big black car stood in wait with the hood peeled up. Nellie glanced at her.

"No one ever comes down this road. Do you think they could use some help? They've got to be lost," Nellie said. She ran up to look under the hood.

"Who are you?" a male voice asked.

"That was just the question I asked myself yesterday," Nellie said. Elsa stayed back.

"That wasn't a rhetorical question linda quera."

"No my name is Nellie not Linda are you a Mexican? You don't look like a Mexican," Nellie asked, "But you have an accent."

"Who are you woman?" Pepe, the red wolf asked. Elsa waited.

"I'm a stalker," Nellie said.

"For the love of all that is wicked I get stick on the road with a crazed stalker."

"Not crazed, am I crazed Elsa?" Nellie asked. Pepe came around the car.

"Rogelio who are you speaking to?" Maria shouted, "It's hotter than the lowest level of Hell. Why haven't you fixed the damned car yet?" Pepe exhaled.

"I'm trying Mama!" Pepe called.

"No you're not! You can't talk and wipe your ass at the same time are you drunk?" Maria shouted. Pepe rubbed his forehead.

"No, but I swear I would give my first born to anyone who gave me a shot right now, a shot to the eye, to the heart any place that would make me dead," Pepe said. Nellie fished in her pack and withdrew a silver flask and passed it to him.

"Here you go, poor dear. You've a tough Mama, huh. My Grams could peel paint with her shrieking," Nellie said. Pepe opened the container and took a swig. He blinked.

"Whiskey, you drink woman?" Pepe asked.

"My name is Nellie and…" she said.

"Yes, yes, whatever your name is thanks for the shot. I got to fix the car, or I'm going down," Pepe said. Elsa leaned over the engine.

"To Hell you mean?" Nellie asked, "Have another hit." Pepe drank another shot. Elsa tapped the engine, and it started. Pepe ran around.

"You did it!" Pepe said.

"You smell like a cantina boy," Maria said. Elsa stepped back. "Elsa dear what have we here?" Maria approached Nellie.

"Mama don't do it," Pepe said. Pepe drank another shot.

"Why didn't you tell me we were going to break down and be rescued by my Elsa and who are you sweet girl?" Maria asked.

"Nellette Cameron, ma'am, it's nice to meet you." They shook hands, and Pepe's eyes squeezed closed as he ran his hands through shiny copper hair pulled into a ponytail. His gray gaze shifted to his mother, and he held his breath.

"What a polite and lovely girl, who are you?" Maria asked.

"I'm a stalker," Nellie said. Maria smiled.

"Excellent we don't have a stalker what kind of prey?" Nellie considered.

"Well, rabbits, deer and humans," Nellie said.

"And what do you do with them when you catch them?" Maria asked.

"Mother stop, we're not this desperate!" Pepe said.

"Hush, go on dear." Pepe frowned at Elsa.

"Well I kill them and then I cook them in a stew or make sausage out of them. Deer make great sausage," Nellie said.

"What about the humans dear?" Maria asked.

"Oh, well, the humans I just started doing that. I always say one can't go against one's nature, so I suppose I would just keep them." Maria yanked Pepe in front of her.

"What would you do with him?" Maria asked. Pepe passed the flask back to Nellie, and she refused it.

"A stalker great, she drinks now if only she played cards, she'd be the perfect wife for me," Pepe said.

"I love cards what kinds?" Nellie asked.

"What is strip the cards mean?" Maria asked. Elsa took Nellie's arm. The older woman shook Pepe.

"I don't know?" Pepe said.

"Think boy what kind of card game is that?" Maria asked.

"Do you mean strip poker mother?" Pepe asked.

"You play cards naked?" Maria asked.

"No you play cards and whoever wins the hand takes off a piece of clothing until someone is naked. I love that game," Nellie said.

"He's very good at cards girl," Maria said.

"So am I. When will you deliver the baby to me?" Nellie asked. Elsa turned to her.

218

"What baby?" Maria asked.

"Rogelio said he would give his first born to the person that gave him a shot. It was me. When do I get the baby?" Nellie asked. Pablo came around the car.

"I'm dying in the heat, and you're meeting a beautiful woman?" Pablo asked. He had a gas can.

"Not just any woman that's his woman of Elsa's clan," Maria said. Pepe frowned as he handed the flask to Nellie.

"No I want the baby. You better not be lying. I know people red headed man. You have my baby!" Nellie said. She stomped away.

"Mama when will I meet my girl?" Pablo asked.

"I don't know mijo. I hope soon, but I fear it will be a little while," Maria said.

"Why am I always the last one?" Pablo asked. Pablo frowned.

"There are others still waiting my pet. She said she knows people what kind of people, bad people?" Maria asked.

"Maybe, we know the same people. How am I going to give her a baby?" Pepe asked. Maria shook her head as she entered the vehicle.

Elsa glanced at Nellie. "I've not a clue what made me say that to the ginger," Nellie said, "Do you know what that…ginger means?"

"It is a slang term for a red head, not always meant as a nice term." Nellie exhaled.

"My Grams was a ginger, and I adored her. Gingers are wild and…strong and…passionate…who are you?" Nellie's gun aimed behind her. Mano stood with his brothers. His handsome face creased into a frown.

"You would shame me woman in front of my leader?" Pepe asked. Nellie stepped in front of Elsa.

"Do not think because you're a handsome, wild ginger that I will be so foolish as to kiss your ass, well, I might do that, however, what I won't tolerate is nastiness, ah crap that's all you know." Elsa turned Nellie and Mano appeared in front of them. His black eyes slid across her face. Pepe pulled at Nellie, and she put the gun at his heart.

"Kill me pretty one for I fear that would be an easier sentence than I will face this evening alone without you," Pepe said. Nellie dropped her arm.

"Your sticky words do not affect me," Nellie said.

"Your blue eyes quiver as does my heart," Pepe said.

"I think you've been around Alfonso too long," Pablo said.

"Hush she likes him," Maria said.

"Come Pepe, we've more important things to do than stand in the heat wasting time," Mano said. Pepe kissed Nellie's hand. Elsa took Nellie's arm, and they started away.

"Speak to her you stupid fool Manuel," Maria said. Elsa turned back, and all that remained was a tornado of dust.

Chapter 12 Madness comes to call

Elsa didn't check in with Abrim. She had broken the routine when he refused to listen, when he broke his promise to always have time for her. He grew tired of the arrangement. She searched the world for her old friend and found him in a village not far from his home. Time and space shifted, and she stood a short distance from him at the top of a hill. He sawed a log. His powerful arms labored to make a workable piece. Even for a man of sixty-two he was powerful and strong. The sweat rushed over his belly and soaked his pants.

A team of men built a house. In the distance, a burned shell lay as a reminder of Patricia's militia. Sweat dripped off of his ponytail as he pushed the limits of his strength. He did his best to work himself into exhaustion.

In an instant, she was next to him. He spun and found; he was alone. He chucked the board away and then moved to a bucket of water. He dipped his hands into the coolness. As he pulled his hands back she arranged for him to see a pair of sad, dark eyes, in a familiar face. He looked away and when he looked again all, he saw was the bottom of the bucket. "Take a break all of you!" he shouted.

He stomped into the nearby woods and the screech of a tree being rendered from the ground drifted to her. He yanked them from the earth with his angry mind. His workers ignored the sound never would it occur to them to disobey their beloved leader. He chose them with intent and knew them to the core. She appeared in the forest where he ripped the branches off and cast them in a pile. He hadn't chosen her. He would never have chosen her. She didn't obey him.

On the next tree she placed a table with water and food so that he could refresh himself. He circled passed it and went on to tear other trees down. She went back to where she didn't belong and waited for the next disaster.

The day passed away, and night came. Elsa remained isolated. She paced in the darkness. She needed to go home, but she was no longer alone. Life was different. A knock sounded, and Elsa turned.

"Miss, a letter came for you," Joel said. He passed the yellow envelope to her and closed the door. There was an address from Mexico. She extracted a black envelope, and her heart dropped to her stomach. She sat at the table and opened it. The sender missed no points. The document was perfect and executed in the exact manner as was the tradition with the exception of the sponsor. Elsa wanted to vomit. Lettie stood outside her door and paced. Elsa yanked the door opened.

"You want to see me?" she signed. Leticia's eyes shifted to the ground, and she chewed her lower lip.

"Uh, no…you're busy. I don't want to disturb you with…" Lettie whispered. Elsa searched for an answer in the young woman's face. Lettie squeezed the fabric of her shirt in clenched, white knuckles. "It's just that…well, you're the One and…" Elsa stepped back. She closed the door and moved to the couch.

"I won't take much of your time. I know you have more important tasks than listen to my problems…I don't mean any disrespect…" Lettie took a deep breath.

"Take your time," she signed.

"You're pregnant," Lettie whispered in Elsa's mind. Elsa bit her lip and the taste of blood flowed. She swallowed.

"So are you," Elsa replied in like. Lettie stood straight. "I've searched my whole life for some part of the past, some part of my family and now…a part of my family grows inside of me."

"I have lost all that was my past, even my memories are fading, but Leader…" Lettie said as they communicated this secret. Elsa had lost her place with the girl and now was regulated to the leader.

"No matter who the father of my child…" Elsa replied.

"Leader you carry the heir of the Black Wolf, even if he were an ordinary man which he isn't, we have a problem, and I have his brother's child in me. What do you think will happen when they find out?"

"We have many problems have you considered what the Fighters will think of this treason?" Elsa said to her in their thoughts. Lettie frowned.

"No all I thought was of Chino and how proud he is and oh, no!"

"No one will take my child from me unless I am dead which I am going to try to prevent. I will not blame you if you choose to go some place else."

"I want to stay with you, and I hoped you would feel the same," Lettie said. She relaxed. "Isabella is she with child?"

"No, she isn't pregnant, neither is Susa. They resisted the charms of the Clan. You may change your mind when I tell you of my next dilemma." She dropped the page on the desk.

"As long as we're together I can face it," Lettie said.

"Samuel has petitioned for a bond of marriage," Elsa signed. Lettie's expression collapsed, but she held the tears in check.

"I am certain that his bride will be very happy. She is a lucky woman to have such a handsome, generous, brilliant man for a husband."

"I'm glad to hear you feel that way," Samuel said. Lettie jumped. David appeared with him and stood at the back of the room.

"I wish you much happiness and success in your new life, Fighter Samuel," Lettie said. Sam smiled. Elsa took Lettie's face.

"Oh I plan to," Sam said. He was so much like Juan today.

"Sam has chosen you, sweetheart," Elsa signed.

"Me why?" Lettie asked, "He thinks of me as no more than a manly woman that...a marriage of convenience."

"Well I prefer of honor," Sam said.

"Send me away, Ma. I can't do this," Lettie whispered. Elsa steadied her.

"If your wish is to shame me, impossible I have taken every precaution, there is no choice, Fighter Marras you're mine," Sam said.

"Why don't I have a choice?" Lettie asked.

"You do," Elsa signed.

"Sure she does, unless she wants to dismiss her father's last words to me," Sam said. Lettie turned as Sam held up a medal. "He gave me this and do you know what he said, sure you do." Lettie raced passed him as he held the medal out of her reach.

Lettie's memories echoed in Elsa's mind. "I will give this to the man who will have my blessing to marry my beloved daughter. I will know the right one Leticia," Jose said.

"You are a self-centered man whose desire to suffer is great." Sam tensed.

"I am honor bond to my teacher to do what is right for his daughter. I will be a good husband," Sam said.

"You are a foolish boy, and you break my heart. I will not be a part of this."

"I didn't expect you to understand mother," Sam said.

"What you expected was a fight, and you will get it. Even with the devil at your side you won't win," Elsa signed.

"Why can't you be on my side?" Sam asked.

"I am on your side."

"She will come to understand why I have done this," Sam said.

"When you force a woman to your side, she is a prisoner always looking for an escape," Elsa signed.

"I have a lot to offer," Sam said.

"She doesn't want to hear your side Sam save it for someone who cares about you, her son instead of a stranger," David said. Samuel walked away. She took a ragged breath and turned to the window. David's hands slid over her shoulders. She faced him. He needed a fix, and she reached up. He stepped back.

"Your poison is so sweet, but I've lived without you, and I will again. You've never lived without your son. How will you manage?" He blinked away.

Morning brought no solution as Lettie sat by the window. "This way sir," Joel called. The door opened, and Juan entered with Sam and David. Lettie leapt to attention.

"Fighter Marras it is an honor to see you so well," Juan said.

"Leader Stein," Lettie said. He walked passed to the window and glanced across. Lettie's gaze followed his to another window, to Elsa's room. Nellie pushed a silver cart into the room and stopped by her.

"Lettie I was asked to bring you tea," Nellie said.

"Who asked you?" Lettie asked. Nellie sat out the shiny white cup and saucer. Another plate sat to the left.

"Elsa," Nellie said.

"How is she?"

"Better now, she's eaten a bit," Nellie said.

"You've gotten her to eat?" Juan asked.

"You'd be surprised what a lady will do if asked the right way, yes, she ate for me."

"Like what?" Sam asked.

"Oh, well four slices of toast, an egg, some oats, a few things," Nellie said. A luscious muffin with giant blueberries sat upon Lettie's plate as Nellie poured out tea.

"That's a lot," Lettie said.

"Oh, no she was still hungry," Nellie said.

"How did you know that?" Sam asked.

"Oh, I know hungry like you know beautiful women that never say no to you."

"My mother is beautiful and she never says yes to me," Sam said.

"Aw well one's mum that's different," Nellie said. A thick fabric napkin went next to the plate.

"And I seem to be hearing no from Fighter Marras," Sam said.

"Beautiful, yes Leticia is that, but she's different," Nellie said. The petite blond stepped back.

"She's a soldier," Sam said. Juan's gaze remained fixed upon the distance window.

"Does she sleep Miss Cameron, right now is she asleep?" Juan asked. Nellie shifted.

"No," Nellie said.

"We must pace ourselves to gain endurance so that we can finish the race. Nothing ever done in a hurry is ever mastered," Lettie said. Juan turned a smile to her.

"Your mother's practical advice and your father's strength that is why you will suit my purpose well Fighter Marras," Juan said.

"Leader?" Lettie asked.

"With power comes privilege and I am your leader and as leader, I am honored to assign your position in the Fighter's group," Juan said.

"My job, leader," Lettie asked. Her gaze traveled to Sam. He was unhappy, but he would hold his tongue.

"Yes your assignment is to protect the one thing that is most important to me, more important than my life, my reason for existence." Lettie's gaze fell on the older man.

"I am to be the guardian of the Crown Prince?" Lettie asked.

"The Crown Prince, oh, Samuel, no. Your job is to protect my One, to keep her safe and well," Juan said.

"I am to be paid to protect Ma? I would do that for free."

"Never do anything for free it cheapens you. A woman with your skills should be paid, and I will pay you to do what you want. Now first thing you are to remain in Texas," Juan said.

"With Samuel?" Lettie asked.

"With my One, this is her home, where she is safe from…enemies. She likes you and some of the others I approve. Samuel you will remain to be the guardian to Fighter Marras," Juan said.

"Leticia and I are to be…" Sam said.

"Equals, Crown Prince, yes I see your father's humor. He wasn't funny don't piss me off Fighter Marras," Juan said. He stepped to the door.

"Leader Stein are you ordering ma to stay in Texas?" Lettie asked. Juan turned a serious handsome face to her. Sam looked much like his uncle save for the blue eyes. Juan's were ebony.

"How do you order a wild bird not to fly?" Juan asked.

"You put it in a cage," David said.

"Where surely you will watch it die," Lettie said. Sam frowned.

"You feed it and care for it, and soon it will adapt to a new life," David said. Lettie clasped her wrists.

"To live as a prisoner or die what an easy choice," Lettie said. Nellie left as did Juan.

"I'll be right out David," Sam said. Lettie went to the window and stared across the expanse to Elsa's room.

"You will take the position?" Sam asked.

"Do I have a choice?" Lettie asked.

"Only if you wish to be free," Sam said.

"Free from what?" Lettie asked.

"The Leader will not accept no," Sam said. Lettie turned to the handsome man, and the thought came to her.

"You will be made a Commander before this night is through, what an honor and all it will cost is your soul," Lettie said. Sam's eyebrow raised, and he smiled.

"Not my soul my knowledge, my loyalty," he said. Her eyes drifted to the outside.

"You will gain nothing, but pain. Listen to what your mother says and you might be spared," Lettie said.

"All lives have pain Fighter Marras."

"Your mother just can't be right can she?" Lettie asked.

"When has she ever been wrong?"

"So why not listen to her?" Lettie gripped her shirt.

"Some pain must be experienced for the good of the community if we care only for ourselves, then all will suffer," Sam said. He used her father's words against her.

"The order of things cannot be confused. First must come self, then family, then community for without self, there is no physical form to grow society," Lettie said. His blue eyes narrowed.

"I don't recall your father ever saying that?" She strolled to the table.

"Did you ever meet my mother?" Lettie asked.

"I did and was honored by her quiet nature," Sam said.

"What was my mother to my father Crown Prince?" Lettie asked. Samuel walked to the door. "You don't know?" He turned back and glanced at the table where Nellie's gifts remained untouched.

"You haven't eaten since you arrived," he said.

"What was Ana Marras to Jose Marras, Fighter?"

"She was what I hope you will be to me," Sam said.

"Which is what?" Lettie asked.

"A stone in my shoe on the million mile walk to my fortune," Sam snapped. Lettie turned from the table and went into the bathroom.

Lettie lay upon the tile floor and counted to a thousand. The tenth time would be her last. "One thousand and I hate that Crown Prince."

She rolled up and went to the room. She glanced through the window and across the way. Elsa rested as best as they could rest which wasn't rest at all. Lettie exhaled, but her anger stirred in her gut.

On the table was a pretty box with a huge ribbon of blue, her favorite color she approached and the card said from Sam. She circled away and came back. The tea was cold. She wrapped her fingers around it, and the tan liquid bubbled up, too hot. She sat it aside. She took the box and opened it. A giant cookie sat among the papers. It was crowned with chocolates and pecans. A cookie such as this would be wonderful, warm and gooey. Tiny threads of steam came up with the sweet aroma. She took the treasure from its nest and bit it. The soft chocolate swirled as she bit another chunk. The crunchy pecans burst their flavor to mix with the chocolate. "I was asked to check on you."

Lettie glanced up at Samuel. "I'm fine," Lettie said. She swallowed the cookie. Samuel frowned. "Sorry that was ugly talking with my mouth full. Who asked you to check on me?"

"The leader," Sam said. He came across the room, and she stood. She replaced the treat in the box.

"You spoke with your Ma? I'm so glad…"

"My mother isn't speaking to me," Sam said. His distress jerked at her stomach.

"She's just a bit tired and…" Lettie said.

"You think you know my mother better than I. You just met her five minutes ago!"

"No, it's just that I thought…"

"Leave the thinking to people that have the skills!" Sam snapped.

"My apologizes Fighter Stein it's just that I was trying to help." He turned on her.

"You believe you can help me with my mother?" His clenched fists flexed.

"I might be able to relate some feelings she's having…"

"You dare to compare yourself to our One?" Sam asked. Lettie moved to him and looked into his eyes.

"Yes, she is our great leader, but she is a woman first, Sam. She's worried for you can you not understand?" Lettie asked. Her fingers danced across his face. His expression softened.

"What would you know of being a woman?" he asked. His arms spilled around her back. It was a question, not an insult.

"I know being a soldier is easier than a being woman and Ma is both. We are women, whether we look the part or not," she said.

234

"So tell me woman something about you?" he asked.

"That cookie was beautiful and the only thing that would make it better was to share it," she said.

"You liked my gift?" he asked. He was neither confident nor sure of himself as he proposed the question.

"Yes it was the best cookie ever," she said. He captured her mouth in a hungry kiss, and she cleared the floor as he pulled her closer. She pulled back and pecked his cheek. "Thanks Sam." He put her back, and she stepped to him.

"Commander Stein do you have time to speak with me," Juan said. The handsome leader's gaze shifted to his Uncle.

"Yes, sir at your convenience, my leader," Sam said.

"It can wait," Juan said.

"No, I was just speaking to Fighter Angel, uh, Lettie, Leticia," Sam said. Juan glanced at them.

"I think it's called kissing Commander," Juan said. Sam straightened, and Lettie saw the shift in his face.

"If you will forgive me Leader, I was just thanking the Commander for the lovely gift he sent me. I will beg your forgiveness commander for any embarrassment I have caused." Sam's head snapped in her direction. Pride spread through him. He was proud of her. Samuel, the Crown Prince smiled.

"I am pleased with your response," Sam said. He was sincere and Lettie frowned. She had to find a way to quiet the telepathic signals.

"I will see you then Commander?" Juan asked.

"Yes my leader," Sam said. Lettie ran after him and clasped Sam's face, she rubbed the chocolate away and licked her fingertip. Sam leaned closer. "That was hot my Angel. You were right about my promotion I'll show my appreciation later."

"Does that work with your little trail rats because I'm not impressed. Be yourself commander and save us both some time," Lettie snapped. He leaned in and kissed her cheek. He limped away.

"What's wrong boy. Why are you limping?" Juan asked.

"I've got a rock in my shoe Leader," Sam said. He glanced at her.

"Well get rid of it," Juan said.

"Never my Leader, it is a sacred rock it brings me luck," Sam said. Juan's gaze left them and traveled across the hall. Elsa stopped outside her door. Her long dark hair fell about her face.

"Elsa have you forgotten all sense of tradition when you come into this place without values?" Juan shouted. Elsa glanced down.

"Do not shout at her Stein," David said. Elsa looked upon the ugly giant, and he crossed to her. Juan got there first and Lettie second. Juan extended his hands, and Lettie stepped between them.

"Do not forget your place Fighter Marras," Juan said.

"My place as was assigned by you was to protect our One, and I have accepted that honor, even if it means I fight you Leader," Lettie said. Juan grimaced.

"You would fight me?" Juan asked.

"I would fight anyone and you," Lettie said. Juan charged, and Elsa pushed her aside and the Fighter's young leader stopped as she greeted him in their tradition. She pressed a kiss to either side of his face and bowed. Juan lifted her, and they entered her room. David stomped away as Lettie went to the door. Sam yanked her back. "What do you want Commander?"

"You, but I will settle for some time to deal with my Uncle, return to your room."

"No," she said. He pulled at her hand.

"In case you missed it that was an order, Fighter Marras," Sam snapped. Lettie gripped his hand as he spun her toward her room. She glanced back and rushed him. He caught her.

"Promise you'll let me help her?" His expression was serious. "Please Sam!"

"Yes, now go before you're reassigned," Sam said. She kissed his cheek and ran into her room. She glanced back, and Joel Byars eyed her. She closed the door and turned off all the lights to wait.

Late the next afternoon Lettie and Elsa found Sam in David's office. "I've made my decision, Samuel. You don't have my permission to marry Leticia." Sam stood.

"You're not giving me your blessing?" Sam asked.

"Elsa don't use your anger with me to punish Sam," David said.

"This has nothing to do with him. My bond supersedes yours," Elsa signed. The Crown Prince was angry.

"Mother made a bond with you Leticia?" Sam asked.

"Yes, the Fighter's bond of Kinship," Lettie whispered. Sam's eyes widened.

"And you agreed?" Sam asked.

"Yes," Lettie whispered. She didn't even know the bond existed until Elsa brought it to her attention.

"What is a kinship bond?" David asked.

"A Fighter's bond of Kinship is made between two fighters. It's not done often and has to do with rank and protection. I can only think of one other instance where it has been applied," Sam said.

"I still don't know what it is," David said.

"It's a very serious bond of commitment to protect and care and love the other Fighter and for my Ma to make it mean she's serious," Sam said. David shook his head.

"So she's going to be her mother? She protected the girl the other day so what's the big deal?" David asked. Elsa glanced at Sam.

"In our world it's a giant deal to have a Fighter's bond of Kinship with the One. Elsa is a Fighter, a female fighter, one of only two. Lettie is the second. Elsa's rank in our world is third, some say second to the highest, so Elsa has the power to press her will on just about anyone for Leticia's sake," Juan said.

"So Leticia gotten in with the big dog, so to speak, so who are the other two fighters with this bond?" David asked.

"My Grandfather took this bond with Ma," Sam said.

"Why?" David asked.

"To protect her from the other Fighters, it was my mother's idea." Elsa eyed David.

"Yeah I can see Elsa wanted this," David said.

"No, my mother Alicia wished to protect ma from all the others that wanted to kiss and touch her," Sam said.

"That was Alicia and she was right. She was always right," Juan said. Elsa clasped hands with Lettie.

"Yeah and I can see old man wrinkles not wanting anyone else to touch Elsa, so of course he agreed," David said.

"He's not old," Elsa signed. Juan eyed Elsa.

"Grandfather didn't want to do it," Sam said.

"O.k. I'm game. Why didn't he want to be hooked up with a beautiful, hot, young woman?" David asked.

"The way I understand it, Ma didn't want him for a teacher or anything else and since she didn't fear him, well, that, and she hit him in public," Sam said. Lettie bit her lip.

"Our leader is a prideful man," Juan said.

"What changed his mind?" David asked.

"When all his best fighters were laid up including Juan from trying to deal with her, he decided in order to preserve their way of life she had to be his...challenge," Sam said.

"I was pretending so the others wouldn't be so mad at her, not that she cared what they thought," Juan said.

"They should have kept their hands to themselves. I didn't need them to show me whatever it was they were trying to show me, like I'm dumb. Your Grandfather is a gentleman which can't be said for all fighters, but then I do bring out the worst in people, don't I Lettie?" Lettie nodded.

"So the only recourse left to Sam if he chooses to take Leticia for a wife is the final count," Juan said.

"What is that Samuel?" Lettie whispered.

"Ma will fight my sponsor, and if she wins you are free, but if he wins you're mine," Sam said. Elsa went to the door, and her gaze went to Lettie.

"What do you mean fight?" David asked.

"A fight to the death," Sam said.

"A physical fight, no!" Lettie said, "She can't fight Juan."

"I'm not Samuel's sponsor," Juan said.

"You have to be," Lettie said.

"David will fight Elsa not me," Juan said.

"No, he will have to fight me because it is my job to protect her," Lettie said. Juan went to the window.

"This time the fight is hers not yours," Juan said.

"They deserve to have better than they do in Mexico. They've lost their families they should have peace and quiet. They can have that here with me, Elsa," David said. When Elsa's pregnancy became known she'd be in greater danger than she was now and Sam too was being sought for a role he didn't want. They would be hunted. David quested for evil soon evil would quest for him. David cupped Ma's face. "I can help you sleep stay with me tonight."

"No," Elsa signed. She walked out of his office.

"Why is our union worth all this?" Lettie asked.

"Why can't you accept my help?" Sam asked. Lettie slapped him.

"You're a self-centered boy, and you break my heart." He clasped her to him.

"Breaking your heart would be a feat since it's locked away in the dark and no one can find it," Sam said. Lettie pushed him off. "Do you hate me girl?"

"No, Crown Prince it is not you that I hate someone else has that honor," Lettie said. She left to find some peace.

The wind shot Elsa's hair up as she floated passed the windows. In the distance, the chimes rang out to equal one. The dark forest beckoned her to enter. Window six ended at the corner. "Samuel I will not fight your mother!" She shimmered through the thin cracked window of the past which in the present was a three-foot brick wall.

"You can't beat her in any fight, and I will lose my chance, don't you see?" Sam said. Juan lingered by the opposite window.

"What?" David asked.

"Elsa has made a move that neither of you have the sac to go through with and by that she will win Leticia's freedom," Juan said.

"She could never be sure I wouldn't do anything to win," David said. The shadows wrapped tight around Elsa as she waited.

"It was a calculated risk," Juan said, "Baby is good."

"That is wrong leader, she is your…" Sam snapped. Juan turned on the younger man a clear glass with golden liquid at the bottom.

"My equal, no you're wrong she's better than me at everything, including impressing father. Do you know what it's like to love and hate someone so much you would cut your own heart out?" Juan asked. Elsa emerged from the shadows.

"Hell doesn't even cover it." Juan raised his glass and shot the liquor. Elsa grabbed him by the neck. Sam swept her out of his leader's reach, even as Juan stood still and allowed her touch.

"Mother you can't," Sam said. Juan released her.

"Samuel stand down!" Juan shouted. Elsa's fingers whipped to Juan's mouth. She closed her eyes. He removed her hand. "You should be sleeping Dear…" His ebony eyes crashed into hers. His thumb caressed the back of her hand.

"You came to see me?" David asked. Juan smacked his lips.

"She looked for me right, Elsa?" Juan said.

"Yes." Juan blinked.

"Why what do you want?" Juan asked. He went back to the window his back to her. Elsa turned to Sam.

"Your leader will choose the weapon I am to use in battle those are the rules," Sam said. Juan came back.

243

"I am Second and so the choice lands on my father," Juan said.

"You are the leader present so it is your choice, and I choose the day of the battle which will be today," Elsa signed. Juan's jaw jumped.

"The long sword is your weapon fighter de las Almas," Juan snapped.

"Leader, no she's never used the long sword, not even in practice. You know she can't do this!" Sam said.

"So then you win by default. I approve of your choice as does Leticia's father, and if you cared, I have these," Juan said. He held up a stack of letters. He pushed them to Elsa, and she refused them.

"Tell Senor Gracia, I will battle him with the long sword at two this afternoon."

"You haven't slept and you can't beat me at this and Juan knows it. Let me help you, Elsa," David said. She went to the door and he countered her. "I can help you without being contaminated." Elsa looked away. "You know what I mean." Juan laughed.

"You're smooth ugly man," Juan said.

"He's not ugly," Elsa signed.

"The rest of the world thinks he is, don't know what you see when you look at him," Juan said. Elsa forced her eyes to him, and the maggots came to life. She swallowed as he touched her face. A maggot crawled onto her cheek and traveled to her ear. She looked

244

deeper, and the red light winked and the maggots disappeared. She exhaled as the giant bug evaporated. The edge of the red light pulsed, and the color seeped out to white as her power entered him. She pulled free before he engaged full strength. His street countenance was back as she walked passed him into the hall and out the window.

Elsa blinked, and rough hands snaked over her body. Her hands were bound, and her head was covered by a cloth. She exhaled as her clothes ripped away. "You animal, you can never do anything right can you?" A fire penetrated Elsa's mind as she was assaulted, she screamed as the shame cut into her. She jerked, and the rejection ripped into her mind. She would end this torture. She stood a giant man stared at her, his eyes lit from within. "What's wrong," he asked, "Elsa, I'm getting Sam?"

"Who's Sam?" Elsa signed.

"Samuel get in here now!" he shouted. Elsa backed up, but he held her. A tall handsome man ran from the room, and she pushed away from them. She jumped to the window and reared back she would be free.

"Leticia, mother no!" a male shouted. She hammered the glass, and the window rushed her face as she fell into space. A second later the earth crashed to her. She jerked to stop and landed softly in the wet grass. Sunlight blasted her eyes, and a man's scream ripped into her.

She slipped her hand in her pocket and found a card.

Juan's scream vibrated through Lettie as she rushed into the room. Samuel gripped her. "Ma just jumped out the window." Lettie jerked to the broken glass and ran. Sam jerked her back.

"She's not dead!" Lettie shouted. David was gone, and she jerked out of Samuel's grip. She jumped the steps down two at a time until she reached the front door. It blasted open as she reached the bottom. David entered with Elsa. Lettie went after him. "Let her go!" Elsa jumped from his arms and ran. Lettie caught her as Susa and Nellie came running up the hall. Each took hold of her, as she convulsed.

"Elsa!" Juan shouted. Elsa ripped free and leapt through the air. Juan caught her and shook as he held her. The women approached. "Back up that's an order!" Her leader's arms were around Juan's neck.

"I need an explanation!" Lettie turned to the voice. Abrim Stein stood in the foyer with them. Lettie's gaze came back to Elsa. Her powerful leader clung to Juan.

"She's fine father," Juan said.

"Now you want to lie to me?" Abrim asked. The elder leader reached the couple. He went to take Elsa from Juan, and she shook her head and forced her face into his shoulder. Juan blinked and then lifted Elsa into his embrace. As her hand came free blood dripped on a playing card, an ace of spades. Lettie raced to her and Elsa shrunk away.

"She's frail Fighter Marras. I will call you soon," Juan said. Abrim yanked Elsa free, and the woman's scream pelted Lettie.

"Let her go let her go!" Lettie shouted. Sam had her as the other two women raced to Elsa's side. The screams drowned out every sound, but the rapid wild thumping. Lettie jerked free and ran to the window, but Samuel caught her and held her.

"It's all right honey, stay still bebe. Ma needs you," Sam shouted. He heard his mother's screams? The silence bonged into her mind as she whipped around. Juan had Elsa again, but Abrim stood his ground. He was ready to fight to the death if necessary. Lettie stumbled to Elsa, and the woman grasped her. They limped away, and Lettie looked back. "She jumped out the second-story grandfather."

"What I'm going to see her!"

"She doesn't want our help father. She's never needed any of us," Juan said. Abrim slapped Juan. Elsa broke free and jumped between father and son. "No get back if you get hurt, I'm going to…"

"Die," Elsa signed. Juan stomped away, and Elsa collapsed. David lifted her, and Lettie ran after them

Raymond stared at the back of the house up to the broken window and then at the ground.

Elsa leapt out of the window filled with pain and confusion. Mother's demons merged in Elsa's mind, and Elsa didn't deal well without sleep. He stepped back to see his work. He was pushed to arrive in time to prevent her death. Mother had sent him to the rescue again. All he had time to do was prevent the crash. "Joel, get in here!" Melvin called. Raymond turned to the man, one day soon he would end the life of the rat man, one day very soon.

Elsa lay among the pillows on the grand bed. "She needs to go home, Lettie," Nellie said. She turned to the blond.

"I don't know where home is for her," Lettie said.

"Don't you?" Nellie asked. The woman fluffed the pillows and drew the blanket closer to Elsa.

"She has a house in Texas at least that is what is rumored and even Leader Juan says it," Lettie said.

"That is a place where she has slept, home is a different place for her," Nellie said. Susa entered.

"How you know?" Susa asked. Nellie's hand rushed through her blond hair.

"I just do and I think I can get there," Nellie said.

"So we go," Susa said.

"Nellie you're needed in the kitchen," Beatrice said. Lettie glanced at the red head as

Nellie went to the door. "You need to remember who saved you from the streets Nellie it wasn't that woman."

"I know where I came from and being here hasn't changed that Beatrice I am still what I was," Nellie said.

"I'm just being your friend. David wouldn't like you're going against him and you don't know him like I do," Beatrice said.

"Is that a threat Ms. Stone?" Elsa signed. Lettie blinked as Beatrice backed up and turned to the bed.

"No, all I'm saying is Nellie is wanted in the kitchen," Beatrice said.

"Oh my," Nellie said. Elsa slipped onto the floor, and Lettie went after her. They helped her back into bed.

"I guess Sam wins," Beatrice said.

"I will be there in one hour," Elsa signed.

"You're crazy David has practiced with the long sword for years even at your top condition you lose, just quit," Beatrice said.

"She not quitter," Susa said.

"You're a fool," Beatrice said.

"Stone get in the office now!" Wayne shouted. Beatrice left. Elsa signed.

"Maybe she's right Wayne," Nellie translated.

"No, fighting for your family isn't wrong even if you fail you're still a winner in my book," Wayne said. Elsa leaned back and exhaled.

Lettie approached the room of the leader. Many times she had spoken with her father about the wealthy man. Her mother had treated him for injuries, and her father respected him, but she had never really spoken to him. She inhaled and prayed he would see things in the same light as she did. She knocked, "Enter." She went in and closed the door. He stopped his writing and stared at her.

"Leader I need…well…" she whispered. He straightened.

"How is Leader Elsa?" he asked.

"She is ill and weak and strong and fierce…"

"So you're not sure how she is?" he asked.

"No, I'm certain that she is ill, and…she fights Gracia to give me a voice, since I do not want to marry…well, not that he's not nice or handsome or…"

"Are you sure you are the daughter of Ana Marras, you do not sound like a daughter of hers?"

"I do not want Elsa put in harm's way. I want the final count to be canceled."

"So you are agreeing to marry Samuel?"

"No I…that is the only way to stop the final count?"

"Yes, if you admire Samuel so much why not marry him?" Lettie watched the old man's face. She wouldn't betray Elsa.

"I will marry your grandson please. Ma, needs to go home, and I'm not sure where that place is?" Lettie said. He wrote on a piece of paper and handed it to her.

"This is the way home for her. I will inform Samuel of your decision," he said. She nodded and left the room.

Lettie made the arrangements for the car to come and get them for the journey. She waited as Elsa rested. She informed them of the agreement. The door opened, and Samuel came across the room. "I'm glad you have agreed to what is…"

"I only agreed…never mind what I think doesn't matter to you."

"Of course it matters to me…" Lettie looked at him, and he glanced away. "You will see that this is the correct course of action."

Lettie moved down the hall, and Sam followed her. "Oh, Samuel!" The pretty blond ran into Samuel's arms, and she kissed him. Lettie glanced down. She turned back when she felt Elsa's presence. Elsa dropped Samuel with two punches, the young woman cried.

"Get up! Now!" Elsa signed. Abrim, Juan and David came to them, and Lettie moved into position. She stood at ease as Elsa's expression changed to one of fury. She signed.

"Get of my house Sophia Cantu and never return," Lettie said. Sam turned to her, and Elsa brought his attention to her.

"Do not move until I say!" Elsa commanded.

"But…but Samuel and I are…" Sophia said.

"You heard the leader, move. Delia take your niece and Joaquin and leave now!" Abrim said. The Cantu's moved to comply with the leader's command.

"Stop!" Elsa signed.

"She said stop!" Lettie commanded.

"Tell her of your decision Samuel!"

"Sophia, Leticia and I are married," Sam said. The pretty blond dissolved into tears and her aunt took her away.

"Lettie prepare to leave, in fifteen minutes," Elsa signed.

"Yes, my leader," Lettie replied. She dared not look back as she went passed Susa and Nellie.

Elsa stood before her son. "I will expect an apology and a correction of behavior toward Leticia, do not pressure her to make a commitment, she isn't ready for," Elsa signed. Abrim stood to the side, and she went to greet him as was their tradition. He stood tall as she kissed his face and bowed to him. "Do you wish to see me before I leave my leader?" she asked.

"Yes, in my room," he said. She followed him into his room, and the door closed behind her. "What punishment will you give Samuel?"

"Punishment for what his stupidity, his lack of concern? You can't fix stupid my leader," Elsa signed.

"You think he is stupid for keeping his promise to a dead man?"

"The only reason there is a union between him, and Lettie is that he forced her hand. She did this to protect me, and I will protect her."

"The kinship bond nice touch, but I don't think it is appropriate to use it against your son," he said.

"Would I do anything different than you have done my leader did you not use it against your son?" she asked. He clenched his teeth.

"Should you be punished for being insubordinate?"

"If you wish, yes I should, what is my punishment, leader?" She waited.

"Will you postpone your trip home or would you like to be punished after you return?" Abrim asked. There was no such place as home for her or the others, would she take them to a barren piece of cold stone when they deserved so much more?

"I will accept my punishment at your convenience leader," she signed. He nodded and went back to his desk. The fatigue washed over her, and the room spun, a moment later he was there to comfort her.

Raymond appeared in mother's office. "Yes, mother?"

"Love is being punished why?" she asked.

"For insubordination," he said.

"What kind of punishment find out!" He appeared in the hall. His shift was about to begin, and he approached the desk. Melvin rose, and he glanced at Sam.

"He been there all night?"

"Yes, I hear his mother is being tortured," Melvin said.

"She is not being tortured," Lettie said. Samuel was close enough to hear her. "Unless you consider service to another as torture."

"She has to serve him? This is the United States we don't have slaves here anymore," Melvin said.

"Nor do we have them in Mexico, and he is serving her," Lettie said. Raymond took his place at the desk.

"He is being kind to her?" Raymond asked.

"Yes, whatever she wants he will do for her," Lettie said.

"That's the oddest punishment I've ever heard of," Melvin said.

"You wouldn't understand our ways," Lettie said. Raymond glanced at Lettie as she went up to Samuel. "You have been relieved of punishment. I pleaded your cause and the leader released you into my care, if you mess up I will be punished. You are to report to your room where you will find your dinner and your work." Samuel nodded.

"I appreciate your concern, Angel." They walked away, and Melvin watched them.

"Punishment from a beautiful woman with dinner where do I sign up?" Melvin asked.

"Not sure it's as simple as that," Raymond said. Melvin walked away. Raymond centered himself, and peacefulness overtook him. It was something he never felt until that very moment. He got up to do his rounds and blinked into mother's office.

"So he is serving her is he?" mother said.

"Do you feel…" Raymond asked.

"Peaceful, yes, which means he is touching love. He is a wicked old man. She's sleeping, and he's holding her. I will never understand why she feels this way with that man!" The jealousy gripped Raymond. "You will need to work on that Raymond. There are many men who wish to be in the presence of love." Raymond blinked back to the mansion and stopped at the door to Elsa's room. The door opened, and the old man loomed in the way.

"Move along." Raymond walked on, so many men to kill and so little time.

Lettie stared out the huge window in the sun room. The sun crested above the ridge. A table was set next to her ready for tea. The mountain ranges, in the distance, a grayish blue and the grass colored a vivid green. She pressed her fingers to the glass. It was cool. Time shifted and the life she knew was somewhere lost in the past. "Leticia?" Lettie turned to face the green wolf, his grin wicked.

She looked behind him, and he followed her gaze. "Afraid your fiancé will catch you with the father of your child?"

"Samuel is my husband. The traditions of the Fighters make me his…" she whispered. Chino frowned.

"If you were mine, I wouldn't be wasting my time with anyone. Have you eaten?" She stood to put distance between them. He grasped her hand, and she pulled away.

"Please leave all you will do is cause a war between our clans."

"You expect me to walk away from my child do you really feel that from me Fighter, maybe among your men that is the way, that is not wolf clan. I will kill him before I allow him to take what is mine!" She shifted away, and the tea cup flipped over the steam came up, and she reached for it. The sleeve of her blouse fell back. She snatched at it to cover the red scars on her wrists.

"You're so beautiful. You've nothing to hide." He rubbed her wrist. "Mama says beauty is from within. Outside life changes us, but inside, we're always beautiful." She gazed into his green eyes, and he cupped her face. A cart rattled in the hall, and Lettie held her breath. "I will always protect you!" he said. He leaned in and kissed her forehead and just as the cart turned he disappeared. Nellie approached.

"My word sit down you're as pale a ghost. Sit I'll pour you a cup of tea," Nellie said. She sat at the table.

Elsa came from Lettie's room. The young woman was alone. Sam was missing. Elsa searched for her son. Lettie was alone two nights in a row. She opened the door to Wayne's office. Bea held Wayne in a tight embrace, and she kissed him. She watched them for long moments and then slammed the door. Bea glanced up, and her face turned red. "I was just speaking to Wayne," Bea said. Elsa nodded. Wayne stepped back he wasn't happy, he wasn't different.

"Where is Sam?" Elsa asked.

"I don't know," Bea said.

"Is Bca your girl Reilly?" Elsa asked.

"No," Wayne said.

"No, I'm not we were just…" Bea said.

"Never mind, I'll find him." Elsa signed. Elsa wandered down the hall and found the room she wanted. There was whistling coming from the bathroom, someone was happy. She wasn't. "You need to help your son," John said.

"You looking for Sam?" David asked.

"Which one John?" Elsa asked.

"Samuel, he needs your help," John said. The ghost shifted, and she turned to David. The maggots no longer crawled upon his flesh. His eyes searched hers as she turned back to his dead father.

"What has he done John?"

"He did nothing more than you have done to save Leticia and Isabella and countless others. You break laws and rules without consequence. Why are you different than my son?" John replied.

"Sam helped him do what?" Elsa asked.

"He gave me the power of sign, of your sign," David said, "Why has father not gone into the light. What is keeping him here?"

"Where is Sam, John said we need to help him?" David grasped her arm, and they appeared in a room. Sam lay still as death and Elsa went to him. David shook him, but he remained still.

"Lettie!" Elsa screamed through her mind. A second later Elsa brought the girl into the room. She ran to Sam.

"Ma, what's happening?" Lettie asked.

"Samuel gave me the power of the sign. He transferred the power…physically. Why is he unconscious?" David asked.

"Your pain, evil went over to him during the transfer," Elsa signed. David frowned. Lettie went to Sam. She straddled his body, and Elsa took her hand.

"Wait if it hurt Sam, it could…"

"Ma, we have no choice," Lettie said. Elsa squeezed her hand, and Lettie pressed her mouth to Sam's. Elsa powered up and sent her power coursing through to her son. She would need to keep enough to save her and Lettie's baby. She sent the message to Lettie, and it was agreed they would give as much as possible and pray it would be enough to get Sam back and not die. The darkness came, and Elsa fell away.

Anga pitched forward as the pain came, and she screamed in her mind as the darkness filtered in, it lasted but, a moment and then the light returned. "Raymond!" The man appeared. "What is happening with love?"

"I don't know. I'll find out, hang on mother."

Raymond went to the room where Elsa was housed it was empty and next he went to Leticia's room, and it too was void. He concentrated and arrived at a darkened room. "Angel wake up!"

"Help her Samuel, I'm taking your mother to my room. Go easy in giving back the power," David said. Elsa was still in David's arms, and Raymond followed them, invisible to anyone. David laid Elsa on the bed and removed her clothes. He dropped his own on the floor and took her close. He kissed her mouth and face. Raymond leapt forward, and his vision was blasted with light. He was back at mother's house. He fell upon the floor and screamed in rage.

"I couldn't let you do what you wanted, Raymond, but I will now offer a choice. She stays with David and lives, or you bring her here, and she dies. Alexander what would you do?" mother asked. Raymond eyed his brother, who also felt the jealous rage.

"Bring her to me!" Alexander shouted.

"No, that is why I am the leader. We will live with this new…misery," Raymond said. Mother nodded.

"You just saved four lives," mother said.

"Four?" Raymond asked.

"Elsa and Leticia are pregnant," mother said. Raymond let the information eat its way through his gut.

"Who is the father?" Alexander asked.

"I don't know. It's complicated," mother said.

"Does she know?" Raymond asked.

"She thinks that she does, but in this world of nightmares all is not revealed, so we shall see," mother said, "Would you like to be reassigned Raymond?"

"No, mother I will return now."

"Not yet, come to me," she said. Raymond went to her and bowed his head. She put her hands on his face, and the power surged into him. Pain rippled into his mind, and he found darkness.

Lettie came to in the dark. She pressed her hands to her belly and listened. "Our baby is still inside of you," Sam said. His face glowed in the dark. A maggot slide across his cheek and she snatched at it. The gooey inside dripped out of her fist.

"Samuel I must tell you something," she whispered.

"All I need to know is that you saved me, and that you will see I will be a good father and husband," he said.

"You don't want to know the truth?" she asked.

"The only truth that matters is that you are mine, and I will fight to the death to protect the two of you," he said. The tears slid down her face.

"Did Papa suffer…very much?" she asked. He drew her closer, and his hard body pressed against her.

"He said, take care of my daughter, tell her I'll find Mama and the kids…we'll be waiting for her," Sam said. His tears dripped onto her face, and she rolled into his embrace. He kissed her head as she grieved.

Elsa jerked awake and David caught her. "Easy."

"Lettie is…with Sam?" she signed.

"Yes, she's fine and so are you. Our baby is safe. I'm not sure how, but you've given me the family I didn't know I wanted."

"David I need to tell you…"

"Nothing you say will change my course. I will fight to the death to keep the two of you safe," David said.

"I can't stay…" she signed.

"You can do better than me I'm sure. Is my father unhappy?" She rolled closer.

"We are born to die, David. You could no more stop his death than create his birth. We have power, but were not God you could never stop his journey or his fate," she signed. Tears splashed down.

"I should have done more." She kissed the tears from his face and patted his chest.

"His happiest time here was the time he was with you," she signed. David frowned.

"So he's staying around because I've failed him somehow?"

"No, he couldn't come here until he came to meet me, and he remains because he doesn't think that there could be a better place than this," she signed.

"Is he going to Hell is that why he stays around? Does he know he's dead?"

"I don't know where he's going, and he knows he's dead. He's not ready to leave you just yet," she signed.

"He tore up my house when I went after you that day?" She didn't answer. "It seemed to me that he would respond that way to my behavior, he never let me get away with anything," he said.

"He knows that you love him," she signed.

"He doesn't like some of the things that I do."

"That's right or some of the people in your life."

"He wants me to put them out because they're bad?" She shifted closer to his warmth.

"You would have to start with me," she signed.

"They're not as bad as you," he said.

"I want to sleep, please?" she asked. He leaned in and took his time with his kiss and his power. She slipped away.

"We're going after them!" Chino said.

"Are you prepared to kill her son?" Pablo asked.

"And what of the giant who keeps Elsa de las Almas, do we kill him?" Pepe asked.

"He's mine and yes we kill them all if necessary," Manuel said.

"She will never make it easy for you, son," Alec said. Elsa adjusted to the dimness where she stood.

"She will adjust to life within the wolf clan," Mano said.

"She is a powerful woman, and you don't have the will or the power to break her, hijo," Maria said.

"That is why I choose her to renew our clan," Mano said.

"If you kill Samuel you will never win her to your side," Maria said. Mano paced against the wall where a fire cracked.

"He will never give me, what is mine," Chino said. Maria rose and glanced in Elsa's direction. She left her sons and went out the door.

"When do we leave?" Chino asked.

"Three days," Mano said. Elsa shifted away and when she returned she was alone in the bed. David was in his office and Samuel with him. Elsa traveled to find Lettie. When she came into Sam's room, Lettie embraced her.

"Are you all right?" Lettie asked.

"Yes, the wolf clan means to take us in three days," Elsa signed.

"Samuel will not allow that," Lettie said, "Let them come, and we shall see who is the stronger of the two groups."

"You are prepared to kill the father of your child?"

"No, but I also will not allow him to harm my clan."

"There is another way, but it will require that you and Susa and Isabella join me, along with Nellie, in two days we leave," Elsa signed.

"You know I would follow you to the ends of the earth, but what can change this where no one is killed?" Lettie whispered. Elsa touched her face. The sadness lived there in those beautiful dark eyes. Elsa left her with her thoughts.

Chapter 13 The One Eyed Man

Nellie came to the desk where the guards were stationed. Joel stared straight ahead. He was a quiet one. She moved passed and collected the linens and placed them in the hamper. "Excuse me I'm looking for…" Nellie came up to the man.

"For me," Nellie said. He turned. He was a giant of a man with a black eye patch and one hard gray eye. He was the man she imagined and Elsa said was an ally, her imagination didn't begin to cover what he was like in person, handsome and tall.

"Excuse me?"

"You are Leonard Longeria you are looking for me," she said.

"Have we met? No I would remember someone like you."

"I am Nellette Cameron. Mister Longeria Elsa said to expect you this afternoon, you're a half-hour early. I'll take him where he needs to go Joel," Nellie said. He followed her to the room where she collected another set of sheets.

"When will I see Elsa?" he asked.

"When she is ready as is the routine. This is your room, coffee machine to your left. I've turned down the bed, and made a scotch, neat. It's on the desk. Everything you need is in this room."

"Not everything sugar, wow that's my brand of scotch, thanks."

"You're welcome. Dinner is served at six. I don't like tardiness. It's rude," she said.

"I'm not going to be here for dinner."

"I can bring it to your room if you prefer."

"No, I'm never anywhere very long."

"That is what Susa says, you will be here at least until Friday, if you wish to see Elsa." She went out the door as he finished his scotch.

Nellie's day ended as it had for the last ten years. Dinner dishes were cleared, and her prep for the next day was complete. She washed her hair and brushed it out as she listened to music. The house was different since Elsa came to them. The house developed a case of eerie silence, the quiet of a forgotten tomb. Nellie finished her hair and put the brush away. Her door swung open, and the giant Leonard came forward. "May I help you sir?" He glanced at her.

"Uh, I thought this was the way out," he said. He lied he had known just where he wanted to come. How strange that her little gifts were so active since Elsa and the other women showed up.

"To exit the building is back out to the left, a sharp right and the front door. I'll let Elsa know you left," she said. She collected the tea cup and put a bag inside.

"I just wanted to get some…"

"Fresh air, same directions as before." She opened a door and took her dinner out.

"That looks good I guess I missed dinner," he said. She pulled another free and put it across from her.

"Please join me if you like," she said.

"I don't want to disturb your time off."

"What's done is done, would you like another scotch?"

"Sure," he said. He sat at the table as she delivered the drink. She picked up her fork.

"Do you usually eat two dinners you don't look like a big eater?"

"I eat one dinner I assumed since you don't know anyone here that you would somehow find me," she said.

"It's damn good. You've a great chef," he said.

"Thank you, I'm the chef and anything else that the family might need," she said.

"You Mrs. Gracia?"

"No, I'm the housekeeper. David isn't married, neither is anyone who lives here, well of the original people that live here," she said. She finished up her dinner, and she brought him a plate of dessert. "Don't feel pressured if you don't want it." He scooped up the sweet and grinned.

"So how long have you known Elsa?" he asked.

"Not long, she saved my life," Nellie said.

"Really she saved mine a long time ago," he said.

"What did she save you from?"

"A tall bridge over some deep water I was at the end, at least I thought I was, turns out I was just at my beginning," he said.

"Well I guess I was stuck, but now, well, what to do with all this freedom."

"Elsa will help you with it. Thanks for the dinner and the drinks. Hey, why don't I take you for…" She stared at him. "Dinner?"

"No, please leave," she said. He went to the door.

"Sorry if I did something wrong, Nellie," he said.

"Goodnight Mr. Longeria." He left, and she stared at the door. He was nothing more than a leaving man, not someone who would ever be happy with a little no one like her. Nellie curled up on the bed with one of her books to read about heroes and legends. She glanced toward the door. That's what he was a hero. She turned the page to where she left off, and the words seemed so flat. She sighed and tried not to think of her new life.

A light knock came. It was midnight. "Come in." Elsa entered, and Nellie smiled. She pulled a cup and started a coffee within a minute the hot brew emerged, and she turned. A tall pale man stood to Elsa's right. "Who are you?" She raised her pistol.

"No need for that girl I'm already dead," he said. She took Elsa the coffee and came around to face him.

"Nellette Cameron." She held her hand out to him, and he shook hands with her. "My word but you're cold as…"

"Death," he said.

"Yes, well you don't look like a normal ghost," she said. Elsa stared up at her. "Ghosts are supposed to be wispy and such."

"You read too many novels. I'm John Dalton, David's father. Don't you wonder why you can see me?"

"No, I've seen ghosts before, just not like you. I suppose they're all different and…"

"Nellette Cameron will you hush. You can see me because you are…like one of those heroes in those books you read, well, except that well you're real, and they're not. You have gifts."

"I've always had my little gifts that's nothing new," she said.

"Now you have big gifts," he said.

"All right now what will this cost me?"

"A lot to begin with you're homeless, but you've been there before, maybe you've never left that place," he said. Nellie glanced about the room, beautiful and comfortable. Elsa took her hand.

"We're homeless, you and me and Susa and Lettie. John thought if he came to see you well, we've a…mission to do, and you will experience many wonderful things. Some will be scary, but you'll be fine I'll be with you," Elsa signed.

"Is Beatrice gifted?" Nellie asked.

"You know the answer to that, your life has changed, just accept it, and it will work out," John said.

"Why haven't you gone into the light?" Nellie asked.

"Mind your business girl," he snapped. He moved away.

"You don't see it but a light is there waiting for you," Nellie said. He waved her away, and Elsa grinned. The door swung open and Leonard Longeria smiled.

"You didn't knock what if I hadn't been decent?" Nellie asked. His happiness spread to his eyes.

"You're the most decent woman I've ever met, although Elsa likes you that's a bad sign," hc said.

"Don't think I am impressed with your good looks and charm," Nellie said.

"Who got charm not you," Susa said. Leonard squinted at her. "Oh, me so scared." Lettie followed them in and shut the door.

"Leonard Longeria this is Leticia Marras Trevino," Nellie said. Lettie shook hands with him.

"You're married to Samuel?" he asked.

"Yes," she said, "Have you met my husband?"

"Not yet, uh, I guess I'll see you Friday, I have a quick trip I'll be back by then, and I'll check in with Nellie," he said.

"All right, be careful," Elsa signed.

"I always am, ladies," he said. The women circled Nellie and she took Elsa and Lettie's hand, a pale blond joined them, Isabella Maldano. Nellie nodded at her. They had never met. How did she know her name, well another mystery to be solved? It didn't really matter she sensed this was her place, where she belonged.

Nellie blinked, and they were in a room. The handsome ginger sat at a table with his friends. A flash of lightning and a clap of thunder shook the house and then nothing.

Elsa smacked her fist onto her open palm, and another shot of thunder rumbled so close and loud that the furniture rocked. Littered on the ground at her feet were her clan and the leaders of the wolf clan. She went around first to Alec and pressed her mouth to his temple and then to each of the men connected to her hunters. She took from them the memories of her clan. She repressed every thought and feeling they had and then moved on to her friends. She started with Nellie and came to Leticia. She leaned down and when she took Lettie's memories of the green wolf, she took also the images of her families' murders, the photos of her mind of them at that moment were squeezed into a tiny ball and pressed deep into Lettie's subconscious. She took the green wolf's ring and Mano's ring and sent them to her pack. Isabella was the last to receive the forgetting, the blond blinked. "Are they dead? What have you done Fighter?" Maria asked.

"They live, but they won't remember each other, for a while, maybe they will never remember," Elsa signed.

"How did you do this?" Maria asked. She touched the faces of her sons and wept.

"It is a gift that I inherited from another transfer, many years ago. This way, I am able to keep your clan from certain death. My leader will not abide by my decision."

"You had no choice my son would have you, one way or another."

"I made a choice. I could kill everyone in this room, and no one would ever know, but me. They would just disappear. My power is the reason that you came to me for help, no?" Elsa signed.

"My doubts vanished when I discovered you were the second in command to Abrim Stein, you would have to be very powerful to come and go as you please with such a difficult man. He was powerful when Alejandro took Patricia from him, but he was unstoppable 15 years ago and the only thing that changed was you coming to his life," Maria said. She paced by the bodies of her clan. "We lost so much."

"If you had not been soul warriors you would be gone, not even memories would remain of you," Elsa signed.

"We deserve better than scraps and cast offs of the Fighters."

"I will defend my clan," Elsa signed.

"You gave your word to protect us!"

"I will keep my word Wolf mother that is why I am here."

"Will they ever remember?" Maria asked.

"Their will is strong, if they want they can bring back any memory. The past isn't lost to them, just misplaced, and I pray it will give us enough time…for the children to be born," Elsa signed.

"Wolf children?" Maria asked. She sent the wolf clan to their beds and returned the women to David's home. "What if I tell your secret?" Elsa sighed.

"Would they believe that Abrim's second in command would save their lives, we are sworn enemies, and they won't believe you and when you insist they will put you away, and I will be forced to punish them in order to keep my promise."

"Should I thank you Fighter?" Maria asked.

"Not yet, let's pray this works." She leapt forward in time and checked on each of the women. She returned to David's room and exited into the hall. Joel Byars stared ahead as if lost in some dream. Loud music played, and she followed the sound. She stopped beside the desk and touched his face. He was very warm. He turned weary eyes to her. She waved and smiled. He glanced down. She patted his arm and went around the corner.

Raymond disguised as Joel stood to the left of the men. He was told to stand by in case the boss needed anything, what could he need he held the whole world in his arms with the beautiful Elsa. "Mother is leaving soon," Samuel said. The younger man shifted.

"Maybe things have changed," David said. Raymond exhaled.

"If my grandfather could not hold her no one can. Her fidelity, her word everything belongs to him, her leader and that is why she will leave this house and take the women with her," Sam said.

"Women which women?" David asked.

"Lettie of course and Nellie now, Susa and…"

"Why is the curse here?" Marcus asked. Elsa's other son, Marcus joined the men and Sam shook his head.

"Her name is Isabella and you better not call her that in front of mother unless you like punishment," Sam said.

"She has always been close to the girl. That is the rumor, I'm not sure that I believe it," Marcus said.

"It's true and her mother is close to Ma as well," Sam said.

"If that is true why does the girl suffer at the hands of the other girls, and the women don't speak with her mother, if they were as close as you say, then they would be popular," Marcus said.

"I don't know the answer to that, but soon she will leave and Isabella will go with the others," Sam said. Elsa sat at a table in her worn clothes and old shoes with no makeup quite the opposite of the other women in the room. She sat at a table and frowned. Raymond moved back and out of the room. He approached with care, and she glanced up.

She signed. "Mother...I need to do something I can hear her stomach growl from across the room, please help me," he whispered the thoughts into the air.

"You can read her sign you've always been able to read her sign," mother called. He exhaled the fear.

"How can I explain that I am able to do this without suspicion she is so smart."

"It is on your resume that was sent to the security man it's handled, just do what is in your heart Raymond." He moved his hands behind him and there appeared a brown sack. He brought his hand around.

"Are you enjoying the party Miss?" he asked. Her pretty eyes went to the sack. She seemed to consider.

"Is that your lunch?" she signed. She looked around.

"Yes, miss it's my lunch," he said. Her head jerked back to him. "In another life I was a teacher…to deaf children, but alas my choice was to be a hero or starve, and I was selfish. This is why I am now in security." She smiled.

"We are meant to be survivors. Your lunch smells delicious."

"Really? Just a poor man's leftovers, a couple of peanut butter cookies and some milk, nothing fancy like the food at this party." She put her head down. "Would you like to have it?" She gave him a smile that would make him cut off his right arm, and she nodded. He gave it to her, and his heart swelled as she placed it on the table.

"Give it back to him!" He glanced at Beatrice Stone, and Elsa's beautiful smile slipped away.

"No Miss, it's yours, no strings," Raymond said.

"Did you think that was a request Byars get that away from her now!" Beatrice said.

"No, ma'am it belongs to her," Raymond said.

"What's the problem here, Bea?" Wayne asked.

"I gave him a direct order to get that food from her, and he refused," Bea said.

"And I will refuse you as well. I will pack my things and leave, but she keeps the lunch," Raymond said.

"You're going to lose your job over something as stupid as this?" Bob asked.

"Yes, if that is what is required, then I will," he said. Elsa's gaze went across the room to Gracia.

"I don't want Joel to lose his job because he gave me his lunch, David, please?"

"Will you eat it?" David signed. When had the giant learned the sign of the Fighters?

"Yes," she signed.

"Then he won't lose his job," David signed. She flashed him a beautiful smile and the other security men and Beatrice glanced at their boss. Elsa smiled at Raymond.

"Thank you," Elsa signed.

"No problem, miss," Raymond said. He walked back into the hall and to his desk. Mother would be unhappy with him.

"Good show Raymond, love will reward you for your kindness," Mother said. Raymond sat at the desk as his brother's jealousy bled into his mind. Raymond grinned to know his sibling suffered, and that he was to blame.

Elsa ate the last peanut butter cookie and drank the last swallow of milk. "Ma, my leader would like to see you," Sam said. She wiped away the crumbs as she nodded and threw away the sack.

"I believe the dear one would be a good choice for the charity auction my leader, of course we will clean her up so that she is given the respect that she deserves," Delia said. Elsa met the gaze of Samuel and Marcus, frowns creased the handsome faces of her sons. She approached and greeted Juan as was their custom with two kisses and a bow. Delia frowned as Elsa stepped back.

"You wanted to see me leader Juan?"

"Dear one you look lovely," Delia said. The woman wore a flowing red dress cut down to her belly button. Elsa nodded. "I'm sure our leader Juan has expressed his gratitude for your good fortune in rescuing Leticia…" Elsa glanced away as the tears jerked out of her.

"Why do you cry? You did what no one else could, you saved at least one and…you did the best you could…"

"It wasn't…wasn't enough," Elsa signed. She turned and walked away. She found a dark quiet spot and came apart, so much power and so little control.

Raymond knocked on the door for the third time. The door opened, and a sleepy Nellie stared at him. "Please Nellie come quick it's

Miss Elsa. Somebody has to help her." Nellie perked up.

"Where is she? Show me?" They ran down the hall, and he brought Nellie to the little dark corner. Nellie cradled the powerful Elsa as she wept in silence.

Raymond blinked to mother's office. "I made it better…I brought comfort to love, mother." The tears streamed down the evil woman's face as she suffered the loss that love did.

"Why didn't you comfort her?" Alexander asked.

"You never cease to amaze me with your stupidity Alexander, how could he comfort her?" mother shouted.

"She's broken and frail. He could have done something."

"He did something he brought love…here is a riddle. What did Raymond bring love? The one who can answer correctly will be rewarded with a wish, a powerful wish, but I warn you if you take the chance and you fail I will bring you severe pain, worse than any you might have imagined. Go and think about it," mother said.

Isabella left the room where Elsa had put her and went to stand at the entrance to the party. Elsa's misery swirled through her mind as she watched the people of her father's clan. The Fighters were all gathered in the room dressed like they were at a special occasion. A small group of young Fighters' scrambled about looking for something. "Find her now!" Juan shouted. It enraged him when Elsa cried, nothing like the tears of a woman to make a powerful man feel weak. Marcus the fair came in her direction, and she popped into Elsa's room. The door bounced off the hinge as he glared at her. "Have you seen mother?"

"Yes, she's about this tall and very pretty," Isa said. He clutched something in his hands, and he wouldn't give it to her without trouble, and she met his gaze.

"I don't need your smart-ass remarks right now the leader is having…"

"Kittens, wow I want to see that," she said. She leapt at him and snatched the object out of his hands and ran for it. He pounced in her direction, and she flew away.

"Give that back to me you useless little curse!" The insult sank into her head and she frowned. She ran to the left and then to the right and she made a mad dash right into the middle of his little peacock friends. She slowed down enough so that he could catch her and he went to searching her body with quick movements. His hands were warm, but it only lasted a minute when he was jerked away and her brother crashed his fist into his face. She jumped between them and held her brother's fist. "Stop, bubba," she said. He stared into her face with her own eyes.

"No one can man handle you!" He defended her not out of pride, but from concern, and she blinked.

"I know. I started it. He called me a useless curse and that hurt my feelings not that I didn't know that he felt that way, but you can't say it to my face. I wanted to punish him, so I brought him in here and made an ass of him." Marcus would have preferred a beat down than what she just said in front of all of his friends. "I appreciate your defense of me even though you hate me." She turned to Marcus and handed him the medal. He glared, and she stuck her tongue out at him. "Baby!" She walked into the hall.

"Elsa, you need to stay away Juan is planning to honor you for rescuing Lettie, and it is only to shame his father, what a jerk. I'll tell them that you left a note they'll be coming to look for me in a minute. What he was asking for it, he's been asking for it, eighteen years of crap from him is all I can stand."

Isabella waited by the door to Elsa's room, the leader had left and Lettie was asleep in her room and so was Susa. Marcus was getting chewed out by his father for being rude, ha, ha. He deserved it. She sat on the floor, and a pair of boots walked up to her. Melvin snatched her off the ground, and his face melted away, and he became a skeleton. Pain erupted from his hand, and she screamed. Marcus grabbed her by the arm. "Let her go!" She leaned into the Fighter with his sweet chocolate scent. She rubbed her face against his smooth neck, and he picked her off like a flea and held her in the air.

"What?" she asked.

"You are a nasty little vermin," he snapped. She jumped up and nibbled his ear, and his expression changed and the chase started again and when she arrived, she spun behind her brother. "She bit me!"

"You liked it, that's against the rules to like your best friend's vermin of a little sister," she said. She stepped around him and faced the Fighter's leader. "Elsa left a note she was…shattered by her failures…" The tears spun off her face, and she glanced down where they collected on the shiny wooden floor. She inhaled and faced him again. "Anyway she left and I don't think she's coming back for a while." The leader's blue eyes glowed when he read the note.

"What was on that note, Isabella?" Elsa asked in her mind.

"Just that you were so sorry to have missed seeing him," the thought twirled around in her head. "It's true."

"Thank you Isabella," Abrim said.

"You're welcome," she said. She glanced at Marcus as she went by, and he frowned. Juan milled about with the Cantu's. Delia hung on his arm, and Isa watched. Joaquin her brother joined them as others came to speak to the young leader. Delia took a step back, and her flesh dissolved to a pile of dirt. Joaquin was next as his sister the skeleton opened her purse and handed him a knife. They stabbed their leader in the back, and blood splashed down his shirt and stained the floor. Isa blinked, and the play continued until he was more blood than anything. She diverted her eyes and Marcus loomed into view across from her, and she read his lips.

"She bit me!" Marcus said. Sam stood next to him.

"Where I don't see a mark," Sam said.

"On my ear, she's such a child," Marcus said.

"So you liked it, did she mention Lettie?" Sam asked.

"That's not funny, haven't you spoken with your wife?"

"She was asleep when I checked on her, she has trouble sleeping, so I didn't wake her," Sam said. Isabella's gaze drifted back to Juan and Delia.

"Did you get the information?" Juan asked.

"He was in Mexico City with your mother, but that changed he's refusing to see her or even speak to her," Delia said.

"Why does she know?" Juan asked.

"No and considering that their lovers it's strange, the old man Alejandro is acting strange, but he's taken care of. He doesn't have long to live. That is why he made Manuel the leader so soon," Delia said, she was no longer the skeleton.

"So the only thing in the way of getting the money is Manuel?" Juan asked. Isa adjusted and sent the thoughts to Elsa.

"Yes, and it's just a matter of time. She'll get him, and then you can take over as leader of the Fighters," Delia said. Isabella glanced down and then up as the sweet chocolate scent came to her.

"What's your answer?" Marcus asked.

"To what?" she asked.

"Yes or no?"

"Drop dead," she said. She moved away and headed for the exit. Her father would never permit harm to come to Leader Abrim and if Juan took over by force he would be killed as would the other Fighters, even Elsa would die trying to protect the old man, and she just couldn't let that happen.

Elsa received the message from Isabella A few days had passed, and she located the Wolf clan leader, but she had many more problems than just his rescue. She waited by the door to the office of Abrim's house. He had returned shortly after receiving her note, and Juan was with him. She hadn't requested a meeting knowing Juan would find a way to avoid it. She entered the office and Abrim sat at the table with Ramon, Marcus, Juan and Sam, who had come home. Lettie was at David's home with Nellie for now, and Sam stayed there with her. "Leader I am sorry about the interruption, but I must see all of you," she signed.

"It will have to wait Elsa, we are in a meeting of the highest importance," Juan said.

"I am resigning from the Fighter's Leader Abrim. I must take better care of myself, and I can't do that as a Fighter," Elsa signed.

"No, you won't do this!" Juan shouted. Abrim's eyes remained on her, and the time for truth was now.

"I'm pregnant I can't lose my baby Abrim, please understand that any good I may have done is only because of you," she signed. Her tears fell, and he stood up. She nodded and gazed into blue eyes bright with some emotion. She touched the lines on his face and the scar across his forehead. Tiny flashes of light popped in her memory like when she tried to remember her family, but this time feelings emerged. The warmth of his arms around her, the scent of his skin, smoky and sweet, a missing piece of her fell into place, and she leaned closer to him. Juan separated them.

"Who's the father?" Juan asked, "You belong to me. I'm the leader. You can't quit." Abrim slapped his son.

"She doesn't belong to you ignorant boy. You want to take from her, but you give nothing in return. I'll live with her decision. Her obligation to you is complete. Her sacrifice for you has been in vain, and that's something you'll have to live with. Now go!" Abrim said. Juan stomped out.

"I'm sorry leader," she signed.

"You've done your best, woman," he said. She stared at the far wall. "Fighter or not, no matter what my bond to you will always remain. There is nothing you can do to change that. Go rest I've business to do," Abrim said. He went to the door as the disappointment crushed her heart. He turned back. "Remember who loves you Elsa," he said. The tiny lights went off in her head as he walked out of the house. Her young sons stared at the table.

"Whatever you need Ma. You have only to ask," Marcus said. She nodded and went out the door. Her heart broke to leave the clan that she loved, but it was the only way.

Elsa walked up the sidewalk and saw the for rent sign. It was the place she wanted and the way she would keep her word to the elder wolf leader. She knocked, and a man came through the door. She wrote on a piece of paper. "Ah, yes, Senorita de las Almas, come in." They entered the cool interior of the building it was a large mansion on the street, and they went up a set of backstairs to an apartment. "Here you are and it wasn't necessary to pay for six months at a time." She wrote on the page. "Yes, now the apartment is connected to the main building, and

in it is a kitchen that you are welcome to use.
The owner doesn't come here much, and he
never uses the kitchen. All of it is available.
Enjoy your stay in Mexico City."

She nodded, and he left. She put her suitcase
on the sofa and went to look at the bedroom. A
window looked out on a room with a sofa and
table next to it. She went back down to the car
and gathered the bags of groceries and went into
the kitchen from her apartment. She opened the
silver refrigerator and unloaded her food. She
placed all her supplies into the pantry and there
was so much room to spare it looked like no one
ever ate there. She found the slower cooker and
cleaned it up to make her stew. She chopped the
vegetables and meat to begin her meal. She
would check on Lettie and Nellie soon. A bread
machine was loaded, and she went to find her
hunters.

She spent several hours with Lettie. Sam
was back, and he had told Lettie of her plans.
Nellie agreed to come with them when she
found them a place to live, big enough for all of
them. It was late afternoon. She raced to the
front door and crossed the threshold to the
porch. "I'd never pegged you for a coward, but
here we are, you sneaking off like a thief,"
David said. He leaned against the stone wall of
his mansion. His gray eyes glowed. "You
weren't going to say good-bye? I thought about

what happened between us, and I figure I was a weak moment in your strong will."

"I have a duty to…" Elsa signed.

"That's crap, the only reason you rescue Juan is for Abrim's approval. You're that old man's lap dog. Did you think I missed the adoring eyes when he appears?" David asked.

"Abrim is my leader," Elsa signed.

"No man acts like he does for a soldier," David said.

"He's always treated me differently, and it hasn't always been good. I worked harder than the others," Elsa signed.

"Just to please him and he loved every minute of it. Now you're running off again to protect his interests and what of Sam and Lettie?" David asked.

"They're coming with me," Elsa signed.

"Yes, back into Hell, instead of living a decent life here with me. What kind of a mother are you to take them back to that dismissal life?" David asked.

"You've no right to judge her," Lettie whispered. Elsa blinked. "Don't listen to him, Ma, he's jealous, and I'd rather be in a black hole full of rats with her than in your perfect little world, Gracia. Ma, please be careful." Lettie retreated back into the house.

"You're tearing my house apart Elsa. Nellie is leaving, and Bea is devastated. Bob's not eating and for what because you're trying to save Abrim's house. He's not the only one who's suffered throughout his life. All of us have, and he has no higher value than the rest of us!" David said. Elsa left the porch as he stared her down. He jumped at her and pressed a kiss on her mouth. He dropped her, and she ran across the yard.

She blinked back into the kitchen in Mexico City and turned off the stew and took the bread from its bin. She put a bowl, and a plate down and brought her supper. A pie went to the oven for later. She spread butter on a piece of warm, fresh bread. She caught movement and looked at the door. Manuel stood watching her with a half bottle of mezcal. "You're the new tenant? I was told you would be here today."

"I'm sorry if I disturbed you," she signed. She frowned and got her paper out to write.

"Your supper smells good," he said.

"You can read my sign?" she asked. Apparently, there were some things from his past that he remembered.

"Yes," he said.

"Are you hungry there is plenty?" His black gaze peeled her apart as she served him a big bowl of stew and brought slices of bread for him. He sat at his place and put the mezcal down next to him. She grabbed a glass of milk.

"You're pregnant?" he asked.

"Yes," she replied.

"You're not wearing a ring are you married?" he asked.

"No," she signed.

"I see a child needs a father, and a mother are you one of those modern women who think they can handle it all?" he asked.

"No, I agree," she signed. He spooned up some stew.

"Will there be a man around later?" he asked.

"I don't have a man, Senor…"

"Manuel," he said.

"All right," she signed. He scooped up the stew with buttered pieces of bread and took a drink from his bottle.

"You're a good cook. Why can't you keep a man?" he asked.

"I never said I couldn't keep a man," she signed. She got up and brought him more stew and bread.

"It is usually quiet here at night, sometimes my clan comes, and we play cards and…"

"Are women going to be here?" she asked.

"No, I'm an old fashioned man my mother on occasion wants to see us, and I don't allow chippies in this house when she is here and she can show up at any moment, so no women, but you," he said.

"Chippies?" she asked.

"Questionable women I don't allow questionable women around my mother."

"But you do have questionable women in your life?" she asked.

"Of course I do. Why wouldn't I?" he asked. He worked on his stew, and she cleaned up the dishes as he ate and drank. When the bottle was empty, another appeared when she turned her back. She took the empty to the trash as she eyed the new bottle. She turned back when she saw the look on his face. She took the pie from the oven.

"Goodnight," she signed. He nodded as she went up the stairs she found her things and showered. She missed the other women so much. How odd to feel that way after all this time without any permanent people in her life, maybe because she was pregnant? She switched the big light off and turned a small one on. She sat on the bed and read she felt sleepy and lay upon the pillow. She wanted only to sleep, and David's kiss brought her peaceful sleep for a time.

The mist rose from the ground like a being come to devour her. Elsa moved among the trees. She kept her pace steady, even as her vision was limited. The fog broke apart as she came over the edge of the jungle. Fear snatched at her heart. The stench of it rose into the air. From the grove of trees, she watched and waited.

Ahead in a clearing the earth gave way to a large hole. A wedge of dirt, dried into rock was evidence of the pit's age. The fear whipped through her mind. She scanned the jungle. The danger wasn't behind her, but in the pit. Her eyes rested on the edge of dirt. She knew its purpose. The dread relentless in its pursuit gripped her in its vice and there was no escape. She would witness what was to come.

The underbrush moved and a soldier uniformed in the way of Patricia Stein's militia, and with a rifle slung to his side stepped through and dragged a woman to the open grave. A small child lay in her arms. He pushed her to the ground, and pointed the bayonet at the boy. The woman placed the baby on the ground and stripped. He motioned her next to the child. She hesitated, and the man aimed at the boy. She lay on the ground and he unzipped his pants and fell on her.

Elsa lunged and fell to her knees, frozen to the spot. She screamed her frustration without a voice. She was helpless and trapped, left no choice, but to watch the tragedy. The boy howled. A wave of terror squeezed her heart. The soldier rose. The woman trembled as he lifted the boy by the hair. She screamed and scrambled to her feet. "Please, not…my only child, Raul. You've taken everything. He's all I have…please. Sir, have mercy on him," the woman pleaded.

She crawled across the graveled ground to him. She clutched at his pant leg. Raul gazed on her with hatred. She held up scratched and bloody hands to catch her son.

Raul threw the baby down. "I'll kill you instead, that way he has time to starve to death," Raul said. The woman stared. Tears rolled down her face as he aimed and emptied his weapon. She fell back and landed in the pit. The soldier chuckled and walked away.

Elsa fell on her face from the force of her determination to get to the toddler who crawled toward the hole. She ran to the pit's edge. She took the child in her arms.

"Please bring…him," his Mother begged. Elsa rocked the frightened boy. He was warm, soft and trembled with fear. The woman's blood mixed with the decay of the corpses that had come before her. "Just…throw…him down. I don't want him…to suffer…" she said. The woman held up her bloody arms. The fear pounded in Elsa's mind with the thought of throwing the boy into the hole. She unbuttoned her shirt and placed the baby next to her. She climbed down the side of the pit. The boy scrambled to his mother's side. The woman pressed her fingers into the boy's throat. Elsa took him back and held him away and shook her head.

"Why…help…him?" the woman asked.

"I must. Your sweet baby belongs to God," Elsa signed.

"God? Is…there a God?" the woman asked. Elsa glanced at bodies of all sizes littered on the ground. Mangled corpses spoke of painful deaths. Elsa shook as she turned to the desperate woman.

"Yes and He has chosen your son for a purpose," Elsa signed. The light of hope returned to the woman's eyes, and the fear passed out of Elsa's mind.

"Mama," he cried. The woman's life seeped away as her blood pooled beneath her. Elsa leaned down so the woman could kiss her son for a final time. His tiny hand rubbed his Mother's face. "Mama."

"I'm Juana Garza…he's…Miguelito. Know peace…my son," Juana whispered. Her eyes slid closed.

"Mama! Mama!" Elsa pulled Miguelito back as he kicked and screamed to get to his dead mother.

"Dear Heavenly Father have mercy on their souls," Elsa prayed.

She carried the orphan out of the pit to a refuge of friends and to a chance at life. The mist appeared to claim her, and she turned to journey to the mountains.

Elsa jerked awake and looked around. She was in her little apartment in Mexico City. "Are you all right?" She glanced over the side of the bed at Manuel.

"I saw you fall off the bed," he said. She stood, and he pointed at the curtain. Down below she saw the sofa and table.

"How did you get up here so fast?" she signed. She knew the answer, but would he tell the truth.

"Up the back steps," he said. No truth, he was a liar.

"Oh, yes I'm all right did you want something, Senor Manuel?"

"I have ice cream to go with your pie." She looked at the clock it was ten p.m.

"Sure you can have it if you want," she signed.

"Yes, well unless you serve it I'll make a mess of it," he said. She went down the stairs and turned a light on in the kitchen. She served the pie, and he sat with her.

"Elsa?" She turned in time to see Abrim. He looked at the set up and frowned.

"Have you eaten leader, I can make you something?" she asked. Manuel stood as Abrim came closer.

"Abrim Stein you know Abrim Stein?" Manuel asked.

"Yes, for many years now, Leader this is Manuel. What is your last name?" she asked. He glanced at her.

"He is Manuel Villanueva Rojas," Abrim said.

"You've met?" Elsa signed.

"No," Manuel said. He sat back down and drank half of the bottle down. Abrim took her arms.

"Come let me show you what I brought you," he said. She followed him back up the stairs. Boxes sat beside the bed. She tore into one and grinned. She hugged him.

"The books for the orphanage, oh, Abrim I'm so happy!" she embraced him, and he held her. "But you don't have to do this anymore. I mean I'm not a…"

"You will always be my keeper, and these books will help the children. It's so nice to see you smile," he said.

"You're the best," she signed. He sat on the bed and frowned. She turned to look, and Manuel sat at the sofa and watched them. Abrim snatched the curtain closed.

"Why are you here?" he asked.

"I needed some time alone, you know to think and this place was available, and I have access to a kitchen and all," she signed.

"Why don't you stay at your little house in El Paso?"

"I needed some place different, until I find a house for Lettie and Sam and Nellie and Susa," she signed.

"How about my house in Presidio? Sam can come and see me from there what do you think?" he asked.

"You've helped me so much already."

"Think about it," he said. She embraced him and he went down the stairs to his limo, and she waved. She came back into the apartment to take care of the dirty dishes.

"You know a powerful man," Manuel said.

"Yes he is a generous wonderful man."

"And what interest would such a man have in a beautiful young woman?"

"He is the bravest, kindness man I've ever known. He's a hero," she signed. Manuel frowned and left. She cleaned the dishes and took a bottle of water to her room. The curtain was closed, and she lay down.

Anga sat back and stared at the calendar, time sometimes stood still in her miserable world. A message arrived, but she had yet to look at it. Business as usual bored her. "Mother Elsa hasn't returned in a week, you said I should let you know."

"I know. She's safe for now," she said. The other two stood behind Raymond, and she turned when she sensed one of them had a thought that might interest her.

"Mother I know the answer to the riddle," Gabriel said. Raymond frowned, he didn't want them taking a chance of getting hurt, and he knew that she would hurt them.

"Do not forget the consequences of failure," Raymond said.

"I am aware master, but I know the answer," Gabriel said.

"You sound certain so go on tell me," she said.

"Raymond brought no love to love to refocus her energies."

"Explain," mother said.

"Nellie is no love and Elsa is love. Elsa couldn't change Leticia's past to work out in her favor, but she can change the present and in this way she would give Nellie the love she needed and even though she failed in the past in the present, she was successful, refocused."

"Very good, Gabriel how long did it take for you to come to this conclusion?" Gabriel straightened, and he became taller.

"I thought on it a day. I had the thought the moment that the master showed us his solution, and I know that the master isn't one to make mistakes and certainly not with love, it made sense but I needed to make sure so I waited," Gabriel said. Alexander's clenched teeth gave away his jealousy.

"Now you arc granted a wish you do not need to decide at this moment…"

"I know what my wish is mother, I want you to send Raymond to wherever love is, and that he should get to spend some quality time with her," Gabriel said.

"What?" Alexander asked.

"No, Gabriel you should keep your wish," Raymond said.

"Why would you do this for your leader?" mother asked.

"It is for a selfish reason. You see if he sees her, and she misses the others which I believe she already does, then love will bring together the other women, and no trust will be with love, and she will be safe," Gabriel said.

"What are you talking about?" Alexander asked.

"No trust is Susa Mendoza, she is…will be my mate, and I don't like where she is staying it isn't safe," Gabriel said.

"Why do you think that Susa is your mate?" Alexander asked.

"Because I followed her when she left the house, and she touched me, I was on the street she passed and she came back with a lunch and a drink and I shook her hand and I was grateful," he said.

"He's right Susa is his mate, and so I will grant your wish, right now," mother said. Raymond blinked away, and Alexander stomped from the room.

Raymond stood at the door to an apartment. He looked around and no one was on the street, so he popped several bags of groceries into his hands and knocked. Elsa was no more than half a mile from mother's mansion. The door opened, and she smiled. "Joel what are you doing here?" she signed.

"It's a long story, but I have some things from Nellie that she said you might enjoy," he said. She opened the door and he came in, and she led him down a set of stairs to a huge kitchen.

"Have you had breakfast I was just making something for myself will you join me?" she asked. He put the bags down.

"Yes it smells delicious." She brought him a big plate of breakfast and a coffee.

"So tell me the story," she signed. She was relaxed and happy, and he wondered what had happened to make her this way.

"Well, I have an old aunt on my father's side of the family. She lives in Mexico City, and she asked me to come and see her, well, Nellie heard me ask Wayne and she told me that you were here as well. She misses you so much and so does Miss Leticia, well then she asked me if I could come and stop by. Well I told her I wasn't sure, but then my aunt had an appointment, and I had Nellie's list and well here I am." She smiled, and he grinned at her.

"I'm glad you came by it's been quiet here, how is everyone?"

"The same I guess, wow this breakfast is great, and the bread my aunt loves bread, and she makes it but she's been sick lately."

"I'll send you home with something to cheer her up. I've had time to make some butter and cajeta. I love it."

"Oh, no I didn't mean…"

"It will be my way of thanking you for being so kind," she signed. Elsa looked up.

"Who's this? I thought you said there wouldn't be any men around here, and this is the second one?" Raymond stared at Manuel Rojas Villanueva, the Black Wolf glared.

"This is Joel Byars my friend from Texas Senor Manuel would you like to join us for breakfast?" He sat down.

"Sir, you have an apartment here as well?" Raymond asked.

"He's the owner of the mansion, Joel," Elsa signed.

"That's nice," Raymond said. He ate his breakfast as Elsa brought the other man his meal. Manuel chugged some of the mezcal.

"What?" Manuel asked.

"It's a little early for hooch, sir," Raymond said.

"Mezcal goes with everything," Manuel said.

"I used to know a man that ate his cereal with beer," Raymond said. Manuel scooped up the egg with some bread.

"There you go," Manuel said.

"He was an alcoholic and he shot himself in the eye. It was gross when we found him, rats were eating him." Elsa reached for the bottle, and Manuel covered her hand.

"If I want to be nagged about my juice, I'll find my mother," he snapped. He got his plate and some bread and left.

"Did I offend him?" Raymond asked.

"I doubt he cares what we think. Here is the bread it just came out of the bread maker and I made a basket for her. I hope it cheers her up," Elsa signed. He drank down the last of the coffee.

"I don't want to keep you just wanted to come by and tell you that you were missed," he said. She put the basket in his hands and reached over to kiss his cheek.

"You made my week. He smiled and they went back up the stairs, and she let him out. The warmth of her love spread through him and he found a small bit of peace. When she locked the door, he went back to mother's house he kept love's surprise a secret until he arrived.

"Mother, love sent you something to cheer you up," he said. She turned and the other two stood behind him.

"She did what is it?" she asked. He put the basket on the table, and she dug in it and found the treats. "Raymond how is this possible?"

"I wanted to take her some things that Nellie mentioned, and I needed a cover story about why I was in Mexico City, so I told her that I was visiting an old aunt who needed cheering up," Raymond said.

"So she did this for me?" mother asked.

"She did. I'll bring it to you in a moment," Raymond said. Mother smiled and nodded.

"Bring enough for all of us, we should share in love's gift," mother said. Raymond blinked away and returned with coffee, and the fresh bread laid out for them. Alexander and Gabriel joined them at the table as mother spread her bread thick with butter and the cajeta. They ate together, and Raymond watched them.

"Don't you want some of this?" Alexander asked.

"It's so good, Raymond," mother said.

"No, she made me breakfast, and she kissed my cheek to thank me for my kindness. I'm so full of love…I think I'll share with mother." He took the old woman's hand in his, and she blinked as he transferred all the love he had been given. The old woman smiled, shyly and ate her bread. Alexander glared at him, and Raymond's heart filled to know he could torture his brother with kindness.

Elsa listened to the sweet music and danced to the left and little to the right. She checked her roasts and iced the two cakes. She wiggled to the left and turned. Manuel stood in the kitchen doorway. She grinned. "Why are you so happy?"

"I've company coming," she signed.

"More men now we need to talk about this. I have a decent house here. Mama comes here and…" Squeals of laughter came from upstairs as she raced to the entrance to the stairs as they came down to hug her.

"Oh I've missed you!" Nellie said.

"Oh, yes Ma, wow, it smells so good," Lettie said. They embraced her and then Susa grabbed her.

"Me smell cake it for me?" Susa asked. Isabella embraced her, and she wiped her blond hair back.

"I smell bread is there goat butter?" Isabella asked. Elsa nodded as they danced around her.

"Me need teach you salsa?" Susa said. She wiggled around.

"Are we going to hear this all-night leader?" Alfonso said. Elsa looked at the opening where Manuel stared at them with Chino, Saul, Pepe and Alfonso.

"Is this the reason you've been hiding out in the city?" Chino asked. Manuel took a hit off his bottle.

"I'm nursing a broken heart you know that," Manuel said. Elsa turned away and swallowed the jealousy. Isabella wrapped her arm around her and gave her a kiss.

"So are we moving to Presidio with the clan leader?" Isabella asked. Elsa glanced at her the wicked little blond tormented Manuel.

"What do you think would all of you come live with me there?" Elsa asked. The women moved around gathering plates and utensils. She took a plate and filled it to the brim with food and bread and walked to Manuel, and he took it and went to the table.

"It seems to me that it might make sense of course David won't like it," Lettie whispered. She had two plates with her, and Elsa watched as she loaded up both plates and gathered some napkins.

"Yeah not think Bob like it either, not know why," Susa said. She had two plates as well. Elsa took her plate to sit next to Manuel, who took a swig out of his bottle. Lettie walked over to Chino, and he took the plate from her and sat next to Lettie. Susa had finished and Alfonso took his plate, and they sat down. Nellie was next and Pepe was served, and Isabella took a plate to Saul and got two tubs of goat butter. They were all seated around the table, and Elsa brought milk and glasses. She took a bite.

"Why does it matter what David thinks or Bob or Leo or anyone else it's not like we're wearing their rings?" Isabella said. Saul's bread disappeared, and she put another piece down for him.

"That's the truth huh?" Nellie said.

"Well, I mean we would be together?" Elsa signed.

"Yes, me miss all you, it crazy huh?"

"I know it's so hard without you Ma," Lettie whispered.

"It's because you're pregnant," Chino said. All motion stopped at the table, and they stared

306

at him. "What look at her with her beautiful skin and glowing face?" Lettie shoved him, and he grinned.

"Don't touch my baby!" He held her close.

"Take it easy, bebe, it was an accident," he said. Lettie put her fork down and moved away. Chino lifted the milk and poured it into the glass for her. She glanced at him. "Doesn't your man take care of you?" Lettie blinked and got up from the table.

"Are we ready to see the movie?" Nellie asked. They finished their dinner and started clearing the dishes. "Come on love, you can help me pick the movie." Nellie took her away, and Chino watched her go as the unfinished glass of milk stayed on the table. Susa and Isabella were next and Elsa gathered the dishes as the men continued their meals. Susa popped her head back.

"We not watching chick flick, nor animal movie?" Susa said. Elsa smiled and shook her head. "Ma, said no me win, not forget the cake." She went back up the stairs and Elsa grinned. A moment later Lettie popped back down the stairs and grabbed the glass of milk and the pitcher.

"We need forks, hurry up. Nellie brought the blankets and pillows we can sit together." Chino watched Lettie's pretty smile. He drank down the rest of his mezcal got up and brought his empty plate to her. He walked away, and the other men left as well all bringing their plates and leaving with their bottles. Manuel stayed until they were gone.

"These women are your clan?" Manuel asked. He stepped close enough behind her to feel his breath in her hair. She turned and took his empty plate.

"They are my family. They are the Soul Hunters," she signed. He nodded. "These men are they your clan?"

"They are my brothers and we are Wolf clan. We're nasty, evil…"

"Enforcers," she signed.

"Yes we are very good at our work, inventive even one might say, we are the real deal," he said.

"You are bad," she signed.

"You are good. We don't mix with your kind," he said.

"That's a comforting thought, I'm sure the Hunters wouldn't want to spit on you much less consider you worthy of our skills, we have choices we don't have to settle for little dogs," Elsa signed. She took the plates and the cake up the stairs and sat with her clan. Her happiness returned as she sat with them eating cake.

Elsa was restless as she woke up and went to the window. Her hunters slept on the floor. Down below, Manuel's head was cranked back, his mouth open, and his eyes closed an empty bottle sat in his lap. He looked pale and unearthly. She blinked down next to him. She ran her fingers against his forehead, and he was very warm. He didn't move as she touched his face. He was unconscious full of his poison. She moved him to his bed and took away his shirt. She reached for his pants and thought better of it. She pulled the blanket up and blinked his pants away. He remained out. She put her ear to his chest and his heart beat strong, and she leaned in to check if he was breathing. She stared down into his face. She caressed his cheek. He had a broken heart that was what he said to his brother, he loved the evil and beautiful Patricia. She closed her eyes and a tear fell, and she opened them to see that it had landed on his face. He stirred, and she blinked away. From the window, she saw him move his hand to his face. She turned away and went back to her bed.

Anga sat quietly, the pain she often felt was returning, but not as quickly because Raymond shared Elsa's love with her. What was she going to do with him, he was a kind man and generous, he didn't fit the mold of her brother's black cloaks, although he did very well with sweet love, even though he was a short man, and he didn't compare with the others, he was so different than all the people that had been in her life, except for love, he was like her. "Mother, there are men here to see you," Gabriel said. She nodded. The wolf clan needed more of her power, and she would take their payment to prolong the comfort. She turned to the three men, but today there were nine.

"Gentleman why are you here?" she asked.

"We heard that you are powerful," Mano said.

"You know that because I gave you the ability to sign, the sign of the Hunters."

"We understand the sign of the Fighters," Mano said.

"All of you understand it and how did you come to learn it?"

"Because the leader shared it with us," Alfonso said.

"And where did he come by it?" she asked.

"You gave it to three of us in exchange for our love," Chino said. Anga nodded something had changed.

"Why did you want it?" Anga asked. Confusion crossed Manuel's face as he tried to think of why he asked for it. "No matter, what can I do for you?"

"There is a woman who lived at the apartment of my home, and now she is gone, I want to know where she went?" Mano asked.

"Do you know who she is?" Anga asked.

"She is Elsa de las Almas. She is the second to Abrim Stein, and she is…beautiful."

"There are many beautiful women in your world Senor Villanueva."

"Not like her, she is also…kind," he said.

"Beauty and kindness don't happen often, so why do you want to know where she is?" Anga asked.

"She needs my protection," Mano said.

"She is a very powerful woman, I doubt that she would need your protection when she is around one of the biggest dogs in Mexico, I hear that he would do anything for her and how can you compare?" she asked.

"I am strong," Mano said.

"And he is stronger," Anga said.

"I am smart," Mano said.

"And he is smarter," Anga said.

"I am young," Mano said.

"And he is old and that does not matter to the fair Elsa. He is a god in her world."

"I feel that we should be together," Mano said.

"Warriors and Hunters don't mix you know that," Anga said.

"I feel that she should be in my presence," he said.

"It is more likely that you should be in hers. She was at the apartment for a reason, to protect you," Anga said.

"It was just a coincidence she was there," Mano said.

"Your apartment has been for rent for years no one will take it even at the reduced rate because you are there your reputation is well known, no one would take a chance unless there was reason and you have a price upon your head, and you know it."

"I want to be back with her," Mano said.

"I will warn you that there will be misery with this choice you want to make, and it will be painful to receive," Anga said.

"Is the price the same?" Mano asked.

"Yes, will all of you take it?" she asked.

"Yes, but only I will go to where she is, the others will wait for a later time," he said.

"In order for this to work in your favor, I will need to give you something that will make her want to be near you," Anga said.

"I can be charming," Mano said.

"No, what I give you will make her want you in an unreasonable way. She will crave your touch and you. Now I warn you that this will turn out to be difficult for you."

"She will want him, even if he is…normal?" Saul asked.

"Do you mean will she want him, even if he is mean, stupid and nasty to her, yes."

"So I don't have to change?" Mano asked.

"Change isn't possible for you or these others so let us begin," Anga said. Saul was the first and Manuel was the last, and she took from them the love she needed to keep the demons at bay and she granted them the Black Wolf's wish.

Chapter 14 A Fighter No More

The sun rose at Elsa's back as she walked up the drive to Abrim's house in Presidio. The tree-lined drive was quiet and beautiful as she came up to the grand wooden doors and she smiled. The other hunters arrived last night.

Elsa came to the foyer of the mansion and saw Nellie. She touched her arm. "Hi! We've been so worried. A package arrived this morning with your name on it. I think you need to see it right away." They embraced.

"It's the books for the orphanage." Lettie and Susa joined them, and Susa frowned.

"Not think so, when Isa coming?" Susa asked.

"When she can," Elsa signed. She followed them to a room, and Elsa stopped when she saw the pine coffin. "Lock the door." She pried the box open and dusted the plastic peanuts out of the way and pulled back a layer of blankets. Nellie gasped.

"Is he dead," Nellie said. An oxygen mask strapped to his face. His eyes closed. Mouth taped shut.

"Check him, Leticia," Elsa signed.

"It's the chap from the apartment in Mexico City," Nellie said.

"It is," Elsa signed.

"I didn't know you could have men packed up and delivered. How much would it cost to get Leo boxed up?" Nellie asked.

"I'd do it for free just to see the look on his face when he came to," Lettie whispered. Nellie giggled. Lettie removed the oxygen mask, but the man remained still, almost as if he were dead.

"He seems fine, Ma. How you plan on hiding him?"

"Why would I want to hide him?" she signed.

"You went to the trouble to bring him here in a pine box. He wears the insignia of the Wolf. One of Rojas' men…" Lettie whispered. Elsa ran her fingers over his forehead.

"I didn't…" Manuel Rojas Villanueva opened his eyes and frowned. He struggled to be free, and the tape came off.

"You've taken me prisoner?" Mano asked.

"Why would she want to do that?" Lettie asked.

"To give me to the Leader Juan, so he can murder me!" Elsa glanced at the others and they went to the door.

"Call us if you need us Ma," Lettie said. Elsa nodded and kneeled down next to the box. Manuel bucked in the tight space.

"If you make a sound all anyone will hear are you choking on your own blood," she signed. Elsa read his thoughts. Enemies couldn't be lovers that would break the rules. He was a firm believer rules were made to be broken. He could charm her like he did all the others, and then she'd tell him anything he wanted to know. Maybe he'd keep her, if she were obedient. She hauled him from the box. His feet were shackled, and his hands cuffed in front of him. She touched the resistant's, and they popped opened.

"How did you do this, kidnap the powerful Black Wolf?" he asked.

"Why would I want you Black Wolf?" He watched her face with expectation.

"Many women want me. However, this is the first kidnapping that I have been involved in. I suppose it was a matter of time, no?"

"I didn't kidnap you Senor Manuel," she signed.

"So how did I get here, where am I anyway?" he asked.

"You are in the House of Abrim Stein. I believe that your lover wouldn't want you to be associated with her husband," she signed.

"Ex-husband and that is the explanation you want to be given a reward for capturing me, so that old man can torture and kill me."

"Torture and random killing are your way, enforcer. You take money from whoever you can to do their dirty work you are a dishonorable man and can never be compared to Abrim Stein who is a hero," she signed. He walked up to her and touched her face. A jolt of power made her jerk, and she stumbled. He steadied her.

"Your Father is a Fighter," she signed. His black eyes glittered. One of Abrim's fighters was the father to this man? She had never met anyone who would even resemble him, even as he looked like his mother, and he was definitely of the Rojas' family.

"My Father is an idealistic fool."

"How do you understand the Fighter's sign language?" she signed. He spun, and she came to face him. He didn't remember how he knew, which, on the one hand was a very good thing as he had a powerful will.

"And what of your lover Patricia, she will not be pleased to know you are in the Fighter's camp?"

"You don't know Tricia. She loves me," he said.

"She only loves herself."

"How would someone like you know about a woman like Tricia?"

"I know more than I care to."

"You know nothing. I'll make her see your plot to destroy her," he said. She smiled wow he wasn't a bad little actor.

"I can take her life whenever I chose. That's not my purpose. She'll meet her fate, but not by my hand," she signed.

"You couldn't understand her. Not Elsa, everyone loves you, wants you. She has nothing left, but me."

"That's by her choice."

"She married a bitter, old man who cared only for his money. He never had time for her. All he wanted was a breeding mare." She slapped him and turned. He eyed her, and she glanced at her clothes and shoes with holes.

"Doesn't the old man provide for you? What did you do piss him off, so he makes you wear those rags? I know he bought the best of everything for Patricia, and he hated her," Manuel said.

"I picked these clothes."

"I've seen better dressed shanty women than you. With his money, you should be dressed from head to toe in diamonds," Manuel said. She adjusted the shirt, and a button fell off. He caught it and put it in his pocket. His sweet manly scent washed over her, sweet Texas Pines.

"The clan leader has more important things to consider than how I'm dressed, Senor Manuel. He's an important, valued man and I'm…nothing."

"You're second in command, and you're the Dear One that's what they call you, how can you be a nothing?" Manuel asked.

"I just am."

"In any world where I exist you would hold the highest of value. In the world where I was brought up second in command means you can't be replaced by just anyone and that means you're someone who needs protection, and here you are in a room, a woman alone with me. I doubt the old man knows," Manuel said.

"He trusts my judgment, Senor Villanueva."

"If I were him my concern wouldn't be with you, but with me, the Black Wolf."

"Should I feel threatened?" Elsa asked.

"Yes, but you don't which is an advantage for me. Where do I sleep?" he asked.

"On the bed," she signed.

"Where are you sleeping?" he asked. She glanced at his eyes. He was uncomfortable and not at all like the suave lover, she thought he'd tried to be with her. Maybe he was only that way with beautiful, rich, powerful women, and she was none of those things.

"On the floor by the end of the bed."

"Sleep on the bed, I'll take the floor. I'm a soldier."

"So am I and you're my prisoner, remember?"

"If you're to be my keeper, I could be a prisoner aren't you going to handcuff me, so I don't escape?"

"No, you're not ready to run yet, goodnight Black wolf." She lay on the soft carpet in front of the bed and closed her eyes and tried not to dream.

Several days passed since she released Manuel from the coffin. Elsa arranged papers and marked in a book. Abrim's house was quiet. Manuel remained a secret, but her time ran out. Nellie came into the room. Her face flushed as she looked at Manuel. "Lettie?" Elsa signed.

"Juan has returned with the Cantu's. He sent to me bring you and Manuel to the library. I don't know how he found out…Sam didn't even know," Nellie said. Elsa glanced at Manuel.

"We'll be along Nellie," Elsa signed. Manuel met her gaze as Nellie left them. "I'll protect you with my life."

"He'll want to kill me? I'm not a child who needs a woman to protect him."

"We shall see who needs help," Elsa signed.

They walked down the halls to the library. She gathered her courage, certain she'd need more than that to get through this situation. She pushed open the tall, wooden doors and entered. All were present except for Abrim. It had always been this way when Juan wanted to do something wrong. Juan was more confident than usual.

She went to a chair as the others were seated. "No, Elsa you're to stand right here," Juan said. She stood before him and faced the others in the room. "I've considered your actions and have decided you'll remain a Fighter. There'll be no further discussion."

"Where is the clan leader?" Elsa signed. He jumped from his seat and got in her face.

"I'm the leader!" he shouted. He could only hold her stare for a moment before he took his chair again. "You'll remain a Fighter, but not as second. Delia will be my Second from now on. You'll follow her every command as if I gave it to you. That includes everyone in this room fighter or not. Also, I've glorious news Delia, and I will be married next month," he said. The tension rose in the people that loved her. Juan laid eyes on her. His skin shimmered as if he disappeared and then his bones gleamed.

"Please my leader, reconsider I'll do as you wish," Elsa signed. Juan shook his head and then seemed to consider.

"Get on your knees and beg me!" Elsa's gaze fell on Sam, and he stopped. Lettie clutched her hands together, but still they shook with rage. Elsa dropped to her knees and bowed her head.

"Please, my leader, I will be, do anything you say," Elsa signed. Juan laughed.

"Why would I want you? Your every move, your every action has been against me. You accuse the Cantu's of being traitors you're the one that works to destroy us. You've brought this animal into my home. You're not fit to spit on. Everything you've touched or been involved in has been to defeat us," he said. She gazed at him she never accused the Cantu's of being traitors.

"I'll do better my leader, please…" Elsa signed.

"You're a worthless animal. You hold no value to me, but as a slave," he said. Juan spit on her and the Black Wolf moved behind her. Elsa's gaze came to Sam. His blue eyes raged. He was moments from destruction. She dropped to Juan's feet and kissed his boots. He kicked her away. Sam came up, and she held him in place by the sheer force of her mind. Juan took Delia's hand, and they left with Joaquin. Sam opened his mouth, and she shook her head. He followed her gaze to the ceiling and saw the device.

"Prepare for dinner our leader will be expecting us," Elsa signed. Manuel pulled her off the floor and wiped the spit off her face. His black eyes burned with some dark, evil fire as he led her back to her room.

Elsa trained on Sam's mind. It was alive with rage. Sam wanted to rip something apart. Anything would do, his every thought based on destruction. "Sam, remain calm, I'll need you. Follow my lead." She approached the double doors of the dining room. Evening had long ago passed away, and she watched him take a breath and sent him strength. He adjusted his coat. The fire burned in his eyes, and then he pushed it down. Nellie and Lettie came up, and she waited for them to enter the dining room, Susa close by. They entered, and she followed. Delia sat on Juan's lap. She giggled as he played with a ringlet of her hair. Sam helped Lettie and Nellie and Susa with their chairs and took his place. Manuel sat across from him.

Elsa pulled her chair from the table. "No," Juan said. She glanced at him and took a step back. "You aren't to eat with decent people your place is in the back kitchen."

"Yes, my leader," she signed. She moved away.

"Wait, come back," he called, "Delia would like for you to kiss her feet as you did mine. Do it!" Elsa went to her knees and pressed her mouth to the woman's shoe.

"Yuck not the top, the bottom," Delia squealed. Delia drove her shoe and heel into Elsa's cheek. Dirt fell against her chin as the heel pinched into her skin. Sam's rage bubbled up in Elsa's mind, and she gripped it. Delia shoved her away with her heel, and Elsa fell and as she rose dirt fell from her face as she gazed at the Black Wolf. "Go peasant, no one wants you here," Delia said. Elsa moved away as she passed Manuel's chair she collapsed at the end of the table. Blood flowed into her mouth. Manuel jumped up as Nellie and Lettie did. Sam wasn't far behind. Elsa drifted to the ceiling in her mind.

"Oh, don't get excited, she's faking to get attention," Delia called. Elsa shook as the vibration of the vision came.

"Get up de las Almas you're a fool," Juan said. Sam's power raged inside of Elsa, but her vision blurred.

"If she dies, I'll destroy everything you've created. I'll kill the Cantu's…" Sam shouted. The scent of sweet pines came to her as Manuel held her close and the blood exploded in her mind. Warm liquid flushed down her face and dripped on her neck. The blood increased in her mouth to drown her.

"Sam oh, my God, Sam she's bleeding!" Lettie screamed from some distant place. There should be pain not just blood.

"Ma!" Sam shouted. He held her close and dove into her into mind and was swept away by the wave of blood. It pulled him down, dragging him under like a rip tide. She forced her way to him and shoved him back to the top, and her hands went over his face. He would drown if they didn't get help. A sweet smoky scent came, and she grabbed it, Abrim. She needed him to pull Sam free.

"What's happening?" Abrim shouted. She reached out for the clan leader, blinded by the vision, and he caught her hand. Sam quivered as she gained control and cut him loose to return to the present.

"Help her, Grandfather," Sam pleaded.

"Elsa, Fighter listen I'm here," Abrim said. His strong arms came around her, but her son was safe and for now, she would float in the river of blood.

Elsa came awake and Sam was with his grandfather. She was blind and the vision still had her, but she could hear. He recounted the last few hours to the old man. Abrim's anger had texture, raw, jagged edges, and it was odd how she could feel his anger like giant slivers of glass. "I'll punish him as he has never been punished before."

"I don't care what you do. We need to help Ma, or she'll die. There's only one man who can help her," Sam said.

"Are you suggesting Gracia, there is another way Samuel," Abrim said. What other way, Elsa wondered.

"He'll help her. He's strong. We need to go now and get there as soon as possible."

"Samuel we all love her, and I can…," Abrim said.

"Do you want to take the chance, she'll die Grandfather. I don't," Sam said. Her son sounded desperate. "Grandfather, Ma has Alejandro's nephew, Manuel. I don't know why, but she brought him here. He tried to help her," Sam said. Let Abrim try, Elsa thought. She struggled to get to the clan leader, but the wave held her down.

"All of you will go then," Abrim said.

"No I don't want to go, I want to stay with you," Elsa screamed in her mind. She tried to move her arms, but she was frozen. The click of Delia's heel emerged. She sensed that Juan was there. He was uneasy, uncertain that wasn't like Juan.

"Has the useless one recovered yet? She's holding up dinner," Juan said. Flesh crashed on flesh. Abrim hit Juan. The sound was like a blast of nearby thunder as he punished his only living child.

"If Ma dies, I'll make you beg me to kill you Delia!" Sam said.

"Elsa and the others are leaving if you follow them or cause them any other harm, I'll kill you myself, Juan," Abrim warned.

"I'll get the car Grandfather," Sam said. The sweet smoky scent wafted over her, and a large, warm hand brushed her face.

"We're going to get you some help. I'm sending you back to Gracia," Abrim said. She fought the blood and raised her hand to touch his face. "Just don't die!" The blood fought back, and she was pulled under and away.

"Don't leave me, Abrim!" She screamed in the nightmare world, but no one could hear her cry as she floated away.

Sirens, screeching tires and car horn blasts brought her out of the nightmare. Still blind she searched for Abrim. "David in here," Sam called. Elsa tasted blood and smelled it. The smell of rain ripped across her face, and David dove into her mind, and he blasted into a wall of blood. "I'm here, hold on baby. I'm here," he said. She shook as he backed out of her mind, where was Abrim? She forced her eyes to focus and stared into the blackest eyes she ever saw.

"Elsa are you awake?" Manuel asked. She touched his face with a bloody hand. He smiled and the blood won again, and he disappeared, but she could hear them.

"He's Manuel Rojas Villanueva. He's ma prisoner. He'll be with us for now."

"She came to and she touched me, maybe I should try?" Manuel asked. The smell of rain came around Elsa, and she felt the wind on her face. Where was the old man?

"We're home, please come back, Elsa, dear," Nellie said.

"She's not as feverish," Lettie whispered, "Don't let her die, David. She's all I've left, please." Leticia's trembling fingers clutched her.

"Were not giving up," Sam said. Elsa had to find the old man, and she let the wave take her away. She was caught on this side of the nightmare unable to return to the present and her body. She turned over in the liquid. It smelled of blood. It was the color of fresh blood it even had the sticky texture of blood. She tasted it, blood, but this much would mean many people died.

She needed answers it had begun in Abrim's house while he was away and right after her confrontation with Juan. It hadn't even been a fight. Juan told her how it was going to be, and she was expected to follow. His plans never worked out that way, he wasn't her leader, and she never obeyed him, why had he thought this occasion would be different? What Juan wanted didn't concern her. She had to find the old man. He was the key to this mess. She jetted forward.

Raymond heard the shriek of terror, and they appeared as Mother convulsed on the ground, blood poured out on the tan carpet from her nose and mouth. Raymond touched her, and she grasped him in a death hold. "Love, my love is bleeding. Someone has hurt my love," mother said. He leaned his head onto her forehead, and the crash like a wave pelted him back. The blood gushed all around him, and the panic set in. Elsa was in blood, floating in blood, covered in blood. He trembled.

"When you come to see things my way girl you will come to know your master," the man's voice echoed into Raymond's mind. "But now I will show you what real pain is, don't you dare cry, or I won't stop!" The strap crossed over his face, and he jumped as it hit him again and again. He heard the soft whimpering sound of a young girl, and mother slipped away, from the pain, from the terror, from the hurt and no one could hear her, crying softly only he had that curse. He tried to send his love to mother, but she flew away to slip from his fingers, back, way, back to her hiding place. Gabriel and Alexander snatched at him, and he came out of her mind with a snap.

His hands were covered in her blood as he rose and collected her. He took her to her room, and he cleaned her face and hands, and he sent the other two away. They were shaken beyond any reasonable sense. As he finished the clean up, she faded away, seeped away until there was nothing left of her, but some bloody sheets and clothes. He exhaled and dropped upon his knees as he mediated to work the pain away to come back to his emotionless self, so he could find where Elsa went.

A siren jerked him out of his thoughts, and a group of people came running into the foyer. David held an unconscious Elsa. Blood dripped on the floor off of her face. She was a ghastly, pale. Her lips were blue as David leaned down and touched her mouth with tender kisses. The others, Sam, Nellie and Susa and Leticia watched. Shock spread over their faces. Wayne pushed passed him with Beto Lamb, a friend of David's and when he touched Elsa, her mouth opened in a silent scream.

David kissed her again and she settled, except for the trembling hands that dripped blood. David bound up the steps two at a time with the fallen Elsa. Raymond's mind spun as his two brethren witnessed the scene though his mind and Alexander shriveled with the images. Raymond exhaled at least she wasn't dead, not yet anyway. He turned and went back to the desk and centered his mind away from the emotions that rolled through his mind. He sat down and stared straight ahead. "Hey, your shift is over, get going," Melvin said. He rose and stumbled into his room where he turned off all the lights and fell upon his knees to mediate.

Above Elsa was clear, empty space, and she didn't know how deep the river of blood ran, but her feet didn't touch ground, so forward was the only option and she needed to pick up speed, if there was an end, she would find it. She surged through the wet and popped out the other side and tumbled onto the ground. It was dark, and she was in the village where Juan grew up at Abrim's house. At the first house, she'd seen the old man. There was one light on.

She entered the house and stood back. Abrim was in the kitchen. "You're totally useless Stein. How ridiculous is it that you're a billionaire, and you've no groceries in your house? You'd starve to death if left to your own devices. It wouldn't be this way if the woman was here instead of in Texas. Now you're talking to yourself," Abrim said. He rummaged through the cabinet. "One can of lousy soup and its chicken noodle I hate eating crap out of cans and especially chicken noodle crap! If she were here I'd have fresh tortillas and fragrant cheese and those nice little cookies she always makes and a savory sopa of beef and vegetables. Nice cups of lemon tea, no coffee with cream her favorite, sitting by the fire in my room, but instead I have crap in a can!" He pitched the soup pot across the room, and it crashed to the floor.

Elsa spun her hand and her left arm echoed with some distance pain, and she ignored it as she brought all his favorites into two sacks she held in her hand. He flung the soup can, and she caught it. He glanced up when he didn't hear the crash. His expression grew hard. "What are you doing here? Do you know what I had to do to get you back to him?" Abrim shouted, "I guess my effort doesn't matter to you. Why are you here?" She raised the two plastic sacks. "Do I look happy to see you?" She shook her head and swallowed the blood in her mouth, but a tiny bit escaped, and she tried to lick it away before he saw it. He missed nothing and charged her, and as he came blood dribbled out of her nose. He dropped the sacks out of her hands and wiped her face. His expression went from hard to pissed. "You're bleeding."

"It's nothing my leader," Elsa signed.

"Nothing my ass, come sit down," he commanded.

"The food I brought it for you," Elsa signed. He hauled her off the ground with one arm, and

330

the other hand grabbed the sacks, and they went around the table. She pulled out of his grasp and went to empty the bags. He pressed her into the chair.

"I'll get it do you think I'm helpless without you?" She shook her head. "Of course I am I was about to eat crap out of can. You know how I hate that. Why is it so quiet when you're not here?"

"Because you're not yelling at me," Elsa signed.

"That's right, who wants peace and quiet when I can have you around bleeding on my furniture and floors causing chaos and bringing orphans into my house?" Another dribble of blood came out of her nose and dripped onto the table. She held the flow back with her fingers. He pressed napkins to her face and the tears came. "You're tired. When was the last time you ate fighter or slept?" She shrugged. He pressed his hands to his face and turned to the sacks. "You're eating now and sleeping right after." He opened the container with the sopa and inhaled. "I don't know how you do this, but the truth is I am hopeless without you Fighter, wait. You're not a Fighter anymore? And here you are bleeding I thought if you gave up being a Fighter things would improve I was wrong."

"You're never wrong," she signed. He frowned as he served up the food he'd wished for and started a pot of coffee. She ate with him and tried to savor the moment. It last for ten short minutes, and he took her to his room and pressed her on the bed. His serious blue eyes looked into hers, and he leaned down and pressed his forehead to hers, and she drifted away.

"She's here father?" Juan asked. Elsa left Abrim's bed and went to the door of his room. The afternoon sun blasted the courtyard below, and she slept, somehow.

"Yes, and don't ask to see her," Abrim said.

"Juan, darling where should I put my things?" Delia asked.

"Get that whore out of my house now!" Abrim shouted. Delia's eyes widened at the clan leader's anger. Juan motioned at the pretty woman to leave, and she retreated.

"I should see her, father," Juan said.

"Why so she can kiss that whore's shoes again, so she can have dirt on her face because you're so big a man you needed to put my Elsa in her place?" Abrim asked. Juan frowned. Elsa emerged, and Juan stared. Blood dripped from her mouth.

"You're bleeding," Juan said. She slapped him and he reached for her left arm, and she cringed as the pain pulsed through her. She jerked away, and he pulled back a bloody hand. "Your arm is bleeding now." Abrim lifted her and slammed the door. He had her on the bed and wiped off the blood with a cloth.

"There's no injury, how is that?" Abrim asked.

"I can't explain, leader, but I must go."

"You're bleeding you've barely slept," Abrim said.

"If I don't go, Abrim your house will collapse and everything you've done for our people will be lost. More people will die if I fail you have to let me go, please." The tears fell like rain on him, and he frowned.

"If you die the people will lose their heart, and I lose," Abrim said.

"You're the important one, Abrim I can be replaced." He grasped her in a tight hold.

"Never say that to me, no one can replace you, go if you must, but Elsa take care because you hold us all in your hands." She nodded and looked down into the courtyard. Juan spoke with Delia and Joaquin. She squeezed Abrim's arm as she left. Elsa opened her eyes. A mist of blood showered down on her. Above her, the ceiling of blood flowed. The mist turned from blood to rain and cleaned her.

She moved forward and a reaper appeared, he motioned to her. "It's time to get Manuel," he said. His voice echoed in the still vacuum. Elsa passed her hand before her, and Mano's room appeared. Her mind was heavy and jagged. She shook him, and he glanced at her.

"Manuel, wake up!"

"Why are you out of bed? You've lost a lot of blood." She touched his forehead, and he closed his eyes. The wind shifted as if they were in a tornado. The wind groaned, and he opened his eyes. They were in the garden of his Uncle's home. "I know what this is?" he said. She stood still.

"You do?" she signed.

"I'm having a nightmare," he said, "This is the part where you try to convince me I'm wrong...go on, try," he said. Elsa shook her head and walked into the house. He stopped her at the entryway. "If this is my dream, I get to say how it goes. Let's go into my room." She pulled him back.

"This is a nightmare. An opportunity for you to learn," Elsa signed. He winked.

"I could teach you some things," he said.

"You must be serious. It's very important," she signed.

"You're such a kill joy," he said.

"Alejandro is dying. You must witness his passing...in this special way," she signed. His expression sobered. He knew about the deception that Patricia practiced, but it had not occurred to him that the time with his beloved leader and uncle would pass this fast.

"No, this is wrong, the doctor said he had six months and this is only one month. You're wrong and I'm going to prove it," he said. This death would change him.

"His time is very near," she signed. He jerked away and ran through the garden. In the blink of an eye, he ran toward a deathbed. He skidded and pushed away from the sight. He exhaled. She took his hand and steadied his mind.

"Elsa, where are you?" Death approached, and Manuel jumped.

"Let us begin," Elsa signed. She turned him, and they faced a door. "Open it." His hand trembled as he turned the knob. They were in the room once again. In the half-light, they could see a large bed in the center of the room. He moved forward to help the old man. Elsa held him back, and Death placed his arm out to separate them.

"No, Manuel. There are some who will come for him," death said.

"Is he dead?" he asked.

"No, soon," Death said.

"Why am I here?" he asked.

"He didn't want his weakness known. In your world, he'd have lost his power. He went to a lot of trouble to keep his secret as you well know," Death said,"Which road will you take? The one your uncle has chosen or the other which would give your people a chance at salvation. You've a chance to see how your life might end, if you don't change." Elsa held Manuel's hand in her right and Death's hand in her left. The wind howled and tore at their clothes and hair. A bright light burst through the middle of the room and from the light, the voices came. Cries of terror, painful moans, and voices begged for mercy. The cries grew in intensity, screams of agony, endless pleas. Other sounds joined the voices, gunfire, metal grinding, bones splintered with agonizing force and the laughter of a madman. Mano trembled, and she gripped his arm.

As the sound grew the man on the bed rose. His eyes mirrored the despair in Mano's heart. Alejandro clawed at his throat as he discovered he couldn't scream. Mano leapt forward. Elsa yanked him back and held him in a steel grip. Alejandro kneeled.

The light expanded and changed to fill the room. From the light walked the victims of Alejandro's life. They came to remind him of his sins. Tortured men came from the light, missing eyes and fingers and hands. Flesh hung from their frames. The people came from the light, too many to count. "Who…are they?" Mano asked.

"Victims of Alejandro's life," Death said.

"They've come for vengeance?" Mano asked.

"No, they cannot pass judgment. They're here as a reminder, of what his life has been. The scales of justice are to be employed," Death said. Mano's eyes never left the scene. The forgotten ones crossed to one side. Their voices went silent. Alejandro gazed, wide eyed. He found his voice. "Have mercy. Don't hurt me please," Alejandro begged. An eyeless man stepped forward and bowed to Death. The reaper nodded. He motioned the others to keep their place as he spoke to Alejandro.

"You'll be given the mercy you showed while you lived," the man said. Alejandro crawled out of the bed onto the floor. He stood before them. His body weak and his skin stretched against his bones.

"I saved you a life of misery by killing you," Alec said.

"It wasn't your place to bring us our fate. You showed no mercy in our deaths. You killed us for money. The truth is exposed as a bright light in the night."

"You were bad people. You did terrible things, and I was your executioner and I suppose this is what I expected." A woman stepped up her right eye a fleshy wound.

"Look at what you've done Alejandro," she said. Alejandro eyed her.

"Sylvia I didn't cause your death," he said.

"You rejected me and…"

"You were married as I recall," he said. A man came up to them.

"Moises you I killed, but you started it, and I finished it and for what a whore that never wanted you!" Alejandro snapped.

The brilliant light traveled to the ceiling and remained suspended like a golden bulb of magic, a second later it popped and the dead remained with Alejandro. The black ooze grasped him and dragged him down into eternity. Death twisted his head as Alejandro yanked his feet out of the muck and stood upon the floor. The ooze grabbed him again. Mano moved to help him when a beautiful young woman stepped in front of him, her eyes the color of a fall sky in her Texas.

"Alicia," Alejandro whispered. Her best friend's smile broke Elsa's heart.

"I love you, Alicia. I'm sorry I failed you," Elsa signed.

"Why are you here Alicia Stein?" Death asked. She smiled at the reaper, and he bowed his head.

"Alejandro tried to stop them when I was captured. He fought them with all his might, but…there were too many of the evil ones," she said. Elsa released her hands from the men's grasp.

"Alejandro didn't hurt you?" Elsa asked.

"No, and I should count toward his punishment, Death," she said, "I'm proud of you of how you handle Papa, of how you love him, and I love you," Alicia said. The tears ran down Elsa's face. She gripped Death and he steadied her.

"He misses you so much. I don't know how to help him," Elsa signed. Alicia's smile was so heartfelt. Elsa touched her face.

"Just love him. The rest will work out," Alicia said, "We'll save you a place. Until we meet again my sweet sister." She stepped to the others whole and glowing. Alejandro watched her with eyes filled with sorrow.

"What now Death?" Alec asked. Manuel watched the man who sheltered him for most of his life surrounded from all sides.

"You have to walk away now," Death said. He moved, and the victims followed him. He looked back as Alicia trailed behind him.

"Keep your promise fighter woman," Alejandro called.

"She will," Alicia said.

"Why couldn't you love me? Why couldn't I be right for you? Why are you so mean to me? Why won't you talk to me? Why am I not important? Why can't you need me?" Sylvia's voice trailed away as the shade of Alejandro wandered away.

Elsa held Manuel as the armor that he wore shattered like glass and splintered on the floor. He wept and suffered as he grieved for an evil man, and Elsa grieved for an innocent woman. Manuel screamed as the grief and emotion raged he fell upon his knees, never weaker than he was in this moment. She ran her hand over his hair, and he looked up with hollow eyes and knew that she saw into his soul, and he trembled for she was the first and would be the last to ever witness this weakness. Across the room, the clock chimed eleven times. He gazed at his Uncle's favorite treasure. An hour before midnight the end had come for Alejandro.

"His fate is sealed forever," Death said, "And what of you young Wolf Leader to which side will you fall when I come for you?" Elsa pulled Manuel up, and he didn't answer. Elsa led him away from the chamber of death and back to the world he knew.

As she came to the stairs, he yanked free and burst through the door of Patricia's room. Elsa ran after him. Mano stared across the bed. Animal sounds emerged from behind the delicate lace. They could see Patricia's naked body twisted around a young soldier. Mano shouted and pulled his knife. He ran to them. "Whore!" Elsa waited for the response. Patricia stumbled from the bed when she recognized his voice.

"Mano? You're alive," Patricia said. The young man came off the bed. "Get out, Fernando." Mano's best friend gathered his belongings.

"Mano, I can explain," Patricia said.

"I see how much you missed me," he said. He stormed out of the room and took Elsa's hand.

"Wait, Mano!" Patricia called.

"Take me back, Dear One of the fighters," Mano commanded. His armor clanked back into place, and he was back to the enforcer, back to the only way he knew. They fell into darkness as time shifted in the shadow of dreams.

Elsa came to in a bloody puddle of dirt. The sun rose through the treetops on its way into the sky. In the distance stood a barn in the middle of a field, gray with age and neglect. She entered the dusty structure and picked her way passed a variety of old, rusty farm tools. Her eyes adjusted to the dimness as she moved to the sound of whispered voices. Only one among the voices did she need.

She stared at the three. They couldn't see her. Joaquin left them. Delia pulled Juan into an embrace. He pushed her away. "Not now," he snapped. Delia pouted.

"Oh, but lover, we need to talk. The old man reversed your order. I should be the rightful Second," she cooed. She slipped her arms around his waist.

"When the plans are finalized, I'll be the only leader. You have to show patience. You should try to win him over," Juan said. He turned and held her. She pouted. Elsa squeezed her hand into a fist.

"I'll try for you lover, but it would help if you came into my room tonight," she said.

"We'll see," he said.

"Do you think he told the bitch, she hasn't been replaced?" she asked. He shrugged.

"It doesn't matter, soon everything will change. Go find Joaquin, tell him I'm ready," Juan said. Delia reached to kiss him, and he pulled away. She left disappointment on her face. Delia's disappointment wouldn't be over if Elsa could help it. His body language, his posture was wrong. He lied to Delia he wasn't ready for whatever they were doing. His resolve was something else. She didn't read his thoughts; she didn't want to know why he turned against her and his beloved father. She moved to hide in the bloody dark.

<u>Chapter 15 The Road of Misery</u>

Elsa crawled out of the dark and light flooded the area. Above her the flow of blood continued to survive. She changed the scene and stood in the jungle. The sound of birds floated through the air. She smelled the rich earth as it came to life. She was invisible to anyone who crossed her path. She wanted to remain unnoticed.

She walked through many villages and experienced the hardships and the triumphs of her people. Poverty was abundant, but somehow the people survived. When she came to the cities there were shantytowns. She knew the cycles with these places. People sold goods or traded. These places were sub-communities and existed independently of the city. The laws of this land, in this place were different.

On the second day, she found Juan. He didn't know she was with him. Abrim traveled with him, his sky-blue eyes so much like Samuel's. Juan turned in her direction. The wind blew across her face as he searched the landscape. By mid-afternoon of that day Juan met with Joaquin and Delia Cantu. They told him where the people were being taken. Delia was to take a group of fighters to this location. She told Juan one of Rojas' generals would be at the camp. It was a lie. The rumor had it the general's brutality outshone Alejandro. All agreed that was a difficult reputation to surpass.

They hoped to kill the general or die in the effort. That would be their excuse to capture Juan. The plan was suicide at the very least. She touched Juan's mind, and the thought occurred to him. "Count me in. When do we leave?"

"No, Juan," she thought. The determination etched in his face and knew she had to try something else.

"We try to take the camp in several hours," Delia said. They moved off toward the jungle and their destination. She appeared at the end of the shantytown as an old, beggar woman. She pulled her shawl around fragile shoulders. An outstretched foot tripped Delia. She spun and grabbed the old woman's arm. "Stupid old hag," Delia barked.

"What have we here? It seems you fancy yourself a queen, ah, but it takes more than royal robes. It takes heart and that's a commodity you lack," Elsa said. Her voice cracked with laughter. It surprised Elsa she could speak, sometimes in the nightmares it happened, never for long and not very often. Delia yanked her off of the ground. "It also takes more than sleeping with the king, but then what would I know of it. I'm an old peasant woman."

"You're a dried up old hag, in filthy clothes," Delia snapped. Elsa looked at herself and nodded.

"Yes, I am. An old hag, yes, but I met a Queen once. She gave me her last loaf of bread and what few coins she had, oh, yes and the coat off of her back. It's lovely, no?" Elsa asked. She turned in the worn shawl to show them. Contempt crossed Delia's face.

"It's filthy and it stinks," Delia said. Elsa frowned.

"It wouldn't do if she returned and saw I hadn't taken care of it," she said, "I'm sure she would help me clean it if she could."

"It sounds like Elsa. Do you know her?" Abrim asked. His blue eyes bright with deep emotion, it was pride for her, and Elsa inhaled. She lowered her gaze. He didn't recognize her.

"Elsa? I'm not sure; she didn't give me her name, great sir. That was all she kept for herself. Long, dark hair, deep brown eyes, a heart-shaped face and slim hands with long fingers," Elsa said.

Juan stared at her. He pulled her to him. The palm of his hand moved across the wrinkled skin to cup her face. She tried to lure him in as he kissed her leather cheek with tenderness. A wrinkled hand squeezed his arm. He stepped back and pressed money into her hand. "Go with God, old Mother," Juan said.

He ran through the jungle followed by the others. At the jungle's edge, Abrim turned back, but by then the old woman was gone. Dollar bills scattered in the wind. Elsa gritted her teeth. Within the hour the whole group assembled. They crept through the trees as gunfire erupted. The fear clutched her heart. She went ahead of them to look around. A train pulled into the middle of the camp. People were herded to a large pit in the earth. This place like all the others was a final destination.

People lined up in front of the hole and then were blasted with a machine gun. Their bodies flew into the pits. She could see some were still alive. They moved among the corpses in agony. Escapees were pulled to the side and chained together. The killing stopped after two or three people were caught. They were shown the consequences of such action. The soldiers of the Patricia's militia dismembered them and pitched them into the hole. The screams of the dying rose and haunted the living. She bellowed at the injustice. Her anger turned her heart to ice. The group of fighters came up behind her. They crept along to the fringes of the buildings. She couldn't find Juan.

A soldier with a machine gun herded a group of children to a smaller pit. From the left came Delia with her conspirators to capture their prey. The man pulled the gun up and aimed. Juan shouted, "Don't kill them!" The soldier turned, and Juan fired. The bullet burst into the man's arm. The machine gun came up, and the sparks of light raced for the target. She shifted time and leapt to push Juan away. Fire burned her left arm. An invisible force shoved her and she landed a few feet away. She screamed.

He fell and she materialized. The anger and frustration came in a thundering wave to wash over her. Her mind turned to an electric current and lanced into the soldier. The surge made him drop the gun. She pictured his heart in her hands and crushed the delicate vessel in her powerful grip; in her vision, blood exploded in all directions. The killer's eyes were open, but his life ended. She felt no satisfaction from his death.

She went to Juan's side. Abrim kneeled beside him. "Elsa, I should have known…you wouldn't give up. Promise…you'll be happy," Juan said. Abrim's eyes searched his son's body as if he looked for something out of place.

"No, you can't die. I tried to stop this. Why wouldn't you listen to me. I've failed you," Elsa signed.

"Promise," Juan said. She nodded.

"You're the Queen of my fighters. Don't ever come…back. Live in…peace beloved." His eyelids fell into place. She pounded on his chest. He opened his eyes and gave her one last brilliant smile. She gathered her strength and pressed her love for him into his mind as his life slipped away.

"I love you Juanito," she thought. She pressed her lips to his in a final kiss. The grief caved in her heart as she rocked him.

"You'll come with us, woman," Joaquin said. Abrim stared at her. The tears in the wise eyes ripped Elsa's soul. Samuel's beautiful eyes, she would have to break her son's heart. She kissed Juan's cheek. She stood to face his betrayers.

"Elsa, no…this isn't the way," Abrim said, "Go! Go!" Abrim shouted. They laughed and Delia kicked Abrim into the dirt, the most powerful man she knew lay helpless. Elsa's eyes fell on Abrim, and he had a wicked, vengeful look, but only for a second as she raised her arms. Her eyes closed.

"Take her!" Delia commanded. Her eyes snapped open, and she twirled. The thunder boomed. The air crackled with electrical force. Two of the men touched her and were thrown back. Delia reached for her. Elsa came up with her knives. Four slashes later and Delia's face was an open wound. Joaquin ran, and Delia screamed again as she followed him.

She moved forward and waved her arms across the land. The trees burst into flame. A group of stunned children huddled in a group behind a small bush. She motioned at them to come to her. Hypnotized they came, a huddled mass of fear.

One of the traitors grabbed a girl to protect him. She turned her dark eyes on him, and he dropped the child. He screamed in agony as fire shot out of his mouth. The children arrived at her side. She pointed to Abrim, and they went to him.

Some of the rest of Juan's group came to Abrim. Grown men, veterans of war, wept for their fallen leader. "Look at the faces that have killed your leader," Elsa signed. They turned to the traitors. Some rose to take revenge on Delia and her group. "No, we finish what we have come to do. They'll answer for their sins. His death…won't be in vain," Elsa signed. Delia disappeared into a truck.

Elsa passed her hand before her and everything exploded. She walked the entire length of the camp and burned all of it. A moment in time and the place turned to an inferno. She freed many people. She appeared on the far side of the camp. Her dark hair moved around her head. From all sides of the jungle the Fighters appeared. Like ghosts from a child's nightmare they came to pay their last respects. She turned back to the fire.

"Juan Carlos!" she screamed. She dropped to her knees as the pain engulfed her. A wild birdcall sounded through the still night, the Fighter's call. She gathered her courage and faced her people. Another voice took up the hail, and another until the sound pounded through the jungle. It pulsed to a deafening sound, and she closed her eyes. The ceiling of blood dripped down. Huge drops fell around her. She jumped up into it as it burst apart. Her body jerked upward as she came back. She gasped for breath and wheezed. "Lettie!" she called. She was alone in David's room. It seemed like hours, but Lettie came, and in reality, it was less than five minutes. "Lock the door," Elsa signed.

Sweat poured off of Elsa's face and body, but she shivered with cold. The pain shredded her mind. She failed, and Juan was dead. Lettie slipped Elsa's robe on. Leticia embraced her, and Elsa crumbled in her arms. Leticia gazed into her eyes and recognized the pain. "What happened? Tell me…it's bad."

"Juan's…dead. A soldier…they were supposed to capture him and kill me…I tried…it didn't work. He…died in my arms." Lettie pulled her close as they cried.

"Does anyone else know?" Lettie asked.

"The clan leader knows, no one here," Elsa signed.

"We'll wait for Grandfather to come. How many are too many to die for a cause?"

"One," Elsa signed, "No one comes into this room until the clan leader arrives."

"Yes, my leader," Lettie said.

"Soon he will come." Lettie nodded as she left Elsa to her grief and regret.

Raymond approached the door and entered followed by the two others. Gustavo stared out the window and stabbed his pen into the desk, the shiny dark wood surface blistered and peeled from the force of the movement. "You summoned me master?"

"Tell me what you know of Elsa's condition?" he asked.

"She is behind a close door. She came into the house covered in blood and the doctor has seen her," Raymond said.

"A lock door stopped you from seeing sweet mercy?" he asked.

"No master, she is no longer in a coma, but she is…"

"In pain," Gustavo said.

"Yes." The master turned to him.

"Do you know what happens when someone spits on one of mine?" Gustavo asked. Raymond looked in his eyes.

"They suffer," Raymond said.

"And what should happen to anyone who kicks sweet mercy, sweet Elsa in the face, to bruise her and cut her. What should happen Raymond?"

"Whatever you want master."

"Come lets us see what I will do," Gustavo said. They followed him into the night and after about an hour they arrived at a large house in the middle of nowhere. They didn't bother with doors as they entered the shadows of a room.

"What have you done, Delia?" a giant of a man asked, his name was Enrique, but everyone called him Henry.

"What you didn't have the balls to do," Delia Cantu snapped. Her face was bandaged in several places.

"You came home covered in blood. Whose blood is this?" Felipe said, the tall man was the half brother to the woman. His blood brother was Henry. Another man came.

"Why didn't the clan leader fight us?" he said.

"What did you do Joaquin?" Felipe asked.

"We tried to capture that bitch Elsa de las Almas all she ever does is get in our way with her good works, and the clan leader is so amazed by her. I almost had her," Delia said. Gustavo took a shallow breath as Raymond, pulled a knife. Gustavo held him back.

"And I'm sure you were a part of this Joaquin," Henry said. Joaquin laughed.

"You are never going to be like our father cowards!" Gustavo came around as he studied his goal. Raymond watched him size up the woman and the man. He snatched at the woman and drew his knife against her throat as her brothers reacted. Gabriel and Alexander fought Henry and Felipe. Gustavo pounced on Joaquin as Delia stumbled to her weapon. Gustavo drove his knife into Joaquin and snatched at Delia. A short sword appeared, and he separated her hand from her arm and she screamed. He came back to Joaquin as Delia's screams pelted the air. Joaquin tried to run, and Raymond countered him and shoved him back to the master. His heart swelled as the vengeance raged.

Gustavo separated the man's hands from his body and watched him jerk on the floor in agony. He returned to Delia and took her other hand, and she screamed and screamed her two brothers couldn't get passed Gabriel and Alexander. Gustavo took a seat and a bottle of wine snapped on the table next to him. Raymond took the bottle and poured it into a small glass and then passed it back. Gustavo sat back as the screams bounced all around them. A strip of tape appeared on each of the victims, and the sound stopped.

"Raymond what should I do with the other two brothers?" Raymond glanced toward the men who had gone still.

"How about a gift for mother? Their talents are raw, but she can mold them to her liking or not," Raymond said.

"Yes, there is one more, Alexander get Norman, he's in the kitchen. He too has some talent Anga might like," Gustavo said. The man exhaled as the two before him seeped to death. He snatched the woman up and looked into her eyes. "You spit in the face of sweet mercy, of sweet Elsa and nobody should ever do that bitch!" His sword appeared and he whacked at her neck, at about the six hit her head separated from her body, and he grabbed Joaquin and eight blows brought an end to the enemy. "Bring one hand of each, so they can be identified." Raymond collected the hands as Norman saw the violence. Raymond walked behind the master as the three new Black Cloaks joined them. They never looked back as the night swallowed them.

Elsa's wait ended on the following afternoon when Abrim arrived. Lettie brought the clan leader to the room. Their eyes didn't meet as she rubbed her aching arm. "I know what's happened. Please accept my condolences," Lettie whispered.

"Does Samuel know?" he asked.

"My son doesn't know yet," Elsa signed.

"Elsa's…in terrible pain I don't want her to die Grandfather," Lettie whispered. Still their eyes hadn't met.

"I know…gather everyone in here," Abrim said.

Ten minutes later all were gathered. Lettie stood by Elsa. David came in last and took a position across the room. The old man's face hollowed with grief.

"Juan was killed yesterday. They were trying to capture him and kill Elsa, but things went wrong. Elsa tried to stop it, but…" Abrim said. The suspicion in Sam's eyes cut her to the soul. Lettie placed her hand on her gun. He glanced at Lettie.

The grief twisted Sam's heart. The pain in Elsa's heart reflected in his blue eyes. The click of guns loading echoed through the room. As the Hunters prepared for her defense, Leticia raised the forty-five. "You'll not blame, Ma for this," Lettie said.

"Do you plan to kill me girl?" Sam asked.

"If I must," she whispered.

"Elsa and I are getting married," David said. They never discussed marriage. Lettie holstered her gun.

"Wait," Lettie whispered. She glanced at Elsa.

"Do you want this? If you don't we can run away," Lettie said.

"No, I don't want to marry him," Elsa signed.

"Then we leave," Lettie whispered.

"Nobody's going anywhere," Sam said. Elsa wobbled and Lettie steadied her. Beto Lamb came to them.

"She's on fire again," he said. David moved to her, and she wobbled back. Abrim glanced at her. She caught her reflection in the mirror, she was pale.

"I'm sorry for your loss, Abrim. If there is anything I can do let me know," David said. The old man stepped in front of David.

"I failed you again leader," she signed.

"No, you didn't. It's your job to keep her safe now David." She shook her head.

"Let's allow Elsa to rest," Nellie said. They filed out and only Sam, Lettie, David and Beto remained.

"You brought me here? How long was I out?" Elsa signed to Sam.

"Yes, three days," he said. Beto glanced at Elsa.

"You're pregnant," Beto said. Elsa turned. David and Sam stared at a different wall.

"I'll check on you later," Beto said. Elsa yanked him back and signed. Lettie nodded.

"She wants to know why you checked." Lettie whispered.

"You're showing," Beto said. Elsa glanced at Lettie. "Your stomach is rounder than normal." Elsa signed.

"She's has been less active lately. She was going to get around to toning back up. She's been busy," Lettie whispered.

"You're going to have a baby, hasn't anything else changed?" Beto asked. Now the whole world would know, and her child would be a target.

"Everything is normal for her, and she's never been pregnant before now, sometimes she misses, but it's normal," Lettie whispered. An oblivious lie, but no one corrected her.

"The test is positive I did it five times to make sure," Beto said. Elsa signed.

"And then you told David?" Lettie asked.

"No, the two of them broke into my office when I wouldn't tell them the results of your blood work. I thought you should know first since you're my patient. Get some rest," Beto said. He left. David hadn't moved or blinked.

"Like I said were getting married," David said.

"No, we're not," Elsa signed.

"You don't want my baby?" David asked.

"I didn't say that," Elsa signed. She disengaged from Lettie and went down the hall to find Abrim. She found the room and walked inside. He stacked his things into a bag. "When do we leave to make…the arrangements?" He stared.

"Elsa we're getting married my baby is going to have a name, my name," David said. He reached for her, and she ran behind Abrim as David tried to snatch her up. Abrim stepped up.

"Stop," Abrim said.

"She's pregnant with my baby, Stein. We're getting married oh and you're done being a jungle rat," David said.

"A jungle rat? Get out of this room, now!" Abrim said.

"This is my house," David said.

"I don't care, move!" Abrim shouted. Sam had come to the room and had David.

"Come on let him talk to her," Sam said. David slammed the door.

"When do we leave?"

"You're pregnant how much?" Abrim asked.

"I don't know."

"How can you not know?" Abrim shouted.

"What do you want to know? When I slept with…" He turned before she could finish her sentence. He came back.

"You could do worse than a billionaire," Abrim said.

"It doesn't hurt that he's fairly young and hot either, but those aren't reasons to marry a man, leader."

"Your baby needs a name," Abrim said.

"It'll have my father's name, my name."

"You need to be cared for and…" Abrim said.

"He thinks I'm a jungle rat, when do we leave?"

"We don't," Abrim snapped.

"We need to bury…your son."

"I already have," Abrim said.

"Without me, I'm sorry I couldn't save him. I tried taking the bullets for him…so you wouldn't suffer, so he would live." He snatched her up, and his hand closed onto her left arm. Something was odd about him.

"You have to stay here! Delia and Joaquin were found this morning. I fear you're not safe," he said.

"Found how?" she asked.

"Murdered that is all I will tell you," he said.

"No, tell me what happened?" She didn't like the way he was acting could he murder the people that killed his son? He could, but had he. She needed to know.

"What kind of a man do you think I am? Do you believe I'd trade two lives for one, even for the life of my son, do you?" His anger was strong and hard, and it pelted her like rocks from the winds of a hurricane. The pain pulsed through her upper arm as he gripped it, and she closed her eyes and forced the memories of Delia and Joaquin's deaths from his mind. He clenched his teeth as she came to know what he had seen, and they were dead when he arrived, long dead, lying in black pools of blood with headless bodies and severed hands. They had been tortured, and her beloved leader hadn't been to blame.

"What have you done I told you no!" She stared into his eyes and popped the three bullets from her arm. Her knees evaporated as they burst through her skin and crashed into his hand. His pulled his hand back and glanced at the objects. "You took three bullets for Juan, in your condition?"

"I didn't know…" Elsa signed. She fell over, and he wrapped his hand and fingers around her bleeding arm. She was up and in his arms. They traveled into the hall.

"Beto Lamb where are you?" Abrim bellowed. She pressed her face against his hard chest as Beto and David came to them.

"I'm here, what is it?" Beto asked.

"Fix Elsa, she took three bullets in her arm," Abrim said.

"Who shot her?" Beto asked.

"Leticia, come out here. No questions stop the bleeding now!" Abrim shouted. David launched in Elsa's direction, and she clutched Abrim's shirt. "Back off Gracia you've caused enough problems."

"Give me my woman!" David shouted.

"She's not your woman and we jungle rats like to take care of our own," Abrim said.

"Will someone tell me how you know she took three bullets?" Beto asked. Abrim's face caved in with rage as he opened his fist with the spent bullets.

"Make her stop bleeding or I'll destroy you!" Abrim said. Elsa pulled on Abrim's ponytail and turned his head. "It's better for them if you don't bleed to death."

"Don't threaten me Stein," David said.

"No more questions come on. Lettie's going to assist you," Abrim said.

"Let's take her to the hospital," Beto said. Abrim grabbed the man and shook him with such force it alarmed Elsa.

"Hey, let him go," David said. Beto got free.

"I don't like you Stein, but I'm going to overlook it to help her," Beto said. They were back in the room, and Beto had disappeared as Lettie cleaned the blood. Beto appeared with Sam and David. Elsa tensed as Abrim held her in his lap. She shook.

"She's got a lot of pain, Doctor Lamb," Lettie whispered.

"I'm taking care of it," Beto said.

"She's pregnant," Abrim said.

"I'm aware I told her," Beto said. Elsa leaned on the leader as Lettie's gentle hands cleaned her arm. She felt the younger woman's confidence in her care and in Lettie's quietness she sank so they could work on her. The leader's scent billowed around her. His fear smelled of sweet smoke from her little house. She focused on that scent and his hard arms around her and escaped into the darkness.

Elsa woke to voices. "Grandfather you can't leave without speaking to her."

"I'm so full of anger I should just leave, Sam," Abrim said.

"She understands anger. She won't understand you leaving without speaking. You're important to her. I found out about Juan's plans, and they didn't include us or her, Grandfather," Sam said.

"Do you think I got to be in my position by being stupid?"

"No, but the reason Juan was to marry Delia was for her father's money, because he planned to cut a deal with Patricia," Sam said. Elsa exhaled as she went to the door. They stood in the quiet hall it was very late at night.

"I know and she took three bullets for him and what will knowing of his betrayal do to her and our people. She says she failed me, I failed all of us in my training of him."

"You knew he was to be captured along with you? They figured ma would try to rescue him, so they'd have her," Sam said. Elsa's hand trembled against the doorknob.

"Did you find out they planned to kill your mother on the spot?"

"No, you knew this?" Sam asked.

"You think I'd go on a suicide mission for no reason? I knew she'd try to save him like she always does," Abrim said.

"So you went along to save her and not your son?" Sam asked.

"I wanted to save them both, and I failed," Abrim said.

"No, you didn't," Sam said. She nodded.

"I'm leaving Samuel take care of your mother," Abrim said.

"One of Juan's mistakes is underestimating Ma. He figured he could turn the Fighters against her. After all, she wasn't very important, just a woman. All she had ever been responsible for were the women and children. Most of those children are now adults and there isn't one she hasn't saved or helped their families, provided for them in some way. He was their leader, but she's their mother. Not one would turn against her, my leader, don't make your son's mistake and turn against her." The tears splashed her hands.

"I'm on the same side I've always been," Abrim said.

"Patricia will be devastated by this loss," Sam said.

"The loss of her son?" Abrim asked. Sam laughed.

"No, not her son, her deal, it's gone. When she's done playing the grieving mother, she'll come after us. She'll kill everyone in this house. They won't take me alive if that happens," Sam said. He pushed his hand through his black hair. Abrim nodded as he went down the stairs. Elsa ran for the window. She shimmied down the side of the house with only one arm and got into the car before he did. He got into the car and slammed the door. She slid out of the dark corner in her pink silk gown, and he drew his weapon. She hated pink. She rushed him, and the barrel of the gun pressed against her heart. He yanked it away and dropped it to his side. She shoved him hard.

"You're not the only one that's pissed. Why are you angry because I failed you and let another one of your children die? Are you pissed because a nothing like me survived…and they didn't? No, you're angry because I'm not the woman you created in your mind no, I'm broken, and damaged and needy. I have needs like any other woman!" Elsa signed. Her arm ached from jerking it around.

"Are you done Elsa?" Abrim asked.

"No, I hate you, go on and hide in your perfect world!" she signed. His expression wasn't angry just stern. She shoved him again. "You better not die or do anything to make that happen!" She kicked open the door to his limo and stepped onto the rocks. She slammed it shut. She ran across the wet grass and tumbled onto the ground and rolled into a sitting position. The door remained closed, and the car still. The window closed. She got up and ripped the bottom half of the pretty gown away and threw it on the ground. She ran to the distance woods until she was out of breath, and the trees swallowed her.

Two hours later she crept into the house, and to the room where her clothes were. She entered the room and searched the chairs. "If you're looking for the rags and old shoes with the holes I gave them to Nellie to burn. You had to see him off didn't you? What did he say to you to make you run into the woods and tear up your clothes?" David asked. He sat on a chair across the room in the dim light.

"Nothing," Elsa signed.

"What did you say to him, you were in the car for a little while," David said. She frowned. "That good."

"I told him I hated him," Elsa signed.

"I bet he liked that," David said. He crossed the room and caught her in his arms. He pulled off her wet gown and pulled his black t-shirt on her. At least, it wasn't pink. He took her into a hot kiss, and she resisted as his mouth trailed down her neck. "We have rules here and rule number one you don't leave without telling me, rule number two you don't wear rags, rule number three you do as I like, and I don't have to be mean to you and..." David said. She shoved him back.

"Let me tell you where you can stick your rules..." Elsa signed.

"Rule number four no ugly behavior, rule...well I'll make them up as I go and do you know why you'll follow these rules? Because Lettie needs to be here, and you won't throw her to the wolves, she needs stability and care and so do you," David said. His turn of phrase about throwing them to the wolves, too bad he didn't know how close he was to the truth.

"You're not man enough to handle me," Elsa signed. He smiled.

"I'm sure no one qualifies to that standard, but I love a challenge," David said.

"Abrim is more than man enough. He's so much of a man I can call him the leader, maybe when you grow up you might equal to his pinky nail, until then drop dead," Elsa signed. She cringed as the pain shot through her arm from the jerking of her sign. He grabbed her and put her on the bed as he kissed her softly. She bit him and still he kissed her. She couldn't get away from him as she let her resistance down, and he held her close. She quivered against him and fought the tears, only one man saw her cry, and it wasn't this one. He pulled her face up, and she glanced away. He jumped off the bed and went back to the chair.

She woke to the smell of rain and turned against his bare skin. "Elsa are you in here?" She shifted beneath the warm blankets.

"What do you want Villanueva?" David asked. Elsa pushed the sleep cobwebs out of her mind, but they were thick.

"I was looking for Elsa. I thought this was her room," Manuel said. David's hand slipped up her back.

"This is my room," David said.

"I'm mistaken then I thought Elsa was in here," Manuel said.

"She's in here sleeping next to me. What do you want?"

"Nothing, it's one in the afternoon I thought she might be awake and…never mind," Manuel said. He left, and Elsa shoved David and stumbled out of the bed.

"Where are you going?" David asked.

"To find him, so he doesn't get the wrong impression." David winked at her as she left the room. Manuel went into a room, and she went to the door, but it was locked. She went back to David's room. He smiled.

"Back so soon?"

"His door was locked."

"Good he got the right impression that you're my woman." She moved to a far corner of the room and lay on the floor. He laughed. "People have been frightened of me for a lot of reasons, but never because I was warm, or they thought my kiss was hot. That's pretty damned good for an ugly man. Wait until I tell Beto." She turned her back on him and struggled to sleep. She slept through the night and through nearly a whole day. For hours, she fought the sleep, but the exhaustion overtook her, and she dreamed.

The birds called to each other in the night and woke her. She was back in the jungle, back in Mexico. Her mind brought her to this familiar place in the cemetery, in the land of memories and regrets. She walked through the rusty gates. Plain crosses made of wood, metal and cement. Proof someone living cared.

She stopped at Alicia's grave. She placed many flowers here over the years. She remembered her friend. Her nickname was Cia. She was the only one allowed to call her that to her face. "I still miss you my sister," she said.

They had become friends after Elsa had helped her friend get a doctor for the gassed people of the village. Alicia's baby boy had been one of the sufferers and Elsa had helped save Sam, even as they'd lost his sweet older sister Lila. Elsa tried everything she knew to help the girl, but it was no use. Alicia grieved for her dead child with Elsa and over that tragedy they bonded.

Alicia was like her father in many ways from her beautiful blue eyes to her stubborn will to take over everything. When Alicia Stein loved someone, she wouldn't be denied and that was the way it had been for Elsa, who had lost her own beloved Aunt. Elsa trusted no one and stayed to herself, but Cia wouldn't have it and over the next five years Alicia loved her. When Elsa decided to become a Fighter, it was Alicia, who encouraged her. There were no female Fighters, and teachers were not so hard to come by as many young men volunteered to teach Elsa in the Fighter's tradition, but Alicia didn't trust them at that time few people knew how to sign, but many a young man was willing to learn. Alicia decided her father was the only one to teach Elsa in the Fighter's way, and she found some way to convince him.

She remembered the first-day Alicia found out she couldn't speak, right at the same time her daughter died. When Lila died in Elsa's arms, her frustration overwhelmed her, and she waved her arms to communicate her helplessness, her failure and through her grief, Alicia stopped her. "You can't speak? You're the girl that's saved Juan so many times?" Elsa nodded as tears ran down her face. Together they carried the dead child into the house. The tears flowed and mixed into the dust on Alicia's grave.

Elsa had Alicia and one of the worst days of her life came when she discovered the butchered remains of her true friend. She had the sense to run back out and stop Juan from going into the warehouse that day. She sent him away, and she prepared her friend for her final trip home. She brought the coffin to the house, and she sent for the clan leader Alicia's father, Abrim, so she could tell him in private. She fought him to prevent him from opening the coffin, and he was three times her size, but she could never live with the pain her friend's tortured body would cause this man she respected and loved. When at last he stopped he wouldn't believe it was her, and she was forced to open the coffin and pull back the cloth to reveal Alicia's beautiful, bruised face and again, she had to fight him to keep him from tearing the coffin apart. The second fight she thought she'd lost, but as she cried for his daughter, he broke down in her arms, and he grieved with such force that all she could do was hold on.

She took him to his room after hours of misery, and he broke every object in the room, except for the bed. He was insane. No one dared go near him, much less spend any time with him, but Elsa remained with him for the two days before the funeral. On the day of the service, she went to him, and he was sullen. "It's time to go," she signed. He'd been the first one to learn to sign so he could speak to her.

"I'm not going," he shouted.

"You must," she signed.

"I said no!" he shouted. She slapped him.

"She deserved better than you! She deserved a better friend than me, but she loved us both, and I won't disappoint her ever again!" He towered over her.

"I'm not going!"

"I better see you by the time we get to the graveyard," she signed. He glared at her with his meanest eyes as she left. She went through the service at the back of the room, and she waited. The procession went into the graveyard, and the minister made his final pleas, and Elsa stopped him as they ready the coffin to enter the earth. She signed, and Juan called to the man. "She said wait! What for Elsa, he's not coming leave it alone," Juan said. Elsa ran back to the house, and she kicked in his door and dragged him out of the room. He pulled back and she punched him, and he fought her. She trained with him for five years, and he would do what she wanted.

She fought him all the way to the graveyard and when they got to the grave, she kicked him back and straightened her black dress.

"I'm sorry we're late, Alicia, but we...came to say good-bye," Elsa signed. She went up to the coffin and kissed the wood where her friend's face would be. She turned back, and Abrim was on his back. "Get up she can't see you like this." Elsa helped him up as the other members of the Fighters and his Second, and the village stared at them. She dusted him off and brushed his hair into place. She wiped the blood off his face and handed him his hat. She put serious eyes on him, and he looked as if he might shout at her or throw her across the graveyard. She grabbed his arm and dragged him to the coffin and pulled a rose from a nearby stand and gave it to him. With trembling hands, he placed the rose on the coffin of his only daughter as they lowered her body into mother earth. When the coffin stopped people dropped clumps of dirt into the hole, and Elsa leapt into the grave and crashed against the wood and screamed in silence. "I'm sorry. I'm so sorry!" she signed. Abrim grabbed her out of the hole, and she fought him to stay.

"No! No! That's not what she would want, she loved you!" Abrim shouted. He wiped the dirt from her face. "As much as apparently you loved her." He hauled her up and took her away. Elsa lay on the grave of her friend and her daughter and grieved like it was just a moment ago. The night was so still.

She forced herself to look to the end of the row. A new grave was added. Juan's name wasn't placed on the wooden cross. Abrim stood at the foot of his son's grave. Where had he come from? She went to him. The pain on the clan leader's face broke her heart. Tears washed down his face. The old man was alone. He came to visit his children, in this small place where his children should have buried him. She wanted to help him make it right, but there was no hope of that. She didn't let him see her. She went to him and held his hand. He didn't know it, but it didn't matter. "I miss you son. I wanted so much more for you. A family, lovely children and old age and a life well spent, but now you'll know none of those things. I pushed you to fight for others, to give and not accept defeat. I wish I could change all that now. If I could you'd be alive," he said. Elsa shook her head. He wasn't to blame, but he'd never accept any other reason. She kissed his cheek and left him to grieve. Juan's grave stood above the others.

"Go with God my dear friend."

Chapter 16 The Fates Visit

Splintering wood and shouts brought Elsa out of sleep. The tears fell as Lettie ran into the room followed by the other women. When they saw her they broke down. Lettie cried bitterly. "You've had a bad dream haven't you?" Lettie asked.

"It got be real bad do this her," Susa cried. Elsa got up as Nellie and even Bea sobbed. Mano came into the room. "Me gonna leave, not now, me stay." The other men followed him in as David pulled on a shirt. Manuel drew closer. She gazed into the blackness of his eyes.

"Mano I dreamed of Alicia, and I was at the grave, and it hurt so much, what have I done?" she signed. She rushed across to him, and his arms opened to allow her in and David stepped between. She shoved the giant as she gazed at Mano, who smiled.

"I don't believe she would want you to suffer, bebe," Mano said. She tried to get around David to him, but the big man would have none of it.

"When did you see my mother cry?" Sam asked.

"Not so long ago," Manuel said. He took her hands. "Alicia would be upset to know you blame yourself…for her death. She would never want you to suffer, she loved you." She got passed David.

"How can you know that?" Sam asked. Elsa leaned on Manuel's shoulder and he patted her back.

"Doesn't everyone love your mother, I mean those people who give her a chance," Manuel said. The evil enforcer comforted her, what a wicked twist of fate for him.

"Yes," Lettie whispered. David separated her from her prisoner. Beto came up to her.

"You shouldn't be so upset in your condition," Beto said. Manuel took her hands.

"He's right, all you should know is sweet love," Manuel said. He gathered her closer and his sweet scent wrapped around her like the softest of blankets. David shoved him.

"Get away she's having my baby," David said.

"Your baby, she can't stand you ugly man," Manuel said. Elsa moved to Manuel as his black eyes glittered with some secret. Her hand went to her stomach.

"She's having my baby, and she doesn't think I'm ugly I can work with that," David said. Mano drifted away.

"You don't know the first thing about dealing with a…monster," Mano said. Elsa eyed him.

"What monster I'll kill it!" David said. Mano turned back to her and smiled.

"You can't kill it because it's Elsa," Manuel said. Elsa sat at the table as Beto went to work on her arm. She watched Manuel leave the room. The others followed him out, and she stared out the window at the fading day.

She was alone in the room, and movement caught her eye. A cold hand sat on her shoulder. Old John stood behind her. "David come to this room now!" His voice echoed, and David appeared.

"Father?" Elsa turned to him somehow he could now see the apparition that once had been his kin.

"Yes, stop staring have you asked her to marry you again?"

"No, she refused the first couple of times," David said. He came up to them and placed his hands on his father's face.

"Look David in his eyes, there is no more pain, he is as he was when you came into his world, his body no longer riddled with the cancer, he is strong and well. What a gift to see him this way." John swept his fingers against her face and smiled.

"This is why you must protect her with your name and your power, who could ever see death and try to bring you peace my son?" David held tight to the man's arm.

"She won't do it. How can I help her if she won't let me?" John turned to her.

"You will marry him and accept his protection, and he will return the graves of your people and your little shack in the woods," John said.

"No, he deserves love and commitment, not me with all my problems and my…"

"Your hurt, he will not always be able to take that pain from you, but there will be moments when you will know peace because of him, and you're wrong you will marry him or he will go to Abrim and tell him who stole your only earthly possessions, and you will never know what they want from you," John said. She shook her head. John placed his hands on David's shoulder, and the giant's expression changed as he saw what the old ghost witnessed.

"Thank you father I will do as you say as I always have. We will marry within the hour, Elsa," David said. Elsa sank into her chair as John slipped through the wall and blinked away.

Raymond came around the bend, and the door to David's room opened. Elsa exited, and the family gathered around. Her eyes were grief filled, and her shoulders were slumped forward. Manuel Villanueva entered the foyer and David signaled for silence.

"Elsa and I were just married about an hour ago. Now under the circumstances we will limit the celebration. We are both very happy." David took Elsa's hand where a wedding band and a giant diamond glittered. Neither one of them looked happy. His shift was over, and he turned Manuel stared at them intent on seeing Elsa's

376

reaction. He moved passed and entered his room where he blinked to Gustavo.

"Elsa has married Gracia," Raymond said. Gustavo nodded.

"Sweet Mercy has graced the ugly man, but to her he isn't ugly, and he is a powerful warrior. What do you feel about this Raymond?"

"Nothing master, I see her unhappiness she was forced to do this." Raymond poured the wine and drank the red liquid and wished for it to be poisoned, but alas it was just wine, and he passed the bottle to Gustavo, who drank from the bottle. His brother shook in the corner from rage and jealousy.

"Well at least you can control what you feel unlike Alexander. The price for her compliance was the return of the graves and the shack that you and Alexander took, but what I want to know is how he knew this since only a few people know what happened. She was threatened with your and Alexander's exposure, and she took the sword through the heart to protect the two of you from Abrim Stein this may work out yet, go see how this happened," Gustavo said. He pitched the empty bottle at the fireplace, and Raymond tasted the next five bottles that would be needed.

Raymond blinked first to the cemetery and with him went all his black cloaks, Alexander, Gabriel, Felipe, Henry, Norman and the newest

Serferino Dorantes. The graves were back, and he looked across the field of stones and to his left stood an old man, and the old ghost laughed as he sat in the dirt. Raymond jumped at him and they went to battle with him, kicking and punching him, and he was as solid as they were and powerful beyond reason. They took their hits and the woman appeared to stand between them, and the old man stood behind her and grinned in his evil wicked way. She ran at them and he retreated to where her old shack was, and it too was back. Gracia had wrung out time to bring back her belongings, he was indeed powerful. The master was never wrong. They looked upon the faded structure, and his arm was clasped, and she looked into his eyes, and he jerked away. He sent the images to the master as he and his men ran through the woods.

Elsa moved up the hall with care. A week passed since Juan's death. She avoided David most of that time. She pushed open the door to the office. Melvin perched a pair of scissors over a package with a postmark from Mexico. She pulled her knife and drove it to his heart. Her hand stopped as David held it in place. "I should check that before you open it," Melvin said. She shook her head, and David removed her from the man. "Sir, I was just trying to…" Melvin said.

"I've expected a package from Mexico, and he kept it from me," Elsa signed. The man shook his head.

"She was about to gut you Hickory if she tells to run in a circle and squeal like a pig you do it! Don't ever touch her," David shouted.

"No sir there might be something dangerous in that package, that's all I was…"

"Out!" David shouted. Melvin scrambled away. Elsa glanced around the room.

"Juan wired Abrim's house," she signed.

"I'll get Wayne to check," he said.

"Make sure the two new ones aren't involved."

"I haven't seen you much," he said. She shrugged. "You're avoiding me, Beto reports you're arm is doing better." She nodded. He kissed her, and she tensed. He smiled.

The halls of the house were long and wide. The house was new and she did her job to keep the family comfortable. Elsa liked the many windows that gave a view of the property, but her favorite room was the sun room at the back of the house. Lettie liked it as well. Elsa came up the hall to the door of the sun room and Melvin peeped into the room.

Lettie was in the room, she was certain of it. She went back up the hall to where Nellie was and found Susa as well. "Come look at this," Elsa signed. They followed her into the hall. Susa started forward as Melvin bobbed around the doorway. Elsa pulled her back. "I'd wager good money that she knows he's there."

"Yeah she know?" Susa signed.

"Fighter Lettie is quiet, lately, but she was her father's very best. She could kill Melvin a dozen ways," Elsa signed.

"He's stalking her Elsa," Nellie signed.

"Yes, but not for the reason you think," Elsa signed.

"He doesn't want to bed her?" Nellie signed.

"That is not what I feel from him, there's something else. David's asking Wayne to check for devices, maybe you could help him with that," Elsa signed. She pulled Susa and Nellie away and went to her room. As Elsa moved away she thought Melvin would come to find trouble.

Lettie sipped the tea Nellie brought. So much was different. Juan was dead. Elsa was pregnant and married to David and Samuel the Crown Prince of the Fighters was her husband. She adjusted the notebook. She tapped the card that Elsa held as she looked out the window the black spade was worn on the card as if it had been shuffled many times. "Leticia, don't forget me!" The pencil froze on the page. She inhaled and the earth, the trees all the scents of home came to her. "Leticia are you listening to me?"

The jungle surrounded her. A tall, blond man with light, gray eyes smiled at her. The warmth of his love welled up in her. "Say you won't forget me," he said. Who was this beautiful, muscled man? She smiled.

"How could I ever forget you?" she asked.

"A prince could come and take you away," he said.

"Were in the middle of the jungle no prince will come here?"

"I want your promise," he said.

"I promise to try not to forget you if a prince should come to the jungle."

"I'm serious," he said.

"You won't be gone long."

"When I come home, I'll have a surprise for you," he said.

"I hate surprises and you know it." He held her close.

"Promise you won't forget me," he said. He smelled of fresh lemons and oranges. What was his name? She forgot, even his name.

"I promise," she said. She kissed him, and he tasted like sweet orange juice. He kissed her, and she felt safe. A moment later his kiss tasted different like mint instead of orange. She opened her eyes. The leader's son kissed her. She pushed him away. "No! Stop," she said. His blue eyes filled with anger. He had her shoulders. She struggled. Elsa pulled him away, and he disappeared beyond the door. Lettie adjusted her clothes and sat at the table. Elsa took a seat opposite her. Lettie poured them each a cup of fresh tea. "I'm different now," Lettie whispered.

"You've been through a lot."

"Yes, but I'm different inside. I see things, feel things in a new way," Lettie said. She gazed at Elsa. "I can see who you really are. I can hear you in my mind. David and Sam and Leo, Susa and Nellie they're like you." Elsa nodded. Lettie's hands trembled. "Can Samuel see what I think?" She held the cup of tea, and the liquid jiggled around. Elsa's breaths were strained.

"No, he can't."

"But you can and you haven't," Lettie whispered.

"I won't those are your private thoughts."

"Samuel would look if he could?" Lettie asked.

"I think he would, but I won't allow it."

"The day you came to me in the prison that's when I changed," Lettie said. She sipped the tea.

"Some people are born open, some closed. It's like a switch I think. I left a part of me with you so you wouldn't die, but by doing that you were opened."

"Can you take it back?" Lettie asked.

"No, when I was a child my Aunt Romalia gave me a part of herself, so that I wouldn't die, but I was born open. I knew you would live if I did it, but not what else would happen," Elsa signed.

"How many times can you do it?" Lettie asked.

"It only happens when it must."

"If Samuel and I don't work out…" Lettie said.

"Nothing about this will change."

"It would be better if I forgot everything about my life before now."

"Better for whom?"

"Everyone," Lettie whispered. Elsa stood and left Lettie.

Elsa sat at the desk and laid her head on her arm. She was so stupid. She made so many wrong turns. She rescued Lettie and she hadn't considered Lettie might love someone else. Lettie loved someone else and now she was going to have a child. Elsa was certain someone else loved Lettie and sooner than later he would come and there would be a war, the first of many wars for her young friend if the wolf clan remembered them.

Elsa changed her clothes and made a cup of chocolate. She removed the package from the safe. The Queen of Los Menos collected the items she requested. It was taken from Abrim's house in the village, removed from Juan's room. Only two people knew of the safe, she and Juan. She pulled the outside sleeve away.

The first thing on top was Juan's will everything he owned now belonged to her. She had even more money than she ever thought she would, and he was dead. The will had a date two days before his death.

The next item a ledger with names and amounts and a CD with all the information; all the names, she knew, but a few surprised her. Jose Marras' totals were moved to Lettie's name. She controlled all the accounts made for the people listed. The Cantu's names weren't listed. There was nothing for them. The rest of the names were for high-ranking fighters and those fighter's families. People that had been loyal from the beginning and The Cantu's should be here, why weren't they? She came to a brown journal and opened it to the first page.

She gazed at the lavish surroundings. She sighed. Nothing was the same. She tried not to think. The journal lay before her.

"I am a Doctor by trade and what you are about to read may seem incredible, even impossible, but I swear on my life it is true. For many years, I have kept secrets. For many years, I have lived in Hell.

A Hell of my own making, but Hell is Hell. When I was a young man, my sole desire was to become a Doctor, to save lives, to perform miracles, in essence, to be Godlike. Do not misunderstand; I did not want to be God. I just wanted some of his glories, and so I studied hard and saw my dream come true. In this place, I chose to practice I was a God for there were no others like me. I was the answer to

384

many a peasant's prayers. I could and did treat their children and many lives I did save, but…many lives I did take.

I am trusted and well-liked by all those around me. I was pleased with myself. In my conceit, I allowed myself to be taken in by a beautiful woman. She was a woman with no rival, and she did desire me and I her. I have heard it said the devil has many faces, and I find there is truth to that statement. For she became my tormentor, and I gave her my soul. In the last couple of years, I have asked myself one question, repeatedly, and it is this, Is there a God in heaven? Honestly, I can say, I do not know and so the opposite question comes to mind, Is there a devil? To this I can say, yes, there is. Yet another question, Are there Angels, of mercy, of light, of goodness? And I answer. I do not know. This query brings another. Are there demons from Hell that come in dead of night, to devour the souls of the innocent? To this I can say, yes, for I am one."

Elsa dropped the book on the desk and laid her head down. She was so tired, and she had fought the sleep too long.

"Cia wait!" The blond reached for Lettie. She kissed him.

"I have to go. Mama doesn't like it when I'm late. We have a guest," Lettie said.

"Here," he said. She placed the object in her pocket. "No, look at it now." She pulled it free.

A heart-shaped locket hung at the end of a heavy gold chain.

"What is this?" she asked. The heart locket took up the palm of her hand, and the dying light reflected off of it.

"Our future, I've the key. I'll show you later. Now go," he said. Lettie raced through the trees, all around her the scenery blurred.

"Leticia!" It was Mama, and she sounded worried. She was in trouble. She came to her worried Mother. "Find Papa quick!"

Lettie stared at her mother as she went into their home through the back door. Men in gray uniforms entered the front door. She glanced toward the fields they would never make it back in time. She decided to disobey her mother and go into the house.

"Where is the whore de las Almas?" Patricia Stein asked, "I know she's here! Lettie couldn't see her mother. She ran into the living room, and two soldiers pulled her back.

"She's not here, please we'll give you money...please don't harm the children," Mama pleaded. A slap sounded from the other room. Lettie counted the soldiers, three inside, and she didn't know how many were with her mother and siblings. Lettie jumped forward. "Wait please!" A shot rang out and Lettie leapt forward again, but the men pulled her into a chair and handcuffed her.

"No Mommy!" Elo screamed. Baby Jose wailed. Then two more shots and the butt of a rifle knocked her back. There were lights, then darkness and no sound. Screams brought Lettie out of unconsciousness. She jumped up. She was home. She ran to the next room. Elsa was on the ground next to her mother. Mama, Elo and baby Jose lay on the ground. She dropped next to them. She checked each one, but they were gone. She lay across their bodies and screamed. Their bodies disappeared and then the shackles held her arms above her head connected to a wall. A dim light beamed down on her. Photos of her father shot to death scattered across the floor. "I'll leave a part of me with you to give you strength." Elsa's voice echoed through the room. Elsa jerked backward like a doll attached to strings. Lettie turned her head, and the prison disappeared. Elsa held her in the room David had given her.

A gold chain and heart-shaped locket filled her hands. "The locket you gave me the other day. What is it doing in my hands, I hid it among my things?" Lettie asked.

"It is from your past," Elsa signed.

"My past…when? I don't have a past. I don't remember anything before you and coming here." Elsa smiled, and all was right. She was safe with her leader.

"Get some rest," Elsa signed.

"As you wish my leader," Lettie whispered. Lettie climbed into the bed and closed her eyes. She wanted just to sleep.

The exhaustion pulsed through Elsa as she lay on the bed. She gave in to the fatigue. She opened her eyes and sensed someone's need. In the dark jungle the birds were silent, and a strange glow lit the night. Two men stood against the light. One tall and thick of body, Abrim and the other not much shorter, but slender, Ramon his Second and the man married to Inocensia her dearest friend.

The tree limbs gleamed orange and yellow. Wood burning drifted in the air as she crept closer. The fire burned in the middle of a clearing. White-hot sparks flew through the air, like souls that escaped from Hell what an odd thought.

"You have news Ramon?" Abrim glanced at the man.

"What is this clan leader?" Ramon signed.

"Clearing some brush to build another house," Abrim said.

"You haven't slept or ate much since your return from Texas," Ramon said. Abrim stared at the flames.

"Do you have news or did you come to piss me off?"

"Patricia has gained power, much more since Alejandro's death. Since Juan's death there has been chaos on our side. She hopes to unite both groups with her choice for leader. Samuel is to be that leader. His reputation has grown over the years. Everyone is saying he should be the natural leader since; Juan is gone. It's the only thing people can agree on," Ramon said.

"Sam won't do it. He believes differently and he doesn't want this burden. He has never spoken the truth, but I know it," Abrim said.

"Patricia plans to force his hand by taking Elsa. She seeks revenge against you."

"She'll not take Sam…Elsa will kill her if she tries," Abrim said. His hands crossed over his chest.

"It'll come to that," Ramon said, "Patricia wants to keep this quiet. Samuel must not be a part of this. If he returns we'll be destroyed to the last child. She sends an elite force, the best of the death squads. They're few, but deadly my leader. You should go to Elsa." Abrim straightened.

"Will she send the Wolves?" Abrim asked.

"I don't know," Ramon said.

"Patricia's best are no match for Elsa. I'm more concerned with Patricia's best killer."

"Villanueva?" Ramon asked.

"I saw how he looked at her. That woman can bring a man to destruction."

"Yes, we've seen what Patricia can do," Ramon said.

"Not Patricia, Elsa can bring a man to do that which is against his will and his senses just to be with her," Abrim said. Elsa shifted.

"If you're so concerned you should go to her," Ramon said.

"Elsa doesn't want my help," Abrim said. Elsa moved closer so she could smell his scent, it brought her comfort.

"How can you be so sure?" Ramon asked.

"She said she hated me," Abrim said.

"Excellent now we're getting somewhere," Ramon said.

"I don't want her to hate me, second," Abrim said.

"Yes, you do, and if she says it one more time she's hooked. How many times has Inoc said she hates me and do you think she does? If she ever stops saying it I'll worry."

"You're a strange man. I don't ever want to hear her say it again," Abrim said.

"You should warn her," Ramon said.

"She'll know and act accordingly," Abrim said. Elsa moved back and walked into the trees. She turned back to the fire. On the far side, a figure separated itself from the darkness and traveled away from the old man. She watched it run through the night. The fire popped and hissed in protest. Her eyes closed as a wolf howled to another.

"What news do you have of Lauro?" Elsa turned and moved closer to the crack in the closet door. Oscar and Felix Dominguez stood by a desk.

"Shouldn't we go get Laura?" Felix asked.

"She moved away two days ago and she took Mimi, they haven't returned to the apartment," Oscar said. Felix paced.

"They disappeared?" Felix asked.

"No, they are two miles north of the store, they're paid up at the motel until the end of the month," Oscar said.

"And you know this how?" Felix asked.

"Just cause I'm not a cop doesn't mean I can't find things tell me about Lauro you found him?" Oscar asked. Elsa adjusted to see the big man, dark circled ringed his eyes.

"Well, there was a sighting of him going north on a bus, to Ohio," Felix said.

"Ohio, they don't know anyone in Ohio are you telling me that he ran away?"

"No, the woman that called said that she saw him with a young woman, he called Eva, but that Lauro was...drugged," Felix said.

"Did she give her name?"

"Yes, Sylvia Cantu, lives in Conroe and I checked it out, she's a nice lady. She was going to visit her aunt in Ohio, she said that Lauro was very uncomfortable with the young woman she thought it was all a bit strange and then she saw the billboards that you put up and recognized him that's when she called," Felix said. Oscar grabbed his coat and his brother followed him out.

"I'm going to get my family back," Oscar said. Felix nodded.

"About time, I'll call you if I hear anything else," Felix called. Elsa followed the car to the front of an old motel. Oscar got out and grabbed the bag of groceries he knocked on the door and it opened.

"Go away," Laura said.

"Not until you hear what I have to say," he said, "First I've loved you from the moment that I saw you move into the apartment. You can guess how disappointed I was when your husband came around the corner. I envied that man for fifteen years and I will for the rest of my life because you loved him and not me." Laura opened the door.

"I never did anything to make you think...I loved Ignacio, I still love him."

"I know, but you said you loved me, maybe not as much as..."

"I love you as much as I did him, that's why..." He pushed into the room and Elsa followed him. He put the groceries on the table and grabbed her up. He kissed her and Elsa turned around, after a moment there was no sound and she left them. She woke in the bed she should be sharing with David, but he was away again. His desire to be a hero was stronger than his want to be her husband. The sadness

392

rained on her and she gathered her pack and went to the door. No one was at the desk as she made her escape.

Elsa walked through the cemetery gates. She resolved to leave the house of Gracia and take the enemy and her problems away from the peaceful home and her Hunters. It took most of the day and into the night to make her escape. She had a key to the boneyard now, David had given it to her as a wedding gift, since this was his land, but she wouldn't break her tradition. Three bouquets of roses stood in front of the graves. The arrangement in front of Romalia's grave was a bright pink, different from the deep red roses placed in front of her parent's graves. She wondered who sent the remembrances. Few people knew of this place or her connection here. It would be a long time before she returned to spend time at home with her kin at least they were back in their place of honor. She sought to engrave the images of the stones in her mind so at least she could revisit the memories. She sighed and turned. Lettie, Susa, and Nellie stood behind her dressed in rags and old worn shoes just like her.

"I knew you were leaving and I went to Lettie and Susa," Nellie said. Elsa nodded.

"We not let you go lone. We help you," Susa said.

"Yes, we have transportation and supplies at least for a few days. It won't give us much time, but more than if we stay at motels," Nellie said.

"I'm not staying at that house when they find out you've left," Lettie whispered.

"They go nuts," Susa said.

"Yep, well we should get started," Nellie said.

"How do you know you weren't followed?" Elsa asked.

"The last time we saw them. They were working late. They don't even know we're alive," Lettie whispered.

"Did you send the flowers?" Elsa asked.

"No, Ma I was going to ask Nellie, but you've been sick, and I wanted to ask you what you wanted first," Lettie whispered. They exited the graveyard. The breeze blew the blooms edges gently.

"What a lovely place," Nellie said, "It's a good choice Elsa for your folks."

"Most people wouldn't describe a cemetery as lovely," Elsa signed. Nellie glanced at the flowers.

"We're all headed for a place like this. I say as long as you're loved, and you've loved someone else it's O.K. in the end," Nellie said.

"Who would guess anyone would meet in a cemetery at midnight. It was a good plan ladies," Lettie whispered.

Elsa gazed at her group. They were all in mortal danger because of her. Lettie grasped her hand. A tremor passed through Elsa.

"Ma, are you all right?" Lettie asked. Lettie placed her arm around Elsa's waist as they left. She glanced back as they passed the gates. Her little world was crowded. They followed the dirt road to a large object. Elsa discovered the transportation was an old recreational vehicle.

"We're traveling in this?" Elsa asked.

"We checked it and it's a good disguise," Nellie said. Elsa nodded as she stood back and examined the thing. All the women entered, and the door slammed closed. She ran back twenty steps. They were better off without her. She turned and ran twenty more steps, and stopped Patricia knew of them, and she would go after them and hurt them. Lettie had lost so much already she wouldn't abandon her now. She ran back to the RV and snatched the door open and jumped inside before she changed her mind. It was dark.

"Damn!"

"Run, Ma, it's a trap!" Lettie shouted. Elsa pulled both pistols and aimed at the shadow figures. The lights flashed on, and the shadows turned into the men of the house, and each held a woman captive, his hand over her mouth. "Bastard you helped him against your own mother!"

"Did you think we wouldn't notice you were gone?" David asked. Elsa glanced at Beatrice, she had been spying on them, and the red head turned away and glanced at the ground. She didn't like being left out of the circle of women.

"Why should you, all you ever do is work," Nellie said.

"Yes, we conduct business, but that doesn't mean we're stupid," Leo said.

"Just neglectful, different and yet the same," Nellie said.

"We're going back to the house," David said.

"I'm not, Susa drive," Elsa signed.

"Where are we going?" Bob asked.

"Not know, we see," Susa said.

"Tell me now," Bob said.

"You get out now," Susa said. She went to the front of the vehicle and started it up. Manuel lay on the floor. Eyes closed hands crossed over his chest beneath one of the beds. Someone had put him out. David had put him out. She touched Manuel's handsome face and sat next to him. The RV rumbled forward as the other women gathered on the largest bed and glared at the men.

Chapter 17 Hard Choices

Raymond made his third round of the night, and the house was too quiet. He checked the office, and the lights were on and the computers were lit as if the men and jumped up and ran. He turned off the lights and went around the corner and up the stairs, and Elsa's door was cracked open. He looked inside and all of her things were missing, and an empty gold envelope lay in the trash with a postmark from Mexico. He went back down the stairs, and Melvin looked at him. "The family has gone on vacation. We're to lock up and wait to be called back." Raymond nodded as he gathered his belongings and Melvin locked the front door of the mansion. Melvin went to his car and drove away. As the tail lights disappeared around a bend, Raymond jumped to the cemetery where Elsa's kin were, staged upon the ground were roses on the graves. He turned to look back, and the old ghost looked back. He gathered his men and went to find the master.

Morning found them at a standstill and Manuel was awake she stared into his dark eyes. The ladies were on the bed, and the men were arranged on the floor of the RV. Leo had his back to her. Bob yelped. Wayne pushed Bob. "Shut up, idiot."

"Uh, sorry boss…you're real ugly in this light," Bob said. Wayne moved around and started the chain reaction as the men tried to get out of each other's space.

"Stop breathing on me, you stink," Wayne said.

"You're not so fresh yourself, Reilly," Bea said. Manuel rolled her beneath the bed with him as the men got rough.

"Stop it, you're going to hurt, Ma," Lettie whispered. David shoved his way to her.

"Elsa where are you?" David shouted.

"She's right here Gracia sleeping next to me," Manuel said.

"Let her go," David snarled. Manuel emerged from under the bed with her.

"Good your awake. We're here," Nellie called.

"Where is here?" Sam asked. Lettie straightened her clothes and braided her hair.

"To our first destination of course," Nellie said.

"Does she have to be so cheerful in the morning?" Wayne asked.

"Not anymore than you have to be nasty. Go brush your teeth already," Bea said. Bob opened the door, and light poured in.

"Hey, turn off that light," David said.

"It's the sun boss," Bob called. David turned to Elsa.

"Tell me why this is important?"

"You can go back to your mansion anytime Senor Gracia," Elsa signed. David was the last one out of the vehicle. The rest of the group stared at their surroundings.

"You lead us to a pile of boards held together by dust and cobwebs?" Sam asked.

"In the middle of God knows where?" Bob asked, "This is where we ended up?"

"This El's home," Susa said.

"This is where you lived when you weren't with us? Did Grandfather know about this?" Sam asked.

"Yes, it was his gift to me," Elsa signed.

"Oh no, Grandfather gives great gifts, and he wouldn't give his best, most important…you boards held together with dust and cobwebs," Sam said. Elsa shrugged.

"He's been here and slept here," Elsa signed.

"Where did he sleep?" Sam asked.

"In my bed, in my room," Elsa signed.

Elsa opened the door, and Lettie followed her. "Hold on, this place looks like it's about to collapse," Sam said. The men entered the house.

"I can't believe you preferred this to our house," Sam said, "I've seen shanty houses better than this." Lettie gave him a look.

"Elsa I need a bathroom to brush my teeth," Bea said. Elsa pointed to the next room.

"What does it mean when a man buys a woman a bed?" Manuel asked. The others crowded around him as they stared into her bedroom. David pushed the others back so he could see, and Sam moved into the room.

"How do you know a man bought that bed?" Nellie asked.

"I know who bought it, Abrim Stein and I know because everything else in this house except for the owner is older than fifty years. This is new and expensive. Elsa won't buy shoes what makes you think she would buy a black mahogany king-size bed of imported wood?" Manuel asked. Nellie nodded.

"It's very lovely. A romantic man buys a bed for a woman," Nellie said. Elsa glanced at David, who frowned.

"I disagree a man buys a bed for the woman he's committed to, more than romance happens in a bed. A bed is for sleeping in quiet comfort, a bed to find solace in time of illness. A bed is a place to plan a future with a woman. It has a much deeper meaning," Manuel said. Nellie eyed the handsome man.

"A romantic you are Mr. Villanueva," Nellie said.

"You were right, Nellie," Lettie said.

"No ladies you've the wrong man," Manuel said.

"What woman wouldn't want a man who thinks of a bed in the way you just described it. Only a certain kind of man could come to the conclusion that a bed is an object to be shared with a woman, he intends to spend his whole life with no matter what," Nellie said.

"Not worry we keep you secret," Susa said.

"Not a soul shall we tell of your weakness," Nellie said.

"It's too bad that the one woman you wish to keep it from can see right through to your bones," Lettie whispered. Nellie left the room, and the other women followed her out. Elsa went to the window as the men left as well. Twenty minutes later Elsa approached the bedroom door.

"We can't stay here tonight. This place could collapse as we sleep," Sam said.

"If Villanueva says one more stupid thing I'm going to drop him off a cliff," David said. The big man frowned.

"I can speak to Lettie maybe she can help," Sam said.

"She's not speaking to you," David said.

"Move I'm going to check on Ma," Lettie whispered.

"Tell her were leaving," Sam said.

"Go on then," Lettie whispered.

"You're coming to," Sam said. Elsa went to the bed and sat down. The memories of Abrim's time with her came back.

"Ma, are you all right?" Lettie whispered.

"Yes, tell them I'll be out in ten minutes," Elsa signed. She pressed her face to the pillow where he had laid his head.

"Elsa, are you taking me back to Patricia? What are you doing?" Manuel asked. She didn't move.

"Elsa let's go now!" David said. She sat up.

"I just wanted a few minutes more," Elsa signed.

"I know so you could dream about that old bastard right?" David shouted. Elsa stood and went out and entered the RV. She sat on the bed as the others entered.

"Keep driving, Susa, what you need is inside the glove box," Elsa signed. She turned her face to the window. Lettie sat with her on the bed as the vehicle moved.

Night came, and Elsa sat among the women. Manuel was among her pretty little sheep, and the Black Wolf wasn't at all unnerved by their grace as they slept. Elsa stroked Lettie's face and moved the hair away. Lettie's face relaxed and she was in peaceful sleep, and Elsa knew the reason well. Elsa took the hurtful memories from her and pushed them so far down Lettie didn't remember them.

Like Leticia, there was another young woman Elsa rescued and left a part of herself with her, so she wouldn't die. Isabella was six years old and captured. The child had been taken to a place of evil where long needles were placed in her ears, and poison blasted into her. She found the girl nearly dead, but Isabella was a Hunter, and Elsa couldn't let her die. So she made the choice to employ the technique her aunt used with her. Isabella lived and Elsa returned her to her mother, Inoc, who herself was a Hunter and a dear friend. At the time of Isabella's rescue she didn't know they were all hunters only that the little girl couldn't be allowed to die.

Isabella's gifts or curses whichever one chose to see them were different than Elsa's and her gifts had to do with memories, retrieval of memories and a unique gift of erasing memories. When she applied her power to the girl, Isabella's power flowed back to her and with it, the ability to erase memories. Elsa adjusted the blanket on Lettie. Her aunt Romalia had shown her the ways of the hunters and had revealed the way the process worked. A hunter telepath passed his gifts on to his heirs. A powerful Hunter or Warrior could and did affect many generations of his family. Elsa's own blood line of Hunters ran through her aunt to her father's family through her. The gifts of a Hunter were often similar in families if a Hunter or Warrior could fly, then offspring would have that ability as well. As they grew in body they also grew into their own unique powers.

All this lead her to an interesting place, one she wasn't sure she wanted to visit. She gained her memory gifts from Isabella, who was Inoc's daughter and Ramon wasn't a Hunter or a Warrior, so Inoc's blood line was where the gifts came, and Inoc's mother was Maura and Inoc's father she knew well. She knew from the beginning who her father was and Inoc recognized another Hunter in her. It had been easy for Inoc to confide in her after she rescued Isabella. Where the two had been good friends before the rescue, they were unbreakable after. Inoc was Abrim's daughter with Maura; his child before he met Patricia, and he kept the secret protecting his beautiful daughter.

Abrim could erase memories, and he was a mighty Warrior, but they never spoke of it because Abrim believed in nothing but his own will. Abrim was a survivor at the highest level, and he taught his fighters to be that way. Do what it takes to win no matter what the personal cost. Do what it takes to live even when all they wanted to do was give up and die. To say he was ruthless would never cover what he was capable of, to say he was cunning measured nothing in his grasp of reality. That he would erase her memories she had no doubt, but for what reason?

Her stomach churned to think of the possibilities. She glanced up, and Manuel gazed at her. He wet a cloth and passed it to her. Her stomach heaved and all the food she had eaten crashed against the back of her teeth. Lettie came off the bed. "Ma!" She grabbed a bag, and Elsa heaved into it as another round overtook her. "I'll get tea."

"If your tea doesn't work I've something we can try," Manuel said.

"Don't try any of your voodoo tricks on her," David snapped.

"You practice the black arts?" Manuel asked.

"Yes, and I've some tricks you won't like," David said. The RV took a sharp turn and stopped. Susa ran over to them.

"You sick, me get stuff, give money, Bobby," Susa said.

"I better get a kiss before you ask me that?" Bob said. Susa wrapped him in a tight embrace and kissed him. She stood back and held out her hands. He gave her his wallet, his pocket change, his comb, his watch and his shoes. She looked through his wallet and nodded. She went to walk away, and he tapped her on the shoulder. She turned, and he grasped her in a kiss and then stepped back. She gave him back his wallet, his pocket change, his watch, his shoes and emptied her pockets. She had lint, two mints, a triangle-shaped coin, and she wiggled out of her bra and put it in his hands.

"Sorry, El," Susa said.

"Come let's see what I can buy you sweet face," Bob said. He shoved all the items she gave him in his pockets. The end of her bra hung out. They left hand in hand. Lettie brought her the tea and Elsa drank it, and it came up.

Manuel moved to help her, and David blocked him. Elsa's eyes remained on the Black Wolf.

"Just lie still or I'll have to use my voodoo on you," David said.

"Maybe its morning sickness," Manuel said.

"It's night time moron," David said.

"It can happen anytime," Manuel said.

"He's right," Lettie whispered. Elsa adjusted and closed her mind to all thoughts of Abrim. Thirty minutes later Susa returned with Bob. "We got stuff," Bob said.

"I smell burgers," Wayne said.

"And fries," Bea said.

"Yes, Susa said to buy you guy's dinner and ginger ale for Elsa," Bob said.

"You got lot girls?" Susa asked.

"Where?" Bob asked.

"You nice me think," Susa said.

"No, I don't have girls or even one. We should eat," Bob said.

"Me drive," Susa said. Elsa watched her friend's face as she went to the front of the vehicle. Bob put his hand in his pocket and sighed. Elsa sipped the cold drink.

Elsa stared into the darkness. When they came to the crossing to enter Mexico, she was ready and presented the papers to the guard. Abrim provided her specials documents that would get her through any crossing without questions and no searches. Abrim had contacts in high places, and it only took one phone call to clear her and her passengers. The others slept through the entire process, and they traveled on into Mexico through bad roads and lonely streets.

Susa drove and Elsa managed to sleep for a bit, but when the vehicle came to a stop, she woke. She went to find her friend. Susa leaned over the engine and looked up as Elsa came to her. "We out gas and engine busted. We followed for while me lost them for now," Susa said.

"How hard did they try to stop us?" Elsa asked.

"Hard, not get pass me, not got lot time. You tell them?"

"Yes," Elsa signed. They entered the RV, and Susa hit the lights.

"Need wake up, El want talk," Susa said. David was the first one up and then Manuel and Sam. The others came awake.

"Where are we?" Bob said.

"In Mexico," Elsa signed.

"What how did we get across without papers and…" Wayne said. The detailed man was law-abiding and only saw in black and white.

"I have ways, but we have a more serious concern," Elsa signed.

"It better not have to do with that old bastard," David said.

"He's neither old nor a bastard. I left your house because I am being hunted by Patricia's death squads," Elsa signed.

"So it does have to do with the old man. She wants you dead to seek revenge on him," Manuel said. Sam turned on the man.

"You should know her plans, no? Since you're her…what do they call you?" Sam asked. Manuel glanced at Elsa.

"I am the Black Wolf I am a Leader like you young Stein," Manuel said.

"No, I meant you're her bitch…her lover, if she wants a dog to beg at her feet that would be you, no?" Sam asked.

"You don't understand our ways Samuel," Manuel said.

"I understand you've whored yourself to please your Uncle and a whore is a whore, anyway you get him," Samuel said. Elsa stood.

"Watch yourself, boy," Elsa signed.

"Yes, my leader," Sam said.

"I hoped to leave on my own to spare you this burden," Elsa signed.

"Maybe you could beat them any other time, but in your condition as pregnant as you are, throwing up and no food. They will not take you alive, but they'll rape and torture you before you die those would be her instructions," Manuel said.

"Susa had to out drive someone following us, and now we're out of gas and the engines blown," Elsa signed.

"Don't ignore what I just said Elsa," Manuel said. He jumped up. She frowned.

"I haven't, but we're in the middle of nowhere with little supplies and a dinosaur to mark are trail. You can't tell me anything about the death squads I don't know. Tell me how to get rid of this vehicle without leaving a trace of it!" Elsa signed.

"Why didn't you tell me?" David shouted.

"Why didn't you tell me Susa, so we could do something before it was too late?"

"They don't trust us," Sam said. Elsa gathered her pack and a canteen and started toward the door.

"Why didn't you just stay behind in your evil little world and keep the Hell out of my life!" Elsa signed.

"Because you're carrying my baby, because…" David shouted.

"We could blow it up," Nellie said.

"No, they still know we stop here and follow," Susa said.

"Is anyone a magician in here cause that's the only way we're going to make this bitch disappear," Wayne said.

"Either way we have to move, we don't have enough weapons or bullets to fight a large group, so our only option is to run, Ma," Lettie whispered. Elsa nodded.

"Gather your packs and the canteens," Elsa signed.

"We don't have packs or canteens," Sam said.

"Yeah, because you were too busy doing your business," Lettie whispered. She walked passed Sam and she helped Elsa out of the vehicle, and they moved down the trail, and the other women followed. All the men joined them except for David. Elsa looked back.

"What's the boss doing back there?" Wayne asked.

"He said to go on and wait five minutes. He's coming," Sam said.

"What's he going to do fold that thing up and put it in his pocket?" Wayne asked. Elsa watched as the others moved away. She waited, and he came over the edge.

"I told you to go on," David said. Elsa waited until he walked passed her, and he came back and pulled her along and she jerked out of his grip.

Raymond and his men watched as Gracia crushed the old vehicle like a soda can. He had shrunk it down to the size of a coin and put it into his pocket. They waited until the group cleared the hill, and Raymond sent his men up the trail and down the dirt road. He erased any evidence that Elsa and her people traveled in this way, and then they moved tracking and following them to correct any little sign that showed the way. Raymond moved forward and stopped he held the others back as the group stopped for a break.

Elsa glanced around. The leaves clapped together in the wind. A bird called from high above. She brushed her fingers against the rough bark. This place was once home, still, it was her home. The leafy arms waved an invitation. "Where is Susa?" Bob asked. Raymond motioned the others to follow to the left and the right of the group, but they stayed far enough back to not be sensed by the warriors and hunters of Elsa's people.

"Here," Susa said. She had all five canteens.

"Where were you? We're being chased by killers, and you disappear?" Bob snapped.

"Nellie's gone," Leo said. Nellie ran up from a different direction with a white sack.

"I'm here," Nellie said.

"What's in that sack?" Leo asked

"Something Elsa asked for," Nellie asked.

"Tell me!" Leo snapped.

"You can kiss my English ass," Nellie said.

"There's an invitation I can handle," Leo snapped. Elsa put her hand on his chest to stop him. The only one of the women that stayed with the men was Beatrice Stone, she didn't fit in with Elsa's hunters, and the woman knew it and was resentful. Trouble would come from that envy, and Raymond vowed to remember for the future.

Elsa glanced at Bob and Susa. Tempers were running high, and the frustration was about to tear them apart. "You have to accept responsibility for this," Bob said. Susa wouldn't look at him. Gabriel took a step, and Raymond shook his head to hold his man in place. It was way too early to expose Elsa to them. "Damn it, Susa talk to me." Susa met Elsa's gaze and glanced down.

"Me know what me did. You know nothin'," Susa said.

"I'm sick of you. The last thing I need in my life is to be associated with someone like you…" Bob snapped. The anger filled Gabriel and spilled into Raymond's gut. His soldier stood in perfect stillness with fists clenched.

"What's going on?" Nellie asked. Bob threw up his fists.

"Not the truth," Bob said.

"What's the truth?" Nellie asked.

"I hate this situation. She's not even my type. Look at her," Bob snapped. Susa's fingers raced to her scar. She walked away.

"That was mean Bob," Nellie said.

"Don't start I don't want to hear any crap," Bob said. Nellie and the others paired off, but stayed close by. Leo went to Nellie, but she wasn't speaking to him. Lettie and Sam weren't speaking. Lettie handed Elsa a piece of bark.

"Chew it, it tastes bad, but it should help," Lettie whispered. Raymond turned to Felipe as he stared at the beautiful, quiet woman, the man's heart bled to see the red marks on her wrist, but he remained still and collected information by watching her.

"You're giving her bark, what the Hell is that, could it harm the baby?" David asked. Leticia gazed at David.

"I wouldn't give her anything to harm her baby," Lettie whispered. David's eyes fell on the quiet woman.

"It's my baby and I'll approve anything she eats or drinks." Elsa glared.

"How many women do you have Gracia?" Manuel asked. Elsa looked at the handsome man. Raymond too wondered why the Black Wolf hadn't escaped. Mother arranged to have him near Elsa, but the vain warrior needed Elsa's protection, and she held his pride in her pocket when she took him to see the last moments of his Uncle's death. Elsa broke the man like a dry twig.

"I have one that's fearful of my kiss because it's so warm. I have one that's afraid to hold me, so she doesn't get lost in my embrace. I have one whose nightmares I take away," David said. Elsa glanced down and turned from them. Alexander's energy came alive, and he hoped that he wouldn't have to put his brother out for jumping forward.

"Three more than I'd have guessed how much did they cost you?" Manuel asked. Elsa walked several steps away with her head down. Like he had any women, no one could ever tolerate his evil. A normal, regular woman wouldn't set eyes on him much less touch him. He was a fright.

"Nothing and there's only one," David said.

"She knows about your money?" Manuel asked.

"Yes, and it has no influence on her," David said.

"She's fat and ugly isn't she?" Manuel said.

"Oh, no she's beautiful and soft, and she smells like the sweetest gardenias in Texas."

"You better go after her an ugly man like you won't get a chance like that again," Manuel said. The arguments ceased as the couples listened to the conversation.

Elsa's face reflected the exhaustion, and she would take them to a Fighter's shelter. Mother warned them not to follow her into the mountain for they would never come out without her. Elsa moved forward, and David spun her into his arms and put a wicked kiss on her mouth. Alexander leapt forward and Raymond snatched him back, and put him out. The others gathered around to wait. Elsa gasped for breath, and Raymond turned. Thunder boomed and a strike of lightening lit the dark sky. David held her and laughed, as he looked up.

"Elsa's this woman you affect," Manuel said. Elsa disengaged, and Lettie took her hand. Manuel stared at her as she collected each of the women. Lettie collected plants and roots as they went and handed her a bark to chew.

"I'm better," Elsa signed. Raymond waited.

"No, Ma it's wouldn't have worked that fast," Lettie whispered. Elsa gazed at David, and he winked. Elsa walked with her head down up the trail and toward the mountains. Raymond reached down and hammered his fist into his brother's face, Alexander gasped as he came back from death. He yanked him up and they continued to follow the group, mending and fixing little displaced branches and rocks knocked aside as the travelers continued. They came to a stop, and Elsa moved into the mountain, and Raymond blinked back to Gustavo's office.

"You almost messed up," Gustavo said. Alexander shifted.

"Yes, master and we need punishment," Raymond said.

"So who wants to be first?" Gustavo asked. His slender hands lay in his lap.

"I'm the leader, I go first master," Raymond said. Raymond fell to his knees and bowed his head. The punishment slammed against his head like an anchor dropped from the sky. It rocketed with a force that left him convulsing and then the others came, but he took the first hit and gained the most power, his chest pulsed like a beast trying to escape from his insides. He inhaled as he listened to mother's black cloaks scream in madness.

Elsa made her way through the dark tunnel they were linked by grabbing the person's clothing ahead of them. She needed no light. She moved with purpose and arrived at a door. They traveled a whole day, and night would find them in a Fighter's shelter. "Ma is the only one who know the way out. Wandering even with a light could get you killed," Sam said. He was warning Manuel, but he didn't need to worry. The Black Wolf wasn't ready to escape. Elsa opened the door and stepped inside. She lit several lanterns, and their shadows cast across the wall as they crowded into the room.

Scattered throughout the area were beds. A stone circle laid out for a fire. A large wooden cabinet stood at one side. Its doors latched closed. "I'd eat dirt just to take a bath," Nellie said.

"I'm a better cook than that. Come on," Lettie whispered. She led them through another door. Water trickled in from one wall and gathered in a pool to swirl out another.

"It's an unusual bathroom, but it'll do," Bea said.

"It's quite convenient," Nellie said.

"The fighters chose their shelters in and around this mountain stream. It's designed for convenience," she whispered. Lettie lit several lanterns. The women finished cleaning up first and went back to the main area, and the men left to take their turn in the water room. Elsa started the fires and Nellie, and Lettie cleaned the rabbits Nellie had killed along the trail. They were placed in a pot with spices from Lettie's packs and wild onions and potatoes.

Elsa sat cross-legged and kneaded the cornmeal she packed and unpacked the cheese. She brought enough to hold her over for a little while, but with the additional people she needed to feed it would be enough for only one meal. She forced the dough into small balls. She set a griddle to heat a half-hour before her preparations. She produced thin circles that were tossed onto the pan. Nellie, Susa and Bea joined them as Lettie pulled a pot from the ashes. "It smells wonderful. I've never been this hungry," Bea said. An hour passed, and the men returned in old clothes found in the shelter that the Fighter's had left behind.

"It won't be long," she whispered. Lettie scooped two cups of liquid from the pot in front of her. She handed a cup to Nellie and one to Bea. Nellie took a sip.

"Tea…oh, it's so good." Nellie drained the cup and refilled it. She took the extra cup to Leo. She remembered her anger and spun back and sat down. Elsa glanced toward the men. They shifted in discomfort. She motioned

David over as she tossed another circle of dough onto the griddle. He sat next to her. She split open one of the breads, pressed a piece of white cheese inside. The tortillas were returned to the fire. A few quick turns and she had a half dozen on the griddle. As she snatched them back into her basket, others took their place.

She took a stack of napkins and wrapped one in each, these, she gave to him. "Pass these along," she signed. He eyed her. Elsa watched the men accept the offering. She turned to the women, who watched the men. The men looked for a sign of acceptance.

"Join us," Nellie said. Wayne marched across the room. She gave him a cup of tea. Sam joined Lettie.

"Come on fellows," Wayne said. Leo, Bob and Mano found places by the fire. Manuel arranged to sit on the other side of Elsa, and she passed him a napkin and he nodded. Lettie handed Susa and Nellie some extra cups, and the tea passed around and the meal served. "These are the best mashed potatoes I've ever tasted," Wayne said.

"Angel is a great cook even when I'm not starved," Sam said.

"When did you capture this many rabbits?" Leo asked.

"When you weren't looking," Nellie replied. She gazed at him.

"Did you strangle them," Leo asked.

"No I broke their wee necks," Nellie said.

"And I thought you were nice," Leo said. Elsa glared at Leo. He rolled his eyes.

With the meal completed and cleaned up, it was time for bed. Nellie and Bea turned the beds down. Elsa watched. She counted five beds and one thin cot. No matter how the math was done, the results would still be the same. Elsa glanced at Lettie. The food she consumed tumbled around and soon would be on the cavern floor.

"Here's how it's going to go for sleeping partners. Sam you got Lettie, Leo you got Nellie, Wayne you got Bea, Bob you got Susa. Villanueva has the cot, and I've got you princess, anyone who doesn't like the arrangements can fight me right now, any takers?" David asked. Elsa went to raise her hand, but Lettie kept her from volunteering. "Excellent, now do whatever mental exercise necessary to get through this lights out in one minute." Elsa gazed at Lettie, who handed her a fistful of bark chips.

Bea came to Wayne. "Which one is ours?" He pointed to the one in front of him. Susa stood next to the one by Elsa's and Bob came to stand by her. Elsa took her hand, and Susa nodded.

"Get in the bed princess," David said.

"I want to be on the outside," Elsa signed.

"Why?" David asked. Elsa's gaze shifted to Susa. "Bob's going to be on his best behavior, isn't he?"

"Yes, sir," Bob said. Elsa met David's gray eyes.

"Still, maybe it's best for the women to sleep next to each other Bob," David said. Susa climbed on the bed, and Bob joined her on the other side. David lay against the wall, and Elsa lay down. Manuel eyed her as she sat on the edge of the bed she would share with David, she laid back and the lights flashed off and Manuel's black brooding eyes were the last thing she saw. Elsa held her breath. The bed was small, and their bodies touched. David's scent dropped on her as his arms drew her close. She pulled to the furthest edge, but there was no getting away as he snuggled closer and laid his head on her shoulder.

Susa's sobs echoed through the cavern. Elsa swallowed the lump. "I'll trade places with you, Edwards," Manuel said.

"The Hell you will," Bob snapped.

"I don't mind being near Susa," Manuel said. Jealousy crushed Elsa's heart and she shivered. David's warm hands rubbed her arms.

"Are you cold, baby come closer," David said. He wrapped her in his tight embrace.

"I bet you don't. Forget it, she stays with me," Bob said. The loneliness closed in and Elsa's exhaustion forced her into a state of wakefulness. The sound of water rushing in the next room mixed with Susa's tears made for a mournful sound. It gnawed at her heart an unmerciful beast. "Don't cry, sweet face, I'm sorry, when I'm worried I say stupid things. I thought my life was good until you came along and showed me I had nothing, hush sweet baby, fall asleep against me," Bob whispered. Susa's sobs end, and Elsa approved of the man's gentle way with her dear, hurt friend. Sleep drifted to Elsa, and she followed it.

Tiny lights popped in Elsa's mind. She inhaled and pressed an urgent kiss to a willing mouth. His strong arms came around her, and she wrapped him in her love. She felt happy. She sensed home and all she wanted was to stay with this man. In his arms, in his warmth, to die in his love was all she ever needed. It was a dream, and her eyes were closed as she loved him. She couldn't open her eyes, and she tried to capture his scent it was like something so familiar, something she knew and loved and couldn't place.

Rustling papers, and gushing water woke her. The rustling came again stirred together with human's breathing in relaxed sleep. She shifted against David, and he sighed. His rain scent ripped across her and erased the memory of the scent in the dream, but the dream scent hadn't been of rain, no something else, and it was lost.

She searched the minds of her family. The next bed held Susa and Bob, and her friend slept in peace. Then Leo and Nellie, Wayne and Bea, Lettie and Sam and all slept. On the end Mano, his mind active and he wasn't in bed.

She appeared on a rock a short distance from where he sat. His back against the door. He rifled through her pack. He found the journal. He turned his sleeve down and several folded pieces slid between the pages. She pitched a rock at him. "If you needed money all you had to do was ask," she signed.

"I've never taken money from a woman," he said.

"Better to steal, than depend on a woman. Not very logical, but I'm not a man."

"I wasn't stealing? I was…" he said.

"I expect to find my things in order, goodnight, Mano." A flash to his right caught his attention and when he looked back she was gone.

A howl stirred the early-morning air. Elsa was on a road. The bare and worn ground from the feet of many travelers lay ahead. The jungle spread out on either side. The underbrush and trees twisted into a dense, murky barrier; a place to hold peering eyes. She walked up a hill. The rutted road cut through to the horizon. The howl of a wolf pack called to his brothers.

Elsa started down the hill. As she took to the road, ghosts moved passed her and materialized into people. From behind her, they came to join in the exodus, the road to the future. She appeared to these travelers, an old, hunched back woman. Her wrinkled, brown skin spoke of life's hardships, experiences seen through ancient eyes. She leaned heavily on a knotted staff. She observed from her position, unnoticed as one of the many.

A young couple moved ahead of her. The man took his lover's hand with tenderness. The woman smiled. "How much longer do you think we'll have to go?" she asked.

"Are you tired of walking so soon, my love?"

"With you by my side I'd walk to the end of the earth," she said.

"You say that now, but I'd have to carry you most of the way." She nodded.

"Not carry me, but I think I should have to lean on you to complete such a journey."

"I'd gladly accept that burden," he said.

"I've heard this new place is wonderful. There's plenty of food and a safe place to sleep and doctors. Do you think it's true?"

"I wonder what it's like to sleep with both eyes closed."

"To never know the gnawing hunger. To watch our children grow in peace. It sounds like Heaven, doesn't it?" she asked. Elsa bobbed her gray head in understanding.

"You have to die to go to Heaven," he said. Elsa hobbled ahead of them and pushed the young man aside.

"Look, Enrique an old Mother. She's the first one I've seen in days," the young woman said. Elsa stopped and took a ragged breath. Enrique guided her from the traffic. The young woman's name was Ana.

"Ana, give her some water. This is a hard trip for an elder," he said. Ana poured her a cup of water. Elsa refused their assistance. Ana grasped Enrique's arm and nodded in her direction. "I meant no disrespect, wise one," he said. She eyed them. Ana helped her sit. She accepted the cup and smacked her lips in satisfaction.

"Good, thank you, daughter," Elsa said. Her voice was back. Ana patted her back.

"Do you think only the young want a better life?"

"No, but it's a long, hard walk," he said. She waved him off.

"I'm as able as you and much wiser. I know how to address an elder," Elsa said. She ambled down the road. They raced after her.

"Please old Mother, Enrique meant no harm…it's just few of us live to be as wise as you," Ana said. Elsa patted Ana's smooth, olive cheek and smiled.

"You were brought up right. You could learn something from this gentle woman, boy," Elsa said.

"You don't move like an old woman," he said. Elsa slapped him.

"My dead husband dared not be so bold. I'd have laid my life down to give him, but one more breathe. You, boy won't disrespect me," Elsa snapped. She took Ana's arm and moved along. He was right, no old people.

"How long have you been on this journey?" Elsa asked.

"For a few months, since the end of August," Ana said.

"What day is this?" Elsa asked.

"Monday, November sixteenth," Ana replied. Elsa considered the date it was August twenty-nine in her world. The crowd bottlenecked, and they were forced to stop. The line inched forward, and the young were taken through a series of gates. They came through the entrance. Ana and Enrique were allowed through. Elsa approached the gate. The guard glarcd. "You can't come in," he said. IIe wore a gray uniform with the militia's insignia. One of Patricia's death squad.

"Why can't I?" Elsa asked.

"Find another place to beg old woman," he said.

"I haven't come to beg. I want to make the trip," Elsa said.

"What use would anyone have with an old woman?" he asked.

"Why am I not allowed to continue?" Elsa asked.

"There's no place for the old where they're going. The young and able are the future. Your time has passed," he said. Elsa watched as the people pass out of sight. She turned from the gate and went back to the safety of the cave.

A wolf's howl cut through the silence of her mind. From the darkness, a wolf pack charged. She waited with patience. A few feet from her they leapt into the air and turned into men in gray uniforms. She raised her arms, and an invisible barrier encircled her. The men dropped upon the ground and snapped at the air. She watched the primal hate glow in their faces. "Give us back our brother," they called.

"He belongs to me," Elsa signed. The leader of the pack stood and motioned the others to stillness. The head of a green snarling wolf lay on his coat. Chino Del La Rosa.

"We'll get him back," he said.

"You'll have to come through me first, Green wolf."

"If it's necessary," he said.

"It will be, prepare your clan, for mine will serve yours death," Elsa signed. She dove into the black abyss and returned to the cave. The sound of water lulled her to sleep.

Chapter 18 Brown Journal

It took most of the day to find their way out of the caverns. They arrived in the city as the sun set. Elsa's feet hurt. Nellie was sick with a cold. Lettie treated her, but still Nellie was miserable. The nausea persisted, and the discomfort plagued Elsa as they came into the town through back roads and alleys. The dark shadows concealed people in a hurry to be somewhere else. Sam led the way. Leo was in front of Nellie. They walked with care, and no one questioned them.

Sam took them through the worst alleys. In every shadow lurked the hidden, discarded people, living on whatever they could. The smell of urine and rotted food floated around them in a fog.

They came out to the main road and kept against a once white stone building. Green mildew grew on the brick. The walls splattered with a variety of yellows, greens and browns. Grass took root in the buckled sidewalk. They passed people lying in doorways. The smell of dirty bodies mixed with those of rot. Elsa stepped over a man. He snored and drooled as he held a picture frame. A family smiled at her from a yellowed photograph. Nellie pulled out of Leo's grasp. He yanked her along as a boy came to her. The child pulled on her shirt. "Please beautiful lady…I'm hungry, give me money?" Nellie dragged her eyes from the sleeping man to the boy.

"Money?" she asked. His clothes were torn and stained. His thin, dirty face was bruised and his scrawny body trembled in the cold night air. "Where are your parents?"

"They were killed…please…anything you can spare," the boy said. Nellie searched her pockets.

"Don't give him anything," Leo said.

"I have to," Nellie said.

"I said don't give him money," Leo snapped. She lost her temper.

"You can't tell me what to do. It's my money. I'll do what I want." Nellie emptied her pockets.

"Please don't do this, baby," Leo pleaded. The desperation in the boy's eyes moved Nellie to dig out every last penny. It amounted to four dollars and thirty-four cents. Terror filled the boy's eyes.

"Don't worry I won't let him hurt you. Get something to eat," she said. Nellie turned to the others. They stopped to watch the boy cross the street.

Elsa stood next to her. The boy placed his hand on the doorknob of a small, white restaurant. A man, dressed in a black uniform slammed him against the nearest wall. Nellie stepped off the curb. "Give it to me," the man demanded.

"What?" the boy asked. The man smashed his fist into the boy's face. Time stopped for Nellie as the man brutalized the child. The man slammed the boy onto the pavement and searched his pockets. He took the money she gave the orphan. The man glanced at them and kicked the boy. Elsa held her in place.

"Do something…call the police," Nellie pleaded.

"He's the police," Leo said. Nellie turned to Elsa, who watched the scene unfold. "We're not in the States," Leo said.

"It's not the country, but individuals who cause harm. We can't judge everyone by this man," David said. A young woman, barely a teen came to the man. She took his hand and pulled his attention away from the boy.

"Who is she? His sister?" Nellie asked. Leo shook his head.

"She's a prostitute," Leo replied. Nellie stared after the girl.

"No, she's just a child." The man slapped the girl. The girl smiled and pulled him to a house. Nellie trembled. The fallen boy was so still. His blood dripped into the dirt. She leapt forward, and Elsa hauled her back.

"Help him," Nellie said. Elsa pushed her back. "If you're afraid I'll do it. How can you be such a ruthless bitch?" The defiance blazed in Nellie's eyes. She stepped off the curb. Elsa pressed her to the ground. Hate raged in the blond woman's eyes.

The anger and desperation rose in the gentle woman. "Nellie, listen, please stay down. When Ma pulls you up don't resist. It's very important," Lettie whispered. Nellie's expression changed. Elsa yanked her up and brought her fist down and arranged to miss her. Leo grasped Nellie's arm. "Bring her," Elsa signed. Elsa took the lead and went to a nearby church. She approached the altar. An old priest turned.

"Confession begins in an hour, my child," the priest said. Elsa pulled her gun. "I can make an exception of course. The confessional is this way," the priest said. She shook her head and nodded at Lettie. Elsa wrote on a piece of paper and included several hundred dollars. She pressed them into his wrinkled hand and stepped to the altar to place an additional hundred in the worn, brass plate. She motioned to them to leave. "Go with God, dear One," the priest called. She turned to him as a tear slipped free.

"May He protect you Father," she signed.

An hour passed and Elsa took them to a set of rusty, wrought iron gates that had once been black. A fence circled a large cemetery. The gate squealed as she opened it. Among the stones were the devotions of the survivors of the dead. Wives and husbands, sons and daughters came to pay respects to those passed from this life.

The small blessings of life served to the dead in their final resting-place. Flowers of plastic, statues of the Virgin Mary and Christ stood by wooden crosses and makeshift markers. Plates that once held meals now littered the ground. Bottles of beer and tequila left untouched. Candles burned in memory for those gone to a better place. She could almost hear the silent prayers sent into the wind for angels to hear. The words and sentiments of ordinary people and the humanity of the living came to this place of death.

She led them to the back and the grave of the unknowns. The earth carved into a big hole. Susa pressed the others back, and they hid in the underbrush it choked everything in its grip.

Another hour passed when they heard someone approach. Two young women came toward them. "I hate this."

"What can we do?" said the shorter of the two. The taller one adjusted her short skirt.

"We could be making money instead of dumping dead children. I think it's time for me to move on," the tall one said.

"Go ahead, you won't find a better place. At least, she feeds us," the short one said. She pulled on the garter holding her stocking's up.

"You've been a whore too long, you don't know what good is," said the tall one.

"I've sold myself long enough to know she treats us well. I was sorry to see Adagilberto killed. He was a nice boy."

"You fight the devil you should be more careful, but he was a good kid," said the tall one. The short woman glanced around.

"Let's go, this place gives me the creeps. I feel like someone is watching us." They swung the sack-covered body into the hole, and the body landed with a thud. The tall one shoveled white powder over the sacks and dusted her hands.

"Who would be out in the middle of the cemetery in the dead of night…except for the dead," the tall one said. The short woman pushed her and started to walk away.

"Don't say things like that, it's bad luck."

"Yeah our lives are perfect. Bad luck, huh? Least we'd have luck. Come on, the police chief is going to wake up soon. We want him to think he had a really good time." They laughed as they moved into the night and out of sight.

Nellie cried. Elsa pulled Nellie to the open grave and climbed in to dig through the layer of lye and listened for the child's heartbeat. She hauled the sack to the pit's edge. Leo and David pulled it out.

"He's still alive," Elsa signed.

"Lettie check him," David said.

"He needs more than I can give him out here."

"Bring him, Sam," Elsa signed. She glanced at Nellie and walked out of the cemetery. They traveled into the jungle, and she called a halt. She removed the cloth that covered the boy, and Lettie came to his side. She cleaned his face as he came around. Nellie stroked his blood-matted hair. Elsa tapped Lettie's shoulder.

"Let's go," she signed. Nellie ran after them.

"We can't leave him," Nellie whispered. Elsa raised her hand. Nellie cringed. She lowered her hand and frowned. Elsa settled on a spot and sat. The boy moaned and cried. Nellie bit her lip. Leo caressed her hand. It went on for an hour when the brush across from them parted. Two figures stepped into view. They wore brown cloaks with hoods their faces hidden in the shadows of the rough fabric. They went to the boy and examined him. Within moments, the crying ended and the larger of the two lifted the boy. Elsa stood and stepped across the clearing. The hooded figures turned to her and bowed. She signed, "Go in peace, my friends."

"Who are they? They look like grim reapers," Bob signed. All of David's people now read the sign, the change came with Samuel's transfer to David.

"Los Menos, people of the dead. Their Queen is stationed at the brothel," she signed. She walked into the night.

Samuel located another shelter. A meal prepared with fresh meat, but nothing was right. Elsa sat in a corner, eyes closed. She moved to her pack and took out a container of ointment and some bandages. She approached Nellie with care. Leo glanced at them. Her big friend was becoming attached to the gentle woman. She applied salve to Nellie's scraped hands and elbows.

Nellie's hurt cut through Elsa. Her wounded heart brought Elsa back to her senses. Often she had to set aside her kindness in order to do her job. She placed the ointment in Nellie's hands.

"I couldn't do what you felt was right. They would have murdered you. It's hard to understand, but you must trust me. You need to live so you can help those that need you the most."

"It's my fault that…" Nellie whispered. Elsa drew a breath.

"As strange as this may seem…your kindness gave me a chance to free him from that life. The chief of police thinks he killed another beggar," she signed.

"But he wasn't…will they feed him?" Nellie asked.

"Yes and he'll be safe," she signed. Nellie swallowed. She rose and went back to finish the meal.

Mano glanced at her as she passed. "How do you do that? You make her care for you with

434

your rough ways. What's a powerful tool, too bad you use it for good."

"Don't test me Villanueva, you'd be hard-pressed to find me in a worst mood," she signed. She went to a bed.

The following evening they traveled in the jungle. Elsa spun and searched the woods. "Prepare yourselves." They jumped into position, but as they came around men in gray uniforms surrounded them. A snarling wolf head graced the right shoulder of his jacket. The green wolf stepped up. Lettie gazed at him and looked away. He remembered her from the apartment in Mexico City.

"We've come for our brother. We've no quarrel with you fighter woman. All we want is what is rightfully ours," the green wolf said. She tilted her head and searched the man's soul. She signed to Leticia to translate, even as he could read her sign.

"He's mine, Chino Del la Rosa. The Black wolf belongs to me."

"He was born to our clan. He'll remain with us until his death," Chino said. He crossed his arms and searched Lettie's face.

"Or at least until you die. You don't give a damn about your clan rights. You want to return him to the whore you've allowed to lead you," Lettie whispered. Chino stared at the beautiful girl. Elsa raised her gun level with his face and signed with the other hand.

"My leader, says you'll never take another breath if you try what you're thinking," Lettie whispered. Elsa realized the girl looked the man in the eye as she spoke for her. She signaled Susa to bring her pack and pulled the brown journal out. She signed.

"What am I thinking?" the green wolf asked.

"I've something more valuable than Villanueva. This book can prove Patricia's involvement in many things. I'm sure she would be very thankful to receive it," Lettie whispered.

"No! I'll go," Mano said. Chino flipped through the book.

"On page twelve, twenty-seven, and forty her name is written. Pitch it to him," Lettie whispered. Elsa raised her arm, and Mano jumped at her. Nellie caught the book as Susa came around and kicked the man. He bounced back and attempted to fight back. Bob aimed. Susa brought her gun around and kept him on the ground.

"You've no idea what you're doing, de las Almas. The journal is worth more than any life. It's the equal of many perished lives…it'll give Tricia more power…please," Manuel said. Elsa nodded to Susa to toss the book to Chino. "Damn your soul to Hell Elsa!" Chino glanced at the man on the ground. He opened the book and found the name on each of the pages she indicated.

"I'll take the trade," Chino said. He signaled the other wolves to follow, and they disappeared into the trees.

Elsa came to Manuel and held her hand out. His face was a mask of rage, and he lunged. Her foot connected with Manuel's jaw. He rolled away and jumped to his feet. The fury danced in his black eyes. She smiled, "You want to kill me? Then kill me," she signed. Manuel lunged and each time he missed, but she never did. He came in for the last time, and she finished him off, with a jab to the face. His head snapped back, but he had the opportunity for a solid push, and she flew into a tree.

Elsa felt David's mind react, and he pulled her back before she smashed into the tree. For a brief moment, she hung in the air and then dropped gently on the ground. His eyes sparkled with unrestrained power. She dropped her gaze.

"We need to make camp," Lettie whispered.

"Not in the open," Nellie said. Samuel yanked Manuel off the ground. He led them to a place that faced the mountain. They set up camp and Elsa placed herself next to the unconscious Mano. They didn't bother with a meal. She ordered them to sleep. As they slept, she untied the prisoner and sat back. Her wait was short as he sat up .

"Why didn't you kill me?" he asked.

"I still have use for you."

"You should have let them take me," he signed.

"She would kill you."

"She loves me, besides, she has need of me in ways she doesn't even know yet."

"You're faith in her is misplaced," she signed.

"I should place my faith in you. A woman who can't speak and whose leader is dead?" he signed.

"My leader isn't dead Mano," she signed.

"The old man is your leader your trust is misplaced. You're lost without that book."

"Never underestimate me, Black Wolf, most everything that happens is because I plan it. I bid you goodnight." She moved next to Lettie to wait.

Morning arrived on the wings of jungle birds. Elsa waited and as she thought of how Mano made his escape, as she pretended to sleep. He watched her face long moments before he left. He needed to leave to make his next move, and she was certain he wasn't done with her just yet. Sam sat up next to Leticia. These people were his family. This ragtag group of ten he would die for. He stretched and took several steps. He spun to search the sleeping faces. One was missing, and Elsa remained prone as he came to discovery.

"Gracia!" Sam shouted. David sprang off the ground, gun drawn. Elsa sat up and watched them.

"What? Are you trying to give me a heart attack?" David asked. Samuel stomped around in a circle.

"Can you count, Gracia?" Sam asked.

"You call me like that to ask a stupid question?"

"Answer it," Sam said.

"You know I can," David said.

"Count the people in our group," Sam said. Wayne and Bob looked at them as David counted. He turned to Sam.

"Villanueva's gone. Why didn't you tell me sooner?" David asked.

"We have to go after him, David. If I'm right, he's going after the death squad to bring them to us, but if we intercept them and defeat them away from the women, then we go back to Texas. I knew he was going to try. Villanueva is the leader of the death squads. He knows how to find them, and that's how he knew what the plan was for Ma," Sam said. Her son was so much like David. The older man could have been his father, except that Alicia only had one love in her short life, and he was Miguel Najeno Trevino.

Samuel wasn't like his quiet, unassuming father. Elsa hoped that as he grew into a man, he would become more like his father, but Samuel was much like Juan, bold and brash. Miguel would never have chosen Alicia for one thing he was ten years older than her, not that he couldn't see the beauty in Abrim's daughter. Miguel could never imagine himself to be graced with such a love as hers. Alicia had other ideas and when Alicia Stein loved someone, they couldn't escape her. She fought her father and brother to be with the only man she ever had the chance to love. Elsa was grateful for her friend's stubbornness because of her, she and Abrim had Samuel to love and now Abrim would have a new great grandchild to adore him.

David trusted Samuel, which was an accomplishment since he didn't even trust her and Samuel too placed his faith in this stranger. She turned to Lettie and put a bark chip in her mouth. "If given a choice, I'd prefer to take the battle away from the women," David said. Elsa sensed the tension rise, in someone. Leticia's face reflected calm, but her heart spoke a different language. She didn't like this situation.

"We'll all go," Nellie said.

"I agree with David," Wayne said.

"We're all going. We're as capable as any man," Nellie said.

"Let's leave your pride out of this. This is a man's job," Wayne said. Elsa cast her gazed at Nellie, and she backed off.

"What if this is a trap to separate us from the women?" Leo asked. Elsa never doubted Leo he was always ten steps ahead.

"We'll be fine," Nellie said. Leo squeezed Nellie as he and the other men gathered.

"We'll be back as soon as possible. If you need me, you know how to get in touch. I'll be back so we can go home Elsa," David said. The men ran through the trees. Elsa brought the women to the business of living and to find their way until the men returned.

Raymond entered the office. He followed Antonio into the master's office. The boy had yet to provide any results for the master and Gustavo asked him to guide him. The problem was that Antonio knew it all and there was no room for any improvement. "Master, we have a plan to yank the first of Elsa's threads." Antonio frowned.

"It's got to be a stupid plan if you came up with it," Antonio said.

"I was the one that came up with the plan, Master Gustavo," Henry said. The giant was a powerful man and more than willingly to gain more power if he could. These new black cloaks would be part of mother's food chain, and if they survived would work well with his plans for the Hunters. Antonio shifted.

"Now I know the plan is stupid. Go on bore father with it."

"Most of the threads that lead to Hunter Elsa are with her, some are scattered, but this thread is a very strong one," Henry said, "You see her connection to Isabella Maldano is as strong in both love and power. Right now, the girl is out of the physical circle."

"Your plan has to do with my Isabella?" Antonio asked.

"She would not claim you if you were covered in diamonds and dripping with gold," Henry said.

"I say that we have a challenge master, to pit one black cloak with another to see who is right," Raymond said.

"I will give a powerful wish to the winner," Gustavo said.

"Then I will take this challenge master," Henry said.

"So will I, so what is the challenge?" Antonio asked.

"The challenge is to get Isabella to accept comfort, food and drink," Raymond said. Antonio laughed.

"Get ready to lose giant for no one knows Isabella better than I do," Antonio said. Gustavo stood, and they appeared on a small dirt road. An old wagon sat by an old building and Isabella loaded the vehicle with old shoes and boxes. Antonio leapt into the dirt and snatched at Isabella.

"Stop working you're going to eat and drink for me!" Isabella leapt out of his way, and Antonio chased her around the wagon.

"Leave me alone!" He countered and caught her, and she screamed. She raised her arms, and Henry jumped to her rescue. He separated them, and Antonio yanked his knife free and Henry got into the way of the blade and it slashed against his forearm and blood gushed out. Isabella pushed Antonio away and the evil little man grabbed her, and Henry roared to life. This time he sent Antonio sailing through an old building and went after him. Gustavo jerked his son back next to them, and Antonio protested. Gustavo back handed him to the ground and glared down at him. The younger man got up and stood next to them. "Come here giant please," Isabella said. Henry came over to her, and she ripped her dress to stop the bleeding.

"I didn't need your help, now look what you've done."

"It wasn't right that he hurt you, lady," Henry said. She sat him on the end of the wagon and proceeded to do the repairs. Her stomach growled, and Henry frowned. "You're hungry."

"Many people are hungry. What is your name, I am Isabella."

"Henry that is what I am called."

"An English name I like it," she said.

"Where is your family?" he asked.

"Far away, I miss them," she said.

"I bet they miss you, does your man know you're alone in the middle of nowhere?"

"Are you looking for a woman?" she asked. Gustavo jerked Antonio back, and Raymond smiled at the giant of a black cloak at a loss for words. He pulled his arm back.

"It would depend on the woman," he said.

"How about me?" she asked. Gustavo smacked Antonio hard.

"You, it's not nice to tease a giant. I know how the women look at me and they think I don't want him, think of all the large-headed children he might give me." Isabella laughed.

"You don't frighten me, and you smell like those little vanilla cookies that they give babies," she said. He grabbed his pack and pulled out a thermos.

"I smell like baby cookies? I'm dying for a cup of coffee. How about you?" he asked. She smiled.

"Yes, but I can't take your stuff," she said.

"It is because I am an ugly giant yes I hear that all the time as well," he said. He held a cup out to her, and she took it and he filled it with the steamy brew. She drank it. "You need to eat I make very strong coffee." He passed her a roll of bread stuffed with meat. She took it and sat next to him and ate it and drank the coffee. He refilled her cup and passed her another bread roll and meat. Antonio hissed like an old tire losing air and Raymond smiled.

"It's very good, thank you. Was that a yes or a no about the woman thing?" she asked. He emptied the thermos and handed her the last bread roll with meat.

"I'm a complicated man see," he said.

"Then that's a no, well I tried, now you must promise me not to fight all the time. A man of your size could be put in jail for beating people down," she said. He got up.

"We just met five minutes ago. Why should I make promises to you?"

"Because you won't like me if you don't and I'll know don't let me hear that you've done it," she said. She dropped the last of the boxes on the wagon.

"When are you going home Isabella?" he asked.

"I don't know," she said.

"I promise not to fight if you go home to your family," he said. She smiled at him and leaned up to kiss his cheek.

"Deal, but it won't be for a few months that I am really home." He nodded, and he put her up on the wagon seat. She waved and drove away. Raymond brought them back to Gustavo's office.

"Very good Henry, better than I could have even dreamed, so you won, what is your wish?" Gustavo asked.

"He cheated father. Raymond helped him," Antonio said.

"Master Raymond did help me, he said that I should consider my goal and find out that which no one else can provide, and that's what I did for…Isabella," Henry said.

"Isn't that the same advice that Raymond gave you Antonio?" Gustavo asked. Antonio stomped away. "You can wait on your wish Henry if you like."

"No, master I know what I want and that is for Isabella to go home as soon as possible," Henry said.

"And how do you think I can make that happen?" Gustavo asked.

"By yanking harder on the thread that belongs to her," Henry said. Gustavo nodded.

"Indeed you wish me to drive her home," he said.

"Or put her in a position that Elsa will not allow," Raymond said. Henry thought.

"She will be put in danger?" Henry asked.

"She's already in danger, and I promise no harm can ever come to her with Elsa around," Raymond said.

"That's right, know your enemy, so they can be conquered, but then again, who conquers whom that we will see," Gustavo said. Raymond retreated with his men.

"Take care Henry that you do not become addicted to the kindness of sweet charity, for it will be a pain that you will need to live with, just ask Alexander what it is like to have so much emotion and no way to control it," Raymond said.

"You are always so quick to judge me and make an ass of me!"

"You don't need any help with that little brother, if you gave me no cause for concern, then I would not need to correct you." Raymond walked on into the night, and they followed.

That night Elsa chose another spot with the mountain at their back. The rocky surface traveled into the sky. No enemy could descend and catch them unaware. The camp faced the jungle.

Elsa lay on her back and took a deep breath. The jungle's moisture filled her lungs. She moved to displace a rock lodged beneath her shoulder blades. She longed for some piece of something, and she couldn't quite put her thoughts to what it was or how to find it. Her mind searched for the memory and found herself back in the dream.

Tiny lights popped in her mind as her mouth pressed against a man's neck. Warm hands pressed her to a hard body and moved against her bare back. She moved her face against the man's neck, and the skin wasn't smooth, but weathered like someone who spent many hours in the sun. She tried to capture his scent, but it was as if her nose was stopped up. His hands weren't soft or smooth, but calloused like a man who used his hands to make a living, but they were warm and gentle on her body. She tried in vain to open her eyes to see this man who she loved with such force, but it wasn't meant, and she spread her fingers over his face to feel every line and scar and still she didn't know him. Her hands moved over his head to his long hair, not too long, just at his shoulders. She kissed his mouth and the taste she didn't know, even though it was a familiar taste like, some wicked little cigars rolled in pear cognac she had to give up. She went in for another kiss to find comfort in him, and the dream changed.

Through the serenity, she heard children's laughter. For long moments, she listened to the joyful sound. It was out of place. No longer in the dream with the man or the camp with the other women, she waited in a line for her turn. A short distance to the left a group of children laughed and played in the sunshine. A tall, chain-link fence surrounded a large open area. Men hammered a structure together. People called to one another. Harmony and peace flowed through the camp. The line moved to the entrance of the fenced grounds. A community being forged out of the raw jungle, and it wasn't a fighter's camp. A section of trees was cleared to build houses.

Her turn arrived, and she stopped. Her skin crawled at the prospect of going through the fence. She bit her lower lip and took a step

back. "It's all right." Elsa turned toward the
voice and recognized Enrique.

"Where is Ana?" she asked.

"Do you know my Ana?" Enrique asked.

Elsa wasn't the old woman he knew, but the
Fighter's queen with her voice returned.

"Yes," she said. He grinned.

"She has made many friends here. Come
we'll get you something to eat and check you in
with the doctor," he said. She forced herself
through the gate. He motioned her along and
smiled.

"Don't be afraid," he said.

"What is this place?" she asked.

"It could be Heaven, but we're all living,"
he said. Elsa shook her head at his enthusiasm.
"I know it's hard to believe. It took me a few
days to accept. Finally, they're helping us
improve our lives."

"At what price?" she asked.

"I can understand your concern, but they've
given us material to build homes and food to
feed the children. Medicine in case we're sick,
even though none of us ever are and doctors to
keep us well…we've found our place," he said.

"What of education and skills to live? What
of the history that has plagued our people?" she
asked. He led her through a door to a room
filled with people and to a table. Laid before
her was a lavish offering. Fruits, vegetables,
steaming trays of beef and chicken and bread,

soups, all the food groups were represented. He pushed her forward, and she took a step back.

"Eat, enjoy, and don't worry. We're finally getting what they owe us," he said. She stepped away from the table.

"What price does this come to?" she asked.

"There's no price, it's free," he said.

"No, everything has a price, nothing is ever free," she said.

"I understand your distrust, for many days I wondered if all this would be here when I woke. It takes time to accept," he said. Another young man approached them.

"Enrique, the Doctor wants to see us."

"I must go," Enrique said.

"No, wait where is Ana?" she asked.

"She has gone ahead to our new home. I'm waiting to join her. I had a letter from her just yesterday. I'll see you later. Accept all these good things," he called.

Elsa tried to find the young woman's presence, some way Ana was out of range. She disappeared to those around her. In the illusion, she was as transparent as a breeze. She moved through the camp. In every way, a paradise to anyone who survived outside the fence. The people outside knew war, disease and death. Each deserved to know peace, to have the basics of life.

Still the camp reminder her of a zoo, the people protected and cared for like a treasure.

In this Eden, there was no sickness, no disability. Food for a peasant class and given freely, with dignity and from the hands of their own people.

The stench of death clawed at her senses. She followed it to its source and found herself on the far end of the camp. Do not enter was posted, on an electric fence the words in red letters in Spanish. She passed through the fence and into the brush beyond. She crept on her hands and knees, through the underbrush. The air reeked of rotted flesh. She came out the other side and covered her mouth as the smell overwhelmed her. She discovered the cause lying in the dead leaves.

She approached, careful not to misstep and came to the first victim, an elderly woman, her skull crushed. Vacant eyes stared into forever. A few feet down to the left a crippled, malformed body, black hair partially covered a face. Throughout the clearing, the impaired and elderly, lay discarded, their hopes never realized. Dozens of unwanted people left to haunt the jungle. The despair sank into her soul at the senseless waste of human potential.

She spun as her rage spiraled out of control. Bent on revenge she stormed to the fence. Fingers gripped the chain-link fence as she pulled herself up and then suddenly she was thrust back to reality. Fear crushed her. She pulled the other woman back into the brush.

Nellie opened her mouth, and Elsa pressed her hand over her face. She slid closer to the mountain and prayed to avoid confrontation. The moonlight provided light to watch the predators enter the camp. In the lead, the Green wolf searched the area, and he motioned the others to look around. Her hand moved to her gun.

Elsa touched Chino's mind. His prey was Leticia. His desire burned through her senses, his longing electric in his plan to capture the beautiful girl. To take for his own a member of her clan, just as she took the Black Wolf. In the raging passion, she encountered something more dangerous than mere lust, a growing love.

Nellie pressed her hand over her mouth as a sneeze overcame her. Lettie moved in front of her as Chino looked in their direction. The other wolves joined their leader. The standoff lasted seconds as the women defended themselves.

Elsa heard Nellie's voice. "Oh, dear Heaven, what shall I do? What else can you do Cameron, go after the brute," she said. Nellie landed on Pepe's back and yanked his head back and bit him.

Chino reached to pull Nellie off. His arm came up knocked her off her feet. Lettie hammered him back. Elsa cleared a path to them and fired. Chino fell and his blood spattered Lettie's clothes. Lettie dropped to

Nellie's side. "I don't want to shoot you, fighter, but I will, come with me," Chino said. He was a short distance from an unconscious Nellie.

He tried to get to his feet. Lettie helped him stand. Elsa fought two of the Wolves, but she allowed them to leave. Chino latched his arm around Lettie's waist, and they made their way through the trees. He turned and howled. Elsa fought her way to them.

Chino moved through the trees with Leticia in tow. The wolf clan allowed their leader a chance to get away. Elsa knew the sacrifice her girl made for her. She came to Nellie and found the journal next to her. He made a trade and one that didn't suit her purpose and took her daughter. It left her with little choice, but to hunt him down like a rabid animal. She would wait, and her opportunity would come.

"Master, Leticia has been captured by the wolf clan," Felipe said. Gustavo pushed his chair back.

"How did that happen?" Gustavo asked.

"Villanueva escaped and Samuel and David decided to go after him," Raymond said. Gustavo stood.

"And what of the women?" he asked.

"They were left alone," Raymond said.

"Elsa agreed to this?" Gustavo asked.

"She was not asked her opinion master."

"Go to them and guard them," Gustavo said.

"As you wish."

"Will we free Leticia, Master Raymond?" Felipe asked.

"No, Elsa will handle that," Raymond said.

"Chino took her. He must want her to ask for ransom," Felipe said, "He is an enforcer maybe someone wants her?"

"He didn't take her for ransom or to give her to anyone else."

"So why would he take her?" Felipe asked.

"Why would you take care her?" Felipe frowned, and they ran through the night to find the women.

Chapter 19 Wolf Clan

The tremor pulse through the Green Wolf as beads of sweat formed and rolled down his shirt. His square jaw clamped together; the pain etched on his olive face. Lettie wiped his face. "We should stop." She helped him sit. "Are you going to kill me?" she whispered. He exhaled.

"No," Chino said.

"What do you want from me?" The lust in his eyes spoke of his desire. She rubbed her scarred wrists.

"Who hurt you?" Chino asked.

"Your leader captured me…I tried to escape," she whispered.

"So you could exact revenge?" Chino asked.

"To kill myself." She avoided the power of his gaze.

"My leader didn't capture you. The Black Wolf takes no prisoners," Chino said. Her attention returned to him.

"Mano is your leader?" she whispered.

"He allows you to call him that?" he asked.

"Yes, Ma calls him that, he's not like I thought."

"Why do you whisper? Do I frighten you?" he asked.

"I'm not afraid of you," she whispered.

"You should be," he said.

"What's the worst you could do? Kill me?"
she asked.

"There are others uses for you," he said.

"You could rape me."

"That's what you see when you look at me?
An animal that can only have a woman by
force?" he asked.

"What do you want with me? You are the
man from Ma's apartment in Mexico City, you
touched my baby," she asked.

"I touched you," he said. He ran his fingers
over a long scar on her forearm.

"How did this happen?"

"I was trying to escape…this life," she
whispered.

"What did your leader expect from my
brother?" he asked.

"A killer," she whispered.

"He's that," he said.

"A man without heart or conscious," she
whispered.

"He can be those things if he chooses," he
said.

"Maybe, but not with Elsa, my leader," she
whispered.

"I'm the only one he allows to call him
Mano," he said.

"You're his Second?" she asked.

"Second what?" he asked.

"You're second in command."

"I'm his brother," he said.

"You're all brothers, no?"

"Yes, but he's my blood brother," he replied.

"You've a blood bond with your leader? Unusual."

"No, we're siblings. We've the same father," he snapped. She stared at his face and body. The resemblance to Manuel unavoidable, he ran his hand over his shaved scalp. His intense green eyes reflected pain and some hidden agenda.

"I should check your injury," she whispered.

"Why?" he asked.

"You'll bleed to death if I don't," she whispered. She moved to him, and he considered her action.

"What do you care?" he asked.

"You're a human being in pain," she whispered.

"This has nothing to do with Mano?" he asked.

"Yes, we're friends," she said. Her hand moved to her baby. She glanced at him.

"Maybe more than friends?" he asked.

"Manuel's not the father of my child," she said, "I'll help you because it's my way."

"What is your name, Fighter?" he asked.

"If you know I am a Fighter, then you know my name," she whispered. She ripped the shirt from his body. He clenched his teeth as she examined him. She patted the sweat from his face.

457

"What did Jose call you, Leticia?" he asked. Lettie glanced at him as a tear fell. He caught it and drank it.

"La Nina, the girl," she whispered.

"You can grieve. I didn't think a Fighter, female or not capable of such feeling. Too bad your people have no conscience when it comes to killing civilians," he said. She slapped him, and he raised an eyebrow. "You're a prideful one." She sighed and poured water onto a cloth to wipe blood from the wound. From her pack, she took some salve and gently rubbed it into the wound.

"Did you know my father was he a good man," she whispered.

"That's an odd question I never met him. I hear he was a teacher," he replied. She pressed a cloth against the wound and the bandage to his back.

"The bullet went straight through. My leader didn't intend to kill you," she whispered. She offered him a cup of water.

"Poison?" he asked. She drank deeply and filled the cup again.

"Don't move your arm too much, drink." She placed the cup at his mouth, and he drank. She picked through her pack and found some leftovers from earlier in the day. She divided the food and gave him a share. She stroked the roundness of her belly.

"You're a strange one offering help to one who means you harm."

"Eat, I'm tired," she whispered. She finished her dinner and took the empty plate from him. "You should try to sleep."

"So you can escape," he said.

"No, you'll need your strength when the One catches you."

"You think she'll come for you?" he asked.

"Yes," she whispered. She arranged her pack and lay down. An hour later she woke to soft groaning. "Green Wolf, why aren't you asleep?" she whispered. He was in pain. She went to her pack and extracted a small bag of leaves. "These will help...I can't prove it's not poison. This plant would harm my child," she whispered.

"I don't want it," he said.

"You must sleep. What can I do to convince you I won't escape?"

"Nothing," he said. She pulled her pack to him and lay at his side. She entwined her fingers with his.

"Please, sleep," she whispered. She closed her eyes and felt him move next to her. "Don't take my generosity as an invitation, Del la Rosa." Some time later she woke to a fiery touch. A fever raged through him. She pulled her hand away.

"No," he said.

"Let me help you. Don't make me tell Manuel I let you die," she whispered. His fingers open. When she offered him the relief for pain, he accepted it.

As morning arrived, Chino's fever broke. Lettie remained awake to watch him. She traveled out to hunt and collect bananas for breakfast. She tended the fire where the meat roasted, and a cereal of wheat cooked. She gathered the banana cakes from the pan and stacked them on a plate. She stirred the cereal. When she glanced up the men stood thirty feet away. She scrambled to the sleeping man. "Chino."

"What?" he asked. She nodded to the trees. He followed her gaze. "They're Wolves. Do they frighten you, girl?"

"No," she whispered. She moved to the fire and turned the meat. The Wolves were statues among the trees.

"What are you doing?" he asked. Leticia stirred more batter. "Making banana cakes," she whispered. From the pot of cereal, she poured some in a cup. She took one of the cakes and ate. He struggled to sit, and she helped him. She filled a reed bowl with cereal and brought it to him. The cakes were removed, and another group started. She watched him drain the bowl.

"Will your men eat with a Fighter?" she whispered.

"Ask them," he said. She moved to stand, and he pulled her down. "From here." She pointed to them and pretended to eat. He motioned them over. They gathered round the fire. Each had a water bladder, round with liquid.

"Is that fresh water?" She asked a giant of a young man with a purple wolf on his uniform. His eyes were blue and his hair red.

"Yes," he said.

"Would you trade some of it for…" she whispered. She searched through her pack for something of value.

"I'll trade for food," he said.

"No…it's free," she whispered.

"We don't accept charity," Chino said.

"I need the water. I'll trade," she whispered. She pulled more cakes from the pan. From their packs came bowls and plates. Chino lost his pack in the fight. She glanced at him. He had nothing.

He owed her for saving his life. She poured out the cereal and cut the meat. The cakes she gave them and saved a portion for Chino. When he didn't move to take the offering, she turned to him. His teeth clenched together. He prepared to argue.

"I'll trade this food and whatever other kindness for your word to protect me and…from harm," she whispered.

"My protection has no price. I give it freely." She challenged him with her eyes.

"Then we can't accept it," she replied.

"I'll trade," Chino said. At the meal's end, each contributed their share of water to her canteen. She noticed the cuts, bruises and other injuries. "It's time to leave, girl."

"Pick any direction, Wolf. It won't matter," she whispered. She tried to help him to his feet, but he pushed her hand away.

"Let us see if we can challenge her," he said. He howled into the morning air and led them through the trees.

They traveled for half the day when she brought up the subject of the men's injuries. "Chino," she whispered. He glanced at her.

"Are you tired?" he asked.

"No, your soldiers are injured," she whispered.

"And?"

"Would you allow me to give them medicine?" she whispered.

"Where did you learn the healing ways?" he asked.

"My Grandmother was a medicine woman. She taught my Mama, and so I learned. It's a family tradition. Except I'm the last one."

"The fighters have a treasure in you. That's why your leader will go to so much trouble to get you back," he said.

"She'll come…because I'm family," she whispered.

"You're also a fighter," he said.

"Yes, but Elsa wouldn't care if I were a peasant. I'm an orphan like so many others, and she's our Mother," she whispered. Chino turned and took her hand.

"You're one of her favorites, aren't you?"

"Yes, may I use my medicine on your men? You'll need every advantage when she arrives," she whispered.

"Why would you help us to defeat her?"

"You can't defeat her, Green Wolf, with or without my help. Nothing I give you, including my life would stop her, but if you take my life, she'll take yours. Have no doubt, only God can stop her."

"So why bother with the medicine?" he asked.

"I pray you see reason. If I can make you strong with my medicine, your people may not be destroyed," she whispered.

"Why would you care either way?" he asked.

"My concern isn't for you, Wolf. It's for Elsa. Taking your people's lives will cause her pain and give her regrets. There has been too much killing." She moved away and continued down the path.

"Do what you want," he said. The march halted.

"Call them over," she whispered.

She anticipated their rejection of her plan. "I'll trade my medicine for a share of a kill," she whispered. Chino nodded, and her examinations proceeded.

As evening drew near the exhaustion weighed her down. "Enough, fighter you must rest," Chino said. His hard face pressed into a frowned as he crossed his arms. His shaved head and mean green eyes made him frightful. He was an attractive man.

"I've one more," she whispered.

"No," he replied.

"Your bandages need changing," she whispered.

"You're as hard headed a woman as I've ever met," he said.

"That's what you like best. Let us get this over with," she whispered. Chino obeyed. She lay on the ground and slept like the dead.

"Leticia, come to me daughter." She turned her head as the echo of the familiar threads of thought, popped into her mind. Her eyes remained closed, but she was awake.

"He won't let me leave, Ma," she thought in her mind.

"I'll take you back even if I must use force," Elsa replied in her mind.

"Wake him tell him I'll trade you for the journal." She pushed his shoulder, and he came awake with a start.

"She'll trade me for the journal," she whispered. The jungle birds called to each other. The breeze cast the trees about. "No, go back to sleep."

"Take her offer, Wolf it's the best you'll get," she whispered. He settled himself and ignored her warning.

"I tried Ma," she whispered. She glanced over his shoulder. "Hello, Mother." He jerked to look back and found himself pinned in Elsa's trap. She pushed his head back to Lettie. He opened his mouth.

"Call them and you're dead," she whispered, "Please don't kill him, Ma. He didn't mistreat me." Lettie stepped over him. She embraced her leader.

"I can't be with you, Green Wolf."

"Because of your child?" he asked.

"For many reasons. Let me go with her. We don't want to fight, please," she begged.

"I'll give you what you gave me, girl. We're even, I won't be so generous next time," he said. She nodded and joined Elsa at the edge of the trees. Lettie sounded the fighter's call, and the rest of the army surrounded the Wolf camp. Chino looked at the multitude of fighters and then at her.

"Go in peace, my brother," she signed. The three other women joined them and walked into the moonlit jungle.

Elsa retraced the steps to the original camp that night. The fighters that joined her were sent back to their families. She took the women to a shelter in the mountain. She wouldn't take a chance the wolf clan would follow them.

As tired as she was, sleep eluded her. There was nothing to do, but lie in the dark. Lettie slept. Her peace of mind returned with the girl. She thought of Ana and Enrique, a happy couple, unlike her Samuel and Lettie. Their hopes pinned on fate and the hand of God. Enrique's enthusiasm was dangerous.

Maybe it took age to see the sharp edges of life. Hindsight grew in the mind as other important images died. Caution nurtured it. The optimism of spirit moved it, and fear kept its watch guiding one through the journey of life and death was the destination.

Alarms blasted in her mind when it came to the camp; freedom was a costly venture and always came with strings. Her purpose was to delay the two young people, and she didn't have a logical reason to stop them. Her duty wasn't to question, only to do. Her problems seemed to multiply. The journey began to take the death squads from her family, and now the nightmare brought yet another fight.

She turned on her side. The other women slept from need; comfort a faraway dream. The danger clawed its way up her spine to lodge in her mind and gnaw at her security. She closed her eyes and allowed the nightmare to take her to walk among the people. Her interest was in Enrique, and as she pictured his face, she appeared in a room. White, sterile, shiny, silver metal was this place. The strong smell of alcohol warned her of some danger. She ran her fingers across a set of glimmering knives. Instruments meant for healing used in the hands of a surgeon.

She found Enrique waiting. His nervousness evident in the way he pressed his fingers into the shape of a steeple. The hopefulness in his heart and the longing for the woman of his dreams pierced the air. She captured these precious thoughts.

From his coat came the letters of his beloved. Her face smiled in his memory and moved through Elsa's consciousness. His desire raged in her heart and pounded through her veins. She went to his side to pat his back and to bring him comfort.

He stood as the door opened and a doctor entered. The doctor's mouth moved, but she couldn't hear his words to Enrique. She read the doctor's mind. "Enrique it's almost time to be with Ana."

"Yes, Doctor. It seems like forever since I've seen my woman."

"I want to give you a shot to relax you?" Enrique nodded. The doctor took out the injection. Elsa probed the doctor's mind, images of screaming people and packages of money splashed with blood appeared from his memory. The face of a beautiful woman walked up to him to seduce him with dark eyes. The curve of face and hip to fill a lustful heart, the devil, Patricia whored herself to bring the doctor to this purpose. She spun to face Enrique.

The trust and acceptance engraved on his face. She twisted her power to appear to him, but it wasn't to be. She screamed at the limits of her curse. The frailty of the human condition that brought hopes and delivered this man to his death, and Enrique took the shot. She wasn't so easily defeated. There had to be another way.

Enrique slumped into a chair. The doctor returned with a form and helped him to a table. The man arranged the form over a manila folder. He signed the page and inserted it into the folder.

She tipped the table. The pages flooded the floor. A picture of Ana slipped into view. She jumped into Enrique's mind and turned his head to look. He gathered them and gripped the arm of the chair as the medication took its toll. In his mind, she pressed him to examine the pages. She felt the medicine dull his senses.

She concentrated her effort to aid him to discovery. He pushed the folder open. They saw the word 'heart' written across the bottom of the photo. Attached to the picture was a certificate of death. Ana's name printed in bold letters. The day of her death marked the day of her departure from the camp. Cause of death a crushed skull. His heart caved in at the information.

She pushed him on, and his fingers slid over other photos. There were pictures of them together at the camp. His hand trembled as he came to a form, with a dollar amount for the purchase of her heart. The price for a pair of healthy lungs stood out as a six-digit number, as much as her heart, worth more than her life. A photo of him caught his attention, the word lungs written in red ink.

He remembered the question she proposed to him. His fist smashed against the table, and he fell across the edge. He sold them to the highest bidder for a hot meal and the comfort of a warm bed. She pulled her mind back as he screamed in agony. The darkness came to claim him, and all was lost.

Her eyes closed, the sweet smile of his Ana, his last memory of the woman, haunted her. She turned and on the wall was a calendar in the month of November, in her world it was August. She returned to the cavern, and the sound of water brought comfort. She still had time.

One more day and Elsa pushed through the underbrush and made her way through the deepest part of the jungle. Here in the cool darkness her mind moved ever forward as she searched for Ana and Enrique. The women followed her without question. Their thoughts were of home, forbidden desires and conflicts of the heart. She found comfort that they would be reunited with the men in a day. She stopped. "Rest, the men will catch up with us soon," she signed.

"Where are we going," Nellie asked.

"To prevent a murder," Elsa signed.

"What can we do?" Nellie asked.

"More than nothing and less than everything. I know what I'm doing Nell, at least some of the time," she signed.

"I know, but I'm just a housekeeper," Nellie said.

"You're not just a maid, Nellie. We all have our purpose," Lettie whispered. Elsa stood. The break was over, and the journey continued. Later, that day Elsa stirred their meal. She glanced to the left and then at Lettie. "We're being followed, Ma," she whispered. Susa crouched, in the distance, and gazed into the jungle.

"Tell the others to stay close," she signed.

"As you wish, my leader." The day wore on as Elsa made her advance and the trackers, followed. In this manner, they traveled and never lost sight of the danger. As evening came to cloak the earth, no attack came. Whoever they were they kept their distance and never posed a threat. Even so, she realized a pattern to their movements. Their destination was a barren section of the mountain.

The uneven terrain and loose rocks slowed them down. She helped Lettie crest a hill as the others caught up. The shallow valley fell into shadows, as the sun made its final descent. She searched for a place to camp. "We'll camp here, Lettie," she signed.

"Yes, Ma," she whispered. They set camp and ate leftovers and then went to sleep.

A howl breached the still morning air. A flock of birds took to wing to pierce the morning sky. Lettie watched the birds disappear onto the mountain ledges.

"Elsa," Nellie said. Lettie turned back. Women and children surrounded them. She stared into each face and found pain and hunger.

"Lettie, take Nellie, do what you can with the sick. Bea, start a fire, find something to boil water in. Susa you're with me," Elsa signed. Elsa trotted into the forest with Susa and glanced back.

"Be careful, Ma," Lettie signed. Elsa nodded and caught up with Susa. They would bring back enough to feed the new arrivals and replace their supplies.

Lettie tended to each with care and efficiency. None of them spoke to her. They accepted her services not with gratitude, but with payment of the only possessions they owned; symbols of their clan. She recognized each item for its true nature; all were symbols of the wolf, objects of all types that showed the animal in glory and strength. She tried her best to refuse them, but without the trade, she wasn't allowed to treat them. An old man approached, and she motioned him forward. A cut on the top of his hand was swollen and very red. She lanced the flesh and the ooze poured out. She gently pressed the surface until all was clear, and she applied her salve and a bandage.

"There you go, I will give you a container of the salve. The wound must be washed, and the salve applied twice a day." His dark eyes looked into hers. He dug into his pack, and she put her hand on his arm. "What is your name Senor?"

"I am Alfaro, Senora. I will do as you say, please take this payment." The wolf face had green eyes.

"You made this for Leader Chino?" she whispered, "You should keep it, for him."

"I believe my spirit guide drew me to create this so that you would have it as a…charm of protection from the great leader Chino." He rose and walked away as Leticia fingered the green eyes in the metal carving. She slipped it into her pocket.

The meat from the hunt sizzled and popped as it cooked. She wondered what Elsa would do to make them eat it. While most of her patients were in good health, food was a daily need not always fulfilled. She longed for a cold drink of water, and an idea came to her. She strolled to Elsa. "Ma, look what they gave me as a trade."

"They're wolf clan?" Elsa signed.

"Yes and they won't accept the food without trading," she whispered. They lived in these mountains and knew where to get what the women didn't have.

"You have a way," Elsa signed.

"We need water and they know where to get it," she whispered.

"Make the trade," Elsa signed.

The trade was more than successful as the women provided them with fresh water. From the kill, they took their share and disappeared into the jungle.

That evening they camped in the ravine. The moon glowed down from the heavens. Susa crouched a short distance away. She turned to Elsa and shook her head. Her gazed moved to Bea.

"She's very nervous," Bea said.

"What should we do?" Elsa signed.

Nellie popped her head around a tree. "We should be in the mountain, this eve." Elsa motioned to Susa to join them. She climbed from the rock to stand by her.

"What is it?" Elsa signed.

"Me not know, somethin' not right," Susa said. Elsa knew well that survival instinct.

"It's not the Wolf Clan," Lettie whispered. Susa shook her head.

"Who else could it be? Maybe it's the men," Bea said.

"Maybe the original enemy, Elsa?" Nellie asked.

Elsa stared into the ebony night. The presence of human minds swirled in a black hole of disjointed patterns. Among the confusion was Abrim's mind. They would be together soon. On the perimeter of peace, she found the threat of evil. "We sleep in the mountain."

Chapter 20 Friends and Enemies

Elsa found no peace within the great stone of mother earth. She ran from the past, afraid of the future and uncertain of the present. She could easily sit in the dark and wait for death to take her, but she couldn't condemn the others to such a fate. How could she justify taking the life of her baby? Her choices narrowed when the little one chose her for a Mama. The fear yanked at her senses. She rubbed her eyes. A fool was one who had no fear and ignored good sense.

"It's time," Nellie said. Elsa took her hand and rose. The debate was over. She moved to the front of the line and took the lantern. She forged through the rock and longed-for Texas. Heaven could be found in the simplest of pleasures like a warm bed, clean sheets and a fat pillow to lounge on.

The guilt galloped into her mind. She knew Heaven, experienced Hell and the places between were distant memories. Time ran out for many a friend and enemy in this shadow world. Still, she moved on, from place to place, from time passed to what could be the future.

Her success wasn't measured by good deeds, but with every breath. Her failures lurked in the shade of her soul, always there to keep her humble. She ran her hand over the cold stone and tried to seize the strength she didn't feel. Her discomforts were of little concern. Her duty dared not be disregarded. Her future lay in every step forward, in every breath gone, in every tear freed.

Knowing the future brought no comfort, only responsibility. The fear she did take with her, a beast, biting and cruel, without mercy. It damned her soul and pressed its desire to kill her. She inhaled, and the jungle tempted her with its aroma. She moved faster, the need to feel the sunshine on her face seized her.

She raced around a corner into the morning light. Her joy short-lived as she came face to face with a soldier of Patricia's death squad. He jumped at her, and Lettie shot him. His brethren joined the fight. She took another one down and lost count of the men who poured into the clearing. They were forced against the mountain. This was a fight they couldn't win alone. A soldier pushed her back. She pulled her arm up as she said a silent prayer.

The man's eyes grew wide as he gasped for air and clutched his chest. In another moment, he fell. The strong electrical current raced against her skin. It was Abrim's mind that saved her. Abrim rode toward her on a giant, black horse, his face full of fury. He hauled her up next to him and plowed through the soldiers of the death squad as his Fighters took up the fight. Lettie came off the ground next, and he drove passed the fighting to another cavern opening.

He dropped them off and spun around to get Nellie. "Oh, my word, but he just snatched me up like a feather," Nellie squealed. Bea and Susa were delivered, and Abrim came to her.

"Don't leave here, understand?" Abrim asked. Elsa tasted his skin on her lips as her face had slid against his neck. She stared, and he leaned down to cup her face. "Don't move from here Elsa, promise!" His thumb went across her mouth as his breath caressed her face. She nodded, and he rode away. His ponytail flew as he joined the battle.

A wolf howl cracked the foggy, morning air. The wolf clan poured out of the jungle to take up the fight. Shadows come to life to help them. From her left, Mano appeared to snap the enemies' neck. Chino raced up to his leader and took down an assassin. The bodies of the enemy littered the ground, and still they came, so many wasted lives. As one battle was won another flared, and the war raged on.

"Ma, why is Mano killing his own men? Samuel said he was the leader of the death squad soldiers," Lettic whispered.

"I don't know," Elsa signed. She searched the battlefield for her leader, but couldn't locate him.

"Grandfather is to the left, Ma. He's off the horse," Lettie said. Elsa found him. A sharp whistle brought the animal to Abrim, and he remounted to be above the battle so his Fighter's could see him. He rallied them and the death squads were crushed, just as Samuel and the other men came on the scene. Abrim rode to Elsa.

"No!" Lettie screamed. Elsa spun. A muscled man with long, blond hair tried to restrain Lettie. With the traditional haircut and dress of the fighters, Adam Maldano had come to collect the woman he loved, but Elsa had erased him from Lettie's memory. Elsa made the hard choice to protect Lettie, to help her, because she loved the girl and all were lame excuses that would piss her off if someone made them for her. She placed the gun at Adam's temple. Lettie screamed again. Elsa saw Chino move toward them, and she held her hand up.

"Release her Adam!" Abrim said. She pulled the hammer back. Abrim snatched the man away. Elsa's free hand stroked the hurt girl's hair. Her wild son landed on Adam. She holstered her gun.

Adam came up and took the vicious attack. Samuel's anger pulsed through her. He unleashed his anger and his eyes bloomed into royal, blue marbles. Adam defended himself and he too had some wicked anger to unleash, and they were a match on the battlefield.

"Adam, you've forgotten yourself attacking our leader." She turned to the man who issued the warning. His tan skin and long, brown hair in a braid the same as when he was a boy.

Another one of her sons, Marcus Nunez, Abrim's adopted son, but the young man was a child of her heart. One of her orphans, she saved him at the age of three from meeting the same fate as his parents and brought him to Abrim. She loved the three-year-old from the moment, she held him. Adam jumped back, and Samuel allowed him to go. Lettie clutched her hand.

Elsa searched the faces for Mano and found him with Chino. "I thank the wolf clan for their help," she signed. He leaned closer to his brother. Chino embraced him and gathered his group. Chino turned to Lettie and bowed. Leticia waved and moved closer. Sam reached to Lettie, and she shook her head as she clutched Elsa's arm. Disappointment crashed into her son's blue eyes.

"Does someone want to tell me why Elsa and the women were alone while they were being hunted?" Abrim asked. His horse wandered away.

"We went after Villanueva, he escaped," Sam said. Abrim moved closer. Elsa stared at him and she bit her trembling lower lip.

"Rojas was coming from the other direction and he got here before you did so who were you following? Your mother gave you permission to leave?" Abrim asked.

"No, he didn't ask my opinion," Elsa signed.

"You didn't consult with your leader Samuel?" Abrim shouted, "Whose bright idea was this?"

"David and…" Elsa signed. Abrim glared, and she threw up on his shiny black boots. Lettie gripped her as Abrim stepped up and Elsa puked on his boots again.

"Leticia what is wrong with my mother?" Marcus asked. Lettie eyed the man.

"Who are you?" Lettie whispered.

"You know me I'm Marcus you grew up with me," Marcus said. Elsa puked again. "Why is my mother ill?" He was as impatient as his father.

"She's pregnant," Lettie whispered. He turned to Abrim.

"I know she's pregnant," Marcus said. Elsa glanced at Abrim.

"You've a son with the clan leader, Ma, why didn't you tell me?"

"It's a long story," Elsa signed.

"Father why isn't she home with you?" Marcus asked. Abrim looked at her. David stomped to them.

"It's not his baby. It's mine!" David shouted. Marcus punched David, and the fight was on.

"Nobody calls my mother a whore, ugly man!" Lettie dragged her away and she was glad to get to a quiet place.

Elsa stood against the stone it was rough and cold as she sipped the water. She was alone in the water room. Lettie didn't remember Marcus or Adam, young men she grew up with, students of her father. When Elsa erased the horrible memories, she took the good ones as well, but it was possible to override the erasure, Lettie remembered the blond fighter and his love even as she didn't know his name and one day she would remember it all when she was stronger.

She took another long sip of the cold water. She was cold and uncomfortable. The third sip was a struggle to keep. "How are you Ma?" Elsa lifted the cup, and Lettie retreated to report to the clan leader. She hadn't told the truth, but she hadn't lied either. She leaned over, and the water gushed out onto the black stone. She gripped the ledge.

"Lettie said you were drinking water," Abrim said. She froze. "Keeping it in is the key, how long have you been like this?" She glanced at him, and he had blood on the corner of his mouth. She moved and swayed. He was to her in the next instant. His body pressed against hers. She inhaled his scent, smoky and sweet.

"Why are you bleeding?" she signed.

"Gracia hit me," he said. She moved. "No I don't need you to fight my battle's woman. I hit him back." She rubbed at the blood.

"I don't want anyone hurting you," she signed. He slipped his left hand over her belly and pressed his palm to her bare skin. He spread his fingers to encompass the roundness of her child. His warmth surrounded her and drove away the cold. She accepted his comfort. Her baby moved, the movement strong. She smiled. "Did you feel it?"

"Yes, you've a strong child growing inside of you, Elsa haven't you felt it move before?" he asked.

"No, that was the first-time Abrim," she signed. He smiled and her heart jerked, he never smiled. She slipped her arm around his neck and rubbed her fingers over his face to his mouth. She leaned up and stopped. There was something familiar about this she didn't like. She pulled out of his grasp and slipped as she tried to get away. He steadied her. His fingers came around the rings that David put on her hand. He gazed into her eyes.

"You should be a happily married woman. Why are you so sad?" She peeled her fingers away from his grasp.

"I'm the same as, I've always been…leader," she signed.

"Nothing has changed for you? Why would you marry him…is there a reason I should know?" he asked.

"I am the same, Abrim," she signed.

"Yes, so you are. Would I ever do anything to hurt you?" he asked. She didn't like the question and walked away. She stopped and turned. He didn't want an answer. It was his way to make her think.

"You can't stop me from loving…just because you're afraid," she signed. He blinked and looked away. She ran back to the main cavern and found Lettie. She dragged her close and pressed the other woman's hands to her belly. Lettie gazed at her. "Is it too soon to feel so many movements?" Elsa signed. Lettie considered.

"Yes, but…" Lettie whispered. The young woman glanced behind her. The old man reached them.

"Why are you here Elsa?" he asked. She frowned.

"If you could control your psycho ex-wife, whore, Elsa wouldn't have to run for her life all the time," David said. David challenged him with his gaze.

"She shouldn't be here, Gracia," Abrim said.

"She's the One. This is her kingdom," David said. Abrim's old, blue eyes shifted to her face.

"You try to use my dead son's propaganda on me?" Abrim shouted.

"You've been so involved in making yourself a hero. You haven't given a damn about the one person who has helped you all these years. You come with your arrogance to criticize her as if she were an ill-mannered child," David said.

"You don't know who you're talking to boy," Abrim snapped.

"You don't want to challenge me old man," David said. Elsa stepped toward them.

"Stay out of this, Elsa," Abrim said.

"Don't use that tone with my wife," David warned.

"She doesn't want to be your wife or your anything," Abrim said. David laughed, and Elsa shook her head.

"Oh, she wants me all I have to do is touch her, and no one else exists," David said. Abrim lost his temper and leapt forward. David grabbed the man around the neck. Marcus and Sam came to separate them.

"Why are you here Elsa?" Abrim asked.

"Well it started out that I was trying to lead the death squad away from the women and now, something has changed. I need to prevent two young people from dying at the hands of Patricia and her greed. My duty won't end until my death," she signed.

"You want to speed it up by placing yourself in danger? Tell me who they are, and I'll help them. You go home where you belong," Abrim said. She burst into tears.

"This is my home, even if you no longer want my help, Juan," she signed. Abrim stared. She realized her mistake and went to run. Lettie caught her. "It's alright Ma." She wiped her face.

"Elsa tells us what we're doing next," Nellie said.

"We should listen to Mr. Stein," Bea said. Elsa drank from the reed cup and Lettie refilled it.

"What we need do?" Susa asked.

"I don't know yet," she signed.

"Who are the young people we're helping?" Bob asked.

"Ana and Enrique," Elsa signed.

"What are their last names?" Wayne asked.

"I don't know," Elsa signed.

"What do they look like?" Leo asked.

"Brown hair, brown eyes, in they're twenties, average height," Elsa signed. Lettie took Elsa's hand.

"You've just described more than half the population," Nellie said. Elsa's stomach tumbled.

"I'll know more later," Elsa signed. Elsa turned to Adam. He stared at Lettie. The determination pressed into his expression.

"I seek an audience with the One," Adam said. He took a place before her.

"You're now Leticia's guardian?" Adam asked.

"Yes," she signed.

"Then I'll tell you of my claim," Adam said.

"Your claim?" she signed.

"I've received consent from my Father, and Ana gave me her consent to marry Leticia. I want you to honor that bond my leader," Adam said. Samuel stopped talking to David. Lettie stopped moving. Leticia's mother had as much of a claim to arrange her daughter's marriage as did her father, since Leticia's mother had a very high ranking among the Fighter's clan.

"I'm pregnant with my leader's son's baby?" Lettie whispered.

"I come from a good family. I've fought in the Fighter's army most of my life. I've earned my place among its ranks. I've money to support her...what did you just say?" Adam asked. Lettie grasped her arm in a death grip.

"Leticia is pregnant with my baby, and she's my wife," Samuel said. Lettie held Elsa's gaze.

"By what law is she married to you?" Adam asked.

"By the only laws that matter, the laws of my land, she no longer lives in Mexico," David said.

"Ma, please don't let either of them take me away from you, please don't let them separate us," Lettie pleaded. When Lettie discovered the truth, she would never forgive her, but for now, Elsa would do all she could to provide security.

"No one will separate us. I promise," Elsa signed.

"I love you more than my life, Leticia, just come with me, and I'll show you the truth," Adam said.

Elsa glanced at Abrim. "She has a say in this, no?" Elsa asked.

"Yes," Abrim replied. She gripped Lettie's arm.

"I'm not your woman, nor have I ever been. You dare to call me a whore in the presence of the One?" she whispered.

"I arranged marriage bonds with your mother as is our tradition," Adam said.

"I know nothing of this bond. My mother is dead. I don't know you, nor do I want to," she whispered.

"Why would I lie? You promised never to forget me if a prince came to the jungle, you promised," Adam asked.

"I don't remember you. I've nothing. I'm an orphan, if not for Ma, I'd be as dead as my mother," she whispered.

"You love me, Leticia. Look in my eyes and know the truth," Adam said. She looked and didn't blink, but her arm trembled beneath Elsa's hand. Adam turned to Samuel. "Has she ever told you she loves you, Stein? Has she?" Adam shouted. She searched her son's face, his expression never changed, but he didn't reply. "Have you ever asked yourself why, Stein? It's because her heart belongs to me! What is your answer Dear One," Adam asked.

"Doesn't matter what she says, my word is law. Leticia's no longer subject to your laws. She's under my protection," David said.

"Shut up!" Adam said.

"Make me," David said. Adam glanced to Abrim. "Well?" Adam was so intent on David, she couldn't get his attention. Her eyes connected to Abrim's.

"The One has a response Adam," Abrim said.

"Yes, my leader," Adam said.

"A bond is a solemn oath and not entered into lightly, but you must know I to have made a bond with Leticia, a Fighter's bond of kinship, and I take that bond very seriously. In order to make this bond with her, I gave up…no I gained responsibility for her. She doesn't remember you and no matter how true your bond is, her feelings must matter and should matter to you. You frightened her earlier, and fear isn't the correct beginning of any marriage. I must deny your request," Elsa signed. He frowned.

"Because she is married to your son and is having his baby that is the true reason."

"Don't allow your anger to mislead you into thinking I need to explain myself to you young Fighter. Know me true I will go against my own son to keep my bond. She asked not to go to either of you, and that is my decision." Elsa doubled over and vomited.

"Ma, where is your bark?" Lettie asked, "It was in your pocket earlier." Lettie searched her pockets.

"Is this what you're looking for?" Abrim asked. He held up the sack of bark chips.

"You dirty old bastard, you touched her!" Abrim and David went to fighting. Lettie helped her to the ground. Elsa leaned on her, and Lettie blocked her view of the fight. If she didn't know better she would swear the old man was trying to piss David off.

"How's he doing?" Elsa signed.

"Grandfather's hitting David, I think he really wanted to hit him. They'll live. You come here," Lettie called. Marcus came to them. "Pretty boy go get the bark chips. You have a girl?"

"My name is Marcus and no do you have someone in mind, and I've always thought of you as sister, the blond is my best friend, and Samuel is my uncle," Marcus said.

"Not me, and I do have someone in mind, but I can't remember her name right now. Very pretty, quiet, not like you go on," Lettie whispered. Elsa glanced at her.

"You remember someone?" Elsa asked.

"Yes and no, I'm not sure," Lettie said. Elsa glanced up as Adam stood over them.

"I was ordered to bring these over here," he said.

"What is your name?" Lettie asked. He remained mute. "Fine, give me the bark chips Storm." His eyes were the color of thunderheads. Adam kneeled down next to them. Lettie placed two chips in her mouth.

"Elsa don't eat that squirrel crap!" David said, "Come here and I'll kiss you, and you won't be sick anymore." Adam stood.

"Don't speak to our leader in such an ugly way," Adam said.

"Stay out of this Maldano," Sam said.

"I'll defend your mother since you seem to have lost your way. Don't disrespect the One with your obscenities she isn't accustomed to such language or behavior. Our leader has never been so stupid with our great lady," Adam said. He walked away from them. David stomped away.

"Ma is he related to Grandfather?" Lettie asked.

"Why do you ask?" Elsa signed.

"That's something the clan leader would do and say. He's marked in the old ways, don't you think?" Lettie asked. Elsa gazed at Abrim, and his blue eyes sparkled with light as she nodded.

The sun peaked in the jungle sky as another day found them miles down the mountain. Lettie wiped the sweat from her forehead. "Ma, when can we stop?"

"We're almost to a shelter," she signed.

A short time later they entered the cool climate of the caverns. The new location was a short distance to the outside, and she needed supplies. "Ma, may I go find a bark?" Ma's concern appeared in her face. "Funny how the mind is, no? I can't remember my family, but if you ask me, which plant to use for a burn, I could tell you."

"Be careful," Elsa signed. Lettie found her way out and approached each tree with interest. She collected roots and other items to use fresh. She examined another group of trees with care. The last one on the row proved to be the one she needed. She peeled off a few strips and turned. A few paces away she peered through the branches of a bush.

The blond man sat on a log. He pressed his forehead as if he had pain. He pulled a photo from his pocket and rubbed his eyes. Something in the way he moved reminded her he wasn't well. She came closer, and he reacted defensively.

"No please…did you want to see me?" Adam said. She turned and inched closer and pointed to a place on the log. "Yes, please sit." She sat carefully and glanced at him.

"Your head hurts," she whispered.

"How do you know that?" he asked.

"You pressed your head. I'm a medicine woman, did you know?"

"I know," he said. He had an oval face and a pale complexion and gray eyes like storm clouds. His scalp was shaved except for a long section pulled into a braid. Her eyes traveled down his body. His arms were hard and his body strong. Long fingers, on big, cleans hands were crossed over his chest. She came back to his face.

"Were you sent to hunt Storm?" she whispered.

"No…why do you whisper?" he asked.

"So no one will hear me," she replied.

"Oh," he said.

"How long has your head been hurting?" she whispered. He smiled.

"You always knew when I was in pain. Where did you get the locket?" he asked. She pulled at it.

"Ma gave it to me," she said.

"Ma? Elsa?" he asked.

"Yes, Ma, it's from my past," she whispered. He nodded. "You would rather have Elsa as the leader than Samuel." He didn't respond. "Samuel doesn't want to be leader."

"I don't imagine he would since he has everything he ever wanted," he said. She gazed into his gray eyes.

"He has never wanted to be the leader. He's not a coward. Ma rescued me when no one else could. She almost didn't make it…sometimes I wish she hadn't," she whispered. In his face was the desire to touch her. She moved back. He rubbed his temples. She touched his face. "Does it hurt here?"

"Yes," he said. She pulled out two leaves.

"These will help, chew them," she whispered.

"Will you accept your usual payment?" She didn't like the question and stood.

"No, they're free," she said. She moved away.

"I can't accept them. You really don't remember me do you? Leticia, who do you love?" he asked. She turned and looked in his eyes.

"I love our leader," she whispered. The hurt and disappointment crossed his face. Butterflies wiggled in her stomach to think the handsome man desired her. He assumed she meant Samuel. She turned back to the trail and found her way back. Samuel placed the meat on a spit over the fire. He glanced behind her as she sat with Elsa. She gazed at him. He stopped moving, his blue eyes bright. She drew him to her with her eyes, and he came. She pressed her face to his, and he kissed her cheek. He moved out of the caverns.

"They'll follow you without question my leader," she said in Elsa's mind. "But Samuel is their war leader just as Juan was. We live in a strange world. They think just because he's a man, he's more powerful than you," Lettie whispered.

"Let us keep that advantage between us," Elsa said in her mind. Lettie gazed across the room. Adam positioned himself, so he could look at her and not be so obvious. He appeared annoyed. If he insisted on looking, she would give him plenty to see and nothing to his liking. She busied herself with the meal.

Elsa turned the cakes. As the final ones came from the pan, she deposited them into a reed container. She sat back. They were ready for what was to come. How would she convince Ana and Enrique and the others to change course, without revealing who she was? She bumped into her pack and willed it to give her answers. She unzipped it and peered inside, on top of the things was the journal. The pages opened to a section that had been marked with other papers. The last entry read:

"On this road to paradise, they were tagged. Led through checkpoints and identified as possible candidates. Only the strongest and healthiest were permitted to continue. They were given papers and code words to get to the next destination. Photographs tracked their progress along the route. At each checkpoint doctors made files for each candidate. In the event, their organs are needed on arrival death certificates followed them to each new place.

My part in this is evil beyond measure; I am their doctor. I encourage the travel and discourage the elders from such a venture in hopes of saving at least their lives. I am a devil. I know not how to escape this madness…one way to stop her…a traitor in her ranks…I leave to another what I do not have courage to do…"

A dark, brown stain spread beyond the page and erased the remainder of the entry. She opened the first of the loose pages. Inside she found some of the death certificates. The doctor's name placed on the bottom, forms filled in the ready. In the next she found photos of the candidates. Among the faces, she found Ana's many times.

She glanced across the cavern at Manuel. His brother called him Mano she had kept that name for him. She held her reasons to detour the travelers. Information she traded for him or the girl.

"If time were replayed, I'd make the same choice," she signed.

"What is the life of two when it comes to saving the lives of the many?"

"We can save them, but until the disease has been destroyed, they're still in danger," she signed. She replaced the items and went to the fire to turn the meat.

Lettie rinsed the reed plates and stacked them to her left. "Here are the last of them."

"Thank you, Mano. Do you have a moment?" she asked. She gathered the remainder of the items and scrubbed them.

"I've more time than I want. What can I do for you?" he asked. He didn't object to being called Mano as his brother called him. She finished them up and he dried them. He ran a cloth over a plate.

"Are you surprised I can dry dishes?"

"I'm not surprised by anything you do, Black Wolf. This situation is unusual," she whispered. He was an enforcer as were his men, he killed for money or power.

"How so?" he asked. She placed a plate atop another.

"The leader of the Wolves drying dishes with a fighter."

"We all do what we must to survive. What I find even stranger is a Fighter's healer would waste her talents on the wolf clan," he said.

"If you wish to insult me, you'll have to do better. Your brother has a better talent for it," she whispered. Mano grinned.

"He would be pleased you think so. I've never seen him so captivated by a woman."

"He's unaccustomed to kindness. I did what my conscience directed," she whispered, "Would you tell me about him?"

"It wouldn't please Stein to know you inquired about another man. Especially about a man, who would kill to claim you? A man whose life you saved when you could have just let him die," he said.

"Chino treated me with honor and respect, even after he knew Patricia captured me. I was unable to thank him. I'll extend my appreciation to you instead, Mano."

"He's one of the bastards my Father can claim," he said.

496

"Your Father is a fighter?" she asked.

"Yes, he's a sainted fighter. He follows all the codes of the fighter's army, but he's a liar and a cheat. Your people respect him, if you truly knew his heart…never mind."

"There are good and bad among all people. I can't judge your father. I don't know him. I know a good man when I meet one and Chino is that and more."

"His mother died when he was a child. Mama knew about him. She sent me to bring him…home. What my father didn't give him, I did. My brother is a man of flesh and blood. He's not a man to play with," he said. Leticia nodded.

"I was honest with him," she whispered.

"Did you tell him who his competition is?" he asked.

"No, he thinks you're his rival," she whispered.

"What?"

"I explained we were friends. I don't think he believed me. I didn't want a war between Chino and Samuel," she whispered.

"So the Green Wolf has no chance?" he asked.

"No, he said he understood," she whispered.

"What did he understand Fighter Marras because I'm not clear about what was discussed?" he asked.

"We came across some women and children in the mountain. They traded some things for my services," she whispered.

"Many people trade," he said.

"Yes, but now I own many images of the wolf, and a man named Alfaro, gave me a small metal carving of a wolf with green stones for eyes, he said his spirit guide drove him to make it, and that it should be a charm of protection from Leader Chino," she said. She searched his face for confirmation. He watched the water run passed.

"It was a test," he said.

"Did we pass?" she whispered. He turned to her.

"Only time will tell," he replied, "What understanding do you have with my brother?"

"Leticia, what's taking so long with those dishes?" Sam asked. She glanced at Mano and waited to see if he would tell of her interest in his brother.

"It's my fault, Stein. I'm not accustomed to drying dishes."

"Thank you, Mano," she whispered. He nodded and left them.

Samuel was angry. "Won't you speak your mind, leader?" He seemed to consider the question and then turned away. "Samuel, I'm not a child, nor am I weak…I can't remember certain things. I won't be treated like…a crazy woman," she whispered. She gathered the dishes and walked passed him to the camp.

Another night found them on a long path, rutted and worn. Tall grass waved in the breeze. There were no humans for miles around. This was where they could change the future of the travelers, the unsuspecting organ donors.

"This is the place," Elsa signed. She glanced at Abrim.

"Even if it isn't were stopping for the night," David said. Adam glanced at David and then at Abrim. Samuel dropped their packs.

"Do what he says Maldano. Now!" Sam shouted.

"Don't shout, Samuel," Lettie whispered.

"Whose turn is it to hunt? I'll do it!" Sam shouted.

"You're in the proper mood. I'll join you," she whispered.

"No!" She slapped him and stormed down the road. Sam followed Leticia. Elsa pulled him back and pointed him in the other direction. She went after Lettie.

"Would you like to discuss it?"

"No, you should be on his side," she whispered. Elsa pulled her around, and she shook her head.

"Even if he's wrong?" she signed.

"Yes."

"I should ask my boy if he would like to talk?" she signed.

"No, you wouldn't understand how he feels…it's a male thing, maybe David or grandfather would be better suited," she whispered.

"I think I've been insulted," Elsa signed.

"Just out manned," she whispered.

They came back to the camp. Nellie set rocks in a circle. Elsa touched the woman's forehead; her illness seemed improved. "Where's David?" Lettie asked.

"He's gone to look for Sam. Try to reason with him." Elsa glanced at Lettie.

"Better him, than me," Elsa signed. Leticia nodded. Elsa took a hooked tool and hacked at the long grass to render sections to pile together. Nellie approached her. Elsa stopped. The others busied themselves in various ways. "Elsa can we talk?"

"Yes," Elsa signed.

"I'm a reader. I've many books in my room. I know I'm just a housekeeper and…"

"You've some concerns?" Elsa signed. Nellie glanced at Mano.

"I don't trust him. Don't you find it odd the soldiers didn't find us until we were to meet up with the men?"

"They were bringing Mano back," Elsa signed.

"Yes, back to us and Leo said they couldn't find him, but he showed up to fight on our side against his own men. How did he know where we were?" Nellie asked.

"He doesn't know exactly what we are doing," Elsa signed.

"Patricia's goal is to capture us then all he has to do is lead them to us. We were lucky to have the Wolf clan and your fighters help us when they did, but next time Patricia comes she'll bring enough men to win. Who will we have?" Nellie asked.

"That's a good question," Elsa signed.

"Whoever you call, we must be certain of their loyalty. If we don't trust the Wolf clan's leader, we can't trust them," Nellie said.

"I'm glad you're with me. How do we get the others involved?"

"We share our thoughts with the women, and then we take it to our men individually. All Manuel will see are couples being close," Nellie said. Elsa smiled.

"You're wicked. I like that," Elsa signed.

"Too much time and an overactive imagination," Nellie said. Nellie left, and she went back to work a large square of bedding grass. Samuel returned with David. They laughed together. She glanced at Lettie, who noticed the change. Elsa squinted in the dying light. Sweat poured down her back. She longed for the carefree life. Abrim sat across the way and noticed the change in his grandson too.

Abrim remained distant he wouldn't even look at her.

She gathered the bundles of grass and walked passed the fire. Nellie was with Lettie soon the other women joined them as they cooked. Elsa knew of a way to call for help. She would contact the Queen of Los Menos. Elsa adjusted. Help was on the way. The evening was still. She positioned them in the direct path of the travelers. They camped early to prepare for their guests. Without question, she knew she could change their plans. They would be disappointed, but they would live.

Nellie's plan worked to perfection. Mano hadn't a clue what was to come, and still he remained smug and certain. He played games this one he'd lose.

Her baby moved, and she rocked it. She separated from the rest of the group to be alone, to think of her plan. She leaned back against the boulder and inhaled. She put a bark chip in, and the bitter tree oil swirled in her mouth. "Why are you out here alone?" She glanced up at Abrim. "Does anyone know where you are?"

"Lettie knows that's how you found out," she signed. He came level with her.

"Tell me the couple's name, and I'll help them," he said.

"They'll need your help when I'm done," she signed.

"No, I'll help them. You go home," Abrim said. He came to send her away and she couldn't leave him to do her duty.

"If you knew where my home was you wouldn't want me to go there," she signed. She stared into his eyes.

"I know where you live. I bought it for you, and I bought the bed you sleep in and I've slept in that bed," Abrim said.

"No, that is the house where I grew up and that's Romalia's house. My home is miles from there," she signed. He grabbed her arms.

"Where is your home?" He sounded desperate and insecure.

"I must show you," she signed.

"So show me!" She pressed her fingers to his forehead and shut her eyes. The cemetery gate snapped into view, and they watched her break in as was her tradition. She ran to her parent's graves and lay between the headstones and stretched her arms out to reach for them. She smiled as she lay in the gravel and dirt. He pulled her to him, and she tensed. His hand slipped over the bare skin of her belly. "That's where you go when you're homesick?" he whispered. His blue eyes were sad. She nodded.

"All I have left on this earth is them, and I don't even remember anything about them. I just want one thing for my own, even if it's just a memory," she signed. He leaned in and gripped her tight. He pressed his unshaved face to hers, and she froze.

She still remembered the parts of the dream, and she relaxed against him. She wasn't very greedy, but she still took more of his comfort and power than she should. He pulled back. "Go back to Lettie. I don't like you being out here alone," he said. He helped her up, and his hand slid away from her belly.

She stepped next to Lettie. Sam and David were nearby. "Ma, where is your sack of bark chips? I want to add more," Lettie whispered. She searched her pockets.

"Is this what you're looking for Fighter?" Abrim asked. She turned, and he held up the bag. He approached her, and Marcus smiled. He turned her as he placed the sack in her hands and held on for longer than necessary. His gaze went to David as she pulled free. She sat next to Lettie and David leaned close enough to kiss her.

"If you want a little honey, baby, just say the word," he said. The heat rushed to her face as he landed a sweet kiss on her cheek. She glanced at Abrim, who didn't seem at all disturbed by David's advances.

Morning arrived and no travelers. Elsa shifted as the worry set in, maybe the group had been captured or diverted, and she'd failed them. She rose and went to Abrim. Marching feet turned Elsa. Sam came to his feet. She moved to the top of the hill and Abrim, and the others joined her. Down the road a bit a line of people moved in their direction. "It's them," she signed.

"That's more than two people there are more than two dozen people," Abrim said. She went to her pack, and he followed her. She turned and placed an envelope in his hands. She withdrew the proof and passed it to Abrim. Sam, David and the others gathered around. He flipped through the pages, and his anger deepened and reflected on his face. Elsa glanced at Mano.

"I'm a witness to prove Patricia's part in this Stein, with Alejandro dead she is to gain all that has been collected and all that will be collected," Mano said. Abrim slammed the folder closed.

"This is your proof to turn them away from the journey, my leader," Elsa signed.

"Where did you get this information?" Abrim asked. Patricia's writing and involvement were clear.

"Do you doubt me? Do you doubt when I tell you this truth?" Elsa signed. He didn't respond, and she walked away.

"Am I relying on you that this is fact?" Abrim asked. She turned.

"I swear it on my life," Elsa signed.

"Then nothing else needs to be said," Abrim said.

Susa placed a pan on the edge of the fire. The meal was near complete. "Meet your new people, so they may know their hero, my leader." He came to her.

"I'd rather they meet my hero, come let me take you to them," Abrim said. Elsa added leaves to the boiling water to make tea. Wayne and Bob stood by another fire. Bea stirred others pots.

"No, I should remain here, my leader, I'm no one," Elsa signed.

"Are you still sick?" Abrim asked.

"No, not since…" Elsa signed.

"I lifted your bark chips from you last night?" he asked. She nodded, and Lettie gazed at her. "Come we do our best work together."

He took her hand, and they traveled over the hill. The lead group arrived, and Ana and Enrique were in the group. "We haven't seen people in days. We've a camp over the hill, please join us," Abrim said. They came into the camp, and Abrim held her hand.

"Senor your wife, my Ana and I we think we know her from some place," Enrique said. Abrim entwined his fingers with Elsa's.

"I don't believe it's possible you know my…Elsa. I don't allow her to leave my sight very often. A beauty such as hers could be stolen, and my world is very dark when she's away," Abrim said. He had a wicked gleam in his eyes.

"All men think their wives are the most beautiful, no? I do no one compares to my Ana, but I'm certain…I know the elder from the other day Ana…the mean, uh, demanding, old fashioned, the one that didn't walk like an old woman," Enrique said.

"Enrique!" Ana said.

"She had these eyes that could peel the flesh off a man's bones you know the kind of woman, I mean Senor?" Enrique asked. Abrim searched Elsa's face.

"Oh, yes I know a woman like that, but it couldn't have been a relative of my…Elsa's she has no blood kin left alive, and as you see she's far from old, although, mean, stern, demanding and old fashioned describe her well," Abrim said, "These are my people." They turned to look at the travelers.

Elsa watched a man shift to the back of the crowd. He had dark hair, a dirty face and brown eyes, and he was different than the others. Lean, wiry and with an arrogance that didn't fit the stance of a poor man. Abrim motioned him closer.

"Who are you people?" the man asked.

"Friends," Abrim replied.

"That's all you told us. Friends from where?" the man asked.

"The north," David said.

"North of where?" the man asked.

507

"Here, what is your name friend?" Samuel asked.

"You're no friends of mine. Why are you delaying us?" he asked.

"We want to share our food with you," Nellie said.

"They're fighters." Someone said from the crowd. Elsa scanned the group and saw Mano in the middle. The man jumped on the information.

"Come on, we want nothing from them," he snapped. She smiled a welcome to Ana.

"I'm tired Enrique can we stay?" Ana asked.

"I'm hungry. It wouldn't hurt to accept their offer," Enrique said. He moved closer.

"They're criminals, traitors to our country. We're asking for trouble. The government is giving us what we're due," the man said.

"All we have are promises. I'll wait and see," Enrique said.

"Don't be stupid Salazar. Why would they help us? We're in the way of their plans to overthrow the government," the man said.

"They're probably not fighters," Ana said. Elsa nodded to Samuel to tell the truth.

"We're fighters," Sam said.

"See they admit it. They kill the poor every day," he said.

"We leave that to the forces of Patricia Stein. We've never killed innocent people," Samuel said.

"They're lying," the man said.

"We've no reason to lie. What do we have to gain?" Leo asked. Elsa watched Mano make his way back. He stared at the man.

"Do I know you?" Mano asked. He came to the man and caught her eye. "I do know you, Fernando Ochoa."

"Who are you?" Enrique asked. Mano turned to him.

"I'm Manuel Rojas Villanueva, Lieutenant Commander of the Freedom Forces. The nephew of the late General Alejandro Rojas," Mano said.

"He's a traitor, don't believe anything he says," the man said.

"Who has he betrayed?" David asked.

"The…government," Ochoa said.

"Wrong answer, you know better, Nando. We've friends in high places, but we never, ever implicate them in our dealings," Mano said. He laughed. "Never send a boy to do a man's job and especially an ill-trained boy. She's not going to be pleased."

"What are you talking about? I don't know you," the man said.

"How does he know your nickname?" A petite woman stood by Ana, her large eyes suspicious.

"Patricia, won't like you're having a woman on the side," Mano said. The woman turned to him. "They're lovers you see."

"You lying bastard!" the petite woman shouted.

"Take her a cup of tea, Lettie. Offer her some comfort," Elsa signed. Lettie pulled the woman to their side.

"If he'd lie to Mona, he could be lying to us, Enrique. Maybe we shouldn't trust him," Ana said. Elsa looked at Abrim.

"We just met these people," Enrique said. Mano fished in his pocket and pulled out his wallet. He thumbed through the items and passed an identification card to Enrique.

"He's who he says he is," Enrique called.

"So what, it's a trick," Nando said. Mano dug through the wallet again and handed him a photo of himself and Fernando, in uniform, arm in arm, in front of a cantina.

"Why would you betray your friend?" Enrique asked. Mano glanced at Elsa. A smile marked his face, but anger warped his eyes.

"Revenge, a friend doesn't screw your woman while you're away," Mano said, "Did you think you could ever replace me, Nando?" Elsa's gaze went to Abrim to see if he cared that the younger man was Patricia's lover. His expression remained the same.

"I was always the better man, Manuel, and now I'll be the only man," Nando said. He drew his gun. Mano turned to him and grinned.

"See you in Hell, amigo," Mano said. Mano held his arms wide. Fernando fired, but Elsa was

510

faster as she fired both 9mm's into the man's head. None of her Fighters moved as she sent the man to his death. She pulled up her weapons, and the one with her injured arm dropped to her side. Her gaze met Manuel's, she just saved his ass in front of witnesses, not good in his opinion, his opinion didn't matter.

Amid the screams and smoke, Elsa sat for a cup of tea. She glanced at Mano. "You didn't think I'd let him kill you, did you? This alliance isn't over until I say," she signed.

"You're welcome. You could never live without me," Mano said. The people joined them. Before Abrim could present the proof a voice called.

"We've come to rescue you!" Elsa turned to Patricia. The woman always preferred to make an entrance. "They'd kill you my friends and take your belongings, but we shall take you to a safe place."

"Show them the picture's Abrim," Elsa signed.

"Oh, my God, Enrique, look," Ana said. Patricia's men couldn't be counted there were so many, and they were surrounded.

"Give up de las Almas. You've fallen into a trap you can't escape," Mano said. The Freedom Forces raised their weapons, but the Wolf Clan wasn't among the ranks.

"Come to the winning side Manuel," Patricia cooed. Elsa raised her gun to his face.

"Lettie now!" Elsa said in Leticia's mind. A whistle pierced the air. Los Menos appeared like shadows of death in their brown cloaks. Through the air like a phantom their Queen flew, sickles at the ready. She took three lead lieutenants to their deaths. Guns fired and shouts rang as the battle came alive.

Elsa's eyes never left Patricia's area. Patricia watched her as well. Mano tried to change sides, but Sam caught him with a kick, and David finished him with a punch. Los Meno's cloaks were pushed back. Their heads covered in black cloth with a skeleton's head painted on the face. Their Queen came up and killed two in front of Adam. She jumped around and killed three in back of Marcus.

The bloody tide changed, and Patricia took two steps back. Elsa moved with her. Patricia turned and ran. Elsa leapt forward. Patricia cleared the battlefield as Elsa caught her. Patricia swung and slammed her fist into Elsa's jaw. Elsa came back enraged and pressed her knife across Patricia's face and came around to her to cut her throat. Patricia's knife whirled toward her. Abrim hauled Elsa back. Patricia got up. "No!" Abrim shouted.

She fought the old man, but he wouldn't free her. Patricia ran through the trees as Elsa struggled with Abrim. Far, in the distance, a vehicle picked her up and disappeared. Elsa pushed away from Abrim. "How could you love her? She killed Lila and Alicia. Her plot killed Juan!" Elsa signed.

"She didn't kill them," Abrim said.

"Her actions caused their deaths. She killed Lettie's family. She shot a baby in the head, Abrim. How could you love her?" Elsa signed. His face lost color as they both knew she spoke the truth.

"I don't love her. I never did," Abrim said. She glared.

"You just saved her life and for what? You've a family. You've Sam and Marcus and all your Fighters and a new little great grandchild to love. You've Inoc and your grandchildren. You've so much family. You're not like me…I don't have anyone."

"I didn't save her life, I prevented her killing…the baby…your baby. I love you and only you for the last fifteen years, and if you had died a few weeks ago I'd have found a way to die as well. I can't imagine a life without you," he snapped. Elsa took a step back as one hand went to her mouth and the other to her stomach and her unborn child with another man. He turned bitter eyes away from her.

"Go, home Elsa." All the pain and strain of his life converged on his face to make him look an old, old man. It broke her spirit to see him this way.

"Come with us!" she signed. He shook his head.

"I've work left to do, but I'll see you…maybe." She rubbed her palm over his face as if to erase the look that came upon him, but nothing changed.

"Don't do this to me," Elsa signed. He pulled her along as the rest of the family came up to them. She wanted to continue the conversation to ask questions, but he walked to Marcus and left her on the battlefield.

Some of the soldiers ran, and the rest lay dead. Los Menos prepared to gather the dead and take them to their final resting place. Their Queen looked on. The brown cloaks covered them, but the Queen's cloak remained laid back against her shoulders.

Abrim returned with Marcus. "Elsa where have you been I looked everywhere for you…I love you," David said. Elsa stared at the man. "You don't think a man like me is capable of love?" Elsa raised her hands to sign, and death took her by the hand. Elsa turned. Death needed comfort and love. Death placed her head on Elsa's shoulder, and she embraced death. Death accepted her comfort. The Queen pulled away, and Elsa kissed her black cloaked cheek. She stared into the woman's pale gray eyes. "I'll see you in a few months?" Elsa signed. Death nodded. "You'll know where to find me?" Death nodded again. Death could always find her. Marcus moved closer.

"Ma, maybe it's not such a good idea to be so anxious to want death to visit you," Marcus said. Her handsome son gazed at death.

Elsa pulled the cloak over the death mask and adjusted the sleeves of the cloak. The Queen retreated and joined the led group that carried the dead. She glanced at her group and searched for injuries. There were some, but all were minor. "That's Snake Crow."

"Is that a girl, it walks like a girl," Marcus said.

"Yes, younger than you," Elsa signed.

"That was wicked what she did with those weapons," Marcus said.

"Those are the least of her abilities," Elsa signed. He stared at the group as it disappeared, in the distance. The travelers stood to the side and seemed lost. Abrim glanced at her.

"Show them, lead them to a safe place," Elsa signed.

"Samuel, I'm sending Marcus with you," Abrim said.

"Yes, Grandfather," Sam said.

"I know you'll help your Mother and try to keep a better handle on her location from now on," Abrim said. Sam nodded. Lettie followed Elsa down the path, and the others followed.

"Where are we going, boss?" Nellie asked.

"Texas," she signed.

"She said Texas we're going home," Nellie said. Susa nodded. "Oh, thank the good Lord."

Elsa glanced back at the old man, but he moved on to his next task.

"Remember who loves you, Elsa," Abrim said. The memory echoed in her mind as tiny lights popped in her thoughts. The wind gushed up around her and with it came a sound, she strained to hear it, and a woman's scream rushed over her, and the scene changed. The shriek came again, and Elsa turned. A giant sword hammered down on the screaming woman to separate her head from her body. The head rolled and bounced into a wall. The lifeless eyes stared up, and then a dripping sound. A warm, stickiness surrounded her hands and a drip splashed her shoes. She looked at her hands, and a dead baby without arms or legs bled onto her shoes. She opened her mouth, and the silence roared.

Acknowledgements

To family and friends thanks for everything!

Connect with me online at
ZoylaWrites.com

www.ingramcontent.com/pod-product-compliance
Lightning Source LLC
Chambersburg PA
CBHW031024030726
47497CB00004B/988